Down Among the Dead Men

Ed Chatterton is the prize-winning author of more than twenty children's novels (published under the name Martin Chatterton). In addition to his career as a writer, he has enjoyed international success as an illustrator as well as working as a graphic designer, university lecturer and commercials director. Born and raised in Liverpool, he now divides his time between Australia and the UK and is married with two children.

Down Among the Dead Men is his second crime novel and he is already hard at work on the third in the DI Frank Keane series.

Also by Ed Chatterton

A Dark Place to Die

Down Among the Dead Men

ed chatterton

arrow books

Published by Arrow 2013

2 4 6 8 10 9 7 5 3 1

Arrow Books
Random House, 20 Vauxhall Bridge Road,
London SW1V 2SA

www.randomhouse.co.uk

Addresses for companies within The Random House Group Limited can be
found at: www.randomhouse.co.uk

The Random House Group Limited Reg. No. 954009

A CIP catalogue record for this book
is available from the British Library

ISBN 9780099576686

The Random House Group Limited supports the Forest Stewardship
Council® (FSC®), the leading international forest-certification organisation.
Our books carrying the FSC label are printed on FSC®-certified paper. FSC is
the only forest-certification scheme supported by the leading environmental
organisations, including Greenpeace. Our paper procurement policy can be
found at: www.randomhouse.co.uk/environment

Printed and bound by CPI Group (UK) Ltd, Croydon, CR0 4YY

To Liverpool and Los Angeles

'If we imagine no worse of them than they of themselves, they may pass for excellent men.'

Theseus, Act 5, Scene 1, *A Midsummer Night's Dream*, William Shakespeare

PART ONE

LIVERPOOL

Prologue

Nicky's panicky fingertips trace the cramped horizons of his terrifying new world and deliver the same bleak conclusion he'd arrived at a hundred times already since he coughed himself awake.

This is for real.

The things in his life that he'd attached importance to before this – haircuts, ambition, music, films, attitude – fade away with such rapidity that it makes his head spin. This is the lesson he is learning: there is here, there is now, and everything else is bullshit.

He already has several splinters in his fingers and with his hand once more scrabbling furiously in a futile search for something to give him hope, another jams itself underneath a thumbnail. The pain is excruciating but Nicky embraces it like a friend. For a few sweet seconds his mind is emptied of all but pure feeling, before the nightmare reality of the situation rushes back in a vertiginous pitch-black tsunami of fear and hopelessness and absolute gut-wrenching horror.

The sixteen-year-old, his body trembling spasmodically, lies naked inside a solid wooden box – Nicky won't allow himself to use the word *coffin* – feet flat against an immoveable wall, legs slightly bent and thin arms pressed in tight against his body. He can, by breathing out and lowering his chest, twist his arm up just enough to reach his face.

He fights the urge to start crying again but it comes anyway, his breath erupting in ragged bursts and rebounding hot and sour from the hard surface a couple of centimetres above his damp face. He aches, with a simple childlike desperation he wouldn't have believed possible a few days ago, for his mother to hold him in her arms, his father to scoop him up, to keep him safe, to fight off the wolves.

To get him out of here.

There's something he needs to remember about his parents – something important – but the only thing that penetrates the fog cloaking his brain is the awful dread certainty that they won't be coming for him.

That no one will be coming for him.

Things like this happen to others, to unlucky people you read about and then forget, glad you aren't one of them. Or else to people who'd slipped through the cracks: addicts, drifters, prostitutes. Not suburban teenagers. Not Nicky Peters.

Not me.

Yet, here he is. The evidence is right there that this time it's he who is . . . what, exactly?

With an almost physical jolt the word comes to mind.

Victim.

With an effort of will Nicky slows his breathing and tries to get back some small measure of control. Time passes. Nicky's not sure how long. He wonders if it's something to do with . . . *that*. He can't even think the words, let alone think about what's been going on. What he'd done was wrong – what *they'd* done was wrong – but that wouldn't lead to this, would it? Would it?

He can remember being hurt. Someone was moving him somewhere. His mind is foggy, memories frustratingly intangible. Ghosts at the edge of the forest.

Then there are sounds coming from outside. Someone's there.

The noise brings the tiniest flicker of relief as Nicky realises that he is not, as he feared, buried underground. He begins to sense a room, a space surrounding his box. He opens his mouth to yell for help and abruptly stops himself. He's seen enough movies to know whoever is outside does not wish him well. He knows how this turns out and it makes him want to cry.

Nicky concentrates; he's always been a serious boy. He's got good ears and the sounds gradually form an unwelcome picture.

Someone is working hard. Objects being moved, the scrape of metal on hard floors. A series of ripping sounds; tape being stripped from a reel. The crackle of heavy plastic sheeting. The occasional grunt of effort.

Outside Nicky's box someone is busy.

Panic floods the boy and despite himself he cries out. 'Hey! Please! Help me! Please!'

The movements stop and Nicky hears someone come close. So close he can hear them breathing.

'Quiet, Nicky,' says a soft, soothing voice. 'No one can hear you.'

Nicky begins to cry again.

He knows who's out there.

One

'Fucking get stuck in, Chrissy,' says Jesus and, as always when the big man tells him to do something, Chrissy does as he's told.

The kid shifts his stance and comes in hard with a flurry of light jabs.

Frank Keane dabs his headgear back into position with the heel of his right hand and tucks an elbow tight against his ribs to defend himself. He's already hurting, and as Chrissy ups the tempo, Frank knows it's going to get worse before it gets any better. It's been a long while since he's had a work-out like this and he's feeling every minute of the lay-off.

'Bollocks,' grunts Frank as he rolls with the fresh onslaught. The word is filtered through his gumshield but the kid hears and smiles. At sixteen, Chrissy Cahill is a handy amateur welterweight prospect with several junior titles to his name. Sparring with a forty-year-old, even one with Frank Keane's decent record, is not part of the boy's usual training regimen. Frank's there for variety, a favour to Jesus Penaquele, Chrissy's trainer.

Jesus – only Penaquele's mother uses the Hispanic pronunciation and she's ninety-seven – is a large man in his sixties with a drinker's face and a keen eye for a likely winner. He has lived in Liverpool his entire life.

Back when Jesus was thinner he'd been Frank's trainer, and sometimes more than that in the bad year after Frank's dad had passed. Frank hadn't been much younger then than Chrissy Cahill is now, and Penaquele had let the boy's grief come out in the ring and the gym. It was only later that Frank had realised how smart and caring Jesus had been. Over hot breakfasts cooked up by Jesus's foul-mouthed wife, Val, after early-morning runs, he had talked to the boy about boxing and football; doing what he could to show Frank how to become a man at a time when there was no one else.

Jesus Penaquele took Frank as far as a national junior bout, where they both found out he'd reached the highest level he'd ever reach as a boxer. That was OK; the game was never going to be Frank's life.

Chrissy Cahill's different. He's a real comer, a genuine contender. One last hurrah for Jesus maybe.

Penaquele's ringside now, pacing restlessly, his hands in pockets, his head tilted. For a big man he's sure-footed, unconsciously echoing the footwork of his protégé in the ring.

'Pick it up, Chrissy. Stop playing pat-a-cake with the old cunt. Give him a bit of the good stuff. He can take it. Head like a fucken rock. Just like all coppers.'

A couple of the other kids laugh. Even through the head protector, Frank can hear the edge in the laughter. They all know he's a bizzy.

'Fuck him up, brother!'

Frank lifts his chin and beckons Chrissy towards him. 'Listen to what Jesus's saying. It's OK.'

Chrissy shrugs and bounces onto his toes. 'If you sure, man.'

Frank tucks in tight and tries to call up some of those long-buried ring smarts. *I can't be that rusty.*

The kid hits him with a couple of stingers on the side of the head and Frank works backwards into the corner. He's just about to congratulate himself that he can deal with the boy when he's caught in the ribs with a left he never saw. Frank grunts and realises that the two to the head were just range-finders. Chrissy's moved up several gears and inside twenty seconds Frank's clinging on.

Turns out he *is* that rusty.

'Fucking hell, Frankie,' he hears Jesus shout, 'give the lad a bit of honest work, eh?'

Frank's been boxing long before he was a copper, most of it right here. Nothing much has changed at the Breeze Hill Boxing Club since he started, except for the flat screen TVs on each wall playing classic bouts on a loop and some expensive-looking fitness equipment dotted around the unlovely hall; no doubt the result of some freelance wealth redistribution that Frank chooses not to think about.

The kids look pretty much like they did when Frank was their age. Better gear maybe. No one turns up in anything except the latest and newest. By comparison, Frank's well-worn Lonsdale shorts and gloves are antiques. Apart from Penaquele, Frank's the oldest participant at the club.

Frank doesn't think he'll be training at Breeze Hill much longer. There are plenty of hardcore faces at the club who don't like him being around. Big men, hard men, who congregate around the weight area. Bouncers. An enforcer for the Halligans. These men tolerate Frank on account of his history with Jesus, but no more than that. Coppers don't mix with the boxing world. As the newly promoted head of the Merseyside Major Incident Team, DCI Frank Keane is particularly unwelcome with those connected to the Halligan brothers, both sent away by MIT last year in the Stevie White case.

'You all right, mate?' says Chrissy.

His voice is one that might be used when talking to a confused elderly relative who's having trouble getting out of a parked car, and Frank realises he's been daydreaming.

He taps the kid with a solid right to teach him some manners and it catches Chrissy square on the shoulder, spinning him sideways. He dances back and lifts an amused chin in Frank's direction.

'OK, Frankie,' says Chrissy.

Now the boy steps in close and Frank concentrates on keeping himself mobile. Even so, the blows hurt. Fuck, do they hurt. Chrissy's got steel, no question, and Frank's arms are beginning to wilt under the onslaught. He's blowing. Frank makes a big effort with a combination but his opponent drifts out of range, no effort involved.

'Concentrate!' Jesus shouts. 'The here and now, Frankie. That's all there is, son. Get your fucken head out of your arse and concentrate.'

The 'here and now'. Frank's heard it a million times from Jesus.

While Frank is coated in a fine sheen, his breath hot and ragged in his lungs, the kid's not even sweating. This won't last much longer. Frank hooks the thumb of his glove under the brow of his headgear and brings it back into position. The watching boxers sense Frank's vulnerability.

'He's gone, bruv!'

'Do 'im, Chrissy, lad!'

The kid shifts smoothly into a higher gear and drives Frank back onto the ropes, the older fighter's arms turning to lead under the blows. Frank's puffing badly now and a lethal right takes out his gumshield, opening him up to anything the kid has got.

Enough. It's only training. Not enough to lose any teeth over.

Frank jumps in close and wraps his arms around Chrissy. 'I'm cooked, son,' he pants.

Two taps to the back of Frank's headgear and Chrissy pushes him away.

Chrissy turns and pats his glove against the outstretched palm of one of his mates reaching through the ropes.

Jesus lifts the ropes for Frank and he steps down from the ring as the small knot of onlookers drift back to their training stations. 'Thanks for that, Frankie. Good to see him coping with some crafty old fucker.' Jesus speaks like words are expensive, biting them out in short measure. He has an intense way about him.

'Crafty?' Frank shakes his head. 'There was nothing crafty about that, Jesus. I was surviving.'

Frank takes off his headgear and Jesus hands him a fresh towel from a neat stack in a plastic container. Frank's still got a boxer's build, although his face shows none of the damage that those who stay in the game have. His sweat-coated hair is short, cropped, the speckled grey winning against the black. He looks like he needs a shave – something of a permanent condition.

Frank wanders to the benches and sits down, takes his gloves off and unwraps the bandage looped around his knuckles, the movements smooth from muscle memory. Jesus wanders over and pats Frank on the shoulder.

'Good work, Frankie. Ta.'

'You rate the boy?' Frank picks up the towel and wraps it round his neck, rubbing sweat from his face with the ends.

'He's all right, like, Chrissy. Fucking did you, hey?'

'No argument there.' Frank gets to his feet and has to brace himself against the wall. 'He's got a bit of Izzy Sulah about him.'

Jesus makes a noncommittal grunt. 'Yeah, maybe. We'll see.' Sulah was one of Jesus's hopes – after Frank – who made a bit of a splash.

'You doing OK?' says Jesus without looking at Frank. 'Work good? All that?'

Frank knows there's only one answer Jesus needs to hear.

'Yeah, all fine.'

'Good. Sound. As long as you're happy, hey?'

He walks over to Chrissy, leaving Frank to stretch off.

Frank showers and leaves around eight without speaking to anyone else. He takes his time. Since he and Julie split in January there's no one waiting for him at home.

Two

All Quinner wants, when it comes down to it, is five minutes' peace and quiet to go over the runsheet and tweak the dialogue for the three scenes they'll be shooting – or attempting to shoot – today.

That shouldn't be too much to ask, should it? Not after six years eating a pile of shit the size of the Mersey Ferry to get the cunting thing in front of the cunting cameras.

But here it comes again.

'Quinny! Quinny, you poof! Oi, softlad!'

Dean Quinner tries not to look up but it's tough when the voice is less than ten metres away, has an accent sharp enough to slice concrete and is coming out of the mouth of your knuckle-dragging cousin, Big Niall. Shaven-headed Quinner, thirty, wiry and wired, sharp city eyes red-rimmed with fatigue, has got a million fucking things to do before fucking lunchtime. But Niall won't be denied.

Quinner puts down his script, bulging with loose notes and unfinished edits, for the third time that morning and stalks across to the wooden barrier the location crew have placed across the top of Huskisson Street to talk to Niall. It's almost ten and the day's schedule is already behind. Fucking Noone, the American gobshite, late again. No apologies, just shows at seven, throwing that gleaming smile around like coins to the poor.

Ben Noone's got it, though, Quinner can't deny that and he's glad they got him before anyone else. Tall, dark-haired and blue-eyed, he moves like an athlete, confident in his own skin. He radiates sex. Speaking with him is like being undressed. The American reminds Quinner of a less androgynous David Bowie. There's something simultaneously beautiful and reptilian at work there.

The industry rumour mill is grinding, even while the movie's being shot, and the buzz is that Ben Noone is going to be big – very big – and that can only be good news for their movie. Casting the unknown looks like a stroke of genius. Even Quinner admits Noone's dead right for the part. And, like so many things that have changed since the Hungry Head production money came on board and the movie stepped up a couple of levels, Quinner hadn't had much to do with casting. His film is now their film.

The production is still a relatively small one, an independent production funded by a ragbag of Euro grants, small investors, the Liverpool Film Office and – most recently and most importantly – Hungry Head. Quinner doesn't care, just so long as it means *The Tunnels* gets made.

The movie is built around the Joseph Williamson tunnels: an apparently useless network of brick-lined, pre-Victorian engineered tunnels that sprawl under the Edge Hill part of the city. Some big, some small, most dilapidated, a few restored. Williamson, a rich eccentric, constructed them over two hundred years ago, apparently for no better reason than to give employment to locals. Teams of men stacked curving vaults on top of each other and toiled on winding shafts of brick-lined corridors and echoing caverns.

There's a peculiarly Liverpool mindset at work that Quinner wants to acknowledge in the construction of the vast, pointless labyrinth. He sees in Williamson's folly a complex metaphor for the city and its history.

Big Niall doesn't know a metaphor from a meat pie.

'Quinny!'

'Niall, you have to stop shouting, man. It's fucking up the sound.' Quinner doesn't mention how much it's fucking up his work. Niall doesn't count what his cousin Dean does – writing – as work. Explaining to Niall how his words make the transition from brain to screen would be like outlining the concept of infinity to a duck.

'Oh, right, yeah, soz, man.' Niall makes a zipping motion across his moon face. 'Me lips are sealed.' Niall has someone with him. A thin guy with a narrow forehead and a zoned-out expression. He looks at Quinner with an odd combination of sneer and fascination. He's wearing a baseball cap and Quinner immediately wants to punch him. He has one of those faces.

'What is it, anyway, Niall?' Despite the determinedly languid appearance of the crew, Quinner knows there's tension building with the next shot. It's going to be a difficult one and they all know it. The production only has the street until twelve and so far there have been problems, the latest being a recalcitrant wheel on the tracking dolly. Quinner needs Niall to stop hanging around.

'You know what I want, Quinny.' Niall does his puppy face and Quinner sags.

'Not again, Niall. I explained to you how it works. I can't just get you a job on here, mate. I'm working for them.' Quinner waves a vague hand in the direction of the shoot.

'I thought it was your film, like?' This is from Small Forehead.

Quinner looks at him and raises his eyebrows. 'It is, Niall's Mate Who I've Never Met, but I sold it. Sold the idea and script to the production company. Now it's *their* film. Was mine. Now theirs. Y'see how that works?'

Niall's mate nods. 'Yeah, right.'

Niall's eyebrows knit together and he points at a passing teenager wearing a location laminate around his neck and carrying a can of WD-40. 'That kid's workin' on the film. Who the fuck's he?'

Quinner's about to answer when he realises he's forgotten. Suddenly, the idea of going through all this again with Big Niall assumes the proportions of Hercules in the Aegean Stables. 'He's one of the actors, Niall,' Quinner lies. 'Fucken great kid. Big star soon. Huge.'

'Yeah?' says Niall, his expression brightening. He nudges Small Forehead with an elbow. 'D'yer reckon you could get me 'is autograph, like?'

Quinner nods. 'Sure, man. On one condition.'

Three

Nicky doesn't know if his job has a name but he doesn't care. He is on the set of a *movie* and the fairy dust is strong enough to lend everything he does a crackle of Hollywood electricity, even if all he's doing is lugging stuff from one place to another.

Being on location in Liverpool is a right buzz too, doubly so when Nicky walks past the small crowd of onlookers behind the wooden barriers marking out the filmmakers' territory. He's only grabbing a can of WD-40 from the camera truck but, striding purposefully through the temporary village of support vehicles camped out like an invading army in his home city, the crew laminate around his neck, it feels like it means something, makes what's been happening the past few years fade.

Nicky's black hair is cut short at the back and sides and is fashionably peaked at the front. He's on the small side, and thin, but not painfully so. He dresses sharp, his taste in clothes altering subtly over the past few weeks as he strives to fit in with the crew. Today he's wearing the new waxed biker jacket he picked up from Superdry. It cost a fortune but Dean wears something similar. The Superdry feels good on Nicky but it makes him feel conspicuous. Although no one has made any comment he's still young enough to worry about that kind of thing. He's got his own rolled-up script in the inside pocket of the new jacket, and the edges of it keep catching his skin through his T-shirt, a reminder to him of how cowardly he's been in not showing it to Dean Quinner. All the articles Nicky reads about the movies – and he reads them all – emphasise how important it is to seize any opportunity in the business. So far, he hasn't done a thing other than show up and he's getting nervous that the shoot will finish before he plucks up the courage.

Can in hand, he heads back to Terry Peters, Nicky's uncle and the sole reason Nicky is on set. Terry's the movie's go-to man: the gaffer. He gets plenty of work; the city is second only to London for movie and TV production. Big Hollywood multiplex stuff as well as smaller scale indies like *The Tunnels*.

Nicky hands over the can of WD-40 without saying anything.

'Cheers,' says Terry and uses the lubricant to free up a reluctant roller on the camera track. Terry gives the cameraman the thumbs up and the preparations for the take can begin again. Terry looks very like his brother, Nicky's dad: tall, loose-limbed, with grey, close-cropped hair and an air of capability. He's a man who would not look out of place fronting a house renovation TV show.

'Positions, please,' says Susie, the assistant director. 'We'll try for a take in two.'

Nicky slides back, well out of shot, hyper-conscious of his lowly status, and watches as the crew click into place around the two actors in the scene. Dean Quinner takes up a position next to Nicky, a script thick with loose sheets and Post-it notes dangling from his left hand.

'What's your name again?' It takes Nicky a couple of seconds to realise Quinner is talking to him. Quinner's tone is neutral.

'Nicky Peters, Mr Quinner,' says Nicky. 'Terry got me the job.'

'Terry?'

Nicky points at his uncle. Quinner grunts. 'Oh, right, yeah. I knew that. Shouldn't have had to ask. Lot of things on my mind, y'know?'

Nicky shuffles uncertainly. It's the longest conversation he's had with the writer since the shoot started. A corner of Nicky's script scrapes against his nipple, another gentle reminder from the god of ambition. *Show him.*

Quinner takes out a sheet of paper and a pen and hands it to Nicky. 'Listen,' he says, embarrassed, his tired eyes not meeting Nicky's. 'Sign this for me. Pretend you're signing an autograph.' Quinner turns and gives Big Niall the thumbs up.

'Shall I just sign my own name?' says Nicky. Susie glares at him and he lowers his voice as Quinner nods an answer. 'What's it for?'

'Long story,' whispers Quinner and takes the signed sheet. He walks across to the large man behind the barrier and, after a quick word, comes back to watch the take. He stands next to the kid, both of them caught up in the scene. When it's over, Quinner turns to Nicky.

'What do you think?' Quinner's pointing in the direction of Ben Noone and Jon Carroll, the actors standing in the pool of light.

Nicky's expression betrays his confusion. He's unsure why Dean Quinner is asking him. It takes him a moment to realise that there's no hidden agenda: the writer is interested in his opinion.

'Him, Noone. Is he any good?' Quinner asks.

Nicky's been with the movie for three weeks, almost the entire shoot. As far as he's concerned, Ben Noone *is* the movie. Though an unknown, the lanky American dominates every scene.

'He's great,' Nicky eventually manages to say. 'Different.'

Quinner doesn't reply. Instead he taps a pen against his lower teeth.

Noone is good. The kid's right about that. It's one thing – despite his personal feelings about the actor – that Quinner doesn't have to worry about as far as the project is concerned. It's taken Quinner a long time and a flirtation with alcoholism to get from script to production. Along the way, Quinner has given up more than once, sold his soul more times than he likes to remember, and is now operating at a permanent level of paranoia and gut-sick fear that the funding will be cut, that the movie gods will call in their marker, that *some fucking thing* will happen to deny him his film.

Just let it open, he thinks and says a silent prayer. Just let it open.

Four

'Call that a knife? That's not a knife. *This* is a knife.'

Noone's Hogan impersonation is spot-on but Carter, the Australian behind the bar, shrugs.

'It's a spoon.'

Noone puts the spoon he's holding aloft down on the bar. 'From the movie, man. *Crocodile Dundee*?'

'Never seen it.'

'You're shitting me.' Noone grins but there's no real warmth there and Carter looks away as the American holds his gaze a fraction longer than is comfortable. 'I thought all you Aussies fucking loved that movie.'

'Not me, mate,' says Carter. 'Excuse me.' He moves down the bar to serve another customer.

'Have it your way, baby.' Noone's voice is barely a murmur.

He swivels his stool back to face the loose group gathered round him like orbiting planets. All of them in this particular circle of worship, boys and girls, crew and followers, are younger than Noone.

Watching from his position in the corner, Quinner sees the dark-eyed kid, Terry Peters' nephew, standing awkwardly off to one side of the group. Quinner doesn't make eye contact. He's still mildly embarrassed he didn't know the kid's name when he spoke to him yesterday.

The older members of the production who've made it to Maxie's Shack on Wednesday evening are scattered in loose groups around the bar. Most of the technical crew, including Terry Peters, are absent, pulling a late one in prep for tomorrow's shooting. It's almost nine and tomorrow is the first day of shooting in the tunnels.

Quinner wonders if the kid would be at Maxie's if his uncle was around. Probably not.

Quinner's with Josh Soames the director, Susie Burrows the AD, and Ethan Conroy and John McElway from Hungry Head, a table of empties starting to pile up in front of them. They have plenty to discuss, but despite his best efforts, Quinner finds himself drifting to the conversation around Noone.

The American mutters something in an undertone to the group and flicks his eyes towards Carter. They laugh and the barman flushes but says nothing. Lol Coleman, Maxie's owner, has made it clear that, for the duration of the shoot, weekends excepted, the place is theirs. Movie people are good for business. Good for the image. Even when some of them are dicks.

Carter can't see Coleman but Lol's always around somewhere and he's not a man you want to get offside, so the barman keeps his opinions to himself.

Quinner's watching it all until someone taps his arm.

'We got EightySix booked.' McElway looks at Conroy and angles his head towards Quinner. 'I said, we got EightySix booked, Dean.'

'What? Oh, yeah, right. Sweet.' He turns to McElway. 'Cheers, John. That's really good.'

EightySix is a London edit facility that Quinner's been pestering the production to use. It's another sign of the difference the Hungry Head investment has made. The made-in-Liverpool flavour is starting to become a little diluted but Quinner is philosophical. If going to London means the movie works better then he's got no problem with that.

As the talk turns to editing, Quinner sees Noone raise a quizzical eyebrow at Danny, some local blow-in he's turned up with tonight and who Quinner instinctively knows is bad news. Danny already seems half-cut but Quinner sees he gets Noone's drift right away.

He watches Danny reach into the pocket of his jeans and palm something to Noone with a practised smoothness. Noone winks and washes it down with the last of his drink.

Quinner's not the only observer. John McElway hasn't missed the transaction. He exchanges a fleeting glance with Quinner.

Time passes.

Noone slides his skinny arse off the bar stool. As his heels touch the floor one of the girls in the group positions herself between his legs. Alix, who does something in make-up, has slowly been working on getting Noone to herself for the past couple of weeks without making much progress. She's clearly decided tonight would be a good night to push it a little further.

'You off somewhere?' Alix slides her hands onto Noone's thighs. He stops and looks at her through his aviators. 'Don't you want to stay, Ben? Talk to me?' Alix's fingers are tracing a line ever closer to Noone's groin. She's a looker too, is Alix.

Noone puts his own hands on Alix's thighs and she leans into the touch. She's wearing a short skirt and Noone hooks a thumb under the hem and starts slowly lifting.

'Naughty,' murmurs Alix. She looks around at the rest of them. *Can you believe this?*

Noone continues to lift his thumbs and Alix starts to tense as he brushes a knuckle against her pussy.

'Ben,' Alix whispers. 'Not here.'

One or two of the group start to shuffle uncertainly. Noone leans close to Alix, still grasping her thighs, pulling her in between his long legs. She giggles softly as he whispers in her ear but then stiffens, the skin on the back of her neck reddening, and pushes him away, a startled expression on her face. She tugs down her skirt and backs off.

Noone smiles lazily and winks at her.

'Haven't you figured Benny boy out yet, Alix?' Danny is further down the track than anyone else would go with Noone. He's rocking slightly on the balls of his feet and his head is nodding easily, two tabs in. His Liverpool accent is hardening as he speaks. 'We don't know if he's queer or straight or what, right?' Danny fixes Noone with an unsteady gaze. 'My own view is that he's a fucken psycho. Just puttin' that out there.'

Noone is still smiling and he stands. 'I'm off the dial, man,' he says. 'Just like Danny boy says, darling.' He says the last words in a passable imitation of Bowie. Noone waves his hands in front of Alix's face and she flinches. 'The bogeyman. Wooo.' He swerves past Alix and waves a hand to the watching circle. 'Got to find my latest victim.'

Alix looks around uncertainly while the rest of the circle collapse in uncontrollable, booze-fuelled laughter, far louder than the half-joke requires.

Quinner's been watching and sees Noone make the early dart. The dark-eyed Peters boy says something to him that Quinner can't hear. Noone laughs and after a minute or two walks out. Nicky doesn't stay in the bar longer than a minute before he too heads out. Quinner can't work out if that's a coincidence.

He watches Alix head towards the bar, talking to one of her girl-friends, who has a protective arm around her shoulders.

'Ready for tomorrow, kid?' Ethan Conroy says in a fake American accent and puts his own arm around Quinner.

'Born ready,' says Quinner.

Josh Soames walks back from the bar and hands Quinner a Diet Coke. Quinner takes a sip and leans back.

'I see Ben's getting an early night,' says Soames and exchanges a look with Quinner. Despite the differences in their backgrounds, and Quinner's initial distrust of the plummy-voiced Londoner, the two are becoming closer. *The Tunnels* is their film now, not just Quinner's dream.

'The Thin White Duke? Yeah, noticed that.' Quinner lets his head drop to his chin. 'Must be dedicated.'

'Boys,' says Susie. 'Play nice.'

Quinner makes a who-me gesture.

'How do you think Ben's doing?' McElway asks the question lightly.

'Good,' says Quinner. 'Yeah, good.'

'But something bothers you about him, right?' This time it's Conroy. Quinner looks back and forth between the two producers.

'Is this some sort of trap? Are you fuckers wired?'

The two laugh. Quinner leans forward and rests his forearms on his knees, his drink held loosely in one hand. 'Where did you find him? I mean, I know he auditioned but it was so late in the game that I never really found out if there was a connection before.'

Noone had joined the production at a very late stage. Almost at the same time as Hungry Head came in, the original lead actor broke a leg and the whole thing almost stalled. Instead of waiting, Hungry Head pushed for a replacement. Quinner hadn't been involved in the auditions.

'No, he just showed up,' says Conroy. 'With all the rest. He had some sort of recommendation from Terry, but other than that he was unknown. Knew the city, did a great audition, nailed the accent.' Conroy looks over for confirmation from Soames, who nods in agreement.

'Brilliant,' says Soames. 'No question.'

'Terry recommended him?' says Quinner.

'Yeah, bumped into him somewhere and got talking. I think Terry knew this gig was coming up and passed him on.' Soames leans back. 'And we got him back in with another guy for a second reading and he convinced us. Not that we needed much convincing. And since he signed up the buzz has been building – admittedly that's got a lot to do with our marketing – but I spoke to an agent in LA about something else and Ben's name came up, unprompted. She knew all about him – or more than we'd been pushing – and she's a serious player. You know what it's like in this business. Heat is everything. Don't you think he's working, Dean?'

'He's great,' says Quinner. 'Perfect. I just wish I liked the twat.'

Everyone laughs and Quinner takes a drink.

Conroy and McElway and the others chat and smile about tomorrow's shooting but after the evening's over and Quinner's outside on the street, he can't shake the thought that Noone, the focal point of *his* movie, might be up to something naughty.

Walking back to his flat, it's not a comforting thought.

Five

For Quinner, this is the week when the movie feels like it's shifted into another gear. They've been shooting for almost three weeks but now they're in the tunnels. He's been down here many times before in preparation but now, filming right where he first got that electric crackle and the idea for the story sprang into his mind, the whole enterprise makes sense.

It'll work, he thinks. *The Tunnels* will work.

He makes his way through the location trucks parked outside the visitor's centre and heads down to the first set-up of the day. Despite the late night at Maxie's and the ongoing rigours of the shoot, Quinner feels energised, positive.

Just inside the location barriers he sees Terry's nephew, Nicky. The boy, carrying a loop of cable, waves a shy hand in Quinner's direction and he winks back. For the first time, Quinner notices Nicky's wearing a jacket like his own and wonders if the kid bought it deliberately. Teenagers do that, don't they, Quinner thinks. He can remember aping Liam Gallagher's walk during the Oasis years. The memory still makes him blush.

But if Nicky's trying to look like Quinner – like the script writer on the set, not the actors, or the director – that's interesting. Although he and Nicky Peters have greatly differing backgrounds, Quinner senses the kid might have some of the fire you need in this business.

Quinner reaches the large gallery in which Soames and his team are going to be shooting a conversation between Noone's character, a slaving ship sailor who has drifted into Williamson's orbit, and Williamson himself. An older, dependable character actor, Dave Losey, is playing Williamson. Quinner's worked with

23

Losey before on a TV soap and waves although doesn't approach him.

The technical crew have been setting up overnight so that time isn't wasted. Today's schedule is heavy, technical and demanding, and by seven the atmosphere is already jagged. Nerves are frayed and Quinner stays in the background. On set he is no more than a sounding-board for Josh Soames and his team. It might be Quinner's baby but he is not a technician. He gets a coffee from the catering truck and wanders inside, finds a brick ledge some metres back from the action and checks his notes.

He already knows Noone's late. Josh had texted as much half an hour ago.

Like I could do anything about it, thinks Quinner. You cast the fucker, you deal with his shit. He can feel his stomach knotting and fights to keep calm. You can only do what you can do.

And then, here he is, the main man, smiling, charming, apologetic and ready to work. Noone, in costume and make-up, looks brighter and more alert than anyone else.

Quinner doesn't look up as Noone walks past.

'You all right, la?' says Noone in a perfect Liverpool accent and pats Quinner on the upper arm. 'Can't hang about here all day, there's a fucking movie to be shot, right?'

Quinner smiles but says nothing.

'Gentlemen!' says Noone as he steps into the pool of light. His accent has changed again; a Victorian Englishman. 'To work, by God!'

Josh shoots a look at Quinner and shrugs. 'Places,' he says. 'Let's get moving.'

By eleven they're on schedule and with some good material safely filmed. The scenes Quinner's sweated on train journeys, in cold flats, at cafes and bars, are brought to glowing, vibrant life right there in front of him. Noone delivers on take after take. He might have been a wildcard casting with some questionable social habits – Quinner has heard a whisper that Alix isn't doing his make-up any more – but he has to admit that Soames and the others had been on the money about the American. When Quinner had first seen Noone he'd had doubts about the actor being able

24

to play a period piece but he seems to inhabit the costumes and role flawlessly. There's an unforced quality to his work that Quinner has only previously seen with experienced performers. Noone's a natural, perfect from the first take.

'Break,' calls Susie Burrows. 'Set up scene six.'

The technical crew begin dismantling the tracks and lights and moving them to the second location, just a few metres round the bend of the tunnel. The actors wander to chairs, reading their scripts. Noone drifts to the table set up by the caterers and fusses over a coffee. He selects a pastry and stuffs it into his mouth.

'Happy?' says Josh Soames and Quinner nods.

'Working really well, mate. I don't have anything useful to add.'

Soames, looking every inch a director – glasses, two-day beard, expensively rumpled clothes – wanders off, happy. 'It's having a good script, Dean,' he says as he goes, 'that makes my job easy.'

Quinner sits back and stretches, pleased enough to take the compliment whether Soames means it or not.

As he does, he sees Noone moving in a shadowy area behind the set. A leather jacket is draped on the back of a chair and Quinner watches Noone slide his hand inside and remove something. Noone slips what he's taken into his pocket and drifts away to make easy conversation with Bea, the continuity girl.

Quinner looks around.

What the fuck?

No one apart from himself seems to have witnessed the theft. For a few seconds Quinner runs through the sequence again to check it had really happened. He knows the jacket isn't the actor's. Their clothes are in the wardrobe and make-up trailer parked outside the tunnels.

Quinner sits back. This will take some thinking about.

An hour later and he finds out whose jacket it is.

Chris Birchall, one of the sound men, is cursing that he's lost his wallet. The theory is it's been dropped during the setting up and Nicky is detailed to see if he can spot it anywhere.

'You seeing everything all right?' Noone's voice is low in Quinner's ear and he jumps.

'What?'

They're standing ten metres or so from the little knot of excitement around Birchall.

'You getting a good view of all the action? From here, I mean.'

Quinner looks at Noone closely. The guy doesn't seem to be worried. Amused, if anything.

'Are you all right, Ben?'

Noone laughs softly. 'Never better, Dean. I'm just asking you if you like what you see.'

Quinner steps a little closer to the American. He can feel the challenge on a basic, instinctive level and Quinner's never been slow to back himself. 'Yes, I did,' he says, looking directly at Noone. 'I've been watching everything very closely. Good performance. Very smooth.'

There's a pause in which the two men hold each other's eyes in the way which usually precedes a confrontation. It's Noone who breaks the moment.

'Well, best get back to work, Dean. No rest for the wicked.'

Quinner reaches out and puts a hand on Noone's upper arm.

'That last take you did?' says Quinner. 'I reckon you could do that again. Make it better.'

Noone looks for all the world like he's considering Quinner's suggestion as a menu choice. Fish or lamb, sir?

'Nah,' says Noone, smiling a movie star smile and shrugging Quinner's hand off his arm. 'I got it.'

Although they've been speaking in code, both of them know the score.

You saw me and I don't care. What's going to happen to your movie if you kick up about this?

Quinner's been threatened before but this is different. There's something about Noone's flat acceptance of the situation and the smooth way in which he's controlled the conversation that makes Quinner feel complicit, violated. Dirty.

'Drinks later?' says Noone. He turns away. 'Nice chat.'

Quinner watches him walk off.

This isn't finished, thinks Quinner, and heads out of the tunnels. He needs phone reception.

Six

It's not often that Dean, or anyone for that matter, asks Big Niall to do something for real cash money. They're in Quinner's flat in the Albert Dock, the evening of Noone stealing the wallet. Big Niall's brought his mate.

'No sweat, Deano,' says Niall, beaming all over his stupid face. 'Sorted, bro.'

'Don't ask him for his autograph, right? I just want him followed. See what he's up to. You got that, Niall?'

Quinner's worries about Noone had already been building for days and the wallet thing has pushed him beyond curious. There's something wrong with the American and he isn't about to risk six years' work on *The Tunnels* for it all to be washed away by this tool. If Quinner can find out a bit more about Noone, maybe persuade him to return the wallet, he'll feel a lot better. He's not the type to sit back and let the American screw things up. It's just a wallet but Quinner's been around plenty of thieves before and none of them have ever reacted like Noone if challenged. Denial, violence, whining maybe, but the cocky shrug with which Noone dismissed his guilt has got under Quinner's skin. He takes out a cigarette and lights up.

'Bad for your health, them things, man,' says Big Niall's mate.

'Fuck off,' says Quinner. He takes a drag.

'No, serious, man. Me ma went with lung cancer that way.'

'Sorry,' says Quinner. To his astonishment, Niall's mate bursts out laughing.

'Fucken got you, bro! Me ma's watching some shit at home!' Niall's mate extends a closed fist towards Niall and the two bump knuckles. 'Fucken hooked or what, man?' Niall's mate turns back to Quinner, his face serious again. 'But they are bad for you, no messin'.'

He's wearing the same clothes he was in when Quinner saw him at the shoot in Huskisson Street two days ago.

'He all right?' Quinner looks at Niall and then nods in the direction of Niall's mate. 'In the head, I mean?'

'Don't worry, man,' says Niall's mate. 'I'll be fucken sound, no sweat.' He folds his arms, two fingers outstretched on each hand and purses his lips in a gangsta pose. 'Ghost Ninja, that's me.'

'Are you saying that's your name? *Ghost Ninja?* What's your real name?' says Quinner, then holds up his hand. 'Wait, I don't want to know.'

He turns to Niall.

'Noone will most likely be at Maxie's. You know where that is? Good. Just hang around and see where he goes and get back to me.' Quinner hands Niall some money.

'Here's fifty notes. Fifty more if you do this right.'

'Sound, Deano. No problem.' Niall signals to his mate it's time to leave.

'*Ghost Ninjaaaaa,*' the guy hisses as he passes Quinner, his eyes wide, pupils small. Ghost Ninja spreads his hands out in a gesture that he imagines makes him look freaky and intimidating. He looks fried, and about as intimidating as a Jack Russell.

'Jesus,' says Quinner and opens the door to the flat, already feeling he's making a mistake. Briefing Big Niall and his dickhead mate to follow Noone makes him feel silly, like he's playing a part in a movie. The trouble is, he can't decide if it's a thriller or a comedy.

Seven

Sitting in the corner of the wood-panelled backroom at The Phil, Frank laces his fingers together and stretches his arms out, the punishment he took in the work-out with Chrissy Cahill on Tuesday replaying in his mind with every twinge. His ribs hurt too but Frank likes the feeling; it reminds him he's still close enough to the man he was in his early twenties. Some of the coppers Frank came up with haven't worn so well and the fact that he can give a kid like Chrissy something like a genuine bout is a source of pride, bruises or no bruises.

'Cheers,' says Frank, catching Harris's eye. As she lifts her own glass, Frank takes a pull on his drink and makes a face. He'd asked Caddick for a scotch but the dickwad's come back with bourbon. Seeing Frank raise his head and look round the room like a malevolent prairie dog for the hapless DC makes Em Harris smile.

'Wrong drink?'

Frank nods glumly and then shrugs. 'Tastes like treacle,' he says. 'Not that I've ever tasted treacle.'

The two most senior members of the MIT unit are sitting together while the gaggle of junior officers stand in a tight knot amid a growing crowd and get louder with every round.

Like most Thursday evenings, this one begins with the Major Incident Team gathered for the traditional end to the week. Exactly why the MIT week ends on Thursday no one really knows, but the tradition – one instigated by Frank's old boss, Menno Koopman – has endured and no one is going to change it anytime soon. Attendance isn't compulsory but it is expected.

If either DCI Keane or DI Harris had known how it was going to end they may not have come.

Harris doesn't make it to that many Thursday sessions, seeing them, with some justification, as a throwback to harder drinking, more overtly masculine times. But she's pragmatic enough to know that a complete absence would not help her in building any bridges in the wake of last year's Stevie White affair so she's there along with Caddick, Rose, Theresa Cooper and the others.

Frank's there because he hasn't got anything better on offer. Since January, the Thursdays, along with the odd boxing session, more or less represent his social life.

None of the team ever invites their partners and few would come if asked. MIT, while not as masonic as it once might have been, can still be something of a sealed world. For Harris, that, at least, is a relief. It's hard enough being a black female officer without bringing Linda into the picture.

She and Frank are discussing – what else – work. Frank doesn't know what he's done tonight but he has the feeling that Em's on his case more than usual. Always sharp, there's an edge there tonight that feels different and her eyes look brighter. For a moment Frank wonders if she's doing coke but guiltily dismisses the idea as soon as it arrives. Em's too smart for that; seen too much. But the thought of cocaine reminds him of the White case from last year.

'What made you side with Perch?'

Just asking the question makes Frank realise he's drunk too much. Otherwise he wouldn't be asking. Neither of them has discussed Harris's ultimately unwise decision to choose DCI Perch over Frank.

'I'm not having a go, Em. It's just something we haven't talked about.'

'Can't we just keep it that way? We are English, you know. Not talking about stuff is what we do.'

Frank wags a finger. 'Uh-no. Not tonight. You're not getting off that easy.'

Harris starts to speak but breaks off as Theresa Cooper leans out of a knot of people and asks her if she wants a top-up.

'No. Wait, OK. G & T.'

Frank drains his bourbon. 'Could you get me a malt, Theresa? I'll fix you up. The boy Caddick gets easily confused.'

Cooper smiles and heads to the bar. Her promotion to Detective Sergeant a couple of months ago has put a spring in her step. It's a little unusual for a promoted officer to stay within the same department but Frank's glad Cooper's still with MIT. Seeing one of their own make it up a grade has shaken up the rest of them. He's already seen an improved performance as competition intensifies.

Harris turns back to Frank. 'I don't know. It seemed to make sense at the time. I was worried about you bringing your old boss back into it. I didn't know Koopman. You were taking a big risk involving him.' Harris shakes her head. 'But you were right. In the end.' She leans back and regards Frank coolly. 'Why are you asking now?'

Frank shrugs. 'Just thinking how stupid it is that we're not talking properly.' He waggles his empty glass. 'Plus I'm half-pissed.'

'Half?'

'All right, almost off my tits.'

At the mention of tits, his eyes – he can't help it – drift towards Em Harris's chest.

'For fuck's sake, Frank,' she says, but there's the start of a smile on her lips.

Frank holds out his hands in apology. 'I did say I was half-pissed. Do you know the efforts I go to not to do that at work?'

'Yeah, I do,' says Harris. 'You're not the worst by a long chalk. That sleaze Pete Moreleigh almost bumped into them at the media briefing last week. I let him know how I felt.'

'So we're all good?' says Frank. Although glad to hear of Moreleigh's discomfort, he feels the discussion of Harris's charms is treacherous ground.

Harris softens. 'I'm glad you asked, Frank. And it is stupid we're not talking. Properly, I mean.' She regards Frank. 'How are you doing, anyway? Single life suiting you?'

Harris keeps her tone light but has those big brown eyes fixed on Frank. His persistence in getting some dialogue going again has touched her. From the office chat it's clear that he hasn't exactly had a smooth ride over the past six months. Despite her mention of Frank's single status they haven't discussed his break-up. Until now. If Frank's going into unknown territory with direct questions, why can't she do the same?

Frank shrugs and grimaces. 'Not really. It's OK. Too much work in the new job.' He doesn't know if that's true or not. It's just something you say in that situation, isn't it? The break-up hadn't felt like a break-up. There was no real drama, no big slanging match between him and Julie; things had been deteriorating for months before she finally made the decision. You could feel it in the dead air between them where there had once been warmth and electricity. There were no kids, thank Christ. At least they were spared that particular horror show.

The mention of Frank's promotion cools the atmosphere a fraction. Even through the fog of alcohol Frank perceives the dip.

'What about you?' says Frank.

Harris hesitates.

Linda moved out a week ago. More accurately, Em had asked her to leave. Just for now. As if in silent reminder, her iPhone buzzes against her thigh. It'll be one of Linda's texts but Harris doesn't respond.

'Yeah, all fine.' A direct question doesn't mean she has to give Frank the unvarnished truth.

Cooper reappears carrying three glasses, expertly shouldering her way through the throng. She hands a tall glass to Harris and a small one to Frank.

'Ta,' says Frank. He sips the malt and sighs theatrically.

'Thanks, Theresa,' says Harris and takes a long pull, grateful for the interruption. 'Christ Almighty. How many are in there?'

'Just one,' says Cooper. Catching Frank's eye, and, momentarily unseen by Harris, Cooper holds up three fingers. She winks and disappears back into a wave of laughter from the MIT crew.

'Bottoms up,' says Harris. For some reason, perhaps its proximity to the 'tits' discussion, the phrase strikes Frank as funny and he fights the urge to smile. He loses and creases up on the red velvet chair, giggling like a schoolboy. Harris watches him and drains her glass in one. Frank's got the compact build of a welterweight and a blue-eyed stare that can freeze the blood of a new-spawned plod from fifty paces but right now he looks like a teenager. Although Frank doesn't know it, it's at that point that Em Harris decides where the evening's going to end.

Eight

'C'mon, Niall. Let's do one. This is fucken boring, man.' Ghost Ninja's voice is whiny. They've only been there for about an hour and Ghost Ninja's already sorry he agreed to come, fifty notes or no fucking fifty notes. It's not like *CSI*, man, not like it one fucking little bit. And Jason – Ghost Ninja's real name – has got some decent weed he wants to get into back home. Get fucked up, like nice and proper fucked up, and watch some shit on the box. 'Come 'ed, Nially. We'll be here fucken hours, bro.'

'Wait.' Niall's spotted the guy coming out. Thank fuck. He doesn't think he could stand hearing any more from Ninja the Whinger.

Noone and a couple of people come through the double doors of Maxie's and stand for a moment on the corner.

Niall and Jason slide back into the shadows of a small cut-through between two buildings. Niall stubs his cigarette out on a wall.

'It's deffo him, lad!' Jason's all excited now, the desire for weed momentarily forgotten. 'Fucken sweet!'

The couple Noone is talking to turn away from him and move down the street. Noone immediately heads directly across the road towards the alleyway.

'Fuck. He's comin'.'

Niall grabs Jason and the two of them shuffle along the alley and squat behind a stinking pile of semi-rotted cardboard boxes and fuck knows what else.

'Jesus Christ, la', this fucken stinks!'

'Quiet, Jase.'

Big Niall can't even risk looking. He pulls his head into his collar. And then looks anyway.

He's just in time to see Noone veer left and head down the street towards the river. Niall stands and, followed closely by Jason, lumbers towards the neck of the alley. Forty metres away Noone hunches into the breeze from the river. He's moving quickly.

'This is ace!' Jason's at Niall's shoulder, his rat eyes shining. 'Fucken *CSI*, la'!'

'Come on.' Niall waits as long as he thinks he can and then, staying close to the building line, follows the American. Negotiating the geography of the city is as natural as breathing to Niall and Jason. Which makes the job simple, even through the late-evening club crowds.

Noone moves with purpose, weaving between the swarm of drunken neanderthals hurrying towards the next booze station.

From behind, Niall notices there is never any contact between Noone and those he passes, not even the brush of a nylon sleeve against his leather jacket. When one plodding cow waddles into his path in her too-short white Lycra skirt the American arcs his back and twists sideways to avoid her.

'Where's he goin'?'

'How the fuck do I know, man?' Niall's no Einstein but he's got the edge on Jason. 'That's what we're fucken followin' the cunt for.'

'He's walkin' miles, man. And I thought Dean said to have a word with him.'

Niall shakes his head. 'C'mon, dickhead. We got to wait for somewhere nice and quiet.'

'We goin' to fuck him up, man?' Jason perks up. 'Nice one!'

'Jesus, Jase. Deano said just to follow. We're not goin' to do anything.'

Niall shakes his head. Fucking Jason. Niall's never seen him fuck anyone up, other than mentally.

Three minutes later, they've lost Noone.

One minute he was crossing the street up ahead, the next, gone.

'What happened?' says Jason. 'Where'd he go?'

'Don't you know?' spits Niall. 'You're fucken Ghost Ninja, aren't you?'

'Don't blame me, man. He probably went home. Didn't Dean say he lived round here?'

Niall doesn't know. He thinks so. He hadn't been listening properly. All he'd heard from his cuz was fifty more notes. Fifty he'd already spent in his head.

'Shit.' Niall spins around, up on his toes, scanning the traffic on King Edward Street. As a line of cars move off from the lights he spots something heading down Great Howard Street.

'There!' Niall points.

Jason cranes his head, exposing a raw red spot on his neck. 'You sure? Why's he goin' that way?'

'It's him,' says Niall, already moving. 'How the fuck do I know where he's goin'?'

With one eye on the traffic he crosses to the central reservation and then darts across. Behind him he hears horns blaring as Jason, less decisive than Niall, comes within an inch of the bumper of a black cab.

'Dickhead!' yells Jason as he arrives on the pavement.

'For fuck's sake, bro! Why don't you set off some fireworks while yer at it? Give the feller some proper warnin', like?'

'Sorry, mate,' says Jason, still flicking Vs at the cabbie. 'Forgot.'

Jason peers ahead. On the left side of Great Howard Street he can see a figure silhouetted in the oncoming lights from the passing traffic.

'You sure that's him?'

Niall's already moving. 'It's him,' he says over his shoulder.

For the next couple of minutes Jason and Niall don't say much. Then, opposite a darkened car wash, the man they're following turns down a side street.

Eighty metres behind, Niall and Jason pick up the pace.

At Oil Street, they stop.

'That road's a bit dodgy, Niall,' says Jason. He's hopping from one leg to the other, his head hunched into his hoodie. 'I went to a twenty-first in an Irish pub down here once – rough as fuck – and I cut through this road on me way back into town. It's fucken nasty at night, man. We don't want to go down there.'

'Let's just see.' Fifty quid is fifty quid. He turns to Jason and jabs him in the chest with his forefinger. 'And don't forget, dickhead, *we're* supposed to be the nasty ones.'

Niall looks down Oil Street and sees Noone disappear through a gap in a wall.

If it was Noone.

Niall, despite his confident assertions to the contrary, isn't so sure any more. What would some ponce of an actor be doing dicking about in a place like this?

'Shit.' To Niall's left are the lights from the city. It looks inviting. Down Oil Street, everything just looks black and shitty. Halfway down the street is a single yellow lamp hanging outside some sort of brick building. High walls and barbed wire run along one side, the arse end of industrial units along the other. Every window is covered with iron bars. The pavement gleams with broken glass. Although Niall and Jason don't know it, the area's thick with the ghosts of the High Rip gang. A hundred and twenty years ago sailors were rolled down here in the slums off the Dock Road, shivved or kicked to death, for the coin in their pocket. It hasn't improved much since then. The place is a shithole.

'Fuck this,' says Jason. 'I'm off. Fifty notes isn't enough for this.'

'Go then,' says Niall, hoping Jason stays.

'I will.'

Niall watches him fidget, unsure of what to do. Niall shakes his head and then heads down Oil Street.

'Wait here for us,' he hisses to Jason and then he's gone.

At the intersection, Jason stands for a second. A car blares past, and someone shouts something. A dog barks.

Jason runs.

Fuck *CSI*. Big Niall's on his own.

Nine

Em is lying on the bed wearing nothing. Frank runs a hand through his hair and whistles. It's an image that he's sure, drunk or not, will stick in his mind for a long time.

'Frankie,' she says, her eyes half-closed. She runs a finger lazily across her lower stomach and makes small, slow movements with her hips.

It would take a much better man than he is to resist. And he's technically single. Like it matters. He doesn't ask about Linda.

There are so many reasons that they shouldn't be doing this that his head would be spinning even without being bombed.

But he is bombed and besides . . . *Jesus. Come on. Look at her.*

Frank pulls off his shirt and staggers onto the bed. Both of them pissed as squaddies on a weekend pass.

Em laughs. A deep, warm sound. She rolls Frank onto his back and straddles his chest.

Frank's breathing comes heavier and Em reaches behind her to find his cock. Without taking her eyes off his she runs her fingers along him and he arches his back towards her. His hands cup her buttocks. A natural place. They're softer than he'd imagined – and he'd imagined them often – but still firmly muscled. Harris is fitter than him, scores higher in the annual tests, works out with . . .

'Frank.' Em puts a hand to his face. 'You still with me?'

Frank focuses and makes a noise but he's not sure what he's saying. Christ, he's hammered. Em slides down his body until she's got his cock in her mouth. Now he's awake.

The moments pass like shadows. Frank's licking her, he's in her, there's moaning, sweat. She's angry and hungry. He feels her slapping him at one point and he's aroused and pained at the same time. Her open palm has weight and he feels he's being punished, not just for this and not just for her pleasure, but for unknown past workplace indiscretions and snubs.

Fucker. She looks like she hates him.

He doesn't care. They fuck hard. Harris wants things from Frank he won't give. Pain. Humiliation. Hers and his.

Fuck me harder, fucker.

Her black skin's a novelty for Frank, his cock for her. He holds her down, her wrists pinned above her head as her legs wrap around him, pulling him in deeper.

Where's Linda? The thought slides in and then out again and is lost only to return, with interest, later.

Drink, the great denier and giver, this time smiles on him, granting him stamina, and she comes first, bucking under him and holding him stiff-armed, eyes fixed on his in that glazed, unfocused death stare. *Un petit mort.*

Cunt. Fuck. Bastard. Do me. Fuck me. She's swearing a blue streak and when she can feel Frank coming she moves him out. *Come on me*, she hisses, positioning him across her, his slick cock sliding over her breasts. She takes him and strokes and pulls and then he comes. *Oh yes*, she says and slides his cock into her mouth again and Frank feels the pleasure and the pain and the familiar Catholic guilt.

She holds him in her mouth too long, until he has to pull out, and they lie spent in a puddled tangle of sheets and come and sweat.

Later, he's not sure when, they fuck once more and then it's dark.

When his eyes open there's grey morning leaking in from somewhere.

Frank's more worried about the hangover he knows is coming. By all rights he should be a broken man. He rolls over in bed and sees the s-shape of Em under a sheet, her back to him, one smooth arm draped over her hip.

He watches enough to check she's breathing and rolls onto his back.

'You'd better go.' Her voice is heavy with sleep but clear. Frank waits but there's nothing else.

'Sure.' He collects his clothes and leaves the bedroom. He dresses in the small living room, the air thick with stale wine. On the coffee table two bottles and a couple of glasses look like props from a play. The blinds are closed and Frank leaves them that way. He registers that the room is pleasant, unremarkable – no easy psychological readings to be gained.

He takes a glass of water from the tap in the open-plan kitchen and drains it in one. In the bathroom he squeezes some of Harris's toothpaste onto his finger and runs it over his teeth. His tongue looks like roadkill and there's a redness to one side of his face, the trace memory of last night's slap.

In the bathroom cabinet – *thank you, God* – paracetamol, and Frank takes three. He can't help but notice the bottle of blonde hair dye, the two toothbrushes in the glass. Harris's partner, Linda, location unknown (by Frank), relationship status uncertain.

This was a mistake.

He closes the cabinet and steps out into the hall of the flat. He waits a few seconds for something from Em but there's nothing. He shrugs his jacket on and silently leaves, his spirits sinking as the door closes behind him.

Falkner Street is cold and empty, Harris's flat a short stumble from The Phil. The distance, Frank considers, may have been a contributing factor. If Harris had lived a taxi away they may have had a chance to consider.

Fuck it.

It happened and it was good. He'll deal with the consequences later. Frank looks at his watch. Four-thirty am.

He walks down Falkner to Hope and turns towards a cathedral; the Catholic one, fittingly. Anxious to postpone any soul-searching until completely necessary, he hurries towards Hardman Street and drops down the hill towards the city centre. On the opposite side of the sloping street the looming Dutch gothic roof of The Phil blocks out the disapproving cathedral. Frank is watched by a passing patrol car, which slows to a crawl as it approaches. Close up, the uniform at the wheel raises a hand in recognition, but Frank, intent on invisibility, ignores him.

A street-cleaning crew is at work mopping up last night's debris outside The Fly In The Loaf. Four men in fluoro jackets hose down the pavements, all of them smoking. A straggle of clubbers limp up Hardman in flimsy clothing, their conversation loud and rich with *fucks* and *twats* and *'ey dickheads*. A girl with the figure of a supermodel and make-up as thick as that of a kabuki actor squeals something to a friend behind her as Keane passes and he flinches. Jesus. Her voice scrapes his skull. The group disappear towards the university district, singing a song Keane doesn't recognise. The squealing supermodel puts a finger under the clinging Lycra of her micro-mini and shows her arse to the patrol car. She's not wearing underwear.

Frank feels approximately eight hundred years old.

Thoughts of a clean-living alternative self pop into his head, as always at times like this. A fresh, ascetic Frank, walking across some unspecified breezy, bracing moor. A sober Frank. A Frank who is happily married again. A Frank who doesn't drunk fuck his colleagues.

A different Frank.

Halfway down Hardman he turns into a side road and into the warm embrace of The Majorca.

The twenty-four-hour taxidrivers' caff is packed with the post-club-run drivers but Frank manages to bag a seat in a corner. Enzo lifts one of his chins in acknowledgement and tea the colour of mahogany appears like magic. It's followed by a full English and more tea. At five-thirty or so, and feeling slightly more human, Frank goes through the usual routine of offering to pay Enzo before leaving without money changing hands.

'Be good, Frank,' shouts Enzo as the door to The Majorca rattles shut.

It's time to go home.

Ten

When Noone notices the two clowns clumsily following him from Maxie's he places the big one right away. He's the guy Quinner was speaking with at the top of Huskisson Street on Tuesday.

Noone briefly considers ignoring the two guys following him, just slipping inside his flat and letting them fade away, but then the familiar, half-welcome anger hits him hard.

Checking that the two guys in hoodies and trackpants are still behind him, he turns past the street leading to his apartment block and drops down onto the Pier Head.

The Liver Building is lit from below, a white-iced cake against the night sky. He walks north and crosses the dual carriageway onto Great Howard Street. Here the buildings begin to lose their scrubbed-up appearance. He walks past a shuttered car dealership and a ragtag collection of half-boarded shops and businesses. Looking back over his shoulder to confirm that his tails are still in attendance, he turns left down Oil Street, a dank, dark road connecting the parallel traffic arteries at either end. The street's deserted, and hemmed in on both sides by ancient brick walls oozing oil and mysterious industrial-yellow chemical pus. The glass-flecked road is patched and re-patched and what pavement there is is treacherous underfoot, even in the dry. About fifty metres from the junction with Waterloo Road there's a hole kicked through a breezeblock wall into a derelict triangle of no-man's-land between two corrugated engineering sheds. It's pitch black and he slips through taking care to be observed. One last glance back up Oil Street tells Noone there's a conference taking place. He waits at the gap in the wall and watches as the smaller of the two would-be trackers walks away, back towards the city and out of view. After a moment the big guy starts walking down Oil Street and Noone smiles to himself.

One will be easier.

Big Niall is conscious of his own fear but there's no turning around now, not after telling Jason he was carrying on. The feller he's following has gone from view but Niall's pretty sure he saw him dive through a gap in the fence. Trying to be clever.

Niall slows as he closes on the gap in the wall. He glances back up Oil Street in the direction he's come from and sees no one. For a moment he considers abandoning the plan, giving Deano a call and saying they lost him. Then he squares himself up, a working man doing his job, and steps through the gap in the wall.

As he does, something metallic connects with the side of his neck and he slumps to the floor, everything reduced to a simple horizon of pain and panic. Then there's a second hit and Niall's not thinking any more.

He comes to less than four minutes later.

For a few brief, euphoric seconds he feels nothing except puzzlement. He staggers back through the broken breezeblock wall into Oil Street before the excruciating pain from his hand hits home and he opens his mouth to scream. Except there's something inside, something blocking his mouth. He spits the object out into his hand.

And now Big Niall does scream.

Eleven

The morning crawls past like a beaten dog.

Somehow, Frank's not really sure how, he makes it to lunchtime and knows that's it for him. Stacked desk or not, he's taking a sickie this afternoon and getting some sleep. One of the advantages of his promotion is a little more leeway at moments of crisis like this. He'd had a call from Harris about two hours ago but let his mobile go to answerphone. In his hung-over state he doesn't know if that's because he wants to avoid her, or if he just wants to avoid hearing her say that's all there will be after last night. Either way, he doesn't pick up.

Bed is a must or he's going to fall down. He's only taken a couple of steps out of Canning Place when it happens.

'Frank Keane?' says a voice behind him.

'Yeah?' He turns and sees a blonde, thirty maybe, good-looking, wearing her hair short, razor-cut on the sides and back. He only has time to register her angry, contorted face before she throws a cup of cold vinegary-smelling liquid in his face.

'Burn, you bastard!'

'What the fuck!' Frank wipes stinging fluid from his eyes, his vision blurred, panic already building.

'Who'll have you now, you bastard! Burn, you fucker! Burn!'

Acid.

The word flashes neon in Frank's mind and he feels himself shrink. He swivels, panicking, into the Canning Place foyer just as his eyes begin to seriously hurt. The security door is locked and the plod on the desk looks at him blankly for a moment until Frank, his eyes streaming, screams, 'Open the fucking door! Do it!'

There's a fumbling second or two wasted before the buzzer sounds. Frank pushes through the security door and runs, stumbling, for the bathroom across the width of the foyer, each valuable second allowing the acid to take hold. He slams into the toilets like a drunk, banging his shoulder on the tile wall, his panicky fingers scrabbling uselessly for the taps.

Fuck, fuck, fuck, fuck.

He squeezes his eyes shut and wonders if they'll ever open again.

And then there's water and he splashes it over himself, frantic, can't get enough, quick quick, turns on another tap and fills a second basin while he's got his face under this one. Plunges his head under and opens his eyes, willing the water to wash away whatever filth that crazy bitch threw. He holds it as long as he can and then stands. He rips his jacket off and then his shirt. His shoulder feels sore and he scoops handful after handful of water onto the skin. He can't tell if the pain's from the hit against the wall or from something else.

Acid. *Shit.*

'You all right, boss?' It's the uniform from the desk. Hastings.

Frank doesn't trust himself to speak; the adrenaline is making him tremble so much but he manages to blurt 'hospital'.

Hastings clatters out and as the door opens Frank can hear the commotion in the holding area. A woman's voice, hysterical, the bass voice of the duty officer talking.

Frank's breathing slows a little and he risks a look in the mirror, expecting to see some molten horror show. A wave of naked relief sweeps over him as he sees no obvious damage. He continues to cradle handful after handful of water onto the affected areas. His pants are wet and he takes them off too. He tries to replay the woman throwing the liquid over him. It hit his face, his shoulder, a little on his forearm and hand.

Panting, Frank leans on the porcelain of the basin and tries to get himself under control. His heart is banging around inside his chest cavity as if it has broken free of its moorings. Hastings comes back in and Frank stands.

'Er, we've got a car outside, sir. Be quicker than an ambulance.'

Frank nods. 'You get her?'

44

'She's been taken to the holding cells, sir.' Hastings hesitates, uncomfortable. There's something else.

'What?' barks Frank. Deep down, he already knows.

'The woman who attacked you? She's DI Harris's partner. Linda Black.'

Frank nods and then puts his face back under water. He holds it there, his eyes open, as long as he can.

Christ. What a day.

Twelve

By Friday, Dean Quinner's regretting involving Big Niall and his cretinous mate in this thing with Noone. Sleep, never a frequent visitor for Quinner, hadn't come easy last night and when the morning arrives, things don't look better. Lying awake, his decision now looks like one of the dumbest things he'd ever done.

What if Niall ends up hurting the actor? Won't that be as disastrous as anything that would happen if the theft came to light? It's only a fucking wallet. Quinner wonders if it's himself he should be worrying about, not Noone. What kind of lunatic puts his faith in someone like Niall?

Shit.

Quinner looks at his watch and reaches for his phone before stopping, his hand in midair. Anything that's happened will be over by now. It can wait. With luck the big idiot won't have done anything and Quinner will be able to call off the dogs with no one any the wiser.

He leans back in the chair and closes his eyes. As he does, the quiet of the flat is cut by Quinner's ringtone signalling an incoming text. Quinner reaches across the coffee table and picks up.

It's from Niall.

Quinner presses 'open' and the message appears. There are no words. Instead an animated hand walks onscreen, forms itself into a fist and then flips Quinner the finger.

Quinner closes the phone and switches it to silent.

Fucking Niall.

Thirteen

The doctor at the Royal, a young Asian woman wearing a headscarf who looks more tired than Keane, sees him immediately. A uniform from Canning Place drives him direct.

'No permanent damage.' The doctor peers into Keane's eyes using a powerful light which feels more painful than the acid. 'You'll need to make a follow-up appointment with an ophthalmologist to double-check in case there's been any tissue scars caused by scrubbing at the eyes, but I think you'll be fine.'

She stands and passes Frank a paper towel.

'Thanks.'

Something occurs to him as the doctor turns to leave. 'What was it she threw at me? Do you know?'

'Not sure. But I would guess something like surgical spirit, or white vinegar.'

'Vinegar? I could smell vinegar but I thought acid just smelt like that.'

'It does, sometimes. But in this case I think your attacker may have been just trying to scare you.'

Frank levers himself off the examination couch.

'She succeeded.'

The doctor smiles bleakly and leaves.

Frank picks up his damp jacket and looks at his watch.

Fifteen minutes later, he's walking down Copperas Hill towards Lime Street. He could call a car but the walk will help clear his head. He cuts past the faded grandeur of the Adelphi and then through the shoppers on Ranelagh Street, heading for the Pier Head. There are a few half-glances in his direction at the damp patches on his shirt.

His phone rings as the Cunard Building comes into view.

It's Harris. Frank hesitates before pressing the answer button.

'Frank,' she says and he knows instantly that she has heard. 'Where are you?'

'I'm going to sleep. Call me in, say, three weeks.'

'We need to talk about Linda. She's in the lock-up at Canning Place. I just got a call from her. What happened, Frank?'

'Didn't she tell you?'

'Yes, sort of. Not really.' There's a pause. 'She mentioned acid.' Frank hears the fear in Harris's voice. It's not something he's ever heard before and it's something he'd rather not hear again.

'She threw what I thought was acid at me. Outside HQ. It wasn't, but I had a nasty couple of minutes until I worked that out. She knows. About last night. Did you tell her?'

'No. She was in a car outside the flat when you left. She'd been there all night.' Harris sounds as vulnerable as Frank's ever heard. 'We've been having some trouble recently. Linda's . . . well . . .'

'It doesn't matter. Get her out as quickly as you can. I'll call Canning Place and speak to the duty officer.' The thought of getting into all that crap now doesn't bear thinking about. 'I'm not pressing charges. It wasn't acid and neither of us needs any more attention, do we?'

Harris doesn't reply for a moment.

'She'll be sorry, Frank. If that's any help.'

'Do what you need to do, Em. Take her home. And you stay home too. We both need some sleep. I'll be back down at Stanley Road tomorrow. If you get in before me look after everything.'

'OK,' says Harris. There's a pause.

'I enjoyed last night, Em,' says Frank. Even as he's saying it the words seem flat. But it's all he's got. 'I don't regret it.'

'Yeah,' says Harris and ends the call leaving Frank looking at the phone.

He crosses the street towards the hulking black Mann Island monolith squatting next to the Liver Building, lets himself in using the security card and heads to the third floor. The apartment blinds are closed and the place is a mess compared to Harris's flat.

The block of apartments and offices is relatively new, built in a rush of misplaced pre-GFC confidence, and is generally regarded by the citizens as a hideous eyesore. Buoyed by a couple of pay rises, and what now appears an inexplicable phase of optimism around the time that Liverpool became European Capital of Culture, Keane had bought a small flat in the development, hoping to rent it out and watch it steadily increase in value. It was a decision he has spent almost two years regretting: he'd seen the investment stutter and fade, and renters had proved more elusive than the Yeti. After the split with Julie he'd moved in, thinking it would be temporary, that he'd get somewhere more permanent, but here he was. Now, alone in the flat, dog-tired and smelling of vinegar, Frank wonders what kind of relationship he and Em might have after what happened.

Frank goes into the bedroom, takes off his clothes and gets into the musty bed. He's asleep inside two minutes.

Fourteen

Once she'd spoken to Frank, Em takes Linda back to the flat. Linda lives in Aigburth but Harris's place is closer.

Linda, her crying jag subsided, is almost catatonic during the agonisingly embarrassing process of getting her released from the building. Harris will be using up almost all her brownie points to limit the fallout from this. And, after last year's disaster with Perch, she doesn't have too many left in reserve.

'What's going to happen?' says Linda as they reach the flat on Falkner Street.

For once, Em doesn't have an answer. A wave of fatigue sweeps over her.

'I'm not sure. Frank told me he's not pressing charges but there could still be trouble. You attacked a police officer, Lin.'

Linda starts to cry again and Em guides her into the bedroom. She undresses her and puts her into bed. Em goes into the bathroom and finds her sleeping pills. She takes one, fills a glass of water in the kitchen and walks back into the bedroom.

'Take this,' she says and Linda swallows the pill without a word. Em goes back into the living room, checks her watch and calls MIT. Linda's attack on Frank will be all over the place and Harris is in no shape to deal with it.

'I'm sick,' she tells DC Rose in a voice that stops any amusement in his voice dead in its tracks. 'I'll be in over the weekend.' She rings off before Rose replies and puts the phone on to charge. She undresses and gets in beside Linda. The two women have their backs to each other but lie close together, skin to skin. Em's not quite ready to let Linda off the hook but wants her to know it will be OK. They both have things they need to say.

'We'll talk when we've had some sleep,' says Em and closes her eyes.

Fifteen

Quinner's phone beeps and he checks the message. Two words: Ghost Ninja.

Before he can reply, the phone rings.

'I'm outside, man,' says Ghost Ninja.

'Then why did you text? Wait, never mind. What is it?'

'Buzz me up. I need to talk to yer.'

'I'm not in the mood for this shit. Not today, mate. You'll have to get Niall to sort you out. It was a stupid idea anyway. Tell him to leave it now. It doesn't matter.'

'I can't,' says Jason. 'You need to talk to us, man.'

Fuck.

'OK,' says Quinner. He moves to the intercom and opens the door for Niall's mate. He can see him on the CCTV camera shuffling gormlessly in the foyer. His eyes keep darting to the sides.

'And it's not the money, man,' he says once he's inside. 'It's Niall. He's been . . . well, he's been all weird since last night.' Ghost Ninja drops his voice conspiratorially. 'The mission! *You* know. Followin' that feller.'

'For fuck's sake, stop hopping about.' Quinner shakes his head. 'You're making me feel dizzy. And what do you mean about Niall?'

'It was fucken mental, brother. Niall just dived right in. Fucken mental.' Jason points vaguely in the direction of the city. 'Down on the dock road, man. Not good. Bad juju.'

'Bad fucking juju? What the fuck are you talking about?'

'Niall!' Jason looks at Quinner like he's stupid. 'That's what I'm tryin' to tell you, man. Niall's all . . .' Jason's voice trails away as he struggles to articulate it.

'Niall's all what?'

'He's fucked up, man. Proper, *good-style* fucked up, I mean. No messin', chief. Like somethin' off the fucken telly. Or the films! Yeah, like in the films.'

Quinner looks at Jason and purses his lips. He tries to remain calm but it's difficult. 'What are you talking about? What's happened to Niall?'

'You'll have to see, man,' says Jason. 'You gotta see.'

'All right . . . Ghost Ninja.' Quinner shakes his head. 'Wait. I'm not calling you that. What's your name? Your real name.'

'Jason. Jason Reeves.'

'Listen, Jason Reeves, we'll call round to Niall's now, OK? He still above the shops in Old Swan?'

Jason nods. 'Yeah.'

Outside the flat Quinner gets a cab. On the journey over to Niall's Quinner makes the cabbie stop at the pharmacy for some paracetamol and a can of Diet Coke. His headache's been building since this morning. Quinner rips open the foil around the paraceta-mol, wincing at the noise, and gobbles three of the pills. Nursing the Coke he cradles his head as the cab bounces over the potholes all the way down Prescot Road. He fishes out his phone and calls the production office to tell them he won't be on set today. Sore throat. Like they give a shit. He's the writer.

'You're good at making shit up,' says Jason. Quinner doesn't reply. He wants to ask Jason some more questions about last night but is wary in front of the cabbie. He should have done it back at the flat but it's too late now.

Big Niall lives above a bookie's facing a busy intersection. When the cab pulls up Jason hops out, an excited expression on his weasel face. He looks like a dog presenting its owner with a dead rat. Jason presses the bell for Niall's place and holds it down. Even with the noise of the street, Quinner can hear the bell upstairs.

'He's not answering the door.' Jason looks at Quinner.

'No shit,' says Quinner. 'Have you tried his phone?'

Jason shakes his head. 'He's lost his phone.'

Quinner hesitates. 'Lost it?'

'Said he had. Then he just, like, stopped talking.'

'Let's give it another go.' Now he's here, with Jason prancing around like a spaniel, all Quinner wants is to leave. But he can't. Not without seeing what his dopey cunt of a cousin's done.

They push open the battered outer door and head up the narrow stairs to a small landing. Quinner knocks on the door.

'Niall, it's Dean.'

Nothing.

'Niall, you twat. Open up!'

'Told yer,' says Jason, his eager face at Quinner's shoulder. 'He's been like this since this morning, man.'

'You sure he's in?'

Jason's head bobs. 'Deffo.'

'Niall!' yells Quinner, so loud it makes his head throb.

An age passes. And then the door's cracked open an inch. Niall's eye appears and looks at Quinner and then at Jason.

'Well, aren't you going to let us in?'

Quinner realises that Niall's thinking it through.

'For fuck's sake, Nially.' Jason's voice is all false jollity. 'Let's in.'

The chain is lifted and Niall opens the door.

The flat's cramped, the rooms above the shops having been almost endlessly subdivided, but tidier than Quinner had expected. Niall's got the shoebox in reasonable shape, considering. The giant TV is on but there's no sound. Quinner gets the impression that Niall's been sitting with it like that for some time. He has his hands plunged into the pockets of his hoodie and is staring vacantly at the screen, where two orange-faced morning TV idiots are gurning desperately at the camera.

'How did it go, Niall?' Quinner sits down on the sofa at an angle to his cousin. Jason leans his narrow arse against the window ledge and lights a cigarette, his hand tapping out a doof beat against the sill. Everything feels like it's too close together.

'Your mate here says something happened.'

Nothing.

'Come on,' says Quinner. 'It can't have been that bad.'

Niall lets out a long breath. 'I don't want to talk about it,' he says eventually. He fumbles with something in his pocket and pulls out some money, holding it out to Quinner with his left hand. 'And I don't want the fifty. Keep it. I don't want anything to do with any of this shit.'

'I'll fucken have it,' says Jason. Quinner can't work out if Jason's joking. One glance at his face tells him he's not.

'Don't be a dick, Niall. That's yours.' Quinner's starting to get seriously concerned. For a while the three of them sit there, the only sounds the surf from the traffic outside and the rapid rat-a-tat of Jason's hand against the window.

'Can you stop that?' Quinner points at Jason.

'What?'

'The drumming. I've got a headache.'

Jason holds up his palms in mock-supplication. 'Don't we know it. Jesus, bruv, fucking chill, eh?'

Quinner ignores him and turns back to Niall.

'What happened?' he says, his voice low. 'Did Noone do something?'

Niall shakes his head. 'I don't know.' His voice is almost inaudible. 'I didn't see him.'

Quinner looks over at Jason, who shrugs.

'How do you mean?' says Quinner.

Niall lifts his head and, for the first time since he sat down, looks directly at Quinner while he's talking. 'We followed your feller, just like you said. He headed towards the Pier Head but then carried on down towards the docks. I couldn't see if it was him or not for definite. We'd lost him for a bit.'

'But we picked him up again,' pipes Jason, eager. 'Then we saw him turning down this side road. Spooky as fuck, man.'

'Jason didn't fancy following him.' Niall's voice isn't accusing.

'I'm sorry, Nially,' says Jason. He takes a drag on his cigarette. Quinner notices how young he is. 'Weren't even sure it was him, though, were we?'

'No, we weren't.' Niall looks in the direction of the TV and then back at Quinner. 'But I didn't want to look soft in front of Jason. So like a prick, I followed this guy.'

'And you're not sure it was Noone?' Quinner's getting a bad feeling about this.

'No,' says Niall, 'I'm not. It was dark down there and for all

I know your man went home and we followed some other fucker. Anyway, like I said, I followed him to this street. It was fucken scary as shit down there.'

'Yeah?'

Niall nods. 'Horror movie scary.'

'And?'

'And nothing. The feller wasn't there, not what I could see. If it was this Noone guy, he'd gone. I turned around to get out when something hit me. The next thing I know I woke with me head on the floor.'

There's more. Quinner can sense it. Something bad.

'What else, Niall?'

Niall starts crying silently. Jason stops smoking and stares at Niall like he's turned into a unicorn.

'Niall?' says Quinner, putting a hand on his cousin's shoulder. 'What happened?'

After an age Niall lifts his right hand from his pocket. His hand is bandaged. He raises it and holds it up for Quinner to see. Niall's index finger is gone.

'Christ,' whispers Quinner.

What the fuck had he got into?

Sixteen

'God Almighty.'

Like a diver placing his toes at the end of the high board, Frank Keane stops in the doorway and contemplates the once-pleasant, high-ceilinged suburban bedroom which now resembles an abattoir. He puts both hands on top of his head and lets out a long sigh that he tries not to let anyone hear.

This thing had been called in around eight but Frank had let Theresa Cooper start things off with him coming in as Senior Investigating Officer. It was only a little later that he had second thoughts and decided to see for himself. He and Harris didn't speak much in the car. They haven't spoken, other than what is strictly necessary, since the phone call on Friday. Although Frank went into work earlier today he spent the time at Canning Place. Being Saturday the place was quieter and no one mentioned anything about acid or vinegar or Harris.

She pushes past him now and negotiates her way across the blood-spattered floor towards the dead woman tied to the bed. The room is ripe with the stink of chemicals and blood and death. A familiar smell.

Frank gets into gear and moves into the bedroom, sliding his hands into latex gloves he takes from his jacket pocket. Harris already has hers in place. Both officers are wearing disposable covers over their street shoes. Not quite the full rig, but it'll do. With another body hanging in the garage, almost certainly the husband, neither of them thinks this will be a tricky case. Still, Frank tucks his tie inside his shirt just above the second button. He doesn't want to be careless.

'They were dentists?' says Frank. One of the techs had mentioned it downstairs.

'That's right,' Harris replies absently. 'They work – worked – together.' She looks down at the body. 'Jesus. Theresa wasn't exaggerating.' Her phone rings and she looks at the number before answering. 'I'll call you back,' she says and ends the call. Frank glances her way and then back to the bed.

'I think we need overalls,' says Frank, almost to himself. He looks down dubiously at his street clothes. 'This much blood . . .' He lets the sentence trail off. Harris doesn't seem to have heard him. Frank might think it's his little secret that he's squeamish but Harris is confident that most of the Merseyside Major Incident Team already know and don't care.

McGettigan, the SOC photographer, is shooting a wide-angled image from a corner of the room. He's wearing one of the pale blue protective suits. Despite the amount of gore in the room, and McGettigan's bulk, Frank can't see a spot on the man. Maybe they'll be OK.

After getting what he needs, McGettigan looks up from behind his Nikon. 'She's all yours, DCI Keane. I'm about finished in here. DS Cooper said it was fine to get started. I've done the one in the garage already.' McGettigan nods to Harris, his face colouring before he scurries, rustling, back to the safety of his lens. Keane can't blame him. More confident men than the corpulent McGettigan find DI Harris intimidating, Frank being one of them. Harris is used to being regarded with interest, and sometimes with outright hostility, by some of the neanderthals she comes in contact with on both sides of the blue line, but her looks are what most people register first.

'Take your time, Calum,' says Harris, touching the photographer lightly on the shoulder as she brushes past. McGettigan's neck flushes crimson.

Behind him, Frank can hear the soft conversational murmur of the techs working in the rest of the house. He and Harris have arrived late, and much of the initial scene work has already been done. Faced with the horror on the bed, Frank's beginning to wish he had left it entirely to Cooper, like he planned. At least now he can delegate the autopsy to juniors. There are one or two advantages to heading up the MIT unit.

From the street outside comes the rumble of another police vehicle executing a laborious turn in the narrow dead end. The bay windows are draped in heavy, expensive-looking curtains but they can't prevent the red and blue of the car strobes leaking through gaps and flashing up the walls. There's another incongruous sound too: the bass throb of dance music being played loudly in a car somewhere nearby.

Frank tiptoes to the window and pulls back the curtain. About fifty metres away, on the opposite side of the railway line that bisects the street, are two cheaply tricked-out cars full of teenagers watching the action. Despite the barrier of the railway line they are closer than Frank feels is appropriate. He lets the curtain drop back into place and zigzags his way through the puddles of blood onto the landing.

'You.' A young plod loitering aimlessly near the top of the stairs jerks to attention like a startled deer. Keane gestures towards the street. 'Get the fucking ravers across the way moved along and tell whichever attention seeker's got their disco lights on to knock them off. They're giving me a headache. If it's one of the medics, tell them they can go.'

He turns back to the bedroom without waiting for a response.

Harris, as is her custom, is using the video camera function on her smartphone to take a 360. McGettigan will shoot an official video record if he hasn't done already, but Harris likes the scene to be available at a touch.

Christ help anyone who steals her phone, thinks Frank. One look at the image bank and they'd need counselling for years.

Frank finds a relatively clean patch of carpet at the end of the bed and stands, arms folded, looking down at the victim.

She's naked, legs splayed, feet turned slightly inwards, her painted toes clenched. Leather belts have been looped around the iron bedposts and are cinched tightly around her ankles. She has been stabbed repeatedly by someone using massive force. Frank can glimpse bone showing through several lateral slash cuts on her thighs. From the blood spray which arcs out across one side of the room and up a section of wall, it looks like her femoral artery has been severed. Frank feels his stomach lurch again.

Her face is obliterated, pulped. There's no chance of anyone making a visual ID from what remains. Moving around to the side of the bed, and holding his jacket to prevent it trailing in the gore, Frank bends close and notices some teeth scattered across the pillows. He wonders for a moment if there's any significance in her husband having been a dentist. If, as seemed inevitable, the second corpse currently dangling from the ceiling in the garage below had done this, perhaps knocking out his wife's teeth fulfilled some dark orthodontic desire.

Frank puts the brake on this line of thinking and chastises himself for amateur psychology. Koopman, his old boss, wouldn't have approved.

Just look at what's in front of you, dickhead. The pieces may come together later if you get lucky. For now it's enough to record it all.

Frank's queasiness is fading the longer he's in the room. Death's like that: you get used to it.

Some oily dark substance has leaked from the victim's head and joined the blood pooling in the corrugations of the twisted sheets. Like her legs, her hands have been tied to the bedposts using belts wound around her wrists. The belts don't match. Frank doesn't make anything of that, he simply notes the fact.

Harris is inspecting the woman's vagina centimetre by centimetre with the aid of a Maglite torch.

'She'll have been raped. Unless this is a sex game gone bad.'

Frank can't tell if she's making a joke and he's not going to risk Harris's wrath by making the wrong call in reply. Her disposition – never exactly what you might call sunny – can best be described as positively subarctic and has been like that since Thursday.

Since *it* happened.

Almost two days now and there's hardly been a civil word between them. Maybe I should have called her yesterday, thinks Frank. Who knows what's been happening between her and Linda since Frank hit the pillow on Friday lunchtime.

Harris points the beam of light at a relatively blood-free area of skin at the junction between thigh and pelvis. 'Could be dried semen.' She looks up at Frank now, her face a mask. 'See?'

Frank bends closer. There might be something there. He can't tell. 'I'll lay odds he fucked her after she was dead.'

McGettigan, the SOC photographer, glances up at this but says nothing.

Frank thinks she's probably right. From here there's no way of knowing, but when the thing shakes out and the reports are in he's pretty confident this will be the case.

A simple rape would be too commonplace for this charnel-house. Of course the fucker did her post-mortem.

More of them did than people would believe.

What did it matter, after all? Now the wife, the partner, the girlfriend, is that dead thing, and you're going to finish yourself before the night is through, why not go all the way into that yawning black abyss? It's not like there're going to be any repercussions. If he does turn out to be the guilty party, the last thing the tooth-tickler currently hanging from the garage ceiling downstairs would have been concerned with was leaving DNA behind.

Part of Frank worries that these thoughts spring so readily to mind with the solidity and heft of absolute fact. Part of him – the policeman part – is glad.

Seventeen

McGettigan, standing just outside the bedroom door, is loading his equipment back into metal boxes. It's just ticked past midnight.

'I'll get out of your way now, DCI Keane. I've already done the vid.' McGettigan gives Harris a brief nod. Some people connected to MIT still had problems with Harris's role in last year's Stevie White case and McGettigan is no exception. But since Merseyside Police, like all police forces on the planet, runs on an insatiable appetite for infighting, politics and backbiting that makes the Colosseum seem polite, Harris's transgression isn't the worst there's ever been in the department, not by a long way, but people do like to nurse a decent grudge when one comes along and Harris still has a bit of time left in the sin-bin.

'I'm off,' says McGettigan and waddles out of the room. He passes Theresa Cooper on her way in, clipboard in hand, paper-booted and suited. Seeing Frank at the scene is a mild disappointment to her and Frank can read that on her face. Cooper is currently the only female of her rank at Merseyside MIT and she's hoping to angle that singularity into further promotion down the track. Being named lead on this investigation would help – even with Frank Keane as official SIO – but her boss's arrival doesn't bode well. Since taking the disgraced Perch's role at MIT Frank has had precious little time as an investigator. Cooper doesn't know it, but it's precisely this that has brought him out tonight.

Frank's not sure how long he can stick life on the fifth floor at Canning Place.

For one thing, MIT – the Major Incident Team, his unit – are based at Stanley Road. Now his desk is supposed to be at Canning Place, he feels even more strongly that Perch moved his office there for no better reason than to be less than tongue's length away from the brass.

Frank has made plans to have his office moved back to Stanley Road.

He already spends almost every day there, just as he had done prior to promotion, but it's going to take longer than Frank likes to get the forms signed and the protocols agreed.

Still, whatever the reasons, Frank's appearance at *her* crime scene isn't the most welcome news for DS Cooper.

Cooper points at the victim. 'Got a few confirmations, sir. Family name is Peters. Paul and Maddy. Both dentists with a longstanding practice in Southport. No prior domestic call-outs. No criminal records. I've got a couple of the uniforms taking preliminary statements from the neighbours but so far nothing out of the ordinary reported. There's a teenage son too: Nicky, missing. DC Caddick is trying hard to track him down.'

At this stage, with no details made public, Caddick's doing this as discreetly as possible. Frank's sure that'll change unless they get hold of the boy soon. The last thing they need is for Nicky to find out about this horror from some source other than the police. Frank doesn't want to think right now about the son being a victim or, perhaps worse, involved in the slaughter.

'No other children, thank God,' Cooper continues. 'Ferguson's looking at the body in the garage now.' She's all business but the pallor of her skin betrays her. Keane knows how she feels.

'I hate murder-suicides too, Theresa. Did I miss the memo? Married life a bit sticky? Kill the missus and top yourself. Fuck me.'

Cooper smiles weakly. Well, I tried, thinks Frank.

'Anything else?' he says.

'There are ashes in the fireplace in the living room. It's one of those log burner things. Not gas. The ashes look fresh. I took samples and sent them in with one of the techs.'

'Interesting. Not really log fire weather, is it?'

Cooper shakes her head. 'I'd say it was clothing in there.'

Frank nods. 'Probably.' He frowns. 'Maybe the dentist burnt his clothes for some reason.'

'I think they're in the garage,' says Cooper. 'There are some clothes there, anyway. I haven't had time to check the sizes yet but I think they'll be his.'

'Any blood on the clothes in the garage?' says Harris.

'None that I can see. Maybe traces once we look harder.'

Frank frowns. The clothing in the log burner – if the ashes turn out to be cloth remnants – is a puzzler. With the working hypothesis of murder-suicide it would make sense for there to be blood on the dead man's clothes. If he committed the crime, why burn any clothing if you are going to kill yourself anyway? Add the disappearance of the teenager, and the murder-suicide theory is already fragmenting.

Frank turns back to the bedroom. Stick to the job in hand.

'Ferguson's already been in here, right?'

'Yes, sir.'

'OK, well, once he's finished in the garage make sure the miserable Scottish bastard has a word before creeping back to Castle Dracula, right?' Cooper nods. Ferguson is one of the county pathologists. Despite his undoubted expertise, he and Keane have differing opinions, mainly concerning which brand of red team they follow, Ferguson being – despite his birthplace, or maybe because of it – a Manc at heart.

Misery findeth misery, reflects Frank.

'Who called this in?' he says, a little sharply, his mind having briefly strayed to bleak thoughts of Old Trafford.

'The dentist's brother. Only lives round the corner.' Cooper checks her clipboard. 'Terry Peters. Eight-forty. Came round and got no reply. Seems that the family was supposed to be home. The brother got worried and let himself in. He's back home with a uniform. I'm off there soon to get a full statement.'

'Neighbours?'

'No one in on the left.' Cooper inclines her head one way. 'The other side is a doctor. Chief Merseyside cardiologist, no less. I got a short statement but no one there seems to have anything very useful just yet. Heard nothing, saw nothing. A few vague ideas about car movements but so far couldn't say which house they came from.'

Cooper's mention of the high-ranking medic reminds Keane of the Birkdale demographic they're dealing with. Step lightly, dickhead. Doesn't the CC live somewhere round here?

'He came upstairs? The brother?'

'Must have done. Why, sir?'

Frank shakes his head. 'No reason. Just seems a bit funny. Would you go snooping around uninvited in your brother's house?'

'I haven't got a brother,' says Cooper. 'But I know what you mean.'

'And check about a dog,' says Frank. 'If you haven't already. This house looks like it'd have a dog.' He's thinking about the walled garden outside. From what he could see it was well tended but the grass had none of the bowling green smoothness some of the other houses in the street possess. No point in a perfect lawn if your faithful hound is taking a dump there every day.

'No dog,' says Cooper.

So much for the great detective. Frank makes a note to think a bit harder before he speaks next time.

Cooper turns to leave and Frank catches a fleeting gnomic glance pass between her and Harris. Without quite being able to pinpoint why, Frank knows that he is the unspoken subject. There's something prurient in Cooper's enquiring expression.

As Cooper's back disappears down the landing, Frank raises his eyebrows at Harris but she doesn't take the bait, her face blank. Frank puts the moment into the sprawling mental warehouse in which he keeps his vast collection of unanswered questions about women.

'What else?' he says. Even if he and Harris are striking sparks off each other, she is still one of the best crime scene readers Frank knows.

Harris scans the rest of the room. Other than the horror on the bed it's neat and tidy. The bed itself sits to one side of the big bay window and faces the unused fireplace. At one side of the room is a large freestanding wardrobe. The carpet underfoot is good quality, a clean, plain weave, and the space is at once both modern and Victorian – a neat design trick to pull off.

'No struggle,' says Harris. 'Before, I mean.' A row of family photos on the ornamental iron mantel above the fireplace seem to nod their perfectly aligned agreement. Several of the images show a smiling man and woman with a dark-haired child: presumably

Nicky before adolescence claimed him. Some of the frames are dotted with blood. The splatter patterns will be analysed later, although Frank knows that unless something fishy turns up soon, there will likely be very little in the way of investigation into what still might prove to be a murder-suicide. Despite the blood, the frames are undisturbed and the images trace the child's growth from beaming infant to scowling teen as effectively as a time lapse movie. On a side table in front of the bay window a slim vase sits undisturbed, free of dust. A clean house.

Frank stops and turns back to the bed. Something about the vase has raised a question.

At the head of the bed he bends towards a clear patch of sheet and, lowering his nose to the cotton, sniffs deeply.

Harris raises an eyebrow. Frank ignores her and inhales again.

'Fresh,' he says. 'I'd bet they were clean on.' It's another off-note in the scene. 'They've got that washed smell. Expensive cotton too.'

'And?'

'She never knew.'

'Um?' Harris isn't sure what Frank's talking about. He points at the sheets. 'If things were bad between them, would there be clean sheets on the bed?'

'They could have been put on days before.'

Frank shakes his head. 'No. They're fresh.'

Harris raises an eyebrow. It's a point.

She has been at eight of these cases. In almost all of them the physical environment betrays the sense of a world decaying long before the act that ends it. Unwashed plates. Puddled dirty clothes on the landing. Unfed dogs. Domestic call-outs on the police log.

A woman who puts fresh sheets on the bed isn't thinking that the evening could end like this. Not that it makes much difference. Frank's sure when the investigation starts digging they'll find what made the dentist snap. It may not have been anything to do with the woman on the bed. Gambling debts. Mental illness. Liverpool being beaten at home by Wigan. Any fucking thing. Frank can recall a case in which a husband killed his wife and then tried to top himself in a row about the outcome of *Britain's Got Talent*.

Frank opens the wardrobe. Inside the clothes are hung neatly and precisely. His on one side, hers the other. Organised, careful people. Blue business shirts. A few sleek evening dresses. Peeping from between the sober blacks and blues is a flash of shiny red fabric. Frank teases it out and sees it's a PVC sheath dress stiff with buckles and zips. It's not exactly Amsterdam dungeon material but it does raise the possibility that Harris's sex-game quip might have more weight than he first thought. He flicks through the rest of the clothes with more attention, but apart from the red dress, the only other indication of anything kinky is a pair of high-heeled biker boots tucked away behind a line of shoes. He checks the size to see if they're hers. They are, but it's worth a look.

Below the wardrobe are two deep drawers. Frank finds a couple of sex accessories in there but nothing more than in most suburban bedrooms. Harris is going through the bedside cabinets. It's a slower process as, unlike the wardrobe, the cabinets haven't escaped the blood splatters.

'Anything?' Frank says.

Harris holds up two rolled joints and a pair of fake handcuffs.

'Hardly the Last Days of Rome, is it?'

'Might be more,' says Harris. 'There's a computer downstairs.' Harris looks at the dead woman. 'She's been restrained. The two joints might indicate stronger drug use.'

Frank raises his eyebrows. He and Harris had smoked a little on Thursday and neither of them had moved on to inject heroin into their eyeballs, but it's worth noting, he supposes.

'I'm sure Ferguson will check.'

Theresa Cooper comes back into the room. Harris holds up the joints and Cooper taps her clipboard with a satisfied flourish. 'Already itemised. I left things intact for McGettigan and the rest of the techs.'

'All right, Theresa, no one's having a pop,' says Frank. Harris replaces the joints where she found them.

'What do you want me to put on the sheet, sir? I mean with you and DI Harris being here.' She holds up the scene of crime document on the clipboard. Frank knows what she's asking.

'You're lead, Theresa. Like we said, I'll do the official SIO role and DI Harris will also act as a monitor.'

Cooper scribbles her name on the form and tucks the clipboard under her arm. 'I spoke to Ferguson just now, sir,' she says. She cocks her head on one side to indicate she has something of interest to add, as if, now that her role as lead is safe, she can bring a titbit to the table as reward. Keane and Harris wait a beat. 'The husband. There's something you should see.'

Eighteen

The lid of his prison is lifted and Nicky blinks in the harsh glare of a torch beam.

As the light moves off him, Nicky chokes back tears.

Hovering above is a familiar face. One he's seen looking down on him before, often, sometimes contorted in pleasure. Down here, underground, there's only one word Nicky can think of to describe his captor. *Monster.*

'I have to clean you,' says the monster. 'Give you food.' It sounds like an internal dialogue. He's speaking to himself.

He puts the torch down on the floor, reaches in, grabs hold of Nicky's arms and hoists him out like a kid choosing a toy. He closes the lid of the box and sits the boy back down on top of it. Nicky can see that he's been inside a crate of some sort.

There's no question of escape or fighting. Nicky's legs aren't working properly and he's shivering uncontrollably.

The torch, although not pointing directly at him, is hurting Nicky's eyes but after a few moments the boy can see his surroundings for the first time since being imprisoned.

They're inside one of the Williamson tunnels, a long, L-shaped cavern with a curving brick roof and a bare earth floor. It's not one that Nicky recognises.

One wall of the space is slick with wet moss. The others are dry. At the end of the cavern is a bank of rubble pushed into a rough slope. The slope runs up to a small opening. Nicky can't see where the opening leads to, just that it's dark. He can't feel any air moving, which makes him think that there's something in place blocking this area from view.

Next to the crate is a trestle table covered in plastic. There are some tools placed on a smaller table at one side along with lengths of rope and some reels of duct tape. At the sight of them Nicky moans involuntarily.

The monster glances at the table.

'Oh, that. Don't panic, Nicky. They're just props. We're friends, aren't we? More than friends.'

Abruptly he hands Nicky a bucket and tells him to clean himself up. 'You stink.'

'You're going to kill me,' says Nicky. He hadn't planned to say anything but it just comes out. The monster can't do all this and let him survive. There's just no way back from this. Nicky tries to keep his voice steady but he can't. If he lets himself think of his mother he knows he'll collapse so he digs his fingernails hard into his palms.

'Who knows? Now get yourself clean. I can hardly breathe.'

'Why are you doing this? I liked you. Those things we did . . . I won't tell.'

'Shh, quiet, Nicky. Get yourself clean.' The monster tries to make his voice soothing but it isn't working. There's a nervy energy emanating from the monster. Unpredictable.

Nicky does his best to scrape the filth from his body, hardly daring to take his eyes from the plastic-covered table holding the tools. When all the water is gone he stands, his knees bent, darting pain shooting up his legs. The monster looks at him without expression.

'All done?'

Nicky nods.

His captor produces a plastic loop from the pocket of his jacket and cinches it tight around Nicky's wrists, held out in front of him. Nicky drops his hands to his groin, covering himself as best he can. The gut-wrenching terror is starting to return.

'What's happening? What are you going to do? Please don't do this.'

Without warning, his expression unchanged, the monster slaps him hard across the face and Nicky falls to the floor before being dragged upright by his hair. He starts to sob and that makes the monster angry.

'Fucking shut it, you fucking little cunt bastard!' Hissing, the monster's face distorts with fury and Nicky can feel the spittle hitting his face. 'Keep it fucking closed, you fucking got that? Fucking shut it!'

The monster stands back, breathing heavily through his nose. He's tall, the monster, and in the torchlight coming up from the floor, his bloated shadow dancing across the curved brick ceiling, he is a subterranean nightmare, a creature from the depths, the devil himself. Nicky finds it hard to look at the creature's eyes. It's like looking into hell. 'You don't fucking understand. I'm under a lot of fucking pressure.'

The monster's head bobs from side to side, half-nodding, half-shaking, as if conducting an inner dialogue. He keeps clenching and unclenching his fingers.

Then, like a storm clearing, he is calm again. He takes out a bottle of water from a backpack and hands it to Nicky. The boy guzzles it and the monster stops him.

'Slower. You'll make yourself ill.' He bends to the backpack and takes out a plastic-wrapped sandwich. Marks & Spencer, chicken salad. He gives it to Nicky and watches him eat.

'The things I've done,' he says quietly as Nicky sits on the box chewing. His tone is one of bewilderment.

Nicky stands there, waiting. He feels like he's going to be sick and his face hurts from the blow. Curiously, the sudden anger from the creature in front of him makes him feel better. At some gut level, Nicky knows that the violent reaction is because the monster doesn't know what to do with him.

It's something to hold on to.

Nineteen

Frank follows the blood trail leading from the main bedroom and along the landing towards the bathroom filled with white-suited techs.

The house is decorated in that way that Frank always thinks of as being beyond him no matter what the money. It's not that these people are rich, or at least not *rich* rich. It's more that they just seem to have the right stuff. The soft lighting, the sagging but expensive sofas, pictures on the wall that look like they mean something.

He's seen a piano downstairs. The kids round here have piano lessons. Or they can play the piano. Either way, it's not something that was common in the homes he was brought up in. He can remember getting a Muppet trumpet one Christmas and that was about it on the musical instrument front.

Past the bathroom is the open door of what must be the teen-ager's bedroom. Frank doesn't stop. Bodies first, rest of the house later. At the top of the stairs the uniform who he'd sent outside earlier is back along with another plod. Both straighten up at his and Harris's approach.

'What the fuck are you two doing, exactly?' Frank Keane can be an intimidatory presence when required. 'What precise purpose are you fulfilling?'

The uniforms start blabbering some nonsense.

'Vamoose, dickheads,' says Frank and they clatter downstairs. Chastened as they are, Frank notices the eyes of both young men sliding towards Harris as they pass.

He doesn't blame them. Harris is worth looking at and men are, after all, just men.

Still, it never hurts to remind your basic plod of his lowly position. What's the fucking point of rising up the ladder if you can't occasionally make someone unhappy?

'Tea!' He shouts the order after them as he and Harris and Cooper head downstairs. 'One sugar. With.' He doesn't really want any tea but it'll give the idle fuckers something to grumble about and make sure they jump that bit quicker when asked next time. A good DCI's rep is established like fossil fuels: layer upon layer over long periods of time.

From the hall the three MIT officers walk outside. Access to the garage is from the front of the house or via an internal connecting door. Frank wants another look at the outside. In the mild June air, he stops and looks up at the bedroom windows.

'I've been here before,' he says. 'Years ago. A party.'

Not a flicker in response.

'I mean, this exact house. Not just the area.'

Harris sniffs and Cooper turns diplomatically towards the garage, the entrance of which has been masked off by a tent-like structure.

Frank, a man not known for his forbearance, suppresses a sharp flare of irritation at his ex-partner. Harris is, on paper at least, Keane's subordinate and, whatever the erotic events of Thursday – not to mention Linda's 'acid' attack – she is still at work. The two of them will have to deal with what's been happening at some point but in the meantime Frank expects Harris to toe the line. He bites back the sharp barb on the tip of his tongue and also decides it's prudent not to mention the image that jumps into his mind on recognising the house. Himself at seventeen, inexpertly fumbling under a pile of coats on the parental bed with a Birkdale girl – Catherine? Sarah? – treating herself to the thrill of one of the bad boys. He has a mental flash of the girl's long blonde hair, of her hand guiding him inside, the smell of shampoo and cigarettes, the thrill of being young and hard and wanted. And her breasts, oh God, her breasts. The thought still gives him a shiver.

He looks up at the room in which Maddy Peters lies butchered and feels guilty at his trip down mammary lane.

The house looks the same as he remembers but under the white arcs set up by the SOC officers the solid Victorian appears no more substantial than a stage set. Frank gets the impression he could push it over with a decent shove of the shoulder.

The temporary illusion of insubstantiality aside, the double-fronted detached has the air of a divorcee caught in the glare of nightclub lights at closing time. But a divorcee with a good lawyer. The place is well-heeled without being flash.

This suburb, the last one before Liverpool is reclaimed by Lancashire in spirit if not according to the county lines, is where the rich live. Restored red-brick Victorian mansions with landscaped gardens and curving gravel drives dotted with Audis and Jags are generously spaced along the leafy, wedge-shaped tangle of roads between the dunes to the west, the train line to the east and the gleaming white art deco Royal Birkdale Golf Club to the south. The village clustered around the train station is dotted with boutique delicatessens and wine merchants and al fresco cafes. From Birkdale, the Northern Line runs south to Liverpool and then on to unspeakable Speke, the socio-economic demographic falling with every kilometre it travels.

Here in Birkdale, Merseyside royalty – ex-Liverpool and Everton footballers – own the bars and restaurants, most of them only a minute in the Merc from the six-bedroom with pool on Selworthy Road. The population of Birkdale west of the line seems to be composed of these footballers, as well as entrepreneurs, media figures, accountants, lawyers, doctors, or, as at Frank's Burlington Road crime scene, dentists.

'You must have been higher up the social scale than you were letting on, Frank. I thought you were a bit of a scally?'

She speaks.

He supposes he should be grateful.

'She – they were slumming it, mixing with us.' Frank isn't protesting. It's a fact. The area of the city he was raised in – Bootle – bears little resemblance to Birkdale. He can't remember the circumstances of being invited to the party but it was rare then for him to venture this far north, which is why it stuck in his memory. That, and the bedroom fumbling.

Until January, Frank lived three stops down on the train in the equally comfortable neighbourhood of Formby. The only reason he and Julie weren't in Birkdale was that Formby is that bit nearer work.

Frank's no working-class hero and he's never met anyone from his background who wouldn't trade the streets of Bootle for the lanes of suburbia in an eye blink. All that bollocks about the inner-city areas being more real? Fuck that. Frank, just like the street rat footballers who migrate from Croxteth, Huyton and Bootle out to the Wirral, or Cheshire, or Birkdale the instant the first million is clocked up, knows that reality is overrated. Give him the suburbs and trees and safety every time.

Cooper's standing at the garage door trying to mask her impatience, a faithful retriever waiting to show her offering. Harris and Frank move along the drive, past the polished Beemer and a small, equally gleaming Toyota, their feet crunching on the white stones.

The street outside is still bustling with activity. Civilians too, not just the coppers and technicians, of whom there are many. Curtains are more than twitching. Neighbours in tracksuits and slippers gather in doorways and discuss the possibilities in the hushed, excited undertone that comes with violent death.

A uniform standing at the garage entrance lifts the white flap guarding the scene from prying eyes and, ducking under, they almost run straight into the pathologist.

'Evening, Fergie,' says Frank. The Scot glances at his watch.

'You mean morning.'

Frank sighs. This isn't one of those love–hate things with Ferguson. He just straight-out hates the stringy Glaswegian vampire.

'Would it kill you to cheer up a bit? Is it a Scottish thing or just you?'

'Just me. The rest o' Scotland never stops singing and dancing wee merry jigs all the livelong day.' His face expressionless, Ferguson gestures towards the garage. 'He's all yours until they bring him into the Royal. I'm offski.'

'Hold on, I need to know what you know.'

'He's dead,' says Ferguson. 'Same as her upstairs. Time of death from what I can measure here is between three and, say, nine yesterday morning.'

'Saturday?'

'That's what I mean by yesterday, DCI Keane. It goes Friday, Saturday, Sunday . . .'

'I mean it was early hours on Saturday, not early hours on Friday?'

'Correct.'

DS Cooper is moving from one foot to the other.

'You need the toilet, Theresa?' says Harris. Cooper stops moving.

Ferguson takes his car keys from his pocket and jangles them. 'Look,' he says. 'I know you got here late but DS Cooper didn't and I certainly didn't.' Ferguson begins speaking as if to a dimwitted foreigner. 'I. Have. To. Go. Now.' He brushes past Keane and points at Cooper. 'Your lassie here will fill you in on what I know. I've already given her the gist. I've got a long night of sleeplessness lying ahead and I'd like nothing better than to stand here repeating myself – honestly, I would – but with three autopsies in the morning, not including your two, I really do have to fuck off.'

He gives a sort of rictus grimace that might have been a smile and stalks towards the crime scene barriers.

Frank turns to Cooper. 'Lassie?'

Cooper shakes her head and moves inside the garage.

The dead man is hanging from a metal strut which supports the angled roof. He is grey-haired, around Keane's age, naked. His feet dangle a short distance from the smooth concrete floor of the neat, car-free space.

Cooper points to a single wooden chair sitting against a wall, perhaps six metres from the dead man. It looks like it has been placed carefully in position. There is nothing in the room other than a plastic bin containing various brushes and brooms and a rack of outdoor shoes. Frank bends to look at two patches of loose earth scattered on the concrete floor of the garage about two metres apart.

'Well, it's not going to be as straightforward as we imagined.' Harris is looking at the chair.

'It's possible he kicked it and it slid into that position,' says Frank, rising slowly, his hands on his thighs. He doesn't think that for a moment but the encounter with Ferguson has left him prickly and argumentative. More argumentative than usual.

'You think so?' says Cooper.

Frank shakes his head. 'No, not really, Theresa. But it is possible.' He gestures towards the small crumbs of dirt on the floor. 'Any ideas?'

Cooper shakes her head. 'Came in on a car?'

Frank doesn't say anything. He's got an idea about the patches of earth – mud is a useful tool – but it can wait until they've seen everything. If he's right, it does mean they're dealing with a very interesting individual.

Frank walks slowly around the dangling body. Someone had put him there. Someone who had put the chair back against the wall. But this isn't what Cooper's bottling up. There's more.

'Come on then, Miss Marple,' Frank says, motioning Cooper towards the body. 'Let us in on your and Fergie's little secret.'

Cooper can't help herself. She smiles and points at the corpse. 'You'll need a ladder to see it.' Cooper looks round. 'Ferguson had one in earlier. Not sure where it's got to.'

'Oi,' says Frank to the uniform at the doorway, and the copper fairly bounces up. Frank nods in the general direction of the road. 'Go find a stepladder.' As the uniform gets to the door Frank raises his voice. 'Don't use anything from the house. Use one of ours. There should be one hanging about somewhere.'

Harris is peering up at the hanging man. Even without the ladder she's already spotted what Cooper is talking about. She doesn't say anything and Frank notices her tact in allowing Cooper her moment in the sun.

A couple of minutes go past during which Keane and Harris examine the dead man from all angles while Cooper watches. The uniform returns with a flat-topped metal toolbox.

'Couldn't find a ladder, sir,' he says, holding out the toolbox. 'Thought this might work?'

'Yeah, fine.' Frank pulls out a sheet of plastic from a pocket and places it on the floor to one side of the hanging man. 'Put it there, son.'

The uniform places the toolbox down carefully and moves back. Frank tests the strength of the lid with his foot. Satisfied he won't be sent crashing to the floor, he steps onto the toolbox and finds himself at eye level with the victim.

'You see it, right?' Cooper is eager. Frank can see what she's talking about. Set close to the rope that bites into the man's neck are two tiny circular red blisters.

They've all seen the marks before and it changes everything.

Twenty

'Have you spoken to Caddick?'

Frank, Harris and Cooper are back upstairs in the teenager's room. The marks on the dead man's neck have made finding Nicky Peters a priority and turned the murder-suicide investigation into a double homicide.

Maybe triple. Frank's not ready to slide the Peters boy into the slot marked 'suspect' just yet. It's going to be a very long night.

All the MIT detectives have seen marks like that before. Two raised red blisters about a thumb length apart. Whoever strung Paul Peters from his own garage ceiling had been able to do so because Peters was in no position to resist.

He'd been tasered.

A taser placed against the neck in DriveStun mode would, in most cases, render the subject unconscious. In police hands the charge is seldom repeated in case it overloads the system and kills someone. Here, that hadn't been a consideration. Subduing the victim would be of paramount importance. Dead or unconscious, it didn't matter, as long as Paul Peters was out of the game. It was entirely possible, suspects Frank, that when the path report comes back they'll find Peters was hung post-mortem. The taser is making all of them adjust their preconceived ideas about the apparent simplicity of the case. See? Menno Koopman's voice echoes in Frank's head.

McGettigan's already been called back in to do a more detailed photographic record of the bedroom, which is now beginning to assume greater importance in the case.

'Caddick's going round the boy's friends. The uncle's given us some possible names and we'll get some when the tech boys look at his Facebook account.' Theresa Cooper glances in the direction of the computer on Nicky's bedroom table.

'We'll leave it open?' It's a question from Harris, and Frank can see it's got under Cooper's skin.

'Of course,' says Cooper, working hard to keep any trace of sarcasm from her voice. There's no need to tell a seasoned copper like Cooper about keeping a victim's Facebook profile open. The network has become a powerful tool for MIT. For everyone in law enforcement. Frank reflects on the struggle in previous years to get people to carry ID cards. The same people who couldn't contemplate the infringements of carrying an ID card are happy to upload any amount of personal data, lists of friends, phone numbers, emails, to a freely accessible system. Facebook. The policeman's friend.

'I'd ask Gerry to do the tech work,' Frank says to Cooper, softening Harris's edge. 'He's good.'

'OK. He's actually doing it, sir. I already made the request.'

Harris is opening the boy's cupboards. 'Nothing jumping out,' she says. Frank grunts and Cooper says nothing.

'I need to coordinate the coroner's office,' says Cooper. She waves her clipboard in the vague direction of the door. Frank nods. 'And you'll need something for the press in the morning, Theresa.'

'You finished in here?' Harris's voice comes from deep inside the depths of the wardrobe but there's no disguising her tone of disbelief.

'Yes, DI Harris,' says Cooper. 'Would you like a list of contents?' Cooper flicks through her clipboard and starts reciting.

'All right, Theresa,' interrupts Frank. He juts his chin towards the door and makes a shooing motion. 'Point made.'

As Cooper exits, Harris emerges and gives Frank a hard look.

'Cut it out,' he says. He's had enough of this playground shit. 'The attitude's got to stop, Em. Cooper's done nothing wrong and we both know your argument isn't with her, right? I know that it's me who's the target – although as I remember it took two of us on Thursday; no one was putting a gun to your head – but it can fucking stop right now, got it?'

Harris opens her mouth and then closes it again.

'Don't make me make you.' Frank puts some iron in his voice. 'Be professional. That's an order. This is a murder investigation and you're bringing your personal life onto the job.' Frank drops his voice to make certain no one can overhear and fixes his eyes on Harris. 'I won't hesitate in making life miserable, Em, if you keep this shit up. Me, I can understand – no, that's not true, I can't, but who gives a fuck? – but the case and colleagues are off limits.'

For a moment there's nothing. Then Harris holds up an apologetic hand.

'It's not you, Frank. Well, it is, sort of.' She drops her voice even further, conscious of the house full of whispering technicians. 'It's complicated. I don't know why what happened on Thursday happened, but I'll try and not let it get to me on the job, OK? The thing with Linda will take a bit of thinking about. And I'll fix things with Theresa.'

It's all he's going to get and she dives back into the stale air of the wardrobe.

Frank breathes out slowly. He's got a headache coming on and the events of Thursday and Friday are starting to get a bad smell. He doubts either he or Harris have heard the last of it. Frank massages his brow with latex-tipped fingers and switches his attention back to the job in hand.

In contrast to the decor in the rest of the house, the bedroom is dark and brooding – deliberately so. It's been put together carefully. Nicky Peters is giving a very clear indication of, if not who he is, then of who he would like to be. The walls are painted deep red and covered in a thick layer of posters, party flyers, photos and ephemera, one wall completely dominated by a movie poster. *Donnie Darko*.

Even though there are what seem to be hundreds of images on the walls, they all seem to have been carefully chosen and placed. There is no sense of chaos, even though that may have been the boy's intention. An image shows a youth hurling a petrol bomb at a line of riot police but Frank notes that it has been precisely and neatly laminated, as have several others. It's as though the boy's innate tidiness will not submit, even in rebellion.

Frank moves along the walls. Girls in underwear. Drawings. The Japanese tsunami. John Lennon. The Ramones. Some current bands he doesn't know. Some art prints that don't look like art.

Ticket stubs from Creamfields. More movie posters, smaller than *Donnie Darko*. Indie flicks, mostly horror. Frank takes out a small notebook and writes *check content of movies/MO?* There is a book-shelf heavy with film and movie books, and with novels that might have been chosen by a set dresser wanting to indicate sensitivity in a teen character.

Next to the bed is a stacked metal cabinet, exactly like a single stand of school lockers. The four doors have locks but are open. Inside are DVDs, letters, souvenirs, school stuff. One shelf contains a series of green A4 folders. Frank lifts one out and sees it's a film script. *N Peters* listed as writer. He reads a few lines and puts it back. He has no way of telling if it's good. Someone will have to read all of them and give him the short version.

Taped to the back of the locker stack is a matchbox with a tiny lump of weed inside. There are a couple of Rizla packets on another shelf. Underneath the bed Frank finds a small bottle of vodka poking out from between a loose pile of books. Somehow, Frank doesn't get the feeling that Nicky was a drinker. The bottle, the weed, the Rizlas, all have the sense of being placed in position to be found by anyone giving the room more than a cursory glance.

Props.

Might be something and it might be nothing.

'Boss.' Harris is standing at a chest of drawers in the corner of the room. Frank notes the 'boss' but doesn't react. He moves across and looks over Harris's shoulder.

She's holding a receipt from an electronics supplier in Austria.

For a taser.

Twenty-One

'Time for a coffee, Frank? You look like you need one, old son.'

No, I fucking don't.

In fact, Frank had slept well after a tiring Sunday and had thought he was looking in pretty good shape, all things considered. Obviously not, if Charlie Searle's crack was accurate.

'Yeah, sure, sir.' Frank turns and follows Searle's broad back down the corridor towards the bank of lifts. Superintendents requesting coffee expect one response.

Monday morning and Frank's only ducked into Canning Place to pick up his reading glasses before sliding back to the MIT operations room at Stanley Road. Running into Charlie Searle on today of all days, as an investigation starts to pick up traction and Frank's needed in fifty different places, is a bit of bad luck.

'I'm a caffeine addict myself,' says Searle as he presses the up button. There is a pause as they stand there and wait. The big feller's smiling but it's about as reassuring as the curve on a scimitar. Searle's got a face that always reminds Frank of a soap actor. His chin is a shade too firm, his posture a touch too perfect, something generic about his every expression and physical attribute. 'Three before lunch or I'm fit for nothing.' Searle's carrying a clutch of blue-bound folders under his arm. He taps them and lowers his voice conspiratorially. 'If it wasn't for coffee I don't think we'd have a departmental budget this year.'

Frank does his best to make his smile sincere. He thinks he may have brought it off. Just so long as the twat doesn't start talking about football. Time slows to a comatose crawl as the lift doors remain closed.

'Big match on Wednesday.'

Shit.

'Thursday, I think it is, sir.'

'Oh yes, of course. More of a rugby fan myself. Still, I do try to get down to Anfield when I can. Cheer on the mighty Reds.'

The doors slide open, preventing Frank from having to respond. Searle's a foreigner. From London. Speaks like a southern rugger-bugger and compensates with this working-class football guff as if the locals can't communicate any other way. The fact that the superintendent is largely right about that isn't going to interfere with Frank's prejudice.

This promotion caper is going to take some getting used to. How the fuck did Koop cope with this stuff?

Pete Moreleigh's in the lift. He moves to one side as they step in. The same age as Frank, but smoother, and better-dressed, he's risen faster in the administration and is only one peg down from Searle. A good copper, once upon a time. Now he runs the Media Unit and acts like he works at the BBC.

'Superintendent,' says Moreleigh and nods to Frank, his eyes skating back to Searle almost immediately.

'Pete.' Searle makes a show of looking at his watch. 'We still good for the two o'clock DMG?'

'We'd better be.' Moreleigh grins. 'A lot to get through after the balls-up from QE and the rest of the worker bees.' He is also carrying a blue folder and glances down at it as he speaks.

Frank wishes he had a little blue folder. Just to be in the club. He has no fucking clue what a DMG or a QE are and neither Searle or Moreleigh offers an explanation. Frank gets the meaning, though, loud and clear: you're in our world now.

'No rest for the wicked, Pete.'

'Amen, Brother Searle,' says Moreleigh and Frank represses the urge to stick two fingers down his own throat. Or Moreleigh's.

That 'brother' thing is interesting, though. Shades of the old masonics? As a Catholic, on paper at least, and therefore outside the circle of secrecy, Frank's always been aware of the plums that fall to the Brothers on Merseyside.

Searle beams down from his full height. Frank half-smiles back and looks at his shoes. 'We've been getting some calls,' says Searle as the doors open onto the carpeted hush of the fifth floor and Moreleigh heads off in the opposite direction carrying his folder and an insufferable air of having business to attend to.

The place *smells* powerful somehow. How do they do that? Has Tesco's got it in the household fragrance section? Pine Fresh, Sandalwood Forest, Power Trip.

'Calls?'

Searle turns into his office and smiles at a good-looking woman behind a desk.

'Can you get myself and DCI Keane some coffee, Denise?' Denise turns enquiringly towards Frank.

'White with one, please.'

Denise doesn't need to ask Searle's preferences.

Inside the inner sanctum Searle proffers a hand at the seat facing his desk. Frank, an obedient dog, sits.

'Wife, kids, OK, Frank?'

'No kids, sir. Julie's fine.' Frank doesn't make any reference to the split and wonders if Searle's asking him just to gauge his subordinate's openness. Or lack of.

'My mistake.' Searle doesn't look like he's too concerned. 'So, the murders in Birkdale. What's been happening?'

Frank quickly and precisely fills Searle in on what he and his team have been doing since the bodies were found on Saturday night. Searle asks a couple of sharp questions but seems happy with the direction Frank's unit is taking. It's clear to Frank that getting background on the case isn't why Charlie Searle has hauled him up to the fifth floor.

'You mentioned something about calls?'

Searle adjusts the blue folders on his desk and leans back, his arms crossed. He lets a bit of a silence develop.

Jesus, thinks Frank. Do they go on a course to learn this stuff?

Eventually, when Searle judges he's left enough time to impress upon Frank how important he is, Searle begins talking again.

Frank can hardly bear to listen but he lets the noises drift past. Amidst all the greasy polly flim-flam and corporate lingo, Frank gleans that Superintendent Charlie Searle has a looming press problem he's anxious to pass on to Frank like a ticking parcel.

'It's your dentist thing,' says Searle. 'My office has been getting calls from a few journos. Nothing we can't handle, naturally, but, with you being a new boy, I thought I'd better give you a heads-up in case they come your way. It could get nasty.'

'Already? Jesus.' Frank can't believe it. 'The bodies aren't even cold.'

'Well, this is my concern, Frank. You may have a few blabber-mouths on your team.'

Frank lets it go. It's not worth getting into a shit fight. Searle and he both know that big crime scenes are about as easy to keep contained as water in a sieve. Too many people, too many ways for the information to get out there. Rose tells him there's a Facebook memorial page already.

'I'm not sure I understand the extra interest, sir. We haven't done the autopsies yet. And the local press usually aren't too much of a problem. How do you mean, it could get nasty?'

Denise comes back with the coffee.

Searle sips with relish. 'Marvellous,' he says as Denise closes the door behind her. He puts his cup down and fixes Frank with a stern expression. 'The thing is, Frank, these journalists aren't locals. All the tabloids have called already. You know what these bastards are like.' Searle actually shivers. 'Pack of hyenas, all of 'em.'

'Am I missing something?'

All warmth has gone from Searle's face now and Frank can feel the copper behind the bureaucrat, the steel beneath the surface. 'It's the boy, Frank.'

Keane nods. 'What about him? Is there a problem?'

'You could say that. It might turn out to be nothing, in which case there's no problem. On the other hand, if I'm catching their drift, and the situation isn't handled delicately, it could turn into a big fucking A-grade problem.' Searle smiles and fixes Frank with his blue eyes. 'And I'm happy to say that it will be your big fucking A-grade problem, DCI Keane. I have no intention of seeing my name up in lights on this one.'

'I'll bear that in mind, sir. What, exactly, is the nature of this problem?'

Searle frowns and, instead of an answer, asks a question. 'Have you spoken to the uncle yet? The one working on the film? Or anyone else on the production team?'

Christ, Searle might be a pen-pusher but there's no arguing with his grasp. Frank makes a mental note to check on the chain of command at MIT. Someone was going direct. Frank and MIT weren't prioritising talking to the film company yet. Searle knew that. The order of the investigation is not a misstep by Frank: the kid's friends and family members are the obvious first points of contact but Searle's interest means that Frank would be wise to take note.

'DS Cooper will be speaking to him today, I'm sure. And I'll make sure she'll be speaking to the production company too. Get the lie of the land. With the murders looking like a domestic – at least initially – the fact that the boy is earning some holiday money running errands working with his uncle wasn't our priority, not with the resources we have.'

Frank makes a mental note to speak to Cooper as soon as he's left. The movie hadn't been high on his list of priorities. Until now.

'Yes, well, resourcing is always an issue, Frank.'

Searle takes another sip and Frank realises that they're approaching the nub of this conversation.

'You know much about the movie business, Frank?'

'It's full of dickheads?'

'You see, that's really why I've brought you in this morning. You really need to sharpen up your diplomatic skills, Frank. There are more films shot in Liverpool than any other city in the UK. Did you know that?'

Frank shakes his head.

'And it generates a lot of cash and jobs. The CC is particularly proud of our relationship with the film industry, Frank. When you're doing your investigation into the missing boy I suggest that we do as much as we can to avoid getting in the way of the film's progress.'

Frank has to think for a moment before he speaks. 'You're saying we should go easy on the uncle?'

'Not at all, DCI Keane. But the last thing we need is their schedule interfered with unnecessarily. These journos? They're sniffing around for more than the usual blood and sex story. So far the only connection between the film and the murders is the uncle – but it's the production company they're interested in.'

Frank shifts in his seat. He's beginning to feel like a lazy schoolboy. He can't see why the journalists would be interested but it's clear that Searle knows something. Searle's got more background on this case, on his case, than he does himself. It's not a good feeling.

'This production company . . .' Searle opens the file in front of him and flicks a few sheets over. 'Hungry Head. They're part-owned by a name. A celebrity.'

'And the tabloids want to link the murders to the movie so they can bring in the celebrity.'

'Precisely.' Searle closes the blue file and smiles. He lifts his cup and takes a sip. 'Tread lightly, Frank.'

Twenty-Two

After the meeting with Charlie Searle, Frank gets into the Golf and heads for the MIT office in Stanley Road. As always, leaving Canning Place in his rear-view mirror feels good and Frank resolves to get the desk moved permanently as soon as he can. He calls from the car and talks to Cooper about interviewing the movie people.

At Stanley Road he pulls into his spot and heads upstairs. The place is surprisingly empty and all of the officers are on phone calls when Frank walks in. He waves to Caddick, Rose and the others and opens the door to his temporary office.

On his desk is a plate of fish and chips.

Standing next to it is a bucket overflowing with plastic sachets of malt vinegar.

From the MIT office comes a gale of laughter.

Frank walks around to his side of the desk and puts an exploratory finger on a chip. They're warm. Frank takes a sachet of vinegar and rips it open. He sprinkles the contents over the plate and takes a chip. Munching happily he picks up the plate and walks back into the main office and stands in front of the crime wall.

'Very amusing.'

Frank puts the plate down on an adjacent desk. 'Anyone like a chip?'

As the MIT crew gather round somewhat tentatively – Frank not being someone that practical jokes are played on with any great regularity – there seems to be a tacit understanding that the plate of fish and chips marks the beginning and end of any discussion of the vinegar incident. Frank has no doubt it will be endlessly discussed and replayed over the coming months – and he still has to deal with the serious fallout with Em, and perhaps with Searle, should he choose to exercise a bit of disciplinary muscle – but here, at MIT, the matter is closed.

With everyone assembled, Frank passes along Charlie Searle's concerns about the press. Although there isn't a table big enough for everyone to fit around, they make do with pushing a couple of the desks together. Those without chair space lean against adjacent cabinets.

'Hollywood?' says Theresa Cooper.

'According to Superintendent Searle.' Unlike some other coppers Frank has worked with, he seldom refers to senior officers by anything other than their full rank and name if there are juniors in the room. It doesn't sit right with him to do otherwise. Charlie Searle might be a bit of a pole-climbing rugger-bugger but, as far as Frank is concerned, that's immaterial.

Cooper makes an encouraging gesture for him to keep talking.

'Oh, details,' says Frank, 'right.' He smiles. 'It seems that the Birkdale case has attracted interest from the tabloids.'

Em Harris sits up a little straighter. 'Already?'

'Already. *The Sun*, the *Mail*, a couple of others have been sniffing round. Searle's been batting them away since daybreak.'

'We haven't even done the autopsies!' Cooper checks her watch automatically. She's due at the morgue at twelve. 'Fuck me.'

'It's quick for a reason. The missing boy – Nicky – is a film nut. He's working, or was working, on a movie.'

'*The Tunnels*,' says Scott Corner.

Frank glances at the lanky DC. 'What?'

'That's the name of the film. *The Tunnels*.'

For a moment Frank wonders if Corner's the link to Searle. If so, that will have to be stopped. Or, reflects Frank, perhaps I'm a suspicious twat and he's just a movie fan. Frank bends his head and kneads the top of his skull in a futile effort to spark some life back into his brain. Looking down he sees that one of his shoelaces is undone and for some reason this depresses him.

He looks up and sees Harris staring at him. And I need to stop fucking other officers, he thinks. Frank is conscious that the rest of the team are waiting for him to speak. He blinks and comes back to Scott Corner.

'It turns out that this movie is partly funded by a company which is owned by a celebrity.' Frank mentions a name. Someone lets out a low whistle.

'And that information stays inside, is that clear? If the journalists dig around it won't be because we've given them any encouragement.'

'But the boy isn't connected directly?' Cooper frowns.

'That's not the point, Theresa. The reason Superintendent Searle's got his dander up is that any connection, no matter how slight, means that this case is bigger news for the red tops. Celebrity plus murder equals sales.'

Frank pauses. 'And they're leaning towards Nicky being the killer.'

He leans back and folds his arms while everyone absorbs the information. He looks at Theresa Cooper.

'They can't do that,' she says. 'Can they?'

Harris glances up from her files. 'They can do whatever they like, Theresa. The question is, how are we going to handle it?'

Frank gets up and wanders across to the crime wall, still in its early days, almost empty. The wall isn't needed but Frank likes it and he thinks the rest of the team do too. It makes them feel they're in a cop show instead of working in an office, which is something, he supposes. He taps the photo of Nicky Peters.

'What's worrying me is that if the scum are peddling the line that Nicky did mummy and daddy and is now on the run, it might force the hand of our man.'

'Unless Nicky is the killer,' says DC Ronnie Rimmer. 'He had the taser receipt in his room. Into all sorts of weird shit, probably, when we start digging. Druggie, maybe.'

'Are we thinking that?' says Cooper. 'Seriously?' She puts out a hand and counts off on her fingers, point by point. 'Even our average punter wouldn't keep that taser receipt. Weird shit? The kid likes horror movies. Druggie? Less weed than a possession charge. Give me a break, Ronnie.'

Frank exchanges a glance with Em Harris. There's nothing he can read on her face but he's happy to see Cooper spreading her wings.

Theresa is at the front of the table.

'At the moment we're looking for someone who's missing, been abducted, or is a suspect. I'm pretty sure that once the DNA comes in from the labs, Nicky won't be in the frame at all, but that's based on nothing more than guesswork. Until we do get some hard forensics, our public stance has to be that all avenues are being considered. But between ourselves? Unless we pull our fingers out we're going to have victim number three before too long.'

'He's already dead,' says Harris. She looks at the faces around the MIT office. 'What? Oh, don't give me that. If Nicky Peters isn't a suspect he's already dead.'

Frank rubs the bridge of his nose.

'This isn't helpful. I know it's your case, Theresa, but with Superintendent Searle barking in my ear I'm going to put my interfering head on and give you some flat-out instructions for this case, and this alone. All our other stuff will have to fit around this one at least until he's happy. You can get back behind the wheel once we've got over this bumpy bit. Right?'

Cooper sits back and keeps her expression neutral. Admittedly Frank Keane is the SIO on the case, but so far she's getting less leeway than he'd indicated might be the case. Frank doesn't care. It's this sort of political stuff that Theresa's got to deal with as she rises.

'Good,' says Frank. 'Theresa, you go to the autopsies as planned. Get as much from that Glaswegian gobshite as you can. Em, you take the Peters couple and dig into their backgrounds. Finances, social, sex, work, you know the score. You get over to Terry Peters for a good chat. Nice and easy, Nicky's missing, anything you can tell us. But like the Super said: tread lightly.'

Harris says nothing and Frank feels himself redden a little. He glances at Theresa Cooper and then presses on.

'Scott, Peter, you keep on with the kid's mates, the school. Facebook, phone stuff. Talk to Ellie about freeing up some plod to do some door-knocking. The boy might be hiding. Could be injured. Start local and spread it as best you can from there. Make sure the first few streets are covered in detail. Talk to the railway people. The line runs close to the house and I seem to remember a body that was dumped in the bushes not far from there a few years ago. Stayed hidden for months. Get the track searched.'

Scott Corner raises a hand. 'The kid's Facebook page? I already had a quick look. It might be nothing but his relationship status was "it's complicated".'

'Good,' says Frank. 'It might mean something. Keep digging. See if you can find the complication.'

He looks out of the window, frowning. What else? With a snap of the fingers he turns to Ronnie Rimmer.

'Ronaldo. You're not bad with words. There'll be some enquiries from the press coming in, just like we talked about. I know it's not our usual style but I want a press statement that sounds like we know what we're doing. Spend a bit longer on it than usual and remember three things: Nicky is missing and we're concerned. All avenues are being explored. We ask for restraint in all reporting. Play down any connection to the movie. We don't have anything solid right now so we may as well keep Superintendent Searle sweet for as long as we can. If something shows up that does connect the murders to the movie then that's another matter. Right now we don't need to rock the boat. Show me and Theresa before you put it out.'

Rimmer nods and jots a note down on the pad in front of him.

'DC Rose, you run the central file here. Get everything running through HOLMES as usual; that's your responsibility. The data's the sheep and you're the fucking sheepdog, right?' The Home Office Large Major Enquiry System, designed to reduce human error in investigations, has been running for well over twenty years. Every officer in the room is well aware of the requirements but giving one person overall responsibility, as he has just done with Rose, helps ensure the system is adhered to.

Frank looks around the room. His voice takes on an edge and everyone there sits up that little bit straighter. 'I want everything going in and out of HOLMES via a portal on Rosie's computer. That doesn't mean he's doing everything. I just don't want any more data going up the food chain without me seeing it first. Superintendent Searle linked Nicky Peters' working on the film directly to the case and seemed to know we hadn't made that connection a priority.'

'He could just have been responding to the press.' Harris spreads her hands. 'Just saying it's possible.'

'Yeah, maybe,' says Frank. 'But I don't want to assume that's the case. This morning is the last time I want to be surprised by a superior officer appearing to be better informed about our case than I am.'

Frank glares around the MIT office. 'Is that clear?'

There is a chorus of grunts. Frank Keane's assumption that Searle has a mole feeding him titbits rankles. Harris regards him blankly. He's still working his way into the role but things like this are, she feels, a misstep.

Now is not the time to point that out.

'I'll get out to the movie people later this afternoon with Theresa.' Frank looks at Cooper, who nods assent. He checks his watch. Almost midday.

'OK, that's it.' Frank makes a shooing motion with his arms. 'Go. Get me something. And remember . . .'

The entire MIT group wait for Frank's words of wisdom but nothing comes out. 'Fuck it,' he says eventually. 'It's gone.' He sits down and studies the file in front of him as the group breaks up. Em Harris waits for everyone to drift away and then approaches him.

'I'll get over to Birkdale,' she says and pats Frank on the shoulder. 'Let you know if I get anything.' Her voice is warm and Frank – to his astonishment – feels tears behind his eyes.

'Yeah,' he says, keeping his head down, feeling both stupid and redeemed as she walks towards the door. 'You do that, Em.'

Twenty-Three

With the press all over the story, the word gets to Josh Soames about the murders and Nicky being missing on Monday morning and the day's filming takes place in a muted atmosphere.

There's been some discussion about abandoning the schedule but they don't. None of them knows what they are expected to do so they opt for a 'show must go on' approach.

'They were killed on Saturday?'

Ethan Conroy's talking to Quinner in the production trailer outside the tunnels. Both of them are drinking coffee. McElway's talking softly on his mobile off to one side. McSkimming from *The Sun* has been particularly persistent. In fact, it's McSkimming who has given Soames, Conroy and McElway most of the information, Terry having been less than forthcoming in his call to the office.

Quinner nods. 'That's what they're saying. It's hard to get anything concrete from anyone. Susie's calling the police to see what they can tell us.'

'Jesus.'

Quinner leans back against the wall. The news of the murders has put the attack on Big Niall to one side. Quinner hasn't mentioned that to anyone. Yet.

'Do we need to think about saying anything to the press yet?' McElway looks worried. Knowing who the investor is in Hungry Head, the last thing they want is a press feeding frenzy. No such thing as bad publicity? McElway knows that's horseshit.

'We'll have to do something,' says Conroy. 'But not just yet. We can palm McSkimming and the others off for a while. The kid's missing too. We can't say anything about that until the police tell us what's happening.'

'Is the kid on the payroll?' says McElway.

'His fucking name's Nicky, John.' Quinner shakes his head and McElway puts his hands together in a gesture of apology.

'Jesus, what a mess.' Conroy paces aimlessly around the office, the floor creaking underfoot.

'Who spoke to Terry?' says Quinner.

'He called Susie about half an hour ago. Didn't say much. Just that he was at home. It was Terry who found the bodies. He identified his brother early on Sunday and has been speaking to the police on and off yesterday.'

'They're coming in today,' Susie calls out from her desk in the main office. 'Not sure what time.'

Conroy rubs his face and breathes out slowly. McElway finishes his call and joins them.

'The press are going to go to town on this,' he says.

'Can't buy that sort of publicity,' says Conroy. He holds his hands up. 'A joke. A bad one.'

'How are we doing?' Quinner gestures towards the tunnels. Both men know what he means.

'Good. Considering,' says Conroy. 'Noone's behaving himself. Funnily enough it's adding something to the takes.'

Quinner's phone beeps and he checks the message. One of the actors wants a word.

'Are we carrying on today?' he asks.

Soames looks at Conroy and McElway and they all nod.

'What else can we do?' says the director.

Quinner moves to the door and picks up his script from the table. 'Carroll wants to go over something.'

The others begin moving out, the conference over. Quinner's almost inside the tunnels when he hears a voice.

'Dean!'

Quinner turns to see Ethan Conroy waving him back. There's a solid-looking, smartly dressed woman with him and a tall man.

The police.

Twenty-Four

The Peters case isn't the only MIT case Frank has on his desk; far from it. There are six separate commands on Merseyside and MIT's cases cross the boundaries on a daily basis. Much of the paperwork that comes across Frank's desk is made up of territorial red tape. With each of the commands guarding their patch, MIT, like other cross-boundary units, are seldom completely welcome.

After the briefing breaks up Frank spends an hour wading through a wave of emails, letters and memos, his eyes closing almost as soon as he's started. After delegating the task to Cooper during the briefing, he's had second thoughts and has now decided to go to the morgue himself for a chat with Ferguson about the victims. With the appointment at the Royal Liverpool University Hospital weighing heavily on Frank's mind, the call from his old boss in Australia comes as a welcome distraction.

Menno Koopman's voice sounds different. Bouncing up into space from Oz and back down again into Frank's phone lends a halting quality to the conversation, but that doesn't stop either man from talking. Despite the Dutch name, Koopman's as Liverpool as they come, a hardworking copper from the old school but not atrophied in the way some of those who came up with him in the eighties turned out. Koopman retired at forty-eight and followed his dream – or his wife's dream, if you're being picky – to Australia three years back. It had been going great until Koopman's estranged son had shown up barbecued to a crisp out at Crosby beach, the result of an industrial-scale drug deal gone wrong that dragged Koop and his family back into all the murderous Liverpool shite again. It had almost cost Zoe Koopman her life and the body count is still filed under 'rising'.

On paper, at least, Koop's calling Frank about the truckload of loose ends left over from last year's shenanigans. The case against bent copper Perch, the former boss of both Keane and Koopman; the missing drugs; the money; the deaths in Australia; Keith Kite's murder. It's both a policing triumph and a nightmare that will drag on for years.

It's coming up to nine in Australia, almost lunchtime in Liverpool. 'Tread lightly?'

'His exact words.' Frank waits for Koop's response. He hears a clink of a glass and can almost see the cold beer on the other side of the planet.

'What do you think he was getting at?'

'That's what I'm asking, Koop. You don't think I'm still sitting here gassing to you because I'm at a loose end, do you?'

'You're some sort of end, you got that bit right. A fucking knob end.' Koop chuckles. 'It's all a bit different now you're in the chair, eh, Frank?' More voices. Someone's shouting. There's traffic.

'Where are you?' Frank asks.

'A bar. Brisbane. We're up for a few days. Zoe . . . well, we're in Brissy.'

Koop stops speaking for a moment. Frank can hear the background conversation, music.

'Koop?'

'Yeah, still here, Frank. Tiny bit pissed, to be honest, so bear with me. Listen, don't sweat that sort of thing. Searle's always looking to protect his back and every time he sees the tabloids his arse puckers in case he ends up looking bad. People like Charlie dedicate their lives to not looking bad. They'd prefer to look good, but since that would require skill, they settle for just not looking bad.'

'So he passes it on to me?'

'Unless it turns out it's good news – unlikely, but possible – in which case it'll be his baby before you've noticed the adoption papers have been signed. The best thing you can do is leave a paper trail. Email him about every dealing you have with the press so when there's blame you will at least be able to back it up. And if you've delegated it, then you'll have to protect the new boy –'

'Girl. It's Theresa Cooper.'

'Little Theresa, eh? They grow up quick, don't they? Girl, then. But I wouldn't worry too much about it, to be honest, Frank. It's standard Canning Place stuff. You'll have to get used to it if you want to keep your seat at the big table.'

'Yeah, well, we'll have to see about that.'

Frank hears Koop laughing. Frank's office furniture is cheap and plasticky and there's an abandoned flip chart from some departmental hot-air convention in the corner. It has the word 'ACHIEVE' written on it in black marker. Someone has circled this word and drawn an arrow to the word 'BELEIVE'. The spelling mistake makes Frank feel like crying again. He looks out of the window towards the river. A weak, cloud-hung sun washes the skyline in dirty yellow light. Everything he sees looks dirty. Used up.

'What's it like, Koop?'

'What's what like? Are we still talking about your job?'

'No. Australia. Your place. Where are you now?'

'What the fuck is this? Do you want to know what I'm wearing?' Koop lowers his voice seductively. 'Want me to get more comfortable, Frankie?'

'Please don't ever let me hear that voice again, Koop. I'm begging you. You can't unremember that stuff. I just wondered, that's all. It's a fucking miserable Monday on Stanley Road, I've got a desk that's bending under the weight of shit that's piled up and I'm calling you from a room that looks like how I imagine purgatory. Not to mention a few choice developments in the Keane personal life which are better left out of this conversation. Do I have to explain it?'

Frank doesn't have to explain a damn thing. Koop knows that feeling well enough. The dull ache in your gut and behind your eyes, the feeling that the job, the city, the crumbling old island, are all too grubby and overcrowded and mean, that the weather's shit all the time and the roads are crowded and there's litter every fucking where. Cabin fever.

'It's great, Frank,' Koop says. Right now it's what Frank wants to hear. That someone made it past the sentries and the searchlights.

'Beaches?'

'You wouldn't believe it, mate. White sand. Blue seas. Paradise.'

97

There's a silence on the line. Koop can imagine Frank gazing through the grime-caked window at the frayed edges of the city and he's not wrong. Frank's remembering an incident three weeks ago. He'd been across the river checking something out on an over-lapping case in Seacombe with the Wirral Serious Crime Squad. It had been a cold day with little sun, and the location was facing the city. Frank could hardly hear himself think thanks to a road crew operating a jackhammer on the esplanade. Less than three metres from the work crew was a scrap of gritty beach covered in bricks, bottles, litter, broken glass and dog shit. The brown-grey Mersey was slopping at the muddy edges while a family of four – tattooed skinhead father sucking on a doobie, fat teenage wife gobbling from a KFC bucket, two toddlers swigging Coke from an oversized bottle – sat on towels as if it was St Tropez. Frank didn't know if he should laugh or cry. In the end he'd settled for embarrassment.

'Paradise, eh?'

'You got it, son,' says Koop gently. 'Speak soon, eh?'

Frank replaces the phone on its cradle and sits back. He wishes he could have told Koop about Harris and all that, but he didn't. Men don't.

'Shit,' he says to the empty room.

Twenty-Five

Menno Koopman slides his phone back into his pocket and drains the last of his beer.

He's at a pub on the corner of Mary Street. He's spent too long talking to Frank Keane already. Zoe will be wondering what he's doing.

Koop sits for a few moments thinking about his old job and all the stuff that had happened last year. It had been a mistake calling Frank. Just made him feel more shit, not less.

'You using this, mate?' A standing drinker is patting the spare chair at Koopman's table.

Koop stands and gestures. 'All yours.' He puts his hands in his pockets and weaves through the crowd, much thinner on a Monday than it would be at the weekend.

Outside it's cold. Koop still gets caught out by the chill at this time of year.

The apartment they're staying in is only a few hundred metres away. Koop slides the key card over the reader and heads to the lifts. At the twentieth floor he steps out and finds their room.

He waits for a second or two before opening the door.

Inside is a modern, trendy-looking apartment. The place is in darkness and Koop can see the lights of the Brisbane apartment and office towers through the floor-to-ceiling windows.

To one side is the bedroom. Soft yellow light spills from there onto the living room floor. Although he really doesn't need another drink, Koop pours one from the bottle of red wine on the kitchenette counter and moves to the doorway.

Zoe's blonde hair is the brightest thing in the room.

Koop stands and watches her head bob up and down in the candlelight, her shadow and those of the other two people on the hotel bed moving across the walls and ceiling more or less in time to the dull thump of the muted drum and bass music in the background.

Zoe is on all fours. A younger man is fucking her from behind, while she has her head between the legs of a woman stretched back on the bed. Zoe glances up and catches Koop's eye, her face slack with desire.

It's eight months since Zoe had been kidnapped and almost murdered. Her girlfriend, Melumi, had died. Badly.

Perhaps that is it, reflects Koop.

And then: no 'perhaps' about it. He closes his eyes momentarily and listens to the noises from the bed. Soft thumps, low groans, whispered dirty talk combining in an ancient rhythm. Zoe has been fixing up these meetings online more frequently during the past few months and they've been getting successively more and more anonymous. Koop doesn't know the people she's talking to, is not involved in the process, and has tried to do what he can to change Zoe's mind. She's having none of it. Koop can be part of it or not. Koop's been here before, done this before, even *liked* this before, once or twice, but never like this, never with so little passion or humanity. With Mel and with Zoe's other girlfriends, the process was organic, warm. This feels all wrong. What was merely kinky has become bent out of shape. He suddenly knows he can't be in the room.

'I'm going,' he says. 'Home, I mean.'

Zoe looks up again and hesitates. Then Koop sees the cloud pass across her face before she nods.

'It's not you,' he says. *It fucking is.*

'You OK, man?' asks the guy. His partner – Koop can't remember her name – stares at him curiously. Koop doesn't reply. He only came along to keep Zoe safe. Now that feels like a mistake.

'OK, then,' says Zoe. Now she's said it, Koop wants to stay but there's a harsh note to Zoe's voice, one that's become too familiar over the past six months, that doesn't sit right with him. She is drifting out of reach like a tourist in a rip-tide.

Koop turns and slips from the apartment.

Back outside in the bland corridor he leans back against the wall and lets out a long sigh. From inside the apartment he can hear the three on the bed increase their pace. Zoe makes a high-pitched noise, louder than previously, and Koop wonders, with a vicious stab of resentment, if it's done for his benefit.

'Fuck it,' he mutters and walks towards the bank of lifts.

Waiting, Koop checks his watch. Only twenty minutes have elapsed since he left the bar. It seems like days.

The doors open and Koop steps into the empty lift and presses the button.

Once outside in the soft Brisbane night, Koop stands uncertainly outside the block and looks up and down Mary Street.

It's over. He can't do this any more.

Twenty-Six

It's gone twelve on Monday by the time Harris pulls up in front of a red-brick Victorian semi, not quite as grand as the one in Burlington Road, two streets away, but big enough. There are two cars parked in front of the garage and she sees movement behind one of the bay windows.

Harris takes a few moments to compose herself and checks her appearance in the rear-view mirror. By the time they'd finished at the crime scene early on Sunday Frank reckoned it was too late to do a decent interview with Terry Peters, so this is really the first crack at putting some detail in the file. Theresa had done some initial notes last night before accompanying Terry Peters yesterday to formally identify his brother. Although there's a high probability that the dead woman in Burlington Road is Maddy Peters, the victim's face is too disfigured for a visual. A uniform is at the dental surgery with a technician going through the records. It may be days before the official word comes through.

Throughout Sunday, while MIT have been setting up the investigation at base and coordinating the nuts and bolts in Birkdale, there's been no sign of Nicky Peters. Door-knocking radiating out from the murder house will continue this morning. There are no plans for searches to be made anywhere. With the deaths not yet public there is only a trickle of information coming in, mostly from those neighbours who have been questioned.

Harris steps out of the car and walks to the door. She presses the bell and hears the tone echoing through the house. A few seconds pass and then a shape looms through the stained glass. A tall middle-aged man appears, his face showing the strain. He opens the door and Harris notes the micro-second adjustment as he sees the colour of her skin. To her vague disgust, she imagines she catches too just the smallest flicker of sexual interest. Or maybe she's just tired.

'Mr Peters? DI Harris, Merseyside Major Incident Team. My office called earlier?'

'Yes, right. Come in. Please.'

Terry Peters shakes her hand and Harris steps into a high-ceilinged hallway. Peters, good-looking in an outdoorsy way, seems to be holding himself together well enough despite the events of the past twenty-four hours. According to Theresa's notes, he's younger than his dead brother by eight years, although Harris knows this experience will age him fast.

'I am so sorry for your loss, Mr Peters,' says Harris. 'And I hope we can get as much information as possible to help us without causing you too much distress.'

'Whatever you need,' says Terry Peters.

'I understand you went with DS Cooper to identify your brother on Sunday?'

Terry Peters nods. 'He looked better than I thought he would. Sounds stupid.'

'Not at all,' says Harris. 'It's always traumatic and anything that gets you through it is good.'

'Do you have any news? Have you . . . got anyone? Has anyone seen Nicky?'

'I'll get any information to you as soon as I can, Mr Peters. There's not much to report on at the moment, I'm afraid. Hopefully later we might have something.'

Peters closes the front door behind them and motions Harris along the hallway and into the kitchen. It's a pleasant room but she can feel the misery caused by the deaths seeping through like damp. A woman is busy in front of a serious-looking cooking range and Harris realises she hasn't eaten a thing since a snatched coffee at six this morning.

'Smells good,' says Harris and the woman turns. Unlike her husband, Alicia Peters doesn't seem to register Harris's colour. Alicia's eyes are red-rimmed but she seems calm enough, considering. She wipes her hands on a kitchen towel and shakes Harris's hand.

'DI Harris. As I said to your husband, our deepest sympathies.'

'Alicia. Thank you.'

'What are you cooking?' says Harris.

'I know it seems like I shouldn't be doing this, but I have to do something or I'd go mad.' Alicia Peters turns to the stove. 'It's fish pie. A Jamie Oliver. Would you like some? I mean, is that OK? Are you allowed . . .?'

'To eat?' says Harris. 'Yes, they let us eat.' She smiles back. 'You know, I'd love some if there's enough to go round.'

'There's plenty. Liam's out. Gone round to friends.'

When Harris raises a quizzical eyebrow, Alicia Peters nods as if she'd spoken. 'Yes, I know, not great, in the circumstances, but teenagers . . . well, they can be like that. Not that we've ever . . . well, you know. Anyway, he's out and that means more to share. You must think it's odd, cooking, I mean, but, well . . .' Alicia Peters lets the sentence trail off and for a moment looks as though she may start crying again.

'It's not odd,' says Harris. 'I've seen people do lots of things far stranger than cooking in these situations.'

Alicia Peters wipes her eyes with the back of her hand and begins to serve the meal.

'We'll have to speak to Liam too,' says Harris. 'Your son, right?'

Alicia Peters nods but doesn't look up.

Terry Peters looks uncomfortable, as though there's some sort of Home Office police protocol about eating fish pie while conducting interviews. Even so, he sorts out plates and cutlery and they sit at a large wooden table bearing the scars of thousands of meals. Terry Peters starts to pour a glass of white wine but Harris puts her hand over the rim. She notices the wine bottle is half-empty. She can't blame them. It's what she'd have done in the circumstances.

Harris eats some of the pie. It's excellent, and for a couple of minutes she sits in a silence which, if not completely comfortable, is at least bearable. Alicia Peters is too young to be Harris's mother but there's something so compassionate in the way she looks at the policewoman that Harris relaxes completely. This is how I want to live, she thinks, luxuriating in the idea of herself in this environment with someone like Alicia. It's with real effort that she brings herself back to the job and chastises herself for doing the very thing she'd mentally accused Terry Peters of doing when he'd answered the door.

'Tell me about your brother's family,' she says to Terry. 'Just a little background.' She takes her notebook from her bag and puts it beside her plate.

Terry Peters shrugs. 'They're nice people. We were close, me and Paul. Pretty close anyway.' He too looks tearful but coughs and stays in control. 'Lives around the corner. We see them regularly. Not in each other's pockets but enough. Go on holidays together sometimes, and the kids get along.'

'Nicky's their only child?'

Alicia Peters nods. 'Thank God,' she says. 'In the circumstances.' Then she brightens. 'You'll need a photograph of him,' she says. 'I'm sure we have a good one.'

'Thank you, but we have all we need, Mrs Peters. There were some family portraits at your sister-in-law's house we are using.'

'Oh, OK.'

'What sort of a boy is Nicky?' Harris finds she hesitates over using the word 'is'. Alicia looks up sharply but doesn't react. She's quick, thinks Harris.

'He's a nice kid,' says Terry Peters. 'I mean he has the usual teenage things going on but nothing that would cause anyone any problems. Paul or Maddy never said anything otherwise, did they?' He looks at Alicia for confirmation and she shakes her head.

Harris knows the next one is going to hurt.

'So there's nothing that you can think of that might make Nicky want to harm his parents?'

For a second neither of them reacts. Then, as the meaning of the question sinks in, Harris feels the temperature in the warm kitchen drop perceptibly.

'What? No!' Alicia has a hand to her mouth. 'You can't think that, can you? Nicky wouldn't do something like that, would he, Terry?'

'That's insane,' agrees Terry. 'Who's saying that?'

Harris holds up a placatory hand. 'No one at our end, although we have to consider every possibility. Even those we find repellent. With Nicky missing and two people dead we'd be remiss in not considering it. It wouldn't be the first time a teenager has done something like this.'

Alicia is shaking her head from side to side. 'Uh, uh, no, no way.'

'I'd have known,' mumbles Terry Peters. 'I mean if Nicky was capable of something like that.'

'That's what everyone says, Mr Peters.' Harris pushes her plate away. 'Sadly.' She flicks open the file she has set down on the table and picks up a pen.

'I'll need a list of their friends, and their contact details, if you have them. And any activities Paul and Maddy were interested in. Church groups, book clubs, sports teams, anything like that. My officers will be following up with background.'

As Alicia and Terry start to list various possibilities, the kitchen door swings open and a boy of about seventeen comes in. His hair hangs down in a fringe over his eyes and he wears an expression of complete disgust with everything he sees. Ignoring everyone in the room he moves towards the fridge and takes out a can of Coke.

'Liam,' says Alicia Peters. 'I thought you were over at Jonno's?'

'Changed my mind.' The boy turns to go.

'This is DI Harris,' says his mother. Liam grunts in Harris's direction briefly before turning back to the door.

'Liam!' says Terry Peters in a sharper tone. 'Come here!'

The boy doesn't look back. Instead he mutters something under his breath and half-slams the door behind him.

'Sorry,' says Alicia. Terry is breathing heavily. Harris notices his neck is flushed.

'Little shit,' says Terry.

'He's my son. From my first marriage,' says Alicia. 'Me and Terry have been together five years. Terry and Liam . . . well, it's not always been a happy relationship. And it's hit Liam hard. All this.'

'Of course,' says Harris. 'Does Liam know Nicky well?'

Alicia shakes her head while Terry seems lost in thought. For a moment Harris considers Terry Peters. Even under the circumstances there's something off about his reaction to an adolescent strop. The warm kitchen that Harris had been inwardly eulogising suddenly seems off-kilter. She decides to take a different tack with

Terry. She's been too friendly. What needs to happen is for her to get him out of his comfort zone.

Harris gets to her feet. 'I think I've taken up enough of your time at the moment.' She turns to Terry. 'If you could pop along to Stanley Road tomorrow there are a few things I'd like you to go over with my colleagues. Might help with the search for Nicky.'

Terry Peters looks uncertain. 'I'm not sure what's happening tomorrow to be honest . . .'

Harris smiles. 'Well, I'm sure you'll understand that this investigation takes priority. Shall we say ten o'clock?' She holds Terry's gaze and there it is: a tiny flicker of anger and annoyance buried deep below the surface, rising like a fish to a fly.

'Ten o'clock. Of course.' Terry Peters gets to his feet. 'I'll show you out.'

'That's not necessary,' says Harris. 'I'd like a word with Liam before I go.' She turns to Alicia. 'Thanks so much for the food.'

'You're welcome,' says Alicia Peters. The Nigella vibe has gone now and she's watching Harris warily. 'Do I need to be there when you talk to Liam? He's a child, after all.'

'How old is he?' asks Harris.

'Seventeen.'

'Then I think we're fine. This is simply information gathering, Mrs Peters.' Harris points upstairs. 'That way?'

Alicia nods.

Harris leaves the Peters standing on either side of the kitchen table. As the door closes she sees Alicia begin collecting the plates. She doesn't look at her husband.

Harris heads upstairs. On the walls are family photographs. Terry and Alicia's wedding with a younger, sulky-looking Liam. Harris pauses and looks closer at the group of people. Paul and Maddy and Nicky are there in the background, all smiles. There are holiday photos. Portugal, Florida. Liam and Nicky on a boat somewhere, Terry fishing in the background. Liam playing football. One image in particular catches Harris's eye. It's taken on the verandah of a hotel and shows both families. They are dressed in light clothes and have suntans, their arms draped around each other as they pose for the camera. Terry is between Alicia and Maddy. His left hand dangles carelessly over Maddy's shoulder. It may be a momentary illusion, a frozen moment as the pose is formed, but to Harris it seems that Terry's thumb appears to be fractionally under the strap of Maddy Peters' bikini top. Only a cynic would see it as anything other than accidental but Harris, like most cops, falls squarely into that demographic. She lifts her iPhone from her bag and takes a shot of the photograph. You never know.

Liam's not hard to track down. At the top of the second turn in the stairs is a landing and from behind the first door comes the throb of electronic music. Harris knocks and after a few seconds the volume is turned down. Liam opens the door and blinks at her. Harris doesn't wait for an invitation. Instead she pushes open the door and steps into the teenager's room.

'Terrible thing,' says Harris. Up close, alone in his room with a woman of Harris's beauty and authority, Liam's adolescent bravado disintegrates. He sits down on his bed and offers Harris the use of the chair sitting in front of his computer desk.

'Thanks,' says Harris. She looks around the room. It's cleaner than she expected but has the faint rank tang of any teenage boy's environment.

'Have you found anyone yet?' says Liam.

'No, not yet. That's what we're doing now, getting some background to help us find Nicky as quickly as possible. What can you tell me about Nicky, Liam?'

Liam shrugs. 'He was my cousin. Sort of.'

'Was?'

'I think he's dead,' says Liam miserably. 'They don't let them go, do they?'

'Who doesn't?'

'Psychos. Must have been a psycho that did . . . that. I heard it was bad.'

'How did you hear that?'

'Just . . . heard. I dunno. From people.'

Harris lets it go. From past experience she knows it's next to impossible to contain a crime scene in a place like this. Anywhere, really. And it was Liam's stepfather who found the bodies, after all.

'So you haven't heard from him? On Facebook? Text?'

Liam shakes his head. 'Last time was on Friday. He posted a photo on Instagram.'

'Can you show me?' Harris knows that DC Rose will be compiling a detailed dossier on Nicky's online presence, but she wants Liam to warm to her. She may get something more useful that way.

Liam clicks open his Instagram account and scrolls to Nicky's pages. Liam opens a photo showing an arty-looking shot of the outside of a nightclub. Even with the distortions of the filters Nicky has applied, Harris recognises it as Maxie's, a club in the city.

'Nicky was here on Friday? At this club?'

Liam shrugs. 'Guess so.'

'Did he go to many clubs?'

'Dunno. Maybe. Some. He's been going more since working on the film.'

Harris makes a note. If they do ever find Nicky's phone they'll be able to confirm some of his movements but the photo of Maxie's on Instagram is a reasonably precise confirmation of where the boy was on Friday night. It's a small piece of information but a good one.

'What else does he post?'

Liam flicks through Nicky's account. There are images of the movie sets mostly. Actors, technicians, the ephemera of film-making. What comes through is the boy's enthusiasm and his straightforward pleasure in being involved in this world. Harris recalls his bedroom.

'Nicky seems like he knew what he wanted to do,' she says.

'He likes movies.'

'But you don't?'

A faint cloud passes over Liam's face. 'Not as much as Nicky.'

'Your stepdad works in the movie business.'

Liam shrugs again but doesn't say anything. The movie angle isn't getting much response from Liam. Harris changes tack and gets an immediate bite.

'Does Nicky get on with his parents?'

For the first time, Liam is animated.

'It wasn't Nicky, if that's what you're thinking. Nicky wouldn't have done anything like that. He wasn't like that.'

'We hear that a lot,' says Harris. 'But . . .'

'But nothing.' The boy brushes his fringe from his eyes and looks at Harris. There's no awkwardness about him now. 'Nicky wouldn't have done that. Not to his parents, anyway.'

'Excuse me?'

Liam sinks back on the bed.

'Liam?' Harris leans forward, her elbows on her knees, and lowers her voice. 'What do you mean by that? Is there someone who Nicky *would* have harmed?'

Nothing. The fringe returns to its natural function as curtain.

'Liam?'

'No! I didn't mean anything.'

'Was someone harming Nicky?'

'I don't know anything.'

Harris sits back. 'It'll all come out eventually, Liam. Best to tell me if you have any suspicions.'

Liam looks towards the door. 'I don't have any.'

Harris stands. She needs to let Liam get it out himself. Pushing won't do much right now. 'I'll go now, Liam.' She hands him a business card, which he glances at and lets fall to the bed. 'But someone will be back to take a full statement from you tomorrow, OK? And I need you to have a think if there's anything else you'd like to tell us, no matter how insignificant, that could help us find Nicky. We don't have much time. Your cousin needs all the help he can get right now.'

Liam says nothing, burying his head lower between his shoulderblades.

Harris leaves and walks down the stairs. From the kitchen she can hear nothing except the clank of plates being washed. There's no conversation and upstairs Liam has not turned the music back on.

Harris opens the door and notices the bigger of the cars has gone. She walks away from the silent house.

Twenty-Seven

After talking to Menno Koopman Frank heads to The Royal and the morgue. He's already late but that's fine with him. Anything that rubs Ferguson up the wrong way is a bonus.

He calls Cooper from the car but she doesn't pick up and he assumes that's because she's at the hospital already. Even Frank wouldn't use his mobile in Ferguson's autopsy room.

After signing in at reception, Frank heads to the examination room, remembering to put on the protective paper bootees – Ferguson being very insistent about protocols – and pushes open the doors.

Ferguson is bent over the body of Paul Peters, Theresa Cooper standing a respectful metre behind him. Ronnie Rimmer is behind Cooper. Maddy Peters is on another slab being prepped by an assistant. The contrast between the dead couple is stark: Paul Peters' naked form almost unmarked, his wife a horrifying bundle of damaged flesh. Frank is dismayed to realise that the autopsies are far from over. He had hoped to arrive near the end but, judging by the work the assistant is doing on Maddy, they are only just getting started.

'Sir.' Cooper raises a hand to Frank as he walks across to the examination table.

'Dr Ferguson is running late today,' she says as if reading her boss's thoughts.

'DCI Keane,' murmurs Ferguson. 'Change of schedule, I'm afraid.'

'Great.'

Ferguson glances up from his task, a scalpel in hand, and checks Frank's feet for code violations before turning back to his task.

'You don't have to stay, Frank – don't you trust DS Cooper?'

Behind the pathologist Frank sees Theresa Cooper stiffen fractionally. Frank's sharp eyes dart to Rimmer for any sign of a smile but the freshly promoted DS's face is neutral.

'Tactful as always, Fergie.' Frank doesn't expand on or respond to the jibe from Ferguson. Never explain. Theresa will have to deal with any disappointment Frank's appearance may have aroused. Christ, compared to the treatment he'd been on the receiving end of in his career, she's being treated like a princess.

There's silence in the examination room, broken only by the sluice taps being turned on and off by the assistant working on the woman's body. Keane rests his backside against a lab bench and feels a wave of nausea wash through him. He eyes an empty examination slab with something like envy. After a couple of minutes, Ferguson straightens and arches his back, groaning slightly. He turns to the three observers and beckons them over.

'There's nothing dramatic to add, from first examination.' Ferguson points a latex-covered finger at the marks on the dead man's neck. 'As we thought, he's been tasered. If you look closely you'll see extensive localised burning around the contact points. I'm prepared to say that probably means multiple charges. Once we open up his chest and get a proper look at his heart I think there's every chance we'll find he was dead prior to being hung. There's some suggestion of that from the lack of lividity around the rope burns.'

'Had he had sex?' Cooper's eyes flick down to the dentist's groin. 'There was some talk about sex games.'

'No,' says Ferguson. 'Not that I can detect.' He straightens and looks at Frank. 'I don't want to tell you how to do this, but most of the good stuff will be in my report.'

Ferguson resumes his work on Paul Peters. 'And that is still some way off, DCI Keane.'

Frank nods to himself.

Quite suddenly he can see himself as Theresa's seeing him: a helicopter boss. Ferguson's right. It kills him to admit it, but this – delegating – is something he still hasn't grasped.

'Makes sense,' says Frank. He sketches a wave to Cooper. 'All yours, Theresa. Fill me in later, OK?'

As Frank exits, Ferguson turns to Cooper.

'You saw that, right?' says the Scot. 'If anyone argues with me later?'

Cooper nods.

'I saw it,' she says. 'But I'm not sure I believe it.'

Twenty-Eight

After the autopsies, Cooper and Rimmer grab a sandwich at The Majorca before heading to the movie location. On the short journey across town all Rimmer can talk about is the vinegar attack on Frank Keane and what it means. Cooper does her best to shut him up but it's difficult. It's a choice bit of gossip which gives Rimmer a chance to indulge in fevered fantasies. The tacit agreement that the matter is closed has clearly not been accepted by everyone.

'Roy must have crapped himself. I heard she drenched him.'

'Are you still banging on about that?'

'Banging. Very good, Theresa.'

'Jesus. And don't let Keane hear you calling him Roy.'

Keane's nickname at MIT is 'Roy'. He not only shares a surname with a former Manchester United captain, he looks like him too. As a lifelong Liverpool supporter, Frank doesn't take this kind of thing – being named after a United player – in good spirit.

Rimmer's smiling. 'You think he and Harris . . . you know?'

Theresa Cooper shakes her head. 'No, I happen to know they didn't.'

In fact, Cooper strongly suspects that DCI Frank Keane and DI Emily Harris shagged each other senseless last Thursday night, but she's so sick of this juvenile crap that she can't resist throwing a small spanner in the works.

'Bollocks,' says Rimmer. 'You don't go around throwing acid at someone because you don't like the look of them.'

'Vinegar.'

'What?'

'It was vinegar, not acid.'

'Well, Roy didn't know that,' says Rimmer. 'The desk sergeant at Canning Place said he looked like a ghost.'

Cooper doesn't respond but it does no good. Like an early-morning barking dog, Rimmer won't quit.

'Hey,' he says, his face taking on a leery slant, 'you ever see DI Harris's, er . . .?'

'Partner?' says Cooper. 'Her partner, you mean?'

'Yeah, partner.'

'Yes, why?'

'I heard she's really good-looking. Plod who saw it all at Canning Place reckons she could be a model.' Rimmer's eyes take on a faraway gleam and it's not difficult to deduce what he's thinking about.

Theresa hits the brake harder than she needs and Rimmer's head jerks forward painfully against the car's window post.

'Ow!'

'We're here,' she says. 'Dickhead. Now try and at least act like a grown-up. And remember, I'm the fucking DS, got it?'

With Rimmer grizzling in her wake, Cooper heads for a security guy at the gate who directs her towards a long caravan standing among the catering and equipment trucks. Before they reach it the door opens and John McElway steps out.

'DS Cooper?' says McElway, holding out his hand. 'John McElway. You spoke to my office earlier.'

He motions for them to come inside. A man sitting at a table rises and shakes hands.

'Ethan Conroy,' he says.

Conroy looks across to Dean Quinner. 'And this is Dean Quinner, our writer.'

Quinner, standing against a plasticky looking wall, pushes himself forward and shakes hands with Cooper. He nods but doesn't speak.

The five people sit around the table. It's a squeeze and there are a couple of seconds of awkward shuffling before everyone is comfortable.

'Very nice,' says Cooper, looking around the caravan. The two producers smile.

'Welcome to the glamorous world of the movies. What can we do for you?'

Cooper addresses herself to Conroy and Quinner.

'In case Mr McElway hasn't told you, I'm leading the Liverpool MIT – Major Incident Team – investigation into a violent crime that took place in Southport somewhere between Friday night and Saturday evening. We want to talk to the people who know Nicky Peters. See if there's any information that might help us find him.'

'He's definitely missing then?' says Conroy. 'We heard that and then . . . well, some people were saying they thought he was . . . well, we thought he was dead or injured. We heard there'd been deaths.'

Cooper nods. 'Nicky's parents were found dead on Saturday, Mr Conroy. We're anxious to find Nicky.'

'Jesus.' McElway sags in his seat. 'Did he . . .?'

Cooper doesn't reply directly. 'We can't tell you much more than that, I'm afraid. But time is a factor. Can we make a start with you three?'

Rimmer puts a black folder on the table and takes out a pen.

'Sure,' says McElway. 'But none of us really knew the boy. He was just doing some runner work for Terry during the school holidays. I saw him around but I don't think I ever spoke to him.'

'Me neither,' says Conroy. 'I can't remember much about him. Seemed pleasant enough. There wasn't any trouble or moaning about his work. But being Terry's nephew that's what I'd have expected. Terry's good.'

'Reliable?'

'He's been with the project from the start of production,' says Conroy. 'A good man.'

'Had you worked with him before?'

Conroy and McElway shake their heads.

'I had.' It's the first time Quinner's spoken. 'He did the location production on a TV thing I was involved in last year. A soap. Piece of shite.'

'You're a local, Mr Quinner?'

Quinner nods. 'Yes. I spoke to Nicky a couple of times. The lad brought me coffee.'

'Did you speak to him on Friday? He was around?'

'Just a word or two. And yes, he was here all day. Not sure when he left.'

'And did he seem his usual self?'

'Far as I could tell. I made some joke about him being out at Maxie's the night before. Said his uncle would grass him up to his ma if he wasn't careful. Something like that.'

'Maxie's?'

'It's a club in town we've been using as a sort of social base,' puts in McElway. 'You usually get a bunch of the crew hanging out after work.'

'But Terry Peters wasn't there on Thursday?'

'Terry was doing some prep work here in the tunnels.' Conroy gestures towards the visitor centre. 'We started filming here early on Friday.'

'Didn't Terry need Nicky to help?'

'I guess not. Maybe he didn't want the kid up too late. Get in trouble with his brother.'

'But Nicky went to Maxie's anyway?'

Conroy smiles. 'He's a teenager.'

'What time did Nicky leave Maxie's?'

McElway shrugs. 'We weren't late. Maybe ten? I was there – we were there until around ten-thirty. I have a feeling most people had left before us.'

'And he showed up on time on Friday?'

McElway nods.

Cooper checks her file again.

'Is Nicky close to anyone in the crew?'

The three men look at one another.

'Not that I know of,' says McElway. 'You'd have to ask the rest of them.'

'We will, Mr McElway. I just wondered if you knew anything that might give us a pointer. Did anything unusual happen on Thursday?'

'Not a thing,' says Conroy. 'The shoot went really well.'

Quinner mumbles something.

'Sorry?' says Cooper. 'What was that?'

'Uh, there was a missing wallet,' says Quinner. 'One of the crew lost a wallet. Chris Birchall I think.'

'A lost wallet?' Cooper looks puzzled. She waits expectantly for more from Quinner but he stays silent. 'What about the wallet? Are you saying Nicky took it?'

'No! Jesus.' Quinner looks miserable. 'I just thought I should, y'know, mention it.'

Quinner looks out of the window.

'OK,' says Cooper. She leaves a pause.

Now's the moment but it slips past without him saying anything. He's not sure why.

Except he does.

Exposing Noone as a thief might mean recasting his role. With almost a third of the footage shot that's too risky. Not after four years. No need for the coppers to get involved in that. It's not like it's got anything to do with all this murder stuff. And Quinner can't mention the attack on Niall without proof. Even while he's thinking it he knows it's bullshit. The cops need to know but he can't bring himself to say the words, to open the can of worms. Not now. Not when they're so close.

And there's no way Noone's involved in this thing with Nicky.

Is there?

'It's probably nothing,' says Quinner. 'Swede must've dropped it somewhere on set.'

'Swede?' says Rimmer.

'Chris's nickname. He looks Swedish.'

'Was the wallet found?' says Cooper.

'I don't think so.' Quinner leans back against the wall.

Cooper pauses. 'OK.' She looks up at Dean Quinner. 'If there's nothing else . . .' She leaves the statement hanging in the air for a moment but there's no response.

'We'll talk to the rest of the crew in here separately. It shouldn't take too long at this stage,' she continues. 'Thanks for your help. If there's anything you remember that might be of interest, no matter how trivial, we'd like to hear from you.' Cooper hands her card to each of them. 'This has the direct numbers for MIT.'

At the door, Ethan Conroy checks his watch.

'If you wait a few minutes I'll get the crew to wrap things up for today. It'll make seeing everyone easier for you.'

'Thanks, Mr Conroy, that would be good.'

'Anything the production can do to help,' says John McElway. 'We're just as anxious as you to find Nicky and get this dreadful thing cleared up.'

Quinner says nothing and the three men leave the caravan.

As the door closes behind them, Ronnie Rimmer looks at Cooper and raises his eyebrows.

'I know,' says Cooper. 'Quinner.'

Twenty-Nine

Quinner spends the rest of the day feeling like shit. He watches take after take from Noone, who seems as good as ever. Like everyone else, he's been talking about the murders and what it might mean, but Quinner can't see anything different in the American. Surely, even if 'all' he'd done was attack Niall, then he'd be showing something? By the end of the day Quinner's lost some of his certainty about Noone.

And yet if not Noone, then who? Who would have been there waiting for Niall and that little shit Jason? Quinner, a professional writer, would jib at placing someone unknown at the scene who happened to be waiting to slice a finger off. It's too far-fetched, or at least that's how it appears to Quinner in his present mood.

During prep for the final shot Quinner comes up above ground. He gets a coffee from the catering truck and sits in the production office looking at the phone in his hand. DS Cooper's card is on the table in front of him.

After a minute or two, Conroy comes in.

'How's it going?' says Quinner.

'It's going well, considering,' says Conroy.

'Considering what?'

'The murders.' Conroy can't keep the surprise from his voice. 'And Nicky.'

'I know,' says Quinner. 'That's not . . . look, it doesn't matter. How's Noone doing?'

'Good. We're moving a bit slower without Terry but it's pretty close to schedule. Josh is keeping the takes to a minimum and Ben's hitting the mark every time.'

'He OK? I mean, he's not nervous or anything?'

'About what? No, he's great. He's doing fine and the crew love him. Can't have hurt finding Chris Birchall's wallet, either.'

'Noone found it?'

'Yeah, fallen behind some shit, I don't know. Listen, I have to go back out. John's kicking up about something.'

Quinner slumps back on the chair.

If Noone had handed the wallet back doesn't that mean it's less likely he's been chopping people's fingers off? Maybe that dickhead cousin of his wandered into some drug thing. It's not like Niall's some kind of Special Forces guy. Isn't it more likely that Noone had nothing to do with Niall's finger? Perhaps getting caught thieving was embarrassing, and he'd thought better of it and decided to hand the wallet back. Yeah, that was it, that held together better than this skulking around with knives in back alleys. He's a fucking actor, for Christ's sake, Quinner told himself.

The talk with Conroy has gone a long way to soothing Quinner's mind. He's glad he hasn't called the cops.

He checks his watch.

Six o'clock. More than late enough for a drink.

Thirty

Before his mother had died and he'd found out everything and changed his name to what it was now, Noone had often thought he was golden. There was nothing to suggest otherwise. He had it all. Money was just there. He couldn't ever remember thinking about it. The best schools, clothes, vacations. Whatever he wanted.

As a boy he hadn't thought too much about being different. You don't at that age and he had been sociable enough not to stick out. No loner, he found it ludicrously easy to make friends and, later, to find lovers. You just had to say the right words in the right order and have the right teeth, the right skin, the right clothes. No trick to it.

But only Noone knew it was a con. It was no surprise to him that he'd been good at acting when he finally gave it a try. He'd been acting all his life, saying what was required and putting the accepted expression on his face.

He knew that most people did what they did naturally. He'd never found being human natural. In any situation he would have his own thoughts and then a second layer: how would a human react? He would imitate human behaviours. If he appeared normal, then wouldn't that make him normal? It worked most of the time.

His mother had tried but she wasn't cut out for the life she ended up living. She loved him but didn't know what to make of the creature who'd arrived unexpectedly. The money had never been an issue – now Noone knew why – and love hadn't been in short supply either. At least not from her direction. But control and discipline and structure? That hadn't been there. And then later, when drink and then cancer had reduced her to a shell, it was too late. Noone was what he was.

And he'd never forgive her for not telling him the truth. Finding that out had unlocked something in him.

Most of his twenties were spent allowing his desires and impulses to rule, and though there had been violence and there had been arrests, responsibility and blame slipped off him like dead skin from a snake. Until his mother's death he'd never questioned why.

Five years ago in Toronto he'd cold-cocked a guy who came home early and found Noone loading his Ducati motorcycle into a van. The guy – some lightweight hipster biker wannabe Noone was working with in a sports bar on West Queen West – had hit his head and spent serious time in the hospital but never testified, never filed the complaint. Noone had put it down to luck.

In Madrid a year later he'd got in the habit of rolling a few tourists for their wallets – nothing planned, just on the fly when he needed quick money – and there'd been an arrest after he'd threatened the wrong guy who didn't want to be rolled. The case didn't get to court – some mix-up with the chain of evidence – and Noone walked again.

Even the worst time, in London, when that young chick had died on the bad junk he'd given her, had come to nothing when the investigating officer had been implicated in a corruption case. Once that had happened, Noone's supplying charge just seemed to dissolve.

It all fitted in so smoothly with Noone's view of his unassailable place in the world that he'd never stopped to think too hard about how trouble seemed to have difficulty attaching itself to him.

But his mother's death provided the answers and since then Noone's blood has been fizzing with the idea of killing. There's been an energy building in him that he always knew would only end one way. It's something that's been coming his entire life, and since his mother died the question has been coming more urgently, and more often. What does it feel like to be a killer?

Since Saturday morning he'd known the answer.

It was wonderful and it was easy and it is only just beginning.

The big question is: who's next?

Thirty-One

Frank gets to Canning Place early on Tuesday and spends the day coordinating the various strands of all the MIT cases.

With so many on his desk, plus an afternoon in court giving evidence in the ongoing Perch corruption trial, most of the scheduled interviews for the Peters case are postponed until the following day. Frank speaks to Harris about her coordinating efforts at Stanley Road. There's no mention of Linda but Harris does ask him how he's doing. Frank tells her he's fine, which is true. They are beginning to get back to normal, although Frank isn't sure that's what he wants. Drunk or not, last Thursday is fresh in his mind and, stripping aside all the rest of the bullshit, he enjoyed every moment. Em seems to be intent on erasing it from history.

By eight-thirty he's battered the overnight mountain of emails and paper into some sort of shape and is ready to head down to Stanley Road before Searle gets another chance to give him one of his gruesome pep talks. As it is there's a memo fixing a meeting at Stanley at two this afternoon.

Frank gets out of headquarters without running into Charlie Searle and arrives at Stanley Road just before nine. He grabs a cup of coffee from the machine downstairs and wanders into the office. The place seems emptier than it should be.

'Where is everyone?' says Frank. He means, primarily, Harris and Cooper. They have a meeting at nine-thirty and there are the ongoing interviews with the movie people and the other witnesses to be ploughing through. Frank's already had a text from Harris signalling something she wants to discuss regarding Terry Peters. Harris is due to interview Peters with him at ten and he wants to get his head together with her beforehand.

It's Steve Rose who answers. 'They only left ten minutes ago, sir. I called Canning Place to let you know but they said you were on your way down so I figured I'd wait for you to arrive. DS Cooper's at Garston with DI Harris.'

'What the fuck are they doing there?' Frank says, and goes to take a sip of his coffee.

Rose tells him and Frank's hand freezes halfway to his mouth. They've found a body.

Thirty-Two

The white and orange EasyJet A380 morning service to Amsterdam rumbles west towards the Mersey, gathers speed and, improbably free of gravity, lifts its load of hedonists clear of the ground before banking south for Schiphol, skunk, and skin. Below the tilting aircraft, too far away for the passengers to see, the body of a young man lies stark against the gunmetal grey mud at the edge of the river.

Frank pulls his Golf in behind a line of police vehicles on a service road running between the south end of John Lennon Airport and the river. He watches the jet curving past the Welsh hills, which seem closer than usual in the clear summer air.

It's a beautiful day.

Frank hasn't noticed before. He takes a second and draws in a lungful of air. Even the dieselly taint of aircraft fuel can't spoil the bouquet. With the rumble of the aircraft engines still loud enough to have to raise his voice, Frank sees Calum McGettigan sitting on the open tailgate of his vehicle, struggling to get free of his rubber boots.

'You finished already, Cal?'

McGettigan pulls off a reluctant boot, and a fat gob of mud flobs onto one of his photography cases. He talks as he pulls on his shoes. 'Easy one today, boss. Only took ten minutes. In. Out.'

'Can I borrow those?' Frank gestures at McGettigan's discarded boots.

'What size are you?'

'Does it matter? I'll only be ten minutes.'

As Frank starts pulling the boots on, a small man in jeans and a leather jacket approaches. He has a bag slung across his shoulders and is carrying a phone. Frank looks up.

'DCI Keane?' The man is about thirty-five, a little pudgy, his hair gelled, skin poor. His eyes are set deep, black shadows underneath like mascara. His accent is estuary English, Frank's least favourite. 'Steve McSkimming, *The Sun*.'

He holds out a hand. Frank regards it blankly, unsmiling. McSkimming withdraws it like he's used to the reaction. *The Sun* is about as popular as the plague on Merseyside since the Hillsborough tragedy. Frank knew a couple of the ninety-six dead and he's never forgiven or forgotten *The Scum*'s role and the lies about his team, his city. Even Charlie Searle's entreaties to step lightly won't force Frank to play nice with vermin like McSkimming.

'What do you want?' says Frank. 'This is a crime scene. You'll have to leave.' He looks round towards a uniform and beckons him over.

'Come on, Frank,' says McSkimming. 'Work with me and it could be useful. We can help.' He jerks his head towards the body. 'Is it Nicky?'

'Don't call me Frank. How did you get here?'

McSkimming looks at him like the question is beneath contempt. 'It's my job, DCI Keane. We get told things.'

'Been phone hacking again?' Frank hopes he is. The idea that any of his officers are feeding people like McSkimming information makes Frank feel ill.

The uniform arrives. Frank points at McSkimming. 'Get him away from here,' he says. Frank looks at the reporter. 'There'll be a press conference today, I'm sure. The relevant information will be given to you then, Mr McSkimming.'

The uniform starts gesturing for McSkimming to move back.

'You'll have to work with us sometime, Frank,' says McSkimming.

'Talk to Peter Moreleigh,' says Frank. He turns away from McSkimming, biting back the venom.

'Block off the access road at either end,' says Frank to the uniform as he starts leading the journalist away from the riverbank. 'Get some more bodies to help.'

In the borrowed boots he clumps across a footpath and through some scrubby grass towards the mudflats. It's low tide, and about ten metres from the bank three figures are gathered around the body, another child of the city spat out by the Mersey.

Harris, Cooper, and a forensic officer Keane doesn't recognise look up at his approach. His feet make a glooping sound in the black mud and it's difficult to stay upright.

'Give us ten minutes, Phil,' says Harris. She looks at Frank. 'Morning, boss.'

'No more than ten, please, if you can help it,' says the FO. 'Doesn't take long for the river to come in again.'

Harris nods and Phil, stepping gingerly, heads past Frank towards solid ground.

'Fuck,' says Frank. He folds his arms and looks down at the body. 'Who called it in?'

Cooper gestures in the direction of the road. 'Security patrol spotted it about half an hour ago. Left behind on the tide. They didn't touch him. Just called 999 and waited.'

Frank can see why. The body is face up, clothed, mouth hanging open, the mottled skin zombie blue. Something's been at the corpse's eyes. Frank bends down for a closer look, almost losing his balance as he does. He reaches up and holds Harris's forearm for balance.

'Thanks,' he says as she steadies him.

'The fish have been at him,' Harris says. 'Or maybe crabs.'

'Do they have fish in here?' says Frank.

'Good point,' says Cooper, looking at the viscous grey river slopping across the mud. Little oil rainbows lend a toxic sheen to the surface. Frank has heard the Mersey has been getting cleaner but he still wouldn't fancy taking a dip.

'Fair enough,' he says, standing. He stretches his back. 'It's going to be a busy one today. The papers are going to go to town on this.' He gestures towards the shore. 'One of *The Scum* was almost here before me. We've got someone feeding him information somewhere.'

Harris shrugs. 'We're not going to find out who. There's always someone.'

'Suppose so.'

The three coppers look down at the body and are silent for a few seconds.

'Poor lad,' says Frank, staring at the face of the victim. 'He looks different from the photos. Smaller.' There's something about the white skin of the hand against the black mud that resonates with him even more than the charnel-house scene in Birkdale. For the first time the Peters case becomes truly personal. Only four days since the first two victims were found at Birkdale and now they have their third body. The setting at the edge of the water puts him in mind of last year's Stevie White case. That had been drug-related, but Frank's certain this one isn't the same.

'I was sure it was going to be the boy when the call came in,' says Cooper. 'I didn't see this one coming.'

'Neither did he,' says Frank. 'Funny, really, considering his job.'

'He was a writer, not a fortune teller,' says Harris.

The body on the black Garston mud isn't Nicky Peters.

It's Dean Quinner.

Thirty-Three

The office is packed. With the murders in Birkdale to add to their already creaking caseload – and Nicky Peters still missing – MIT was operating at full stretch even before Dean Quinner washed ashore at Garston. Back at MIT before the briefing, Frank calls Charlie Searle and asks for two more detectives from another section to help ease the pressure. Searle assents but reminds Frank of the planned meeting that afternoon.

'Let's make it later,' says Searle. 'Five, OK?' He's not asking and Frank's heart sinks.

'Peter Moreleigh heard from Steve McSkimming,' says Searle. 'He's not happy.'

'Oh dear.'

'I'm not saying you have to like the man, Frank. But maybe throw him a bone now and again? It won't hurt to keep them sweet.'

'All of them, sir?'

'Just the nasty ones. So yes, all of them. Even *The Sun*.'

'I'll try, sir.'

He signs off without mentioning his suspicions that there's someone feeding information to McSkimming and turns his attention back to the briefing.

Dean Quinner turning up dead is a development rich in possibilities. There's a palpable buzz in the operations room as the investigation shifts up a gear. The murder also serves to focus attention sharply onto the *Tunnels* movie production. Everyone at MIT can feel the increase in tension and it feels good, like things are going to happen.

'There are a few changes we need to run through,' says Frank.

He's in front of the crime wall in the MIT office, which is growing

130

fast. The discovery of the latest body will mean a further explosion of information.

'First thing is that myself and DI Harris will assume full control of the case.' Keane looks at Theresa Cooper. 'I know that's a disappointment, Theresa, but that's the way it is. This is no longer a suspected domestic incident and Superintendent Searle has made it clear that MIT should make this case a top priority.'

Cooper, leaning against a filing cabinet, says nothing, but Keane isn't the only one to note the flush on her neck. It can't be helped.

In truth, the investigation hasn't been going well.

The enquiries into Nicky Peters' social and school life have run dry. No bullying they can find. No Facebook trail despite the 'it's complicated' relationship status. No history of trouble. Nothing.

And although Theresa Cooper has been digging deep into the dead couple's past, that too has proven equally arid. A trial separation three years ago seemed to have been resolved amicably. There's some suggestion that Maddy Peters might have been having an on–off affair with someone but there's nothing solid on that so far to connect with the events of last weekend. There are no obvious business or money issues. Both the remaining partners in the dental practice are clean. The couple had a holiday planned to Portugal in July, a regular spot.

Harris has a few ideas regarding Terry Peters but so far they're nothing more substantial than vague unease. She's already detailed Scott Corner to look closely at Terry and Alicia and she has Peters coming back in later today, but neither she nor Frank has high hopes of anything being unearthed.

Quinner being killed does give Frank the opportunity to narrow the angle of the investigation down. With the killing of the Peters couple, there were a multitude of potential ways in which to focus resources, something which always made Frank's heart sink. Many possibilities means that not everything can be covered well. With Quinner, they now know the deaths are connected to the movie.

In Frank's mind it also makes the chances of finding Nicky Peters alive even more unlikely than they had been.

Quinner's been killed for something he knows and Frank can't see, if Nicky's innocent, that whoever abducted him will leave that loose end untied.

'Clearly the deaths in Birkdale and Dean Quinner are connected,' begins Frank. 'The priority for us is still trying to locate Nicky Peters, but we now need to find the link between the Burlington Road murders and Dean Quinner.'

Cooper glances towards Ronnie Rimmer, who flicks his eyes towards Keane. *Tell him.* Cooper raises a hand.

'Theresa?' Frank stops and turns in her direction.

'We interviewed Quinner yesterday with Conroy and McElway at the movie location.' Cooper gestures towards Rimmer. 'Both of us felt he wasn't telling us something. We were due to interview him alone today.'

'OK,' says Frank. 'That's good to know.' He leaves it unsaid that it's that kind of slackness that has marked the investigation. Letting things slide over into tomorrow. My fault, he thinks. Poor work.

He turns back to the wall and taps a finger on a photograph of Terry Peters.

'This is where we are going to start. Terry Peters is the connection between Birkdale and the movie. I know that DI Harris interviewed him yesterday morning. She and I will talk to him again today. Scott and Theresa, I want you to take Terry Peters' background apart. Anything at all.' Frank looks at Harris. 'When we bring him here we'd like some leverage. If he's involved in any way I want to maximise the nerves.'

'He's been and gone,' says Harris. 'He came in at ten and I got him to come back at three.'

'Good,' says Frank. 'We'll get to him then.'

He looks again at the wall before speaking.

'Of course, Terry Peters may not be involved. From what DI Harris tells me, he's got a decent rep among the movie people. What that's worth I have no idea but we're getting told he's a good guy. But I'd like more details on the movie production. Schedules, arguments, money issues, anything.' Keane glances at the two loan detectives. 'I want the rest of the production interviewed solo and in depth. DCs Magsi and Flanagan here will dig into all available records on the cast and crew. Arrest sheets, histories, Facebook postings, websites, whatever you can use. And quickly. Ideally feed anything you get to the interviewing investigators before they talk to the movie people. The more we know the more ammunition we have. We're going to make something happen in the next twenty-four hours, and if that means stepping on some toes, then we will step on as many as we need to. Got it?'

Tread lightly. Charlie Searle's words float across Frank's mind. Fuck it. Searle can't have it both ways. If he has to conduct the investigation like a politician then he'd rather not have the job.

He puts his hands in his pockets. 'I'll be here for the rest of the day. If anything pops up in the interviews I want to be notified immediately, is that clear? No dicking about. If there's a red flag, get me in. We're no longer interested in keeping the movie people sweet, OK? The fucking thing is probably dead in the water now anyway.'

Harris coughs. 'I wouldn't be too sure of that. I'll call the production office to check.'

'You think they'll carry on after this?'

Harris shrugs. 'Lot of money involved.'

Frank shakes his head. 'Well, let's find out. Either way, they're all getting interviewed today and tomorrow. No exceptions.'

Thirty-Four

'Mr Peters.' Frank gestures towards a chair on the other side of the desk. He and Harris are seated directly opposite Terry Peters. There is a digital voice recorder on one side of the Formica-topped desk. With the new investigation into Quinner's death, events have overtaken Frank's schedule and the interview is taking place late in the afternoon. Peters had been sent away and has returned. Although not ideal, Frank's hoping the fractured day will help the interview. Anger can be useful. Makes people less guarded.

'Thank you for coming in again. This must be an incredibly difficult time for you.'

'Yes.'

Terry Peters is taller than Frank is expecting, taller even than his dead brother. He sits and leans forward on the table, his tired eyes taking in his surroundings.

'Not very impressive,' says Frank, reading his expression. 'Apologies, but we're pushed for space at the moment.' In fact, he has picked J7 specifically. He's found its cramped, dismal atmosphere to be very helpful in the past.

Terry Peters shrugs. He makes no attempt to engage DI Harris and she makes no move to be friendly, fish pie or no fish pie.

'Have there been any developments?' says Peters.

'How well do you know Dean Quinner?' Harris's ignoring of the question is deliberate. Prior to the interview she and Keane discussed the aggressive stance they would take. With speed a priority, politeness goes out of the window.

Terry Peters isn't stupid and Frank notes the change in his expression.

'Dean? What's Dean got to do with it?'

'If you can just answer the question, Mr Peters.' Harris keeps her voice neutral.

'Dean didn't have anything to do with . . . with what's happened, did he?' Terry Peters juts his chin out. Frank thinks his reaction looks genuine.

'Would that surprise you?' Frank asks.

'What's he done?'

'How well do you know Mr Quinner?'

Peters sits back and looks from one cop to the other. 'I know him well enough. We worked on a TV thing a couple of years ago and then on this one. It's a small world – TV and movies, I mean – up here. Most of us have crossed paths before. Why?'

'Are you friends?'

'We're friendly, if that's what you mean. I'll have a drink with him from time to time, but it's mostly film business we're talking about.' Peters looks at Frank. 'That's the way it works on location. Everyone's the best of friends for the shoot and then it's on to the next thing. Dean's OK, as far as I know.'

'Do you know if Nicky knows Mr Quinner well?' Harris puts the merest stress on the word 'well' but it's enough to get a response. Terry Peters' face flushes and his teeth show.

'What the fuck are you getting at? Has Quinner done something to Nicky?'

'That's a quick temper you have there, Mr Peters,' says Keane.

'What do you expect? My family's been . . . been fucking butchered. Nicky's gone. If Quinner's got anything to do with it, I've got a right to know!'

'And if you thought he did have anything to do with it? What would you do then, Mr Peters?'

'I'd fucking . . .' Peters stops short. He sits back and a wary look comes into his face. 'Something's happened, hasn't it?'

'Dean Quinner was found dead this morning. Killed.'

Peters opens his mouth to speak, blinks and then closes his mouth again. 'What? Jesus. *Dean?*' He rubs the bridge of his nose. 'I don't understand. What did Dean have to do with what happened to Paul and Maddy?'

Although Frank's take on Peters is that he is genuinely bewildered at news of Quinner's death, he's not quite ready to let him off just yet. Frank opens the file in front of him and glances inside. He lets the silence ripen. No hurry.

'You ever been in trouble with the police, Terry?'

Terry Peters shakes his head. 'I don't fucking believe it.'

'Is that a "no"?'

Peters looks at Keane and Harris in disgust. 'You know the answer already.'

'Domestic assault.' Harris purses her lips. 'You were bound over.'

'I was getting divorced!' Peters looks to the ceiling. 'She put a complaint in when I went round to talk and I ended up punching a window. Just frustration.'

'Your wife – ex-wife – ended up in the hospital.'

'She scratched herself on a piece of glass! What has this got to do with anything?'

'Where were you yesterday evening, Mr Peters?'

Frank's question hangs in the air. Peters cocks his head on one side and furrows his brow. 'You're not fucking serious, are you? You think I killed Dean? Maybe I killed Paul and Mads and Nicky! Throw in fucking Gaddafi while you're at it!'

'Mads?' says Harris. 'Is that your pet name for Mrs Peters?'

It's a wild throw of the dice from Harris. There was something about Terry when she'd interviewed him in Birkdale yesterday, something in the way he spoke about Maddy Peters, and maybe the thumb under the bikini strap in the photo, that prompts her to drop a hook in the water. To both her and Keane's astonishment the bait is taken.

Terry Peters looks like a child caught with his hand in the charity collection box.

'We're finished here,' he says, his voice cracking. 'I want to speak to a lawyer.'

'That won't be necessary, Terry. You're just helping us with our enquiries. There's no need for a brief. Not unless you're planning on surprising us again.' Frank stands and walks over to the wall. He puts his back against it and looks at Peters. His voice is soft.

'You were seeing Maddy? How long had it been going on? It's better to tell us, Terry, rather than have us find it out later.'

Peters is shaking his head from side to side, but neither Harris nor Keane thinks it has anything to do with what he's thinking. It's a reflex action, his subconscious denying what all three people in the room now know. He starts crying. Keane and Harris watch in silence. A lot of people cry in here. After a few seconds, Peters starts talking again in a low, halting voice.

'We didn't mean to. It just . . . happened.'

'Did Paul know?'

Terry Peters shakes his head once more. This time it's clear what he means. 'No! We made sure of that. It was all going to stop.' His face creases again. 'My brother! Jesus!' He buries his head in his hands again and sobs.

'What about Nicky? Did he know?'

'Fuck, no!' Peters looks up and wipes his face with his hand. 'I didn't do anything!'

'It doesn't sound good, though, does it, Terry?' says Harris. 'You didn't say anything to me about this when I interviewed you at home, did you?'

'I'd only identified my brother the day before . . . I couldn't think straight about Paul and Mads and Nicky! And I couldn't say anything in front of Alicia.' Terry Peters looks up at Harris. 'How could I?'

'Still, you should have. What we have to decide is why you didn't. Whether it was, as you say, embarrassment at screwing around behind Paul's back – or if there's more.' She fixes Peters with a stare and lowers her voice. 'Is there more, Terry?'

'It's not like that.'

'You still haven't told us where you were.' Frank's following Harris now and keeps his voice at the same low tone. 'If you want us to believe you, you're going to have to give us more than you have so far, Terry.'

Peters makes an effort to calm down.

'What times?'

'We'll come back to Dean Quinner in a moment. Let's take things in order, shall we? Just go through your movements the evening of the deaths at Burlington Road. Friday evening or the early hours of Saturday morning. You were working late at the location?'

'Yeah, until about twelve. Some of the crew will tell you that. I made a few calls to Ethan as well.'

'And afterwards?'

'Nothing. It was too late to go down to Maxie's, and besides I was knackered. I just drove home. Got there about one. Had a glass of red wine and went to bed.'

'With your wife?' Harris takes care not to place any stress on the word 'wife' but it can't be helped. Peters looks like a whipped dog. He nods. 'Yeah, with Alicia.' Peters turns to Frank. 'Does she have to know anything about this? About me and Mads, I mean?'

'If you're being straight with us about this, it should be OK. We can't promise anything. But if you're messing us about –'

'I'm not!'

'As I said, if you are, then we can't help. If you are cooperating, then maybe it won't come out.'

Frank checks the paperwork in front of him. 'You live just around the corner from your brother, right, Terry?'

'That's right. Sandwell Street.'

'So it'd take you no time to get to your brother's place in Burlington Road.'

'I didn't go!'

'But you did find the bodies, right?'

'You know I did. I called you.'

'Right,' says Frank. He looks at the file. 'Eight-forty on Saturday night and you called in? Was there a reason for that?'

'I do sometimes. Call in, I mean. Just for a drink. Say hello.'

'And if Maddy is alone you might get a quickie.' Harris is brutal.

'No!'

'So that never happened?'

'I'm not saying it never happened. Jesus.' Peters runs a hand over his face. 'I just called round. I wanted to chat. It's been a long week and I like them.'

'Do you think your brother knew about you and Maddy? Did he find you with her, Terry? Is that what happened?'

'Christ, no!' Terry Peters leans forward on the desk. 'Why would I call you if I'd killed them?'

'People do, Mr Peters. They get clever.'

'Well, I didn't. I came in and found them . . . like that.'

'Upstairs?' Harris has her arms folded. Her scorn is palpable.

'I . . . just looked for them. I'd been upstairs before.'

'I bet you had,' says Harris.

Peters shakes his head in disgust but says nothing.

'So you discovered Maddy first?' Frank's looking at his file.

'Yes.'

'But you didn't go in the room?'

'Not once I'd seen it . . . like it was.' Terry Peters' face is stricken. 'I couldn't. I could tell she was dead.'

'You know,' says Harris, her tone reflective, 'if you did kill Maddy your story about an affair is quite convenient, isn't it?'

'How do you mean?'

'The forensics. You admit to sleeping with your sister-in-law. That would explain a lot of things we might find.'

'Well, it is what it is,' says Peters. 'I'm trying to tell you everything.'

'And Paul?' says Harris. 'How did you end up finding him in the garage?'

'After I called the police I wondered if . . . whoever did it was still around, so I looked everywhere. I also wondered where Paul and Nicky were, so I was looking for them too.'

Frank's been quiet for a few minutes. There's something about Terry Peters he can't quite figure. He's come up with a story that to him, a seasoned cop, rings true. He's admitted a few things and owned up to some bad behaviour. But Harris is right about this also being a clever story. Discovering the body and being the lover of the victim – or one of them – gives Peters a lot of wiggle room. Hair samples. Fingerprints. Even semen. All explainable, if not palatable.

But Frank feels there's something they're missing. What that might be, he hasn't the foggiest.

He looks at the man in front of him. He's seen them all through here. Every size, shape, colour and personality. With Peters he just doesn't know.

'Look, Terry. I know you've been through a lot and, to be perfectly honest, your story should be easy enough to check out – and believe me, we will get it checked out – but if you're telling the truth about that, I don't want to waste time digging up useless dirt on you. DI Harris, I suspect, doesn't quite share my belief in you, Terry, so you can be certain she will be thorough. In the meantime, we're investigating the deaths of three people and the disappearance of your nephew and, frankly, I don't give a flying fuck if we step on your toes to get some quick answers. I'm sorry for your loss, and I can only imagine how guilty you must feel about what you and Maddy were up to, but I need you to stop fucking about and start *thinking*. Now, is there anything you can tell us – *anything* – that might help? Let's start with Quinner. Did Dean know Nicky?'

Terry Peters takes a deep breath.

'Well?' says Frank.

'I'm thinking!' He shakes out his hands like a footballer warming up. Harris is staring at Peters intently. He's keeping something back, she decides. Buying time to figure out a way to frame the story to put himself in the best light.

'The only time I saw the two of them together was a couple of days before . . . before it happened. We were shooting at Huskisson Street, a couple of days before we went into the tunnels. Dean was talking to two guys behind the security barrier. They looked at Nicky and said something. That's why I noticed. I try and look after the lad on the set, y'know? Nicky told me later that Dean had pretended to these guys that Nicky was famous. He signed an autograph. I think Dean wanted to get rid of them.'

'What did they look like?' says Harris.

'Pair of dickheads, to be honest. One big one, stupid-looking. One smaller. Also stupid-looking. Dressed like your average scally. Trackies. Caps. Bad skin. Early twenties, maybe?'

'You see them again?'

Terry Peters frowns, concentrating. 'No. That was it.' He holds up his hands. 'If I knew anything else, I'd tell you. Nicky didn't see much of anyone on set. All he wanted to do was watch the shoot. Nicky's a bit starstruck that way. He hasn't been around actors as long as I have. Thinks they're special.'

'And aren't they? Special, I mean?'

Peters grimaces. 'Oh, aye, they're special, all right. Just not in the way you mean. Haven't met one of them who isn't special in one way or another.'

'Who does Nicky like on the set?' says Harris. 'Anyone in particular?'

Terry Peters frowns. 'Not sure.'

'Really? There's no one you can think of who Nicky admires?'

'Well, he wants to be a writer, so maybe Dean. I don't think they ever spoke much, though.'

'Anyone else?'

'No.'

'No one at all?'

Terry Peters frowns as if concentrating. The movement doesn't look right to Frank. A tell?

'He likes Ben Noone, I suppose. Nicky thinks he's the next big thing. But I don't think they know each other.'

'Noone?' It's Frank's turn to frown.

'The lead actor,' says Harris. 'American.'

'Famous?' Frank looks at Harris. 'Should I know him?'

Peters shakes his head. 'No, he's new. Came out of nowhere.'

'You recommended him to Ethan Conroy, didn't you, Terry?' says Harris.

Frank's impressed. Harris had clearly been digging around in some of the witness statements taken by the team.

Peters shrugs. 'I might have.'

'You knew Noone from somewhere else?'

'Not sure where I met him. Just around. When this gig came up, I mentioned it to him.'

Both Frank and Harris pause. A silence falls in the interview room.

'Does Noone know Nicky?' asks Frank eventually.

Peters shakes his head. 'Don't think so.'

'You got anything else, DI Harris?'

'No, I don't think so.'

Frank, arms folded across his chest, his back against the wall, is silent for almost a minute, during which time he's looking at Terry Peters. Eventually he pushes himself upright and then sits back down. 'You can go now, Mr Peters. If you think of anything else, please let us know.' He smiles grimly. 'And if you're fibbing about anything you've said today – if your alibi for Friday isn't as watertight as a fucking submarine – we'll be letting *you* know. Right?'

Terry Peters gets to his feet. He looks like he's been in a war zone.

'You're not going to say anything to Alicia about . . . about me and Maddy, are you?'

'Goodbye, Mr Peters,' says Frank without looking up. 'I can't promise anything.'

Peters opens the door and shuffles out.

For a few seconds Harris and Keane say nothing before Frank breaks the silence.

'Fuck me.'

'Here?' says Harris, deadpan.

It's lines like that that remind Frank how much he likes her.

Thirty-Five

Nicky's out of the box. The monster's moving him.

'It's too close, here,' he says. 'We need to go deeper.'

He's a bit more ragged this time, distracted.

Nicky's weak after another two days in the box. The monster had left water but Nicky had eaten nothing since the sandwiches. After the monster had gone, Nicky had tried banging on the sides of his tomb but no one had heard.

Now, half-delirious, Nicky is pushed up the sloping rubble leading to a dark opening ahead. In his free hand Nicky's captor holds the torch. With the beam of white light bouncing in front of them, they scrabble up and into a narrow shaft. Crouching awkwardly, they shuffle along for about ten metres until they reach a solid-looking wall. Nicky has to stop to be sick.

'Get up,' says the monster. His voice is husky, emotional, and, even over his own filth, Nicky can smell a sour tang on the monster's breath.

'Push it,' says the monster, indicating the wall.

Nicky leans forward and presses his hands against the surface. To his surprise it isn't masonry but grey-painted wood and it falls back easily, revealing a larger cavern beyond. Nicky is pushed roughly through the opening and he stumbles.

'Get up,' says the monster. A hand drags Nicky to his feet. The monster turns and replaces the door across the opening.

The space they're in is piled high with rubble. With the painted wood in place it would take luck to locate the opening to the shaft and the room where Nicky had been held.

Nicky is directed to the left, where there is another, larger shaft which bends upwards and to the right. At the end of this is a space

143

which seems to be a dumping ground for all manner of debris. The floor is under water; Nicky can see the reflected gleam from the torch.

'There,' says the monster. He points the light towards a dilapidated iron box about the size of a small caravan. It's some sort of industrial fridge with thick walls. The tunnels are awash with the debris of past times: piles of smashed china, decayed wooden boxes, old car batteries. How and why the fridge is there Nicky has no idea. It doesn't matter. It is here and he is here and that's enough.

The door is pulled back. Inside the fridge is dry. When the monster places the torch on the floor and takes a knife from his pocket, Nicky steps back, his eyes wide.

'Easy,' says the monster and cuts the plastic looped around Nicky's wrists. He gestures for Nicky to step inside. There's some food and water and a bucket. A blanket. A big improvement. Hope.

'The door and walls are insulated. No one can hear you.'

'I'll suffocate,' says Nicky.

'I think there are some gaps. You might be OK.' The monster's voice indicates that it's all the same to him.

Nicky wants to know what is happening but something tells him not to ask. Curiosity killed the cat, his gran used to say. He never really knew what it meant but it comes back to him now. The less he says the safer he'll be. He just knows it. Besides, not asking, not pleading, is the only thing Nicky has left. And he's puzzled about being moved.

Then the monster does something strange.

He hugs Nicky.

The boy can feel the monster's stubble scraping his young skin and he tenses, fearing a knife in the ribs as he's being held.

'Sorry, Nicky,' comes a whisper in his ear and then he's released. The monster steps away and picks up his torch. Nicky stands naked at the rear of the fridge watching him close the heavy door. It sticks at the last, leaving a sliver of light until the monster kicks it into place. In the dark, Nicky can hear a padlock being placed in position.

'I didn't mean it all to end like this,' says the monster. He's crying. As Nicky listens in the pitch dark to the receding footsteps he lifts a hand to his face to the spot where the monster brushed against him.

He can still feel the rasp of Terry's cheek against his own.

Thirty-Six

It's almost six by the time Frank gets out of the interview with Peters.

A good interview, opening up some lively threads and possibilities and it's gone a little way to lifting Frank's mood. He drives to Dean Quinner's flat at the Albert Dock in golden evening sunshine. The day that had started so brightly – unless you were Dean Quinner – had been a peach. Frank wishes he'd seen a bit more of it instead of being in J7 or behind his desk. Still, some good things had happened.

The meeting with Charlie Searle has been postponed, for one. That felt like a result.

As far as dealing with the press goes, Frank's hoping that Searle may feel it worth stepping in, despite being cautious not to be seen as the man to blame if things go wrong. Frank's mishandling of the persistent McSkimming might be enough for Charlie Searle to take over.

Which is just fine with Frank.

Peter Wills and Phil Caddick are at Quinner's when Frank arrives. It's only ten hours since the body washed up at Garston but it already seems like a side story to the main event of the double killing in Birkdale. Frank thinks this could prove to be a problem, which is why he's making sure the MIT team know that the Dean Quinner murder is no less of a priority. Showing up at the dead man's flat is a way of demonstrating that.

The place has been photographed and dusted on Frank's order, even though there's nothing to suggest this is where Quinner was killed. In fact, Frank's certain that Quinner wasn't killed here. But, with this murder, the focus is now firmly fixed on the *Tunnels* production cast and crew and, so far, there is no crime scene. The river location of the body won't give them much. Quinner wasn't killed there. Current and tide suggest he was put in the water further east but there are marks on the body that suggest Dean Quinner may have been snagged on a passing boat and dragged upstream. Nine times out of ten a body would drift seawards, but the chance of it being different is there so Frank doesn't want to make an assumption that will get in the way of the investigation. He's only sprung for the extra forensics at the flat from his tight budget because now that they have a narrower range of potential suspects, there is more chance of those forensics being useful. With the forensics team having left, Wills and Caddick are going over the flat in detail. They'll take material they find potentially interesting back to MIT for further analysis.

'Anything?' says Frank by way of greeting.

Wills is on his knees next to a stack of blue plastic evidence boxes. He's surrounded by every piece of paper that he could find in Quinner's flat.

'Not much, sir.' Wills looks up. 'Looks pretty clean at first glance. What paperwork he's got is mostly related to the production. Scripts, shooting schedules, that kind of thing. Haven't been through them in detail yet. A few domestic things, the normal stuff. Bills, banking. Nothing obviously personal so far. Phil's sent the computer over to Rose to see what he can get.'

'Just the one?'

'There was only one here, along with an iPad. We had a quick look but there was nothing that sprang out. Might have more luck once Rosie gets into the emails.'

'Phone?'

'No sign of one. There's a landline. Rob Flanagan is accessing the records for that.'

Frank's not sure they'll get much from the landline. Quinner seemed to have been tech-savvy, someone who used his mobile and internet wi-fi to communicate. Increasingly, MIT are finding it's only mobiles that prove useful.

Frank leaves Peter Wills to the paperwork and wanders round the flat.

Quinner seems to have been a tidy man. The place is pleasant but nondescript. It faces the city – the cheaper side. Through a window Frank catches a glimpse of the back edge of the Mann Island monolith. He and Quinner were almost neighbours.

On the walls are movie posters. Mostly indie flicks. Frank recognises some but doubts that Quinner had anything to do with them. *The Tunnels* was his first film.

Ethan Conroy had told them that Quinner had been working on this project for years. His baby. Frank thinks that could be an important piece of information. Parents would do anything to protect their offspring. Perhaps Quinner tried too hard to protect his movie.

From what?

That was the question. Frank's team will investigate money issues as a matter of course, but he doesn't believe that will be a tree that bears fruit. Conroy and McElway are the money men on this film and there's nothing so far to suggest that money troubles, or lack of them, have any bearing. Money's always worth investigating, but with the murders of Paul and Maddy Peters, and Nicky's disappearance, Frank doesn't expect this to be about money.

The Peters murders were personal.

Quinner's murder doesn't feel like that so far, but Frank knows they're connected. You don't have to be a copper to know that. What is interesting, he thinks, is that if you accept that the murders of Paul and Maddy and Quinner are linked, then it means that Nicky shifts firmly into the 'potential victim' category. Frank can't come up with a convincing theory that has Nicky killing his parents, evading capture and then killing Dean Quinner so efficiently. And the fact that the murders of the Peters couple were made to appear, at least temporarily, as a domestic murder-suicide, and that Dean Quinner was just flat out killed, means to Frank that they are investigating a crime more complex than it appears on first inspection.

In the bedroom, Phil Caddick has taken out the contents of Quinner's wardrobe and cabinets and laid them on the bed.

'Phil,' says Frank. He looks at the neatly arranged piles of belongings on the bed. Caddick's going through everything piece by piece.

'Sir,' says Caddick. He straightens up and gestures towards the bed. 'Not a lot, to be honest. No drugs, no sexual material to speak of, nothing.' Caddick lifts a small piece of paper from the bed. 'The only thing that might have anything to do with it is this, but it's a long shot.'

He hands the paper to Frank. It's a taxi receipt dated Thursday, 13 June. Frank shrugs.

'Why? I mean, it's the day before the Birkdale murders, but is there some other reason that makes you think it's relevant?'

'Pete's gone through his receipts. The feller was methodical – all his taxi receipts are in with the rest of the financial stuff – but this one I found in the pocket of these.'

Caddick holds up a pair of jeans. 'They were hanging up. Probably indicates he hasn't washed them since the taxi, otherwise the receipt would be with the others. The taxidriver could have something useful.'

Frank wishes he could be more enthusiastic because Caddick has a fair point. It's just that he has the feeling whoever killed Quinner isn't stupid enough to leave an obvious trail. Like a taxi-driver witness.

'You're right, Phil, it's something.' Frank hands back the receipt. 'Chase it up.'

Phil Caddick turns back to the bed.

Frank leaves them to it. If they haven't found anything at the flat in four hours, there's nothing he's going to do in a flying visit that will make any difference.

Outside, leaning against one of the sandstone pillars overlooking the dock, he calls MIT and gets put through to Steve Rose. He's hoping there's something on Quinner's computer or iPad that might be useful for him in the meeting with Searle.

'There's nothing I can see in the emails,' says Rose. 'Nothing obvious. He's got a lot of emails going to the production office, as you might expect. Older ones are more about the money raising and getting the production going. Not many personal ones. Dean doesn't seem to have been much of a socialiser. His Facebook account isn't really used. From what I can see his browser history is fairly predictable. Lot of film-related stuff. Things on Liverpool, the tunnels, that kind of thing. What porn there is is standard stuff. Hetero, if that's any help?'

'Can you tell me the browser history over the past few days? What was he looking at leading up to this?'

There's a pause. 'Just checking over it again,' says Rose. His voice is muffled, as though he's tucked the phone under his chin. When he speaks again his voice is clearer. 'OK, it's mainly movie-related stuff, I think. Reference sites, Wikipedia, review sites, movie trailers. Lot of Google searches.'

'Can we tell what he was looking at?'

'Mm, yeah, mostly.' Rose's voice is muffled again.

'Are you eating?' says Frank.

'Er, no.'

'For fuck's sake, Rose, put down whatever greasy slab of calories you're shovelling down your fucking throat and concentrate. I can hear your saliva. It's disgusting.'

'Right. Sorry, sir. Er, OK, Quinner was searching yesterday. The last thing in his history is a search on something called USEARCH.'

'Which is?'

'Hold on.' Frank can hear some keystrokes. 'It's a US-based people finder. Background checks, that sort of thing. A pay site, but I can't see anything that indicates Quinner registered.'

Frank moves out of earshot of a passing group of overeaters munching on brightly coloured buckets of chicken. The head of the family is wearing a pair of three-quarter-length shorts that could easily double as a Bedouin tent. 'What the fuck are you looking at?' he snarls at Frank. His son, a teenage blimp of about fourteen, snickers unattractively. The two of them puff out their chests. It's like watching a pair of hippos do an impersonation of Bruce Willis.

Frank reaches into his pocket, produces his warrant card and thrusts it close to the man's face.

'Can you read?' asks Frank. 'Shoo.' He turns and pockets his ID. 'Carry on, Rose. USEARCH?' Behind him, the herd moves on, muttering muted obscenities and slurping soft drinks. Frank turns and motions them away with the back of his hand and the group drift round the corner.

'Well, there's not much else, sir. It's a people finder site.'

'What does he have before that?'

'Some IMDb searches. Mostly on the cast. IMDb is the movie database. Lists previous work, that sort of thing. Couple of searches for Ben Noone.'

'Ben Noone?'

'He's one of the actors.' Rose taps some keys. 'The lead actor, apparently.'

'I know who he is. It's the second time his name's come up today. We're speaking to him tomorrow. Does he come up again in Quinner's computer stuff?'

'Not really. And Quinner's got lots of stuff in there relating to the other members of the cast.'

'Yeah. Probably nothing, but we're a bit light on possibilities. Keep digging, Steve.'

Frank rings off and calls one of the new guys, Saif Magsi. He doesn't want a main MIT officer tied up on a red herring but he'd like a bit more on Noone before speaking to him. Quinner's searches on the American are unlikely to be important but, judging by the pickings on show at his flat, Frank's grateful for any crumbs.

'DC Magsi? It's DCI Keane. Yeah, never mind that. Listen, I want details on Ben Noone. He's due in tomorrow for an interview and I'd like some material. Don't spend too long, OK? It's probably nothing, but just get some material to work with.'

Frank rings off, pockets his mobile and heads for his car.

He passes the fat man he'd had trouble from earlier, leaning over the edge of the dock looking at something in the water. Frank considers giving him a kick up the backside and sending him over. At least that way the day wouldn't be a total waste.

He checks his watch. He's been on the clock since six that morning. He could head back to the office; Christ knows there's enough there to keep him busy till Doomsday. Instead, Frank flexes his arms and decides his work-out with Chrissy Cahill is far enough in the past for him to do another work-out in Bootle. He'd been hoping that Harris might suggest a drink but it hasn't happened.

Boxing it is.

Thirty-Seven

Wednesday.

'DC Magsi!'

If Frank Keane's reputation hadn't reached Saif Magsi's ears before, he is in no doubt now. The DCI's voice cuts across the office like a pistol shot, jerking the DC's head upright from his monitor.

'My office.'

Magsi glances at Flanagan, who shrugs.

'Need a weapon, Mags?'

Magsi's tired eyes narrow. 'Pick on the Paki, eh?' he mutters. 'Why don't you get the harsh word?'

'Luck of the Irish,' says Flanagan. He cuts a look across to where Frank Keane's standing in the open doorway. 'Best get moving, Paki,' hisses Flanagan. He winks at Saif.

'Fucking Paddy,' says Saif and flips Flanagan the finger.

Frank gestures for Magsi to follow him into the interview room. As he reaches the door, Harris emerges, heading for the coffee machine at the end of the corridor. She makes a drinking motion with her hand and Frank nods.

He opens the door of his temporary office and steps through, Magsi close behind.

'Is there a problem, boss?' Magsi's nervy but pissed off too. He's a good copper and, as far as he knows, hasn't done a thing to deserve the sharp end of Keane's tongue.

Frank sits down and indicates that Magsi should do the same. When they are settled, Frank prods the file on the desk in front of him with the end of a pencil, as if it were infectious.

'What do you call this?'

Magsi rotates the file and reads the name on the top inside sheet.

'You asked for this material, sir. As much as I could get on each member of the production.'

'So what the fuck is going on with Ben Noone?'

Saif Magsi looks puzzled.

'Everything's there, DCI Keane.'

Frank picks the file up and reads. 'Benjamin Noone. Age twenty-nine. American. Born Los Angeles, California, 10 July 1983. Current address Flat 213, River Towers, Old Hall Street, Liverpool.'

He looks up from the paper and regards Magsi. Sour doesn't begin to describe Keane's expression.

'I don't know if you think this is some sort of fucking game, Mr Magsi, or if this is how you do things over in your crappy little department, but I don't accept this kind of sloppiness, is that clear?'

Magsi nods but his face is hard. 'That's all there was, sir.' He sits back and folds his arms. 'I know why you're angry and I see now I should have talked to you about this before I gave it to you.'

Harris comes back in carrying two paper cups. She puts them down on Frank's desk and looks at her watch. 'Shouldn't we be meeting Superintendent Searle?'

'It's later,' says Frank, trying not to look too happy in front of Magsi. He takes his coffee and sips it cautiously. Last week he'd burnt his tongue on a brew the temperature of a thermonuclear reactor.

'Have you seen this?' Frank puts down his cup and proffers Harris Magsi's file.

'What?' Harris takes a seat and picks up the file.

Frank dips his head in Magsi's direction. 'This one's had since yesterday to dig up as much info as he could on the production.'

'And?'

'Look at what he's managed to find on Ben Noone. He's one of the actors. Have a read of that.'

Harris reads the single sheet in the file. Her eyebrows rise and she looks over the edge of the paper at Saif Magsi.

'This is it?'

'That's all,' says Magsi.

'See?' says Frank, looking at Harris. He picks up the coffee and, forgetting, takes a healthy slurp, burning his tongue once more. 'Fuck!'

'Always wait,' says Harris. She narrows her eyes at Magsi. 'Seriously? This is everything you can find on Noone?'

Magsi sits forward. 'I'm not dicking anyone around, DI Harris. There's nothing else.'

Magsi looks at Keane, whose expression is shifting from scorn to one of growing interest. Frank thinks Magsi, from the little he's seen, has the makings of a really good police officer. Perhaps that's why he has been so hard on him.

'I checked all the usual channels. The movie company had his address and date of birth. I managed to get his passport details from Immigration Services. He doesn't have any other records. No driving licence, at least not in the UK, no arrest sheet, no parking tickets, no educational records. I checked with the US State Department and found he was born in LA. I did some digging around in the US records that are available online. Same story. No arrest sheet. No employment record. No educational records. No Facebook account. He's not a registered voter. There's nothing more they could give me. Or would give me. He hasn't committed any crimes, is travelling on a valid visa, so the word I'm getting from the Americans is that unless he's a suspect that's as far as they'll go. Is he a suspect?'

Frank screws up his face. 'No. But this has got my interest. What about money, rent, credit cards? Anything on that?'

DC Magsi leans forward. 'His flat is one of the new ones over at Old Hall Street – the big glass box, River Towers? He's been there since it opened six months ago. The place is owned by an American company, Nerex Holdings. Noone isn't listed as a tenant or owner or anything. He's there legitimately, though. I called the company that administers the building and he's staying there with Nerex's consent, apparently. I didn't go any further because there wasn't time. He doesn't have a credit card or a bank account that I can find.'

Frank sits back and looks at the sheet of paper. There's silence in the office. After more than a few seconds have ticked by, Frank rubs the side of his nose and speaks.

'Let's get Mr Noone in tomorrow morning, shall we? Should be interesting at least. In the meantime, DC Magsi, you work on Mr Noone some more. Concentrate on the financials. Credit cards, bank accounts. As much as you can get, within reason. The more we have before we talk to him, the happier I'll be.'

DC Magsi gets to his feet. At the door he pauses and glances in Frank's direction.

'If you're waiting for an apology,' says Frank, 'don't. You should have flagged this sooner. It stinks.'

Saif Magsi says nothing and slips out.

Harris sits in the chair vacated by Magsi. 'What do you think?' she says, tapping a nail on Noone's file. 'Saif's pretty thorough from what I hear, but there must be more on Noone than this.'

'There will be. But I don't want to waste too much time on Mr Noone just yet. Magsi can do some more checks and we'll talk to Noone tomorrow. I want to work through the production and background crew today. You follow up Terry Peters. I'm not happy about him and Maddy Peters. At the moment he's looking our strongest bet, agreed? I'll do a bit of work on Noone's background. It's probably nothing but it's worth looking at. We had something similar with Col North last year, remember?'

'Have you had much experience with the American system?'

'No, not really.' Keane stands up and takes his mobile out of his pocket as he heads for the door. 'But I know a man who has.'

Thirty-Eight

'What did he say when you told him?' asks Menno Koopman.

He and Warren Eckhardt are sitting on the deck at Menno's place drinking whisky. As usual, Warren is wreathed in a thick plume of smoke. Koop tolerates it because to deprive Warren of cigs would be like depriving a fish of water. With Koop living in the lush hills in northern New South Wales there are hardly any neighbours within sniffing distance and most of those who are seem to exist on a diet of dope. They're not going to notice Warren's solo war on the ozone layer.

Since he met the Queenslander during last year's drama – Eckhardt being an investigating officer on the Australian side – Koop has been enjoying his company more and more often. Especially these days, the way things are between himself and Zoe.

Koop doesn't know where Zoe is exactly. She left yesterday afternoon and mumbled something about Brisbane. Business or pleasure, Frank's not sure. Maybe both. Her design company is up there but Frank noticed she'd taken her heels. The bedroom ones.

'Well, once he'd stopped yakking about how shit I am – the usual stuff – he didn't say anything,' says Warren, taking a drink and a drag, seemingly simultaneously. 'I just put a hand inside me jacket and pulled out the little white envelope that'd been sitting there for a week. "Stop talking for two fucking minutes, will you," I said, and pushed the fucking thing across the desk. He looked like he couldn't decide whether to punch the air or punch me.'

'Big moment,' says Koop. He raises his glass in salute. 'Not every day you retire from the force, Wazza. Even a mickey mouse Aussie one.'

'Molly Minchin never forgave me after I got seconded to the

Organised Crime Group. He was pissed off because I didn't bring the dead rat back to his office. No glory. My days were numbered from that point.'

'You made the right decision. I mean, look how it's working out for me.'

Warren pauses and then bursts out laughing. He laughs so hard Koop thinks he might pass out and, love him though he does, he'd rather not have to give Warren mouth-to-mouth resuscitation.

'To retirement,' says Koop and raises his glass.

Before Koop can say anything more he hears the hum of his phone vibrating on the surface of the coffee table. He clambers from the depths of the sofa and reaches across.

'Never a good sign,' says Warren Eckhardt as Koop clumsily manoeuvres his lanky frame upright. 'Phone calls at this time of night.'

Koop puts down the tumbler of scotch and holds the phone at arm's length to read the ID. 'Frank Keane,' he says, looking at Warren.

'Are you going to answer the fucking thing or just look at it?'

'Right.' Koop presses his finger on 'answer'. 'Frank.'

Warren hears a yap of dialogue and then Koop answers.

'Do you know what time it is, Frank? Here, I mean?'

Koop looks at Warren and shakes his head. *Dickhead*, he mouths, waving his watch. The phone squawks again.

'Well it's a nine-hour difference, not seven, and yeah, I am awake as it happens, but that's not the point . . . No, it's OK, might as well talk now as tomorrow. My head won't be right.' Koop takes a sip of malt and listens to what Frank has to say. As the conversation unrolls, Koop's expression sharpens.

'Yeah, maybe. I was in LA for a while. Listen, I'm here with Warren Eckhardt who you know from last year. No, we're not in bed. It's not that kind of relationship. I'm going to put you on speaker. Warren might have something useful to add. He spent some time in the States too. New Mexico, I think.'

Koop puts the phone down on the coffee table and presses the speaker button.

'Warren.' Keane's voice is clear, his Liverpool accent amplified in the Australian setting.

'I have to warn you, we're half-pissed,' says Warren, his smoker's voice softened by the scotch. 'And it was Washington State. I did eighteen months on secondment just after 9/11. Global policing was all the thing.'

Koop raises his glass to the phone and turns to Warren. 'Frank's got a weird one.'

Frank sketches out the lack of information on Noone for Koopman and Eckhardt.

'He's just a witness, right?' says Warren after Frank's finished.

'Correct.'

'But . . .?'

'It smells wrong,' says Frank. 'Don't you think?'

'It does to me.' Koop is looking at Warren.

'Maybe,' says Warren. 'The bloke might just be clean. It happens. But I admit, it does look like there's got to be more.'

'There's nothing in the UK we can find. Not with the resources we've got, anyway. I was hoping you might have a friend I could call. Or you could call. We're getting nowhere through the normal channels and I want some more solid background before we talk to him. That's why I called so late.'

'I can try,' says Koop. 'But I'm not sure I'll get anything more than you can. There's a guy I know who might be able to tell me if the lack of information means something. Sam Dooley. Maybe this Noone is ex-military, something like that?'

'Don't think so,' says Frank. 'He's an actor. But if you can give it a try, Koop, that'd be great. Don't spend too much time. This feller's just a side issue at the moment.'

Thirty-Nine

DC Ronnie Rimmer glances over to Frank's office and, through the open door, sees him yakking on the phone. He's heard Frank mention Koop a couple of times but can't imagine why he's talking to their old boss.

Rimmer balls up a wodge of emails and tries to flip it across the MIT office into Saif Magsi's coffee cup. It's almost ten metres away and Magsi's concentrating furiously on the work in front of him. After the run-in with DCI Keane he's not going to be caught lallygagging.

'Not a chance,' says Rosie, glancing up from his computer screen at Rimmer's attempt. Both coppers sit at the same desk on either side and both have teetering stacks of paper strewn across the surface. It's gone six now and Rimmer's due to knock off.

Rimmer sets himself like a pro and lets the paper ball go. It sails across the room and lands – a fucking office b-ball miracle – slam in the centre of Magsi's coffee.

Hot liquid slops onto Magsi's immaculate trouser leg.

'Fucking hell, Rimmer, you knob!'

'He shoots! He scores!' Rimmer gets up from the desk and runs across to Magsi, his arms aloft. 'The crowds go wild!'

Magsi shakes his head. 'If this doesn't come out you're paying for it, Rimmer. Don't think I'll let it go. Cos I won't.'

'Sorry, mate,' says Rimmer. 'But you have to admit it was a fucking great shot, yeah?'

Magsi nods and holds up his hands. 'Yeah, yeah, I'll give you that, man.' He smiles, happy that he's being immersed in the MIT world.

Still, they are a good pair of trousers.

Rimmer sits back down and stretches. He's been at this all day and the screen in front of him bears the meagre fruits of his labours.

159

He'll be glad to get out of the office. This morning, he and Rose had gone to break the news of her son's death to Quinner's mother in Litherland. After watching her world collapse, and getting what little practical information they could, they'd come back to the office and worked without a break since eleven.

Dean Quinner's life had been laid bare. Phone numbers, jobs, addresses, bank details, friends, family, education, the lot. And then a secondary list of calls that Rimmer's made that day, almost all of them pointless, repetitive fishing expeditions, wrong numbers, outdated numbers, some recipients shocked, others cagey. His eyes are swimming with the information and he knows that his colleagues are feeling the same way. The important difference for Rimmer is that he's finished for the day.

'I'm gone,' says Rimmer. He checks his watch. 'Overtime used up and there's someone waiting.'

Steve Rose simulates a blow job using his tongue to press out the side of his cheek. 'The nurse?'

Rimmer smiles. 'The nurse.' He notices Manda Davies, a relatively new addition to MIT, regarding them sourly. 'And don't be disgusting,' adds Rimmer. 'Christ, Steve, grow the fuck up.'

On his way past Manda's desk, Rimmer winks.

'Dickhead,' she says.

An hour and a half later, showered and changed into civvies, Rimmer is sitting at a table outside the Baltic Fleet on Wapping. It's a fine evening and the pub is full, even on a Wednesday.

Rimmer picks up his bottle of micro-brewed ale and clinks it against Hanna's glass.

'Cheers,' he says and she smiles warmly. Maybe Rosie wasn't so wide of the mark.

Hanna takes a long pull on her G & T and closes her eyes. 'Jesus,' she says, her eyes still closed. She opens them and looks at Rimmer. 'I needed that.'

'Long day?'

As Hanna begins describing the various reasons she needed the G & T, Rimmer sits back contentedly watching her. Hanna's muted

Danish accent is a turn-on and she looks great. There's something about a foreign girl. Maybe, because of the job bringing him into contact with the wrong type of local, he's come to associate the Liverpool accent with trouble. Hanna, a triage nurse at A & E in Walton, is leggy, blonde, and dresses with an understated style that Rimmer finds very appealing.

'Stop it,' she says, breaking off from her story.

'What?'

'You're not listening to me.'

Rimmer holds his hands up in surrender. 'You got me, Hanna. You're so good-looking that it was all I could think of.'

Hanna laughs. 'Of course.'

'Anyway, you were telling me about the nutjobs you get coming in?'

'You *were* listening.'

Rimmer smiles. 'I'm a multi-tasker. I can ogle *and* listen.' He drinks and then gestures with the heel of the bottle. 'Go on. The finger.'

'Well, like I say, this man came in last Thursday, maybe early morning Friday, with his finger missing. Told us he cut it accidentally when he was laying tiles.'

Rimmer shrugs.

'Who cuts tiles at two in the morning?' Hanna has the air of a prosecution lawyer delivering a devastating zinger.

'Maybe he was one of those shopfitters? They work all night sometimes.'

Hanna shakes her head. 'No, this man was not like this. He was not a working man.'

'So you put the finger back on?'

Hanna shakes her head. 'No, he didn't have it. And this is why I'm telling you, Ronnie. He said he lost it when he spat it out.'

Now Hanna does have Rimmer's full attention.

'He spat it out? That's what he said?'

'Yes. But when I asked him about that he changed his mind. He told me he was getting confused and said I must have not understood him.'

'What happened?'

'We patched him up and cleaned the wound, and then we wanted to keep him for observation. This is a big thing, losing a finger, right? But this man won't stay. He left right after we fixed him up.'

'Did you call us?'

Hanna nods. 'The duty manager called the police to report it, but they didn't arrive until after the man has gone.' Hanna fixes him with a pair of large blue eyes. 'What do you think, Ronnie? Drugs? Or maybe the man cut his own finger? Some sex thing, maybe?'

'I don't know.' Rimmer's distracted by Hanna using the word 'sex'. All thoughts of the fingerless low-life disappear as she leans across the table. Rimmer looks at her glass. It's empty, and Hanna is idly playing with a chunk of ice.

'Fancy another stiff one?' Rimmer leers.

Hanna smiles seductively and pulls him forward, her half-closed eyes locked on his. She drapes a hand round his neck, licks her lips and drops the ice straight down the back of his shirt.

Forty

Frank leans back in his chair and rubs the sides of his face.

'Bring him in.'

After a morning checking on any overnight progress – frustratingly there's none to speak of – and driving the rest of MIT's caseload, by the time he's back in J7 at Stanley Road with Harris it's past one, with the actor due in in five minutes.

Em's brought a couple of coffees in from Marco's on the corner of Hardman Street. Another step on the road to peace? Frank's not sure but he's grateful anyway. He slept well last night, feels sharp, and after the bureaucratic slog this morning, the coffee sets him up nicely for what he hopes will be a more satisfying afternoon. He considers asking Harris how Linda's doing but he hesitates and then the moment is gone. He knows he'll have to talk about it soon but this probably isn't the right time.

Focus.

He and Harris have already been through the angle they're going to take in the interview. Harris is yet to be convinced that Noone represents even a remote avenue for the investigation. So far there isn't a shred of anything to connect Noone with either the Peters family or Quinner. In fact, as someone from outside the country, he is, in her opinion, a long way down the list of possibilities. But Harris knows Frank well enough to respect his instinct and there's no denying that Magsi coming up short on Noone's sheet has piqued her interest in the American too. Their experience with the ex-IRA guy on the Stevie White case has left an impression. Like Noone, Declan North had a sketchy paper trail. It's worth throwing a hook in, anyway.

The uniform comes back into the interview room, a tall, athletic man behind him.

'Mr Noone,' says the uniform and leaves. Frank's tidying up his paperwork so doesn't look up at first.

As Noone takes his seat, Harris's first thought is that he's ridiculously good-looking. Clooney when young. No surprise he got the *Tunnels* movie.

'DCI Keane?' The rich American voice rolls around the shabby room. An alien sound in here – Hollywood on the Mersey. A few years back, only just out of uniform, Frank had once briefly met Samuel L. Jackson when the actor was shooting a movie in the city. It had been an oddly unnerving and dislocating experience, as though by being there in the flesh, Jackson was breaking some immutable physical law. Noone's voice has something of Jackson in it.

Frank takes a few seconds to study the man. He looks his twenty-nine years, but that is not a criticism. In fact, thinks Frank, he'll look better with age. His face is open, approachable. He's dressed well, but not overly so. Boots, black jeans, an expensive shirt under an equally expensive-looking jacket. Frank's eyes flick towards Noone's hands and he flashes on the scene in the Peters' house.

What do you think you'll see, Frank? Blood?

Frank puts out his own hand, which Noone shakes warmly. There's no attempt at any masculine posturing by the American, no excessive grip. Neither is there any limpness. His skin is warm, dry.

'Thanks for coming in, Mr Noone.' Frank indicates the chair across the desk. Noone looks at Harris, smiling. 'This is my colleague, Detective Inspector Harris.'

Noone extends his hand. 'Wow,' he says, holding Harris's hand a fraction longer than he had Keane's. Harris doesn't smile back but she has to force herself. I like him, she thinks.

And then: he's an actor.

Frank leans across the table towards the interview room digital recorder.

'We record everything these days,' he says, looking at Noone. 'You have no objection?'

164

Noone shakes his head as he pulls back a chair. 'No problem.'

'DCI Frank Keane and DI Emily Harris. Interview with Benjamin Noone.'

'How can I help you?' Noone says. He sits down, the legs of the chair scraping against the floor. 'Any news on the boy?'

Frank waits a few moments, regarding Noone. He ignores the question.

'We're talking to everyone involved with *The Tunnels*, Mr Noone. As you are aware, Dean Quinner was found dead yesterday morning. Since Mr Quinner was the third death connected with the production – leaving aside the issue of Nicky Peters – we are of the opinion that the killer is one of the members of the production team.'

'You're kidding?'

'No, I'm not. The chances that Nicky Peters and his parents and Dean Quinner were randomly attacked are so slim as to be dismissed. The killer is one of you.'

Noone raises his eyebrows. 'You don't mess around. I like it.'

Frank glances at Harris. You getting this?

'We're not overly concerned with your feelings about anything, Mr Noone.'

'Of course.' Noone looks contrite.

'We can get the obvious questions over first.' Harris looks down at her file. 'Taking things in order, do you have any idea where you were on the evening of Friday the fourteenth, Mr Noone?'

Noone folds his hands in his lap. 'The fourteenth?'

Frank starts to get the curious feeling that the man in front of him is enjoying this encounter.

'The evening the Peters family were killed,' says Frank. 'You must have heard about it. It was the talk of the town.'

Noone pauses before answering and looks at Keane. He holds the pause just long enough for Harris to glance from him to Frank. The animal challenge is there; that instinctive moment that's so hard to disguise and that both Frank Keane and Em Harris have seen a million times.

'Well, of course, we all heard something had happened that weekend, but none of us were sure exactly when.' His words sound sincere but to Frank's ears there's something a little 'off' buried deep in the sentence.

He's on stage. The fucker's giving us a performance. Frank's got an ear for pretence that wouldn't be out of place at a top-flight acting academy. Most decent detectives have it, developed over long hours of listening to every nuance of human behaviour.

'Try and remember,' says Frank.

Noone concentrates. Or appears to. It's hard for Frank to tell. Maybe this is how he is all of the time. People in here react differently. Noone's composure may simply be a defensive reflex, something that's done well for him in the past.

All it's doing in J7 right now is setting Frank Keane's teeth on edge. Which is good. It means that there's something in Noone that Frank's senses are telling him to examine. He wonders if Harris is feeling the same way.

'Friday the fourteenth, last Friday.' Harris consults a sheet of paper in front of her. 'According to your shooting schedule, you were on set that day. The location was the Williamson tunnels. The first day of work in that location, I think.'

Harris looks up. 'That help you, Mr Noone?'

Noone leans forward and puts his elbows on the table. 'Yes, it does. It was the second day in the tunnels, though. We'd started on the Thursday down there. I remember feeling cold – it's damp underground – and I asked Nicky to get me my coat from the truck.'

'You knew him well enough to call him by his first name?'

'He's a good kid. Everyone calls him Nicky. It's a small unit.'

It's Frank's turn. 'Unit?'

'A movie term. Means the whole thing. Everyone shooting the movie.'

'You're not an actor, though, Mr Noone. Not an experienced one. Right?'

Noone smiles. 'Depends on your definition of experienced.'

'What I mean is that this is your first movie. Tell me a little about how you got the role.'

Noone raises his eyebrows fractionally. 'If you think it will help.'

'I do.'

'I've been travelling for a couple of years. Been in the city for the past eight months. The crowd I'd been hanging out with are artsy. One of them knew Dean and mentioned his movie. I thought it would be kind of interesting. I'd always been good at goofing around. So I tried out and here I am.'

'The person who recommended you was Terry Peters, isn't that right?' Harris's voice is even – just someone getting confirmation of something she already knows.

'That's right,' says Noone. 'It was Terry Peters who put a word in for me.'

'Did you know Terry Peters well at that point?'

Noone shrugs. 'Not really. I'd met the guy a coupla times along with a bunch of movie and TV people. Seemed OK. I don't really know him that well now, if I'm honest. How's he doing? With all this, I mean? Must be tough.'

'He's doing as well as you might expect,' says Harris, shortly. She looks down at her notes, rubbing her finger against her lip, and Noone glances in Frank's direction. Although Noone keeps his expression bland, there's something knowing in the gesture that Frank doesn't like, as if the American is inviting Frank to share a male secret at Harris's expense.

'Let's get back to the fourteenth, Mr Noone,' says Harris. 'We've been talking for five minutes since I asked and you haven't told us anything. I'd still like to get your movements.'

Frank curses himself inwardly for not noticing how smoothly Noone had deflected the question. I need to raise my game here, he thinks, and straightens his spine, the fighter coming out of his corner. Chrissy Cahill pops into his mind and he remembers how easily the boy had caught him napping.

'I'd need to check with a few people but I'm pretty sure we'd have been out at Maxie's if it was a Friday. That's been pretty regular since we started the shoot.' Noone frowns as if concentrating. 'If I had to make a guess, I think I left before Nicky.'

'You remember that?' Harris's voice is quizzical.

'I remember thinking that in the US he wouldn't have been at the bar. What is he, sixteen, seventeen? You gotta be twenty-one back home.'

'It's eighteen here,' Frank says.

'Coulda fooled me. Liverpool's pretty easygoing on that score.'

'Can you give us the names of the people you were with that evening?'

'I'll try. There were the guys from Hungry Head, John and Ethan. Josh Soames too. And Dean, he was with them, mostly. A couple of girls, I don't know their names. The boy was there.'

'Did you speak to Nicky?'

Noone looks at Harris. 'I can't remember. If I did, it wasn't anything.'

'Danny Lomax?'

'Who?'

For the first time since the interview began, Frank can sense a trace of unease in Noone. It might not mean anything, but it's there. Maybe Noone's first misstep. Frank decides to push.

Noone shakes his head. 'Doesn't mean anything to me. You meet lots of people at Maxie's.'

Frank laughs and leans forward, folding his arms on the table in front of him.

'Come on, Ben, you and I both know who Danny Lomax is. He's a drug dealer. Your drug dealer.'

Frank's information on Maxie's regular patrons is in the file handed to him by Magsi. Lomax is known to MIT tangentially. Not a big player on the club scene but known. Noone and Lomax had been talking that night, according to the Aussie barman Magsi had interviewed.

'My drug dealer?' Noone smiles. 'That makes him sound very important.' The American sits back. 'Look, I admit I know Danny from the clubs and, yes, I do know he's got drugs. I may even have got some from him, just some recreationals to loosen the kinks. We all do that, right?'

He eyes Frank, amused, and Frank can't help but flash back to the night with Em. They'd both had a smoke. Like Noone said, we all do some of that.

'No. Not all of us, Ben.'

'Really?' The actor smiles gently. 'Whatever you say.'

Harris is reading from the file. 'We'll be talking to Mr Lomax again. For the time being we can just ignore any "recreationals" you may or may not have had. Can we just establish that Nicky Peters wasn't being supplied by Mr Lomax too?'

'Not that I know.'

'I'd like to talk about you some more, Ben. You say you're a traveller. When did that start and why did you end up in Liverpool?'

Noone spreads his hands. 'Why not? It's cool. I was bumming around Europe a bit and someone mentioned this was a good place to come. I came. No big reason.'

'And stayed?'

'That's right. I like the place. It suits me.'

In a funny way, Frank knows what he means. The city does suit the American. Performers like the place and Liverpool loves a performer.

'What started you off, the travelling?' Harris's question sounds more like something from a daytime chat show and Frank wonders if the actor's charm is working too well on Harris.

Noone returns plenty of charm in his answer, smiling at Harris. 'After my mother died I didn't feel like staying at home.'

'Los Angeles?'

'Correct. And if you've been there, you'll know why I like Liverpool.'

'Your mother?' prompts Harris.

'Yeah, she died. Cancer. We weren't close. Once she'd gone I came into some money and lit out for Europe. Nothing unusual.'

'How about your father?' Harris's voice is all concern now. Maybe she should try acting too, thinks Frank.

'My father? He's gone.'

'Dead?'

A flicker of annoyance passes across Noone's face like a digital jump on a screen.

'Not that I know. He wasn't part of my life. Never knew him.'

Before he can pick up on Noone's reply, Frank's phone vibrates in his pocket. He fishes it out and reads the text, holding the phone below the edge of the table. 'Got something,' the text reads. It's from Saif Magsi.

'Carry on without me,' says Frank. 'I'll be back in two minutes.'

Noone's expression is open as Frank gets up and leaves. As the door closes behind him he sees Noone turning towards Harris and smiling. He starts to say something but Frank doesn't catch it.

Magsi's outside in the corridor.

'Didn't want to come in and show you this in front of Noone,' says Magsi. Frank nods approvingly as Magsi hands him a sheet of paper. 'Just came through and I thought it might be relevant.'

On the sheet of paper is a credit card number and a list of monthly statement balances for the past year in the name of Benjamin Noone. The logo at the top reads 'Wells Fargo'.

'It's a prepaid,' Magsi says. 'A Visa card, but topped up before it's used. Wells Fargo's a US bank.' Magsi's immaculate nail traces the statement balances. 'These are just cash payments made inwards by Noone. He can do that at almost any bank without leaving an electronic trail.'

'So how did you get this?'

Magsi looks a little uncomfortable. 'I know someone who can look up that kind of thing. Sort of a freelancer. My brother.'

'Stop,' says Frank, 'I don't want to know.' He rattles the sheet of paper. 'So this is inadmissible?' His voice is level.

'Yeah, sorry, boss. I thought . . . well, it was just pissing me off not finding anything on Noone, and my brother, well . . .'

Frank pats Magsi on the shoulder. 'No, it's fine, Magsi. It's useful. But don't mention this to anyone else, got that? I don't want it coming back to bite us later.'

Magsi nods, relieved.

'And next time, if there is a next time, ask me first, got that?' Without waiting for a reply, Frank tucks the credit card details into his jacket and turns back to the interview room. Inside, Harris is laughing at something Noone has said.

'Cosy.'

Frank sits down and looks at Noone.

'How do you manage for money, Ben?' he says. 'Can't be too much in acting, even in the movies. Not for a newbie like you. What have you been using?'

'There's no mystery. I came into money after my mother died.'

'You're rich?' says Harris. 'River Towers is a pretty swanky address.'

170

'I do OK.' Noone pauses and smiles again. 'And River Towers is overrated. Mostly dodgy property developers and criminals, if you ask me.'

Frank doesn't return the smile. 'Is that where you met Danny Lomax?'

Noone shakes his head. 'Still talking about Danny? You're barking up the wrong tree there.'

'What tree should I be barking up, Ben?'

'I can't tell you how to do your job, DCI Keane, but drugs have nothing to do with this.'

Now the atmosphere is unmistakeable. Harris picks it up too.

'How would you know what is relevant in this case, Mr Noone?' she says. 'Do you have any information for us?'

Noone sits back in the uncomfortable interview room chair and folds his hands in his lap. 'No,' he says. 'I don't think I do.'

To Harris's surprise, Frank doesn't respond to this.

'Let's turn to Dean Quinner.' Frank gives Noone a long look. 'You don't seem too upset about Dean's death.'

'Is that a question?' Noone taps a finger on the edge of the table. 'We weren't buddies, but I liked him OK. I'm not that upset because that's not who I am. I don't get upset very easily. Aren't the English supposed to understand that?'

'Even we manage to squeeze out the odd tear now and again, Mr Noone,' says Harris. 'At the very least Mr Quinner's murder must mean trouble for the movie. You'll be out of a job if it folds.'

'I don't want the production to stop,' Noone replies, 'but it's only a movie. I was brought up in Los Angeles. Movies don't impress me the same way they do most other people. And I don't need the gig. Besides, isn't that an argument for me *not* being involved in whatever happened to Quinner?'

Harris leans across to Frank and points to a small statement on the initial data collection sheet. This was largely gleaned from phone calls made by MIT to the movie people following the discovery of Dean Quinner's body. It's something from Alix Turner, one of the make-up team.

'Someone said that you and Dean were having an "intense" discussion on set. What was that about?'

There.

Noone's nostrils flare and his eyes narrow. Frank registers the corners of Noone's mouth turning down. In a split second the expression is wiped clean and replaced by one of Noone's sardonic smiles. Noone brushes some specks of dust from his sleeve.

But Frank saw.

He saw Noone's true face for a fleeting instant. Even an actor's mask slips from time to time.

And in that instant, every atom in Frank screams one visceral, unalterable fact: this is the guy. Locking eyes with him now, Frank just knows, *boom*, that the affable American across the desk is the killer of the Peters family and Dean Quinner. Frank's not remotely religious, but it is as if the devil has come into J7 in that electrically charged split second and, for Frank at least, the entire investigation shifts emphasis.

This is the guy.

What's more, thinks Frank as Noone regards him with a bland indifference, I'm pretty sure he knows that I know. And he doesn't care.

After twenty years on the force, and coming into contact with some of the worst scum to breathe air, there have been many times when Frank gets this basic, neanderthal reaction. Useless in court, of course, but highly useful when it comes to focusing effort. Frank glances at Harris to see if she's read it the same way but he can't tell.

'What was it?' Frank points at Noone. 'He saw something, didn't he? Or said something you didn't like. What was it? Did he catch you with your pants down?'

'Did Alix tell you that we were having this "intense" discussion?' Noone shakes his head. 'He's the fucking writer, man! And I'm the fucking lead! If the two of us can't have a fucking discussion on set then I don't know who can. She's pissed because I didn't want to fuck her. Ask around. This is getting ridiculous.'

Under the table Harris taps her foot against Frank's, their pre-arranged signal that they should speak.

'We're going to take a break, Mr Noone.' Frank leans forward and presses a button on the digital voice recorder. 'DCI Keane and DC Harris suspending interview with Benjamin Noone.'

172

As Keane and Harris push back their chairs, Noone does the same. Frank holds out a hand, palm up, gesturing for Noone to stay.

'We'd like you to stay a little longer, Mr Noone. If that's all right with you.'

Noone sinks back onto the chair and nods to himself as if Keane has confirmed something. 'I'm all yours, DCI Keane.'

Outside, Harris moves a little way along the corridor before speaking.

'I just want to check where you're going with this. You're pushing him hard.'

'He's the one, Em. Can't you feel that?'

Harris steps back and looks at Frank as if he's mental.

'What is this, the fucking *Matrix*? The "one"? What the hell does that mean, Frank?'

Frank grimaces and holds up his hands in a placatory gesture. 'I know, I know. It's weird, it's flaky. And I know that there's pretty much nothing solid we can put against him yet.' Frank pauses. 'But I also know I'm right about him. You must have had that kind of reaction before? He's guilty.'

'I agree he's not making me ready to strike his name off, but I'm not picking up the same vibrations as you.'

'We sit on him,' says Frank. 'Give the cocky fucker a couple of hours and see how he likes being messed around.'

'That won't do anything,' says Harris to Frank's back. He is already heading for his office.

'Perhaps not,' he replies as he reaches the stairs. He stops and looks back at Harris. 'But it'll make me feel a lot better. Who knows, perhaps he'll have a fit of remorse and confess to everything?'

'I wouldn't hold my breath,' says Harris, but Frank isn't listening.

Forty-One

It's not the first time Ben Noone's found himself waiting in a police interview room. If Frank Keane thinks this shit's going to knock him off his stride, he's mistaken.

If he's honest, this is what he's been looking forward to since Monday.

Once Dean was dead there was no doubt in Ben Noone's mind that the cops would make the connection to *The Tunnels*.

That hadn't stopped him killing the writer.

Ferguson's autopsy won't show it, but as with many before in Liverpool, in the final reckoning it had been drink that killed Dean Quinner.

The vodka he'd been sculling most of Monday afternoon up at The Pilgrim and then at a succession of increasingly blurry bars on the way down to the river ensured his wits were gone when the time came. Maybe, thinks Noone, it might still have happened the way it did, but the condition he was in didn't help.

Sitting in J7, Noone replays the night.

It's past eleven when Quinner, as fried as an egg on a hot skillet, stumbles out of the last bar on Slater Street and heads for home through a dizzying maze of midweek drinkers. Noone watches him bump into a small knot of young lads, all white shirts and gelled hair. They laugh and part for him, pushing him away as if leprous, not yet pissed enough themselves to take offence. That might come later on the two o'clock exodus.

On the pavement Quinner straightens himself with the exaggerated care of the terminally blitzed.

'You can do this, feller,' he mutters, loud enough for a passing girl to hear. She cackles and grabs the arm of her friend. Trailed by

Noone, Quinner heads slowly down Slater Street and picks up a kebab, most of which ends up on his jacket, but he makes it to the Albert Dock without incident. His route takes him past the front of Canning Place Police Headquarters.

Noone is careful to stay out of range of the CCTV cameras as best he can. He's dressed in a high-necked black jacket and a dark baseball cap. He stays on the side streets as much as possible and, because he guesses where Quinner is headed – to his flat on the docks – he is able to tail him from the front. The CCTV footage from in front of Canning Place is the clearest the MIT investigators will find of Quinner. He'd be picked up again on a camera overlooking the Maritime Museum and once more on one belonging to his block of apartments. The twenty-two-second clip shows him stopping and answering his phone. After a few moments he walks out of shot and it's the last time Dean Quinner's seen alive. Later, when Frank's going over the flickering blue and white images on the monitor at MIT, he'll peer closely at Quinner's image again and again as if, by concentrating hard, the end result will change.

Noone, standing in the shadows across the dock from the flats, makes the call as Quinner is reaching for his keys. He fumbles before answering.

'Dean? I need to explain something to you.'

Noone keeps his voice hesitant. He sounds vulnerable, contrite. He is convincing.

'I'm embarrassed about what happened. That thing with the wallet? I don't know what I was doing. Maybe pressure, I don't know. Do you have time to talk?'

Relief floods Quinner. This man couldn't have hurt Niall. He wants to talk. Suddenly Quinner sees what he's been doing: dramatising a small incident into something larger than it is.

'I'm down by the arena,' says Noone. 'Meet me there?'

In his befuddled state, Quinner doesn't click how Noone knows where he is.

He just goes.

The wind's picking up a little as Quinner starts to walk along the river on Kings Parade. For the first time Quinner's aware he's only wearing a thin jacket. To his left is the curving hulk of the Echo

Arena, masking the city from view. At this time of night there's no one there.

Quinner walks carefully, mindful of the river racing past to his right. He's never liked staring at the waters of the Mersey. Here, black as treacle, it slides along the thick stone walls of the river walk without a sound. Quinner sits on a concrete bollard and waits for Noone.

Noone watches him all the way. After Quinner sits down, he checks that there is no one in sight before emerging. The taser is in the pocket of his black zip-up. He folds a gloved hand round it and walks swiftly across to Quinner.

There's no conversation. With a final look up and down the windswept promenade, Noone lifts out the taser and applies it to the writer's exposed neck. Quinner jerks and is still. Noone sits down next to him, supporting Quinner's unconscious form – someone helping a friend a little the worse for wear.

Noone finds Quinner's phone and throws it into the river. Standing, he drags Quinner upright and pulls him towards the low fence next to the water. Noone's much bigger than Quinner and has little problem tipping him over and onto the stone ledge. He hops over the fence and pushes the writer into the water. The tide is high and Quinner's body slips under and is gone. Noone vaults back over the fence and walks towards the city, his cap pulled down low. Less than a minute after Dean Quinner's been put in the Mersey, Noone is gone.

Forty-Two

Theresa Cooper isn't the sort of woman who takes setbacks well, and being deprived of the lead in the Peters case at the Tuesday briefing comes high on the scale of things that seriously piss her off. After the meeting she had driven to the largely deserted car park at a nearby Asda, stopped in the furthest corner and screamed out her frustration for five minutes. Then, checking that not a trace of it showed on her face, she drove back to Stanley Road and continued working.

By two on Thursday afternoon the fire's still burning.

If it kills her, she is going to find out one important thing to help this case along.

Cooper's been detailed to dig around into Terry Peters. The brief has been for background on all the Peters family but, after being brought up to speed by DI Harris about Terry Peters' affair with Maddy, it's Terry she's concentrating her efforts on.

The trouble is that there's virtually nothing. Everyone who comes into contact with him seems to say the same thing: he's basically a good guy.

His only obvious brush with the law has been the case brought by his ex. Cooper reads and re-reads the details and is forced to concur with the version of events that Peters had given in the interview with Harris and Keane: in frustration he'd broken a window and his ex had sustained a minor injury. From this she'd made maximum trouble, bringing charges against Terry Peters and making sure that the case didn't run out of steam. In the end, the punishment reflected what the court believed: that Peters was in the wrong but not dangerous.

After some more digging, Cooper finds the details of the divorce five years ago. The grounds are irreconcilable differences, no mention of cruelty. The wife got the house, custody of the only child and what looks to Cooper's eyes like a decent result. She's about to abandon that line of enquiry when a thought occurs to her. If Terry's ex-wife came out of the deal with pretty much everything, why was there so much bitterness? It could, of course, simply be the residue left when so many marriages collapse, but Cooper wonders if there might be something else.

It's probably worth a trip to Ainsdale to find out what Terry Peters had done to piss off the ex so much.

'Mrs Peters?'

The small dark-haired woman standing in the doorway of her house has her arms folded. 'No,' she says flatly. 'It was. Now it's Ms Flynn. My maiden name. You're DS Cooper?' Her voice inclines to the Lancashire rather than the Liverpool side of things. It can go either way in Southport.

Cooper nods and Flynn invites her inside with a movement of her head.

The house on a middle-class estate in Ainsdale is modern, clean and completely absent of any character. The rooms look like they've been cleaned that morning.

In the living room, the woman offers a hand. 'Stella,' she says. Cooper can't tell if the staccato style is natural or simply the result of nerves. Some people just can't operate normally around the police, although if she had to bet, Theresa is pretty sure that Stella Flynn doesn't come into that category.

Cooper looks at a photo of a serious-looking teenager – was there any other kind? – in a frame above the fireplace.

'Your son?'

Stella Flynn's face blooms into a glorious smile. It transforms her, and it's easy to see the impact she'd have had in her youth.

'Jacob. He's eighteen this year. Hard to believe.'

'He looks like his father.'

As rapidly as it had arrived, the smile vanishes from Stella Flynn's face.

'I can't see it.'

Cooper doesn't say anything.

'Tea?' says Stella and Cooper nods. When Stella heads for the kitchen, Cooper follows her.

'What school does your son go to?'

'College,' corrects Stella, filling the kettle. 'KGV. He wants to be an engineer. Loves making things work properly, does Jacob. Always has done.' She presses the on switch and lifts two mugs from a cupboard. 'Milk?'

Cooper nods. 'No sugar.'

'How has he coped since the divorce? It can be hard for boys.'

Stella bangs the mugs onto the kitchen counter with a little more force than Cooper believes is strictly necessary.

'It was a while ago. He's fine.'

Stella turns as the kettle begins to hiss. 'Look, what's all this about? The divorce? I heard about . . . what happened. But we don't see any of Terry's family since we split up.' Her ex-husband's name is spoken with venom. Stella lifts out the milk from the fridge. 'Obviously I'm sad about it. Nicky's a nice boy.' She glances up at Cooper.

'Were he and Jacob close at any stage?'

'No.' The word is spat out. 'Like I said, we haven't seen anything of them for five years. I spoke to Maddy in the shops once but that's about it.' She faces Cooper square on. 'What's this about? I want to help, but I can't see what I can do.'

'Can we have the tea?' says Cooper. 'It'll be easier with a brew.'

Back in the living room Cooper sips from a china cup and she's right; it does help.

'I am here to ask about the divorce. It's nothing really, just something that I'm curious about.'

Stella looks wary but Cooper thinks she's starting to loosen up a little.

'Yes?'

'Well, it's just that when I dug around in the files I couldn't see why you'd be so set against your ex.'

'He smashed up the house!'

'He broke a window, Stella. According to the report.'

'Well, yes, maybe I did make it bigger than it was.'

'Why? Was there another woman?'

Stella shakes her head and says something under her breath.

'What was that, Stella?'

Stella Flynn looks up. 'I wish it had been . . . another woman, I mean.'

179

Cooper sits up a little straighter. 'Men?' she says and Stella shakes her head more vigorously. Tears well up in her eyes and her cup begins to tremble.

'What was it, Stella? What was it that Terry did?'

'Boys,' says Stella in a voice so low that Cooper can hardly hear her. 'He liked boys.'

Forty-Three

Frank's plan to ruffle Noone's feathers by letting him wait in the interview room doesn't work out exactly as he'd hoped.

Just after three, with Noone waiting in J7, he and Harris take Frank's car to the Pier Head and park outside Bean, a coffee shop Frank's become a regular at. Sitting in a back corner seat – the policeman's choice, facing the door, full view of the room – Frank sips his coffee and tries to relax.

Harris is drinking tea. For a few moments neither speaks.

'How's Linda doing?' Frank says. Even to him it sounds jarring.

'She's OK. Still upset.'

Frank nods and, without thinking, touches the side of his face where the vinegar had hit. That had been a bad moment.

'It was only vinegar,' says Harris, as if reading his thoughts.

'Easy to say.' He looks up at Harris but she just nods. She doesn't seem in the mood for an argument.

'What about Noone?' She jerks a thumb in the general direction of Stanley Road. 'Are we going to talk about him?'

'It's him,' says Frank. 'You can see that, can't you?'

Harris holds her hand out, palm down, fingers splayed, and waggles it from side to side. 'Maybe. When he came in I sort of warmed to him, at first. But that went away. He's too cocky. Even allowing for him being an American.'

'It's him.'

Before Harris can reply, Frank catches the eye of a thickset middle-aged man on the opposite side of the cafe. At Frank's glance he turns his head back to the iPad he'd been reading. Frank keeps looking but knows that with Harris in the room there are always going to be eyes pointed in their direction.

'Was he here when we arrived?' Frank inclines his head fractionally in the direction of the man with the iPad.

'Who?' Harris is confused.

'Doesn't matter.'

'Are you getting enough sleep?' Frank senses sarcasm but there's nothing showing in Harris's expression.

'I'm OK.'

'Theresa's got some sort of bee in her bonnet this morning. Looked like she was on a mission. And she's at the Quinner autopsy this afternoon. She might have something useful for us.'

Frank nods absently. The guy on the iPad gets up and goes to the bathroom. Frank puts down his coffee and gets to his feet, his quads still aching from Tuesday's work-out.

'Won't be long,' he says, and heads towards the toilets. Harris rolls her eyes and sinks back into the leather seat.

Frank pushes open the toilet door. The guy is at the urinal and Frank leans back against a wall. After a second or two, the big man glances over his shoulder at Frank and then back at the empty urinal next to him.

'Can I help you?' he says.

'You're American.'

The man finishes pissing and zips up. He turns and washes his hands at the sink.

'Yes,' he says cautiously. 'I'm American. What's the problem? If you're looking for a pick-up, I can tell you I'm not the guy you need.'

Frank takes out his warrant card. 'You know what this is, right?'

The man seems baffled. 'Look, I have to go.'

'You're a cop.' Frank's making a statement. 'I can tell.'

'You're a fucking nut,' says the guy. 'I used to be a cop. Now I'm a tourist.' Close up, Frank can see the man is older than he'd first thought, his short hair speckled with grey. The guy makes a move to push past Frank and Frank holds out an arm and places a hand flat on the man's chest. As he does, the guy eyeballs Frank and shakes his head. 'I wouldn't,' he says in an even tone.

'A tourist?' says Frank. 'I don't think so.'

The guy sighs and then something happens, something quick, and Frank finds himself on the tile floor trying desperately to breathe. The American has Frank's arm behind his back and a knee on the nape of his neck.

'Stay down,' he says. 'It'll take a couple of minutes to get your breath back.'

He releases Frank and stands. Frank sees the door open and the man leave. Frank tries to stand but can't, not yet. He puts his forehead on the white tile and waits, panting heavily. Just as the American had said, his breathing returns to normal after a few minutes. Frank gets to his feet and opens the door to the cafe. Harris looks at him curiously as he approaches. There's no sign of the American.

'Are you feeling OK?'

Frank nods, the movement making his neck hurt.

'Because you look like crap, Frank.'

'Thanks.' Frank's voice is hoarse and he coughs. 'Just a touch of flu.' Without knowing why, he decides he's not going to say anything about the man in the toilets. He feels soiled by the encounter and embarrassed.

And curious.

Harris waves her iPhone at him. 'We've been summoned.'

Frank takes a drink from his coffee cup and raises his eyebrows.

'Searle's at Stanley Road asking for you.'

'He can wait.'

Harris shakes her head. 'That's not why we have to go. Caddick called about Noone.'

Frank looks up. 'What?'

'He's got a lawyer.'

Forty-Four

The night with the nurse turned out better than Ronnie Rimmer had dared imagine – and he was a man with a highly coloured imagination when it came to sex – and he positively bounces into work straight from her place, wearing the frazzled, triumphant air of a man who got very lucky indeed.

Ignoring Steve Rose's adolescent jibes, Rimmer dives back into the grinding task of assembling the information on the Quinner file. It's not until midafternoon that a name in front of him triggers something.

Niall McCluskey.

Dean Quinner, despite his Liverpool Irish roots, doesn't have too many relatives in the city. Apart from his mother and a younger sister, most of the family seem to have moved to Manchester for some unfathomable reason. But Big Niall, the cousin, is one who'd stayed.

Rimmer is sure he's heard the name before. He goes to work on McCluskey and finds a reasonable file on him. A couple of minor assault charges, some D & Ds, one charge of petty theft and an arrest for public nudity. It's hardly the file of a master criminal but it's something. But Niall's record isn't what is itching Rimmer's memory.

Wasn't McCluskey the name of the guy with the missing finger that Hanna had told him about last night? Half-cut, she'd blurted out the guy's name without thinking, violating several privacy laws, and then asked Ronnie to forget all about it. 'Forget about what?' he'd said. Now Rimmer wishes he'd paid more attention to what she'd been saying than what she'd been wearing.

He takes his phone and dials Hanna's number. It goes onto voice-mail and he leaves a brief message for her to call him. It's only when he hangs up that he realises she may think it's a purely personal matter, so, feeling foolish, he dials again and leaves a second message letting her know this is police business. The two calls, neither delivered very articulately, hardly show him in a smooth light, and Steve Rose lets him know it via a series of snickering one-liners, but it can't be helped.

Next, Rimmer calls Walton A & E. It takes him almost twenty minutes to burrow through the bureaucracy and get someone who is able to tell him the names of the admissions to the department on the night in question. Despite some initial resistance to giving out the information Rimmer reminds the receptionist that the patient in question is possibly important to several murder investigations.

'We already know he received treatment,' says Rimmer without revealing how.

'What's the name again?'

'McCluskey.'

'Yeah,' says the receptionist after a pause. 'Niall McCluskey. Came in at 1.54 am. Hand injury. Discharged himself at 5.10 after he'd been stitched up.'

Rimmer's starting to get a good feeling about this.

He walks across to Frank Keane's office but he's not there.

'He's in J7,' says Manda Davies. 'He and DI Harris are interviewing the actor.'

'I thought that was earlier?'

Davies shrugs. 'It was, but for some reason they left him to stew. He got a lawyer and they're in there now.' She tilts her head and says in a singsong voice, 'I wouldn't talk to him right now . . .'

'Oh?'

She looks up at Rimmer. 'He didn't look too pleased when he came back in. And Superintendent Searle's looking for him.'

Rimmer nods and returns to his desk. Manda's got a point. If Keane's got a moody on, Rimmer knows he'd better choose his moment. Chasing a loose end like this won't be welcomed without something more substantial behind it.

Rimmer grabs his coat. With a bit of luck he can put some more meat on the bones before presenting the offering to Keane.

'I'm going out for a bit,' he tells Rose. 'Fancy coming?'

'Roy won't like it.'

'Suit yourself.'

'Hold on,' says Rose. 'I didn't say I wasn't coming.'

Twenty minutes later, Rimmer and Rose are at Niall McCluskey's place.

'How do you know he's there?' Rimmer's filled Rose in on the details on the drive over.

'I don't,' says Rimmer. He looks up at the flats. 'But I'd bet money that he's holed up inside.' Rimmer's been thinking it through, and the more he thinks about it, the more the whole episode sounds like someone being warned off. Finding out that Niall McCluskey was injured almost immediately preceding Quinner's death, Rimmer's sure he's onto something.

'In any case, someone's got to tell him about Dean.'

'His cousin?' Rose laughs. 'Since when do we break the news to cousins? How about getting some counselling for the neighbours?'

'You know what I mean. Gives us a reason to be here. Quinner didn't have much family still here.'

Rimmer opens the door that separates the bookie's from the bakery and heads up the narrow stairs. On the landing he knocks on the door and strengthens his Liverpool accent.

'Delivery!' He knocks hard again and waits. Steve Rose rocks backwards on his heels, his arms folded. He raises his eyebrows and Rimmer shakes his head.

He knocks again and this time puts a bit of a whine into the words.

'Come on, mate. I can't leave this outside. Someone'll nick it.'

The door opens and Niall looks out.

'Shit,' he says as he sees the two coppers.

'Niall McCluskey?' says Rimmer.

'No,' says Niall, but it's a half-hearted attempt. Rimmer's already pushing past him into the flat.

'Come in,' mutters Niall. 'Make yourselves at home.'

In the living room Rimmer stands in the centre while Niall waits in the doorway. The TV is showing a cop movie, the sound turned down. Rose ambles around, looking at the few items in the room. He picks up the remote and turns off the TV. The smell of recently smoked weed hangs in the air.

'Fond of the wacky baccy, Niall?' says Rose.

'What's all this about, like?' says Niall, ignoring the question. Even he can see that these two aren't here about dope.

'You hurt your hand?' Rimmer gestures towards Niall's bandage.

Niall raises it limply and looks at his hand as if surprised to find it there.

'It's nothing.'

He puts it behind his back. The action is so childlike that it's all Rimmer can do not to smile.

'How did you lose your finger, Niall?' says Rimmer. Niall looks at Rimmer as if he's a mind-reader. 'Has it got anything to do with Dean's death?'

Niall flinches as if struck. His mouth opens and then closes again. 'What?'

'Dean, your cousin. We found him in the river. Tuesday morning.' Rimmer gestures towards the sofa.

'You'd better sit down, Niall,' he says. 'Tell us what happened.'

Niall sits down heavily on the cheap sofa and starts to talk.

Forty-Five

The lawyer's somewhere around forty, blond-haired and pink-faced. His name is Eagles. That's what it says on the card he hands to Frank as soon as he walks back into the interview room. Eagles passes a second card to Harris. Noone is sitting comfortably behind the table, the lawyer standing.

Frank catches Noone's eye and gets nothing back, not even annoyance. The American doesn't even look bored.

Eagles holds out a hand, which Frank shakes, although not with any enthusiasm.

'You turned up quick, Mr Eagles,' says Frank. 'What were you doing, just hanging around outside the building on the off-chance?' He inclines his head towards Noone. 'You know this is simply a routine questioning?'

'Mr Noone wanted someone here to make sure there are no misunderstandings. He's . . . sensitive about his position as a foreigner in a situation like this.'

Frank looks closer at Eagles' card. 'You're with Bilson's? I didn't know you did this kind of thing. Bit grubby for you lot, isn't it?'

Eagles ignores Frank's question. 'Mr Noone is here under his own free will. And leaving him here to stew is not something you do to witnesses who happen to be our clients, DCI Keane. Any further questioning from this point forward will be done in my presence. Now, do you have anything more you want to talk to my client about?'

Frank sits down opposite Noone and looks at him. 'Yes,' he says after a few seconds have passed, 'I think we do.' He presses the digital recorder and updates the time and people present.

Harris takes the seat next to Frank, leaving Eagles standing.

'A chair?' says the lawyer.

Frank waves a hand in the direction of the door. 'Ask the officer outside.' He turns to Eagles. 'Or you can just hang upside down from the ceiling. Whatever's easier.'

Eagles doesn't react and Frank feels like a tool for the cheap gibe. The man's only doing what he's supposed to be doing. Frank gets up and brings in a chair from the corridor outside.

Frank sits and reads the file in his hands. Harris leans across and points at a note Frank has made in the margin. He nods. When he looks up, Noone is watching Harris, the trace of a smile on his face.

'Something amusing you, Nr Noone?'

Noone shrugs. 'Just thought you two overplayed that a little. Too *CSI*.'

'Is that how you see everything? As an act?'

'Isn't it?'

'Are you going to ask my client any more questions?' says Eagles.

Frank doesn't reply. Instead Harris speaks. 'How did you get Mr Eagles' phone number?'

Noone holds up his phone and waggles it between his thumb and forefinger. 'Google.'

'You just happened to find a senior partner at Bilson's ready to drop everything and scurry across to Stanley Road?'

Eagles leans forward. 'I hardly think this is something that needs to be answered. I am Mr Noone's representative. How that happened is none of your concern.'

'Let's turn to the events of Friday the fourteenth,' says Frank. 'You told us you left Maxie's before Nicky –'

'I said I think I did. I didn't really notice. He's only a kid.'

'Where did you go after leaving Maxie's?'

'Back to my apartment.'

'Alone?'

Noone shakes his head. 'No. I was with some chick.'

This is information neither Frank nor Harris is expecting.

'You gave us the impression you left alone.' Harris's voice is even. 'Who was this woman? Do you know her name?'

'I did leave the club alone. I met this girl outside. Bummed a cigarette off her, got talking and she came back.'

'Just like that?'

Noone smiles. 'What can I say?' He folds his arms. 'I think her name was Helen, something like that. Ellen, maybe.'

'Phone number?'

'No,' says Noone. 'She left early.'

Frank makes a note on the file and shows it to Harris. She gets up and leaves the room, Noone watching her as she goes. 'How early?' says Frank.

'No idea. I was sleeping.'

There's silence in the room. Frank waits for Harris to return. He's comfortable with silences in here. They can be very unsettling for some but Noone seems equally at home. Eagles consults his watch, fidgeting. Frank gets the feeling that for him environments like J7 represent unfamiliar territory.

Harris comes back into the room and takes her seat.

'They should get some good footage,' says Noone to Harris.

'Excuse me?'

'The CCTV. River Towers has some decent security. Should be some good footage. That's what you've been out to chase up, right? Smart thinking.'

Eagles leans across and puts his hand on Noone's arm. He whispers something in the American's ear and sits back.

'Just trying to be friendly,' says Noone.

Frank's had enough. He closes the file and points across the table. 'I'll just tell you this straight, maybe it'll save some time.' He fixes his gaze on Noone. 'You did this. I know you did this. And what's more, you know I know, don't you? You don't think there'll be any forensics we can put on you? Prints? We'll find something.'

'I'd been there before,' says Noone, evenly. 'With Terry one night. Met the family. If my prints are in there, that'll be why.'

Frank looks at Harris and then back at Noone. 'You think that'll cover you?'

'I got the full tour,' says Noone. 'Very keen to show off the place. Don't think there was a room I didn't see. I may have had a shower.'

'Nice,' says Frank. He tries to remain calm but Noone is getting under his skin. And he's smart. Saying he was at the house previously negates almost any forensics. Unless he left a bloody print. Even hair samples would be tainted.

'You did this, Ben.'

'We're finished here, DCI Keane,' says Eagles. 'My client doesn't have to sit and listen to these wild accusations.'

Frank ignores the lawyer. 'This isn't a performance, Noone. There's a sixteen-year-old boy out there. Now you've killed him, or you've got him. One of the two. I *know* that. We can wait for this bullshit story of yours to fall apart or we can help Nicky. You can help Nicky. Just tell us and it'll be easier for you in court.'

Noone just sits there. He turns to Eagles. 'Can you believe this?'

'No,' says Eagles, 'I can't.' He stands and places his briefcase on the table, his hands folded across the clasp. 'Unless you are going to formally charge Mr Noone with murder, we're leaving. Right now.'

'The DNA will be in soon, Ben,' says Frank. 'From when you fucked Nicky's dead mother. You remember coming over her, don't you? Your client won't mind giving us a DNA swab, will you?' Frank smiles at Eagles. 'For elimination purposes.'

'We're going,' says Eagles. 'You can get a court order for that DNA swab.'

'No friendly cooperation?' Frank folds his arms behind his head.

'Unbelievable,' says Noone, getting to his feet.

'Was she dead when you fucked her, Ben? I'm betting she was.' Frank's angry, but even in the midst of his rage there's an uncomfortable feeling that Noone's too confident. There'll be no DNA, thinks Frank. I was wrong. He didn't fuck Maddy Peters.

Eagles opens the door to the interview room and steps outside. At the threshold, Noone turns to Keane. 'Good luck,' he says. 'I hope you find Nicky, I really do.' He closes the door behind him. Frank picks up the file and hurls it after him. It bounces off the battered wood and sprays paper across the floor.

Em Harris presses the stop button on the digital recorder and stands. 'Can I just say, you handled that perfectly, Frank. Textbook stuff.'

'Fuck off,' says Frank. 'And it's DCI Keane, Harris. Or have you forgotten I'm your boss?'

'No, DCI Keane,' says Harris. She opens the door. 'I haven't.'

Alone, Frank places his forehead on the Formica surface of the table and lets out a long, low groan.

Shit.

Forty-Six

The day's not over.

After losing his cool in the interview with Noone, Frank runs straight into Searle outside the MIT offices, Peter Moreleigh at his heels like an attentive terrier.

'Sir.'

'The very man!' Charlie Searle is oozing bonhomie. A bad sign. Frank's sure there's a direct and inverse correlation between Searle's cheeriness and the amount of shit about to be dumped in your lap. From the grin that's creasing the slimy bastard's face now, Frank knows he's in for something special. It's also bad that the two of them are still around after five.

'Will this take long, sir?' It's a faint hope but he's got to try. 'Only I've got an update meeting . . .'

'Only take a few moments, Frank. Your office?'

Two minutes later and Searle's sitting opposite Frank. Moreleigh leans his skinny arse on the sill of the window. 'Can't for the life of me understand why you prefer it down here, Frank,' says Searle, casting a dubious eye around the unlovely surroundings.

'Each to his own, I suppose.'

Moreleigh smirks and adjusts the lapel of his suit.

'Fill me in,' says Searle. There's a joke there somewhere but Frank doesn't take the bait.

'I imagine this is about the Peters and Quinner cases?'

Searle nods. 'Correct.'

'I'm on lead for the Peters case and Harris is looking after the Quinner one. They're obviously linked. I understand from DC Rose that the film production has shut down after Quinner's death.'

Searle looks at Moreleigh, who shakes his head sadly. 'We're getting flak from the council on that. Movie production is a cornerstone of the new regime.'

Frank doesn't respond. He waits until he's sure Moreleigh's finished making noises and then picks up the thread as if he hadn't spoken.

'I've got a strong feeling about Noone, the American actor. That's where I've just been. He got briefed up halfway through. Eagles, from Bilson's.'

At the mention of one of the city's oldest law firms Searle raises a quizzical eyebrow.

'Quick work. And expensive.'

'Too quick,' agrees Frank.

'Anything solid on him?'

'Well that's the thing,' says Frank, conscious that he's straying out onto decidedly creaky ice. 'It's the absence of anything solid that's worrying me.' Frank explains to Searle about Noone's flimsy records.

'Seems a bit thin, Frank.'

'We should be hearing from the lab about the DNA material gathered from the Peters house. I've been promised it today. I need to get a court order for a swab from Noone. And I've got a couple of officers trawling the CCTV for evidence to disprove his story. He claims there's a woman he spent the night of the fourteenth with. No name or number and says he picked her up outside Maxie's.'

'Hmm. OK. We'll talk about the DNA swab when we know it's not the dentist's. No need to rock the boat unnecessarily. And surely the brother – Terry – is in the frame too? He was sleeping with his sister-in-law. In my book that places him much closer to the centre.'

Searle might be a bit of a wanker but Frank has to admit he's still a cop under the suit. The blue files mustn't only be for show. The fucker's done some homework on this case and Frank agrees on every point he's made. Terry is a stronger candidate.

Except that Frank knows that it's Noone.

But Charlie Searle and Pete Moreleigh aren't here for a chinwag about progress. If Searle's taken the trouble to get out from behind his desk and schlep across to Stanley Road with Moreleigh in tow, there's a reason. Frank spins out a few more minutes on what's happening with Terry Peters and the work being done on the Quinner case before Superintendent Searle comes to the point. It's Frank's request for more uniforms for the ongoing search for Nicky that gives Searle his chance.

'Ah, yes, Nicky Peters.'

'Why does that sound like it's going to be a problem for me?'

Searle smiles without warmth. 'Because it probably is, Frank.' Searle gets up and stands next to Frank. 'You've had contact with the tabloids on this?'

'Yes,' says Frank, not sure of where this is headed.

'Then you'll know what they're capable of.' This is from Moreleigh. 'We had a call from a journalist at one of the red tops, a chap called McSkimming. Vicious little bastard if his previous stuff's anything to go by.'

'And?'

'McSkimming's going to run a story in tomorrow's paper suggesting strongly that Nicky Peters killed both his parents. They have an interview with Alicia Peters.'

'Terry's wife?'

Searle nods. 'Alicia's making it sound like she's a worried relative. Come back, Nicky, all is forgiven. That kind of carry-on.'

'She's found out about Terry and Maddy.' Frank's nodding his head as if confirming something to himself. 'And blaming Nicky's better than admitting it might be her husband.'

'It could be the husband.'

'No,' says Frank. 'It's Noone, I can –'

Searle cuts across him, all pretence at friendliness gone. 'Cut it out, Frank. We can't support that kind of dumb policing. Both Terry and Nicky Peters are better suspects than Ben Noone and you know it. I want you to get something prepared for McSkimming. They're going to run this story and I don't want the department to look stupid.'

'This is going to put Nicky in danger.'

Searle's expression is scornful. 'For fuck's sake, Frank, if you're right about him being taken by Noone then the kid's dead. And if by some miracle he's not and turns out to be the killer, then he might as well be dead. We're going with the story that we're anxious to speak to Nicky. When he turns up we want to look like we knew it was him all along.'

'And if the DNA from Birkdale is Noone's?'

'Then you'll be right and I'll be wrong. But that's another day and we can deal with that if and when it happens. In the meantime I want a statement that positions us with an umbrella when it starts raining. Nicky Peters is a troubled teen. We're reaching out for him. We understand. We'd like to speak to him. Got it?'

Forty-Seven

It's all Theresa Cooper can do to stop herself sprinting for the car after Stella Flynn spills the news about her ex-husband.

Instead, she forces herself to slow down and get as cohesive a story from Stella as possible.

'You know this, Stella?'

Stella nods. Her shoulders are shaking so much that Cooper takes the cup from her and places it on the coffee table. The last thing she needs at this point is a compulsive-obsessive to get deflected by tea stains on the shagpile.

'I started to get a few ideas about him a long time before it happened. A wife does, you know?'

The unmarried Cooper nods in agreement. 'Go on.'

'Little things at first. A lack of interest in me. Well, that wasn't anything special. Men can do that.'

'But . . .?'

'But he started to show an interest in filming Jacob.' Stella looks up. 'I don't mean the normal sort of filming – Terry works in the business so he's always got cameras on the go – I mean filming stuff that was sort of . . . wrong. There's no other way to describe it.'

'Like what?'

'Well, Jacob was getting older by this point. Maybe nine or ten. Too old for some of the stuff. I found some shots Terry had taken of him in the shower. I asked him about it and he just said it was fooling around. Like a prank thing. I should have been firmer then, but I wasn't to know. Anyway, after that I kept a bit of a lookout for anything funny and there wasn't anything for a long time. It looked like Terry had been telling me the truth.'

'And had he?'

Stella shakes her head. She's crying again. 'God forgive me,' she sobs. 'Poor Nicky.'

'What about Nicky, Stella?'

'I found out – well, suspected more like – that Terry had started helping Nicky out with cameras and stuff. He was always interested in that sort of thing was Nicky, even as a youngster. Made his own videos. Not just filming. He edited them, put them to music and the like. Entered competitions.'

Cooper steers Stella back to Terry. 'And Terry?'

'I came back one day, home.'

'Here?'

'No, where we used to live. Birkdale. It was the weekend but Jacob was off with some school trip thing. I was working at the hospital – reception work – but there'd been some problem with the rosters . . . I don't know. Whatever it was I came home early and Terry was in the back garden with Nicky. He must have been about ten. He was lying on a towel and Terry was rubbing oil on him. It was a warm day and Nicky had shorts on, so I suppose it was technically OK, but when Terry saw me I knew. I just *knew*. He made some crap up but that was the finish of it. I started divorce proceedings straight away.'

There's silence in the room. Theresa gets the feeling that Stella Flynn might crumble away to nothing if not handled correctly.

'But you didn't say anything?'

'I did!' Stella's face flashes anger. 'Of course I did! I told Maddy about it.'

'How did she take it?'

'She didn't believe me. Not Terry.'

Cooper thinks: she was sleeping with him even then.

'And Terry had been clever. Covered his tracks well. Nothing on him, and Nicky never said a word. Denied that Terry had done a thing. For all I know Nicky might not have known if Terry had been fiddling with him. He was only a kid. The family closed off against me – those that knew what I thought, anyway. When he married Alicia I tried to tell her but even though she had a boy herself she was the same as Maddy. Didn't want to know. I could see how

I looked – a nasty, bitter ex-wife trying to stir up trouble. I tried a few times. No one listened.'

Stella fixes her eyes on Theresa. 'But I fucking knew what that bastard was doing and he wasn't going to get to Jacob. I'd have killed him if he'd ever tried to see him again. Killed him.'

'And did he? Try, I mean.'

'Once. The day he broke the window. I told him then that if he ever came back it would all come out, evidence or no evidence. He hasn't seen Jacob since then.'

'What happened when you heard about Nicky?'

Stella fishes a tissue from the pocket of her jeans and blows her nose. 'I heard about Paul and Maddy being killed. It seemed so unlikely that I didn't know what to think. I certainly didn't connect it with Terry in any way. It was only when I heard that Nicky was missing that I wondered.' She looks at Cooper imploringly. 'But what could I do? I don't have anything to back me up. I'm just the ex-wife, right? Who's going to believe what I say?'

Cooper stands up. She's a solid woman and right now looks like she's ready to take on all comers.

'Me,' she says. 'For one.'

Forty-Eight

While Frank and Harris are interviewing Noone, Terry's in the bar of The Pumphouse all afternoon and by six is well on the way to being completely bollixed.

With everything turning to shit, and work halted on the movie, drink seems like the only sensible option.

After the interview with the police on Monday he'd worried that he'd fucked up more than he already had, but they seemed convinced enough by his story about the affair with Maddy.

For a moment, when the black copper had known he was hiding something, he'd thought the game was up. Blurting it out about Maddy turned out to be the best thing he could have done. When they let him go he could hardly believe it and there was only one thing on his mind.

Get rid of Nicky.

Except he couldn't. He'd bottled it. Terry thinks of Nicky down there now, alone, terrified, in the dark. He might be dead, he might not, but Terry knows he can't go down there again. If he hadn't been able to do it before then he wasn't going to be able to do it now. As he sees it he only has three options.

He can talk, tell the police everything and face the consequences. Who knows, he may get points for saving the boy? It's the only choice that will redeem him but Terry Peters hasn't got that in him. The idea of the shame, of the pure hatred that will rain down on him, is overwhelming.

The second choice is the one he'd tried to do and failed. He'd gone down there again the other night ready to tie up the loose ends. Fuck 'loose ends'. *Say what you mean.*

He'd gone down there to kill Nicky.

And it had been impossible. Terry just doesn't have what it takes, despite what he'd said that night at Paul's house.

'I'll take care of Nicky,' Terry had said. 'I'll do it.'

But he hadn't.

Why the fuck he'd ever kept Nicky in the tunnels – like some sort of pet – he didn't know. Wasn't the whole thing bad enough as it was? Nicky's the only real connection between Noone, Terry and the murders and Terry knows he's risking everything leaving Nicky alive.

But it's Nicky, for Christ's sake. Blood.

The last choice, and the one that's foremost in Terry's mind, is to kill himself. The river's there waiting. It would be so easy to drop over the side and let the Mersey take him. He can almost hear it calling. One seductive step over the rail, a few minutes' struggle in the black water and then nothing. No more pain, no more decisions, no more consequences.

Terry closes his eyes but all he can see is his brother's face.

Tell me what to do.

Paul had always known what the right thing to do was.

He had looked after him when they were kids, always made sure that little Terry had been included. Paul had given Terry nothing but trust and love and in return Terry had abused his only son, fucked his wife and then helped slaughter all three of them. He is vermin. He is less than vermin.

He lurches to the gents and is violently sick.

When he emerges, Noone's in the bar.

'I left him down there, Ben.' Tears are running down Terry Peters' face. 'I left him to die. In the tunnels. He's all alone.'

'It's OK, Terry,' says Noone. 'Let's get you home.'

Forty-Nine

Cooper gets back to MIT from Ainsdale around six. She's missed the Quinner autopsy but this takes precedence. Ferguson's results will come through anyway, MIT presence or not. Police attendance is more a habit than a requirement and Cooper's confident she can claim that Stella Flynn's revelations about her ex-husband will cover any problems with the autopsy. Getting anything solid to back up the ex-wife's claims will be another story.

As luck would have it she runs into Harris just outside the MIT office.

'It's Terry,' Cooper blurts out as soon as she sees the DI. She'd meant for it to come out differently but she can't help herself.

'What?' Harris is distracted. Apart from the ever-growing stack of MIT emails and memos, her phone is clogged with increasingly needy texts from Linda. Add to that the fact that Frank's gone off at the deep end in the interview with Noone, and the last thing she needs now is some twaddle from Theresa. 'What's Terry?'

'He fucking did it!' Cooper leans in close, her eyes shining. 'He's a kiddie-fiddler, Em!'

Harris raises her eyebrows, not commenting on Theresa's breach of office etiquette in calling her by her first name. 'I didn't see that one coming,' she says. She pushes open the office door and makes her way to her workstation, Cooper following close behind. 'Explain.'

'It gets better,' continues Cooper as Harris deposits her file and phone on the crowded desk. 'He was sniffing around Nicky Peters. I just came from Stella Flynn's place – Terry's ex – and she spilled the lot.'

'Oh,' says Harris, her excitement diminishing rapidly. 'The ex.'

'Wait,' says Cooper. 'Wait a sec. I know what you're thinking, but this is right.'

'And we have some evidence of this?'

Cooper hesitates.

'We can get it.' She starts to speak urgently, as if by simply conveying how much she wants this she can make it happen. 'We have probable cause to seize Terry's computers, search his house. There'll be something.'

'You mean there *might* be something.'

'It's got to be worth a try.'

'And if there's nothing? If Stella's just stirring up trouble? The papers are already all over this one, Theresa. You know what it'll be like. A sniff that we're considering Terry for the deaths will be enough to condemn him instantly.'

'He's guilty,' says Cooper. 'I talked to Stella and she's not making this up. At the very least, with Nicky still missing, we've got to try, haven't we?'

This last statement is the one that hits home for Harris. Theresa's right. They have to try.

The fact that the information is coming from Stella Flynn is still a problem. It wouldn't be the first time that an ex-partner has caused trouble by making baseless allegations. Harris has to persuade a magistrate to sign off on a search warrant. Usually, this is unforthcoming in the absence of any corroborating evidence.

'He was having an affair with Maddy.' Harris is talking to herself. 'Might be enough.'

'And there's a boy missing,' adds Cooper. 'No one likes being the jobsworth who gets someone killed.'

It's a good point.

'Let me talk to DCI Keane. Get a team together to go as soon as I confirm; nothing heavy, this is just information gathering. And keep it small. No uniforms, plain van. The fewer people who know we're looking at Peters, the better, at the moment. If he is involved we have to be ready to move quickly.'

Harris locks eyes with Cooper. 'If Peters does have Nicky and he gets wind that we're looking at him, it could put the boy in more danger.'

'What choice do we have?'

Harris sits down. 'Let me think this through.' She's quiet for a moment or two. Then she picks up her phone.

'We'll have to grab Peters at the same time,' she says, picking out a number on her phone. She looks up at Cooper as she puts it to her ear. 'DCI Keane's not going to like this.'

Fifty

Frank has had days as stressful as this before – the day of the vinegar incident springs to mind as a case in point – but so far Thursday is really shaping up to take the prize.

The Quinner investigation, two further lines of enquiry opening up after the interviews with Terry Peters and Ben Noone, and then being sandbagged by Searle and Moreleigh over tomorrow's press conference.

Oh, and he's almost forgotten being put on the toilet floor at Bean by the mystery Yank tourist.

So when he leaves the meeting with Superintendent Searle to find Harris, Cooper, Rimmer and Rose all clamouring for attention like a pack of hungry chicks, Frank's initial reaction isn't good.

'Later,' he says, after unloading a selection of his favourite expletives in Rose and Rimmer's direction. As the more junior of the four they cop it first. It's unfair, but Frank's just not in the mood for fairness. All he wants is to get a beer in front of him and forget about MIT for a few hours.

It's Harris who gives him the wake-up call. Almost pushing him into the privacy of one of the interview rooms she closes the door.

'On Sunday you told me straight not to let my personal life affect my work. Now I'm telling you the same. You may be a DCI but as a friend I'm telling you to shut the fuck up and listen to what we've got to say. Just because you're having a bad day doesn't mean you can opt out. Now, if you stop dicking about and start thinking, you'll see that this case is unravelling fast. If we act, *now*, instead of whingeing like a grounded teenager, we could make some real progress. Theresa and the others have fresh, proper information.

The case is breaking in front of you, Frank. Don't fuck it up by acting like a complete tit.'

Five minutes later all members of the MIT unit are in the briefing room. A chastened Frank – Harris being completely right about everything – is all business.

First up is Cooper. In a few short sentences she outlines the developments from Stella Flynn and the preparations she and Harris have made for gathering evidence from Terry Peters' house. The request for a search warrant is in with the magistrate and Harris is expecting an answer soon. She'd stressed the need for expediency in the emailed brief and followed it up with a call.

Frank scratches his head. 'You're right,' he says. 'Let's do it. Just as you've arranged, small team, no waiting. As soon as this meeting's over you go.' He looks at Harris. 'I think we might still be barking up the wrong tree with Terry but we can't take that chance. Get the search warrant. I'll deal with the fallout from Searle.'

Harris says nothing but Frank can tell she's happy with the outcome. For a fleeting second the unchivalrous thought occurs to him that Harris is manipulating the situation to harm him with Searle. He dismisses the idea as quickly as it arrives and turns to Ronnie Rimmer.

'Before we move on to Peters, let's hear your news, Ronaldo. You look like you're going to wet yourself.'

Rimmer's less assured than Theresa Cooper but he manages to give Frank the gist of what led him and Rose to Niall McCluskey.

'In his mouth?' Frank looks sceptical.

'That's what he says.' Rimmer jerks a thumb downwards. 'We've got him downstairs in case you need to talk to him. I think he was happy to be somewhere safe.'

'And he's saying that Noone did this? After Quinner asked him to play the heavy?'

'Not quite. He says they followed Noone, lost him, and then thought they'd picked him up. When McCluskey went down Oil Street he thought he was following Noone but couldn't swear to it.' Rimmer hesitates. 'He thinks he was tasered.'

Frank stands a little straighter. 'Oh?'

'Says he felt like he'd been punched in the chest but there's no markings on him. According to him, that is. I haven't checked yet. But he brought up the word.'

'Good,' says Frank. 'Very good. Is McCluskey willing to be examined by a doctor? There might be evidence of being tasered.'

'We'd have to put some pressure on,' says Rimmer. 'The feller's shitting himself. I'm not sure he'd give evidence against the guy he thinks cut his finger off.'

'Still . . .' says Frank.

'Yes, exactly,' says Rimmer.

It's Harris who speaks next.

'We've got to bring Noone in as well.'

To her surprise, it's Frank who's against it. The guy who's been pushing Noone as 'the one', isn't sure.

'We can't,' says Frank after a long pause. 'I want to, but we can't. On the face of it we have hearsay evidence against Peters and Noone, but the witness statement against Noone comes from a known criminal.'

'With a missing finger,' says Cooper.

'Agreed,' says Frank. 'Which can't be a coincidence. But with Noone being so heavily lawyered already, and with McCluskey being sketchy on the ID, I want to make sure we have something firm before we bring him in. The idea of this fucker sliding away again is giving me the heebie-jeebies. I'd like a little more before we move on Noone.'

Tread lightly.

The phrase slides into his head and Frank curses himself inwardly. Is this how it happens? How you start moving from being the copper to being the politician? For a moment he sees himself as the old Frank would have seen him: the spineless pole-climber making sure he can kick down.

Fuck it. It can't be helped.

He turns to Rimmer. 'Good work on this. We'll take in Peters and see what turns up. In the meantime I want Magsi and Flanagan to watch Noone overnight. You can get some officers back in to take over later; I'll square the overtime with upstairs.'

Frank looks at Cooper.

'That's all. Go and get Peters.'

Fifty-One

Noone's not driving his own car. Not this time. Since the killings last weekend he's already learned a lot and is determined not to make any more rookie errors.

He doesn't need to hot-wire anything. A street acquaintance in Madrid had told him the best way to get a car was this: you find a house in a middle-class neighbourhood that looks like it has several people living there who drive cars. If there's only one car on the path, knock. Carry a clipboard or a file, something that looks like you might have a reason to call. If there's someone in, make some bullshit excuse about a charity or sales and move on. When you find a house that doesn't answer, break in and take the car keys. Most people leave them in the hallway or kitchen, somewhere they can get to them easy.

This is the second time Noone's tried it and it's worked exactly as described both times. After leaving Stanley Road with Eagles he gets a cab to Aigburth and nails a car second house he tries. On the way back into town he texts Terry Peters and finds that he's at The Pumphouse. In total it takes him less than an hour from leaving Stanley Road to arriving at the pub.

The interview with Keane had been interesting but, like a great shining neon sign flashing in front of his eyes, Noone came out with one thing on his mind: stop Terry.

Noone puts on a baseball cap and a pair of glasses. He's dressed in blacks and greys, nothing distinguishing his clothes from a thousand other people. In the pub he keeps his head down and avoids glancing round. He doesn't order anything and speaks only to Peters.

Terry's drunk and easy to persuade into the car. It's perfect.

'New?' he says as Noone pours him into the Mazda. 'Wouldn't have said this was your sort of car.'

Noone says nothing and Peters is asleep by the time they get to Seaforth. In the traffic, Noone reaches Birkdale by six-thirty. He turns the car into Sandwell Street and pulls into Terry Peters' driveway.

'Wake up.' Noone pushes Terry with the heel of his hand. Terry's too drunk to notice but Noone's already dehumanising him: keeping his sentences short, touching him only when absolutely necessary, not using his name. 'You're home.'

Terry wakes with a start. He blinks at Noone and then up at his house. Noone swivels his head around to check but the high hedge that runs across the front of Terry's house shields them from view.

Terry opens the door and steps out unsteadily. 'Thanks for the lift,' he says.

Noone gets out of the car. 'Let me help you.' He places one hand on Terry's arm and with the other he finds the taser in his pocket. 'Alicia home?'

Terry nods.

'Anyone else around? The kid?'

'No,' says Terry. 'Liam's staying with a friend for a few days.'

Terry's fumbling for his keys when Alicia opens the door. At the sight of Noone she smiles uncertainly.

'Alicia,' says Terry, 'this is Ben. A friend from the movie.'

Noone smiles, his best feature, and Alicia waves them inside.

'You're drunk,' she says to her husband, who is struggling to remove his jacket.

They're the last words she'll ever speak.

As Alicia turns, and with Peters temporarily helpless, Noone punches her hard in the face with his right hand. She smashes sickeningly into a small table with a vase of flowers on it and slides to the floor, a thick streak of red marking her progress down the wall. Terry Peters, his arms still in the sleeves of his jacket, can do no more than lurch to one side as, with his left hand, Noone takes out the taser.

Peters makes a sort of animal cry as Noone applies the taser to his exposed neck. The American presses the switch and Peters drops to the floor as if swatted by a giant hand. Noone steps closer and administers a second jolt. Peters twitches and then is still.

Behind him Alicia Peters, her jaw broken, moans. She makes a meaningless gesture with her left hand and attempts to crawl.

Noone notices with interest that he has an erection. He feels energised, not as euphoric as when he'd killed Paul and Maddy, but it's still a rush.

He takes three steps across the hall. Alicia Peters twists her neck and her eyes widen at the sight of Noone looming above her. Blood drips from her mouth. Noone places his feet either side of the injured woman, reaches down and touches the taser to the back of her neck. There's a small whimper from Alicia and then she too lies still.

Noone straightens up and checks his watch: six-thirty-five. He listens for any noise in the rest of the house. Terry might have been mistaken about the stepson, but there's nothing.

Satisfied he's alone, Noone checks his appearance in the hall mirror, dotted here and there with blood from the blow which broke Alicia's jaw. He straightens his collar and relaxes his shoulders. He pushes a strand of hair carefully back into position and lets out a long slow breath.

Checking that neither of the Peters is showing any signs of life, he turns and peers through the stained glass set into the front door. There's no one outside and the suburban street – what he can see of it at least – is deserted. Noone opens the door, taking care to leave it unlatched. He walks calmly down the three steps to the driveway and across the front of the house to the garage. The door slides up easily and Noone drives the stolen Mazda inside. He closes the garage door behind him and re-enters the house through the interior connecting door.

It takes him no more than three or four minutes to load Alicia and Terry into the Mazda. Terry, being the heavier, is more of a struggle, and Noone ends up just leaving him halfway in. It won't matter.

Back in the house Noone finds a kitchen store cupboard. He rattles through the various cleansers and bottles of bleach without finding what he's looking for. Irritated, he stands and checks his watch once more: six-forty-four. This is taking too long.

In the cellar that runs beneath the house Noone finds something he can use: a can of petrol for the lawnmower. He gives the red plastic container an exploratory shake and finds, to his satisfaction, that it's almost full. He unscrews the cap and fixes the flexible spout in place. He sprinkles petrol sparingly round the cellar and then heads back upstairs. He goes from room to room pouring the petrol over everything, making sure he covers each room. In Terry Peters' office he adds extra to the computers and filing cabinets.

Downstairs Noone goes back into the garage and spreads the last of the petrol over the occupants of the Mazda. He opens the petrol cap and returns to the kitchen, leaving the connecting door open. Noone opens all the gas jets on the stove. In the living room he does the same with the gas fire, taking care not to let it ignite. Happy that the room is filling with gas he walks down the hall with the petrol can, upending it on the rug. He checks the street one last time through the window. It's clear.

Noone tugs the visor down on his cap, replaces the glasses on his nose and winds a scarf he's taken from the Peters' bedroom wardrobe around his neck.

From inside his jacket he takes out a cigarette lighter. With the front door open, Noone flicks the lighter and a small flame appears. He touches it to the edge of the hall rug and watches as the petrol-soaked wool ignites. Noone makes sure it is fully alight before carefully closing the front door behind him. He walks calmly down the steps and out of the driveway without looking back.

As he reaches the end of Sandwell Street he hears the first window breaking. Twenty paces later as he crosses the road that heads west to the dunes, Noone hears a loud explosion behind him, followed rapidly by two more. An alarm goes off briefly before there is a fourth, much louder explosion that he can feel even from a distance of eighty metres. He looks back and sees a great plume of flame and smoke reaching high above the suburban rooftops. A tree in the adjacent garden to the Peters' place is on fire.

Someone starts screaming. Noone turns and continues towards the beach. He crosses the coast road and is in the dunes less than four minutes after starting the blaze.

He stops and listens but can hear nothing of the carnage he's left behind. The evening is a fine one and the only noise comes from

211

a couple of gulls wheeling over his head. The sea is too far out to be heard.

Noone loosens the scarf and drops it to the sand, then starts walking south towards Ainsdale, Formby and Liverpool beyond. After a few hundred metres Noone sheds his cap and his glasses and buries them in the sand. He takes off his jacket and tucks it under his arm. He rolls up the sleeves of his shirt, every inch the rambler on an evening stroll.

It's twenty kilometres from Birkdale to Crosby but Noone is in no hurry. The journey takes him just over four hours, almost all of it through the dunes. It's slower that way but he sees fewer people, and those he does see can be easily avoided. At Crosby he walks past the iron men on the beach as the last of the light fades before cutting across back roads to Waterloo train station. There he takes a train into Liverpool and arrives back at his flat on Old Hall Street by midnight.

Inside he showers, gets a cigarette and pours a glass of red wine. Naked, he stands looking out across the city lights, noting with detached interest that though he feels calm, the hand holding the glass is trembling with adrenaline. In the darkness of the room, the tip of his cigarette glows red as he replays the killings in his head.

Fifty-Two

The MIT meeting breaks just after six-fifteen.

Cooper, Harris and the officers she's detailed to do the evidence and seizure at Terry Peters' place stay behind for their final briefing. As discussed, it's a small team. A van is obtained from the pool and they go over the details of how the seizure's going to happen.

'I'm not expecting any trouble, here,' says Harris, 'but this is a murder case. We'll get a couple of armed response officers in attendance but they can travel separately and will not get out of the car unless needed. Theresa, you fix that, OK?'

Harris checks her watch and picks up a phone to chase the search warrant. At this time of day there's always the possibility that the request will slip through the bureaucratic cracks as someone heads home.

Cooper's on the phone to the armed response unit but has one ear to Harris's conversation.

Harris puts down the phone and smiles.

'Got it.'

The team grab what they need and assemble downstairs.

By six-fifty they are on their way to Birkdale in a plain white Transit. Behind them are two armed officers in a blue Ford.

Harris is looking out of the window at the flat farmland dividing Liverpool from Southport when the call comes in about the explosion in Sandwell Street.

'Is that us?' says Cooper.

'Put the lights on,' Harris tells the driver. 'Doesn't sound like there's much point in arriving quietly now.'

Both vehicles turn on their blues and get to Birkdale in less than ten minutes.

'Jesus,' whispers Cooper as they close in on Sandwell Street.

'It's a fucking war zone,' says Harris. The MIT team park on Trafalgar Road and approach Sandwell Street. There are already four fire trucks there and a number of ambulances and local police vehicles. The focal point of all the activity is number 18.

There's nothing left.

Where Terry Peters' house used to be is a smoking black hole. The houses to both sides are badly damaged and on fire. A large tree is alight in the front garden and the road and surrounding gardens are littered with broken bricks, glass, splintered wood and concrete. Fragments of household items are everywhere and the air is thick with the smell of burning. Slate roof tiles are embedded in flowerbeds and cars. There isn't a single unbroken window in any of the other properties in Sandwell Street. Three cars are on fire, one of them lying on its side. None of the MIT unit can see any casualties but that doesn't mean there won't be any. With this much destruction there has to be.

'Get back!' A fireman, bulky in his protective gear, waves the MIT team away.

Harris flashes her badge but the fireman doesn't look interested. 'Get back,' he repeats, flatly. 'Gas,' he adds, by way of explanation. 'There could be more explosions. A broken main, maybe.'

'I need to speak to your coordinator,' says Harris, ignoring the fireman's words. 'This wasn't a gas explosion. Not one that involved a faulty main, at any rate.'

'No?' says the fireman. 'You an explosive incident expert, are you, love?'

Harris steps in close and speaks so only the fireman can hear. 'In this case, yes. Now stop being a fucking dickhead and get me someone in charge. Now. We're not going any closer to the scene so you can relax on that score. This is important.'

Three minutes later, Harris is in deep discussion with the senior fire officer. They need to know that there's overwhelming evidence that this is a deliberately lit fire.

While Harris is talking, Cooper retreats to a relatively quiet spot in the gardens of a retirement home on Regent Road and calls Frank Keane.

'Is it Terry Peters' place?' Frank says as soon as he hears Cooper's voice.

'Yes. There's some damage to the neighbouring properties but it's number 18 that's gone.'

'Peters?'

'No sign,' says Cooper. 'I can't see a car outside if that's any indication.'

'Shit,' says Frank. For some reason he thinks that Searle will be blaming him for this. His next call will be to the superintendent. An incident of this size changes everything. McSkimming and his like will be descending on the scene already.

'What do you want us to do, sir?'

'Send the armed unit back. They're not going to be any use. Get DI Harris back here as well. You and the other two stay. I know there won't be much work you can do on the site itself for a while but get what you can in the way of information. Check the cab companies and trains. See if there's anything that pops up quickly. You never know, our man might have been sloppy.'

'Yes,' says Cooper. 'Sir?'

'Yes?'

'Who are we looking for? I mean, it might be a dumb question but do you think this was Terry? Or someone else?'

'I don't know, Theresa. Get what you can and work on the assumption this was Terry Peters' doing. It's the likeliest explanation.'

Frank rings off. If Terry Peters doesn't show up inside number 18 fried to a crisp then he'll retire. There's only one person who Frank believes is behind this.

Ben Noone.

Fifty-Three

Frank calls Charlie Searle at home with the news.

To his surprise, Searle is nothing but professional. There's no bleating about things that might have been done differently. If anything he's pleased that Frank's MIT were on their way to Sandwell Street before the explosion. No one could say they weren't on the right track.

'You must have been close, Frank,' says Searle. 'And this puts Peters right in the frame for the lot, doesn't it?'

This is where it was going to get tricky.

'It does look that way,' says Frank.

'*Look?*'

Frank takes a deep breath. 'I still think Noone is involved in this.'

'Noone?' Searle's voice is incredulous. 'Are you still barking up that tree, Frank?'

Frank hears Searle put his hand over the phone and speak to someone. When he comes back on, the superintendent's tone is markedly brisker.

'Have you any evidence to back that claim up? Anything?'

Frank outlines the story brought in by Rimmer. Almost as soon as he's finished, Searle is on him.

'That's it? You're telling me that this actor cut off this McCluskey's finger?'

'We're almost one hundred per cent.'

'Christ Almighty, Frank.' Searle sounds tired. It's worse than being patronised. 'Does McCluskey have form? Wait, don't tell me, I know he does.'

'He does, sir,' says Frank. 'But he has lost a finger. And he says Noone did it.'

'He says he *thinks* Noone *might* have done it. You told me he lost Noone in Oil Street. It could have been anyone.'

'Someone who just wanted to send a warning? I don't think so. I've got DC Magsi and DC Flanagan watching him.'

Frank hears a deep intake of breath at the other end of the phone. Then Searle starts talking.

'Listen, DCI Keane. And listen fucking properly, you fucking half-wit, because I'm not going to repeat myself. You've got sweet fuck-all on Noone, absolutely fucking nothing except a fucking bad case of amateur fucking sleuthing. You *know*? That's all you have? I'm not even going to comment on the load of old flannel coughed up by this fucking McCluskey wanker. While you're scurrying around chasing some fucking nonsense involving this fucking *actor* – God help us, an actor – there are serious fucking crimes taking place under your fucking nose. Half of fucking Southport is in fucking flames! You do know the fucking CC lives nearby? Christ knows what fucking Terry Peters has been up to. Investigate *that*. Get fucking Magsi and fucking Flanagan back where they're fucking needed instead of sitting on their fucking arses watching fucking actors. *Actors*. Jesus! I don't want the fucking CC to find out we responded to this incident with anything less than fucking nuclear weapons when something like this happens in his own fucking back garden. Got that? Say the fucking words, Frank.'

'Nuclear, sir.'

'That's it. Keep repeating that fucking mantra until it's dribbling out of your fucking nose. I'll be doing an early press conference at Canning Place tomorrow morning and you'll be there with fucking bells on doing exactly what I'm fucking telling you. There'll be no mention of anyone else in connection with this and we'll be proceeding with our enquiries on the assumption that Terry Peters is our man. Peters. If Peters isn't inside the house, then we're looking for him. I want you to get that information out to the general force. We're looking for Peters. Can you imagine the fallout if Peters turns up killing someone else and we're fucking chasing some fucking American clown because you've got some touchy-feely bollocks about him? Now, pull your fucking finger out your fucking arse and do the fucking job you're fucking paid to do.'

Searle hangs up, leaving Frank looking at the phone.

Fifty-Four

When Noone wakes on Friday morning a thought occurs to him that makes him laugh out loud.

He's a serial killer. More than one makes you a serial killer, right? Five is definitely serial killer.

None of it's been planned or anything – not properly planned – not like in the movies when some crazy lives in some shithole and has some sort of psycho kink. He just drifted into this thing after his mother died.

From that point it had almost been inevitable.

Noone lies back and tries to see if he feels any different and, after a few minutes' consideration, comes to the conclusion that, other than a pleasant sense of accomplishment, he doesn't. There are no regrets, that's for sure. In fact, if there's one thing he knows, it is that he's going to do this again. Fuck, it's too much of a goddam rush to let something like this go.

And there's a tickle of an idea working its way into his mind. Something that's been nagging at him like a half-remembered word is now taking form.

He'd been in Liverpool almost a year before he met Terry. It had happened just like he'd told that cop. The two of them had been at a bar and a girl Noone had been sleeping with introduced them. She'd been working on some piece of TV crap that Terry was the location manager for. Noone had sensed something in the guy right away. Something truly dark.

OK, Noone had to admit he hadn't known just how dark the sneaky fucker had been but it hadn't taken long to find out. Over the next few months, after Noone coming into his orbit, and with the drug intake increasing, Terry had given Noone an insight into what a genuine freak was like.

The man fucked anything that moved and managed to keep a lid on everything. He fucked girls from the movie, had a few women around the city. He'd go with men too. He was even, Terry revealed one night, fucking his sister-in-law. Felt bad about that one but the sex was terrific.

But even Noone had been brought up short when Terry Peters, stoned off his gourd on some high-grade skunk Danny Lomax had supplied, had let slip he had a thing going for young boys.

One of whom was his nephew.

Even now, Noone squirms at that memory. Had that really been him? It didn't seem possible really, looking back. But he'd done it. Noone doesn't even regard himself as bi. It was the repulsiveness of the thing that attracted him initially. Could he really do this? Become one of that tribe?

It turned out he could.

He and Terry began seeing Nicky together. The boy was already in the zone; Terry had seen to that, had been grooming him since he was ten.

And working on the movie, seeing Noone in the lead, had made the transition from idol to lover a smooth one.

It wasn't like the boy was a child. He was sixteen. Legal. Terry Peters might have been a fucking paedophile but Ben Noone wasn't. Noone's rationalisation was enough for him to try it.

Then, on Friday night, he'd given Nicky and Terry a lift home. The boy's parents were out until two, Nicky had said.

They'd have the place to themselves.

Had he thought it might end with a killing at that point?

He must have done, at some level, he supposed, even allowing for the fact that Noone doesn't believe in any of that psychobabble. He'd had the taser with him. He could have gone to River Towers with Terry and Nicky with zero chance of being disturbed. He could have locked the doors at Burlington Road, taken more care, done a thousand things differently, but he hadn't and he'd killed that family and then killed Dean and Terry and Alicia.

And he'd gotten away with it, just like he'd gotten away with everything else in his entire life.

This felt like a beginning.

Fifty-Five

Terry and Alicia Peters had been in the house.

The theory that Charlie Searle is busy selling to the assembled press in room 21b at Canning Place is easy to understand. Hedged by all the usual phrases used in these situations, the message was clear: Peters had most likely killed himself and his wife after realising he was going to be outed as a child molester and killer. Needless to say, Searle wasn't actually saying the words but, by gesture and silence, makes it clear to the pack that that is what had happened.

Frank tries not to say anything. It's safer that way. McSkimming's near the front and he's looking at Frank.

'Do you believe that Terry Peters was responsible for the deaths of Paul and Maddy Peters?' says McSkimming. He's looking at Frank but it's Charlie Searle who answers.

Searle oozes sincerity. For all Frank knows, he is being sincere.

'We think that's a possibility, yes,' he says. 'But we will be considering all avenues of enquiry. At the moment the evidence does seem to be pointing in a certain direction.' He pauses. 'In domestic cases such as this terrible tragedy it is often found that the perpetrator is closer to home than we imagine.'

'Is it true that police are investigating allegations of child abuse related to this case?' This is from McSkimming again. His face betrays nothing about his paper planning to run Alicia Peters' story pointing the finger at Nicky. In an instant, Nicky is back, painted as victim this time. Another unapologetic tabloid flip-flop.

'We can't comment on ongoing investigations in any way that could influence the outcome,' Searle intones. 'But it is an area we will be examining.'

221

'Are you in contact with Operation Vector?' asks a journo from the *Mail*. He's referring to a high-profile anti-paedophile operation run by the Serious Organised Crime Agency in London that has had success identifying predatory abusers.

'We are aware of Operation Vector,' says Searle. Before the *Mail* journalist can follow up with another question, McSkimming tries again.

'Is Terry Peters one of the names on a list of suspects and, if so, why wasn't this information acted upon earlier?'

Searle pauses and Frank glances in his direction. McSkimming clearly has some inside information. The details of Terry Peters being on the Operation Vector radar have only just come in. Frank hasn't even had time to digest the intelligence.

'It's been confirmed that Terry Peters' name was on Operation Vector's lists, but not, so far, as a suspect. His computer ID had been flagged as a potential line of investigation, although it had only been graded as a level three investigative route, level four being the lowest. He'd have been investigated but not as a priority. Our best information did not identify Peters as dangerous. In hindsight, clearly that information appears to have been incorrect, but we simply do not have the resources to investigate all potential suspects identified by Vector. At the last count there were in excess of eighteen thousand names on the list.'

Searle talks calmly and clearly. He's selling the line to the press. Peters is your man. He's the killer.

McSkimming looks happy enough. Child molesters sell papers. Especially ones with a tenuous link to Hollywood.

Nobody mentions Ben Noone.

Fifty-Six

The next week goes past too fast for Frank's liking.

While a convincing case is being built nailing Terry Peters as the killer – with a succession of witnesses coming forward to give evidence of his sexual duplicity and appetites – Frank is getting nowhere with his solo mission to get evidence against Noone. Even when Damo Smith, one of the hardest of the hard men at the boxing club, talks to Frank one night after his work-out, it's more evidence against Terry Peters. Ordinarily, Smith, who fronts the controlling agency behind most of the city's nightclub doormen – and therefore the front-line drug trade – wouldn't speak to Frank. But this is different. Nobody likes a paedophile.

'Peters is a fucking kiddie-fiddler,' says Smith. 'Nothing you can take into court, but Danny Lomax let something slip about Peters asking him about some muscle-relaxant drug. The cunt tried to tell Danny it was for some woman but Danny said he knew it was iffy. Told me he'd seen something between Peters and the boy one night in the bogs at Maxie's. Like if he'd been there two seconds earlier he'd have seen them at it. Said he didn't have anything to do with Peters after that.'

That's it from Smith. All of it pointing to Terry Peters.

Frank had had hopes about the CCTV footage from the night of the first killings, but it's inconclusive. A car that may have been Noone's can be seen in the appropriate locations, picked up by traffic cameras and the odd security camera, but nothing is concrete. No numberplate, no face ID. The CCTV footage from River Towers, along with any key card records, has proven to be useless. No images of any kind have been saved and the electronic data storage system which could identify the entrance and exit times of residents wasn't working that night.

There's nothing from the forensics. Going out on a limb, Frank raided the MIT coffers and sprang for a rush analysis of the key evidence from the initial crime scene. There had been no semen. None of what little forensic evidence there was could be connected to Noone. Eagles had even supplied independently witnessed DNA material from the American – 'as a goodwill gesture' – to the investigation.

Nothing.

DC Rose's examination of Nicky's computer has been thorough. There are no references to Noone. No incriminating images. No diary entries.

Nothing.

Niall McCluskey's missing finger had been found, wedged in the grating of a kerbside drainage grid. It backed up McCluskey's story but only in that it confirmed where he'd lost the digit. Frank had had the area gone over by a team looking for something to connect it to Noone but they'd come up short again.

No new witnesses connecting the American to the case.

No new leads.

No forensics.

Nothing.

And he's not getting any support from MIT.

Frank strongly suspects that Harris and Cooper have lost any enthusiasm for Noone as a player in this, along with every single member of the MIT unit. And most of them had none to begin with.

Even Frank is starting to lose the concrete certainty he had back in the interview room.

One Tuesday Frank gets a call unrelated to the case. Jesus is dead. Heart attack at the gym.

The funeral is a proper Liverpool one. Tears and flowers and then, later, drinking and swearing and laughter. The ceremony and burial are in Litherland and afterwards everyone squeezes into Jesus's spotless little red-brick at the top of Guion Road. The last time Frank had been there, as a teenager, the house was overshadowed by the hulking oil refinery at the top of the dead end. Frank can remember the contrast between Jesus's flowerbeds – filled with a riot of clashing colour – and the rusting black metal monster looming over the roof. The refinery's gone now, the land cleared for something else.

Frank spends time in the kitchen mostly, helping Jesus's wife, Val, wash up. Val cleans furiously, washing and talking and drinking whisky as a stream of wellwishers come and pay homage. Every second person tries to wrestle the dishwashing sponge from Val but she's having none of it, reserving her most venomous retorts for the most concerned enquiries.

'Let me do that, Val; come on, girl, put your feet up.'

'Fuck off. You'd only get it wrong.'

Some of the funeral guests eye Frank warily. There are people here he's put inside in the past. Some dangerous players too. Only his proximity to the widow keeps the drunker ones at bay as the afternoon progresses.

'I always knew he'd go like that, the stupid fat fucker,' says Val. She attacks a chocolate-smeared plate with venom. Frank knows that Val fed Jesus an uninterrupted diet of chips and pies and white bread for the whole of their long marriage.

And: 'Imagine dying of a heart attack at the gym. I thought you were supposed to fucken get fit at them places?'

As far as Frank's aware, Val's never been to Jesus's gym once. He wonders what will happen to it now.

Around three, Frank hangs up the towel.

'I've got to go back to work, Val.'

Val breaks off and wraps her arms around Frank. She smells of whisky, strong perfume and cigarettes. 'Make sure you eat more,' she says. 'There's not a fucken pick on you. You're skinnier than a Chinaman's knob.'

'I thought you said Jesus was too fat?'

'Don't be fucken cheeky.' Val plants a wet kiss on Frank's cheek and holds him close. 'Go on, see you, Frankie. Next time it'll be my funeral.'

'Or mine.'

A woman comes in with another stack of plates and Val resumes her duties. 'Fuck off then,' she says, her back to Frank.

He weaves his way out of the house and goes back to Stanley Road because he doesn't know where else to go. He spends an hour shuffling paper and staring out of the window. Frank hadn't given Jesus much thought until he died. Now it feels like an unexpected hole in the road has opened up in front of him.

Eagles, Noone's lawyer, calls just as Frank's considering getting drunk. The lawyer tells Frank that Noone's going back to the US tomorrow.

'He will, of course, be available for any further witness statements.'

Frank hangs up without saying another word and looks at his watch. It's late. Too late to be here, that's for sure. He looks across the almost deserted MIT office to where Harris is typing. Frank catches her eye and she mimes lifting a glass to her mouth.

'It's Thursday,' says Harris.

Frank could kiss her.

'Did you ever consider you just might be wrong, Frank?' Harris says as the two of them are walking towards the Albert Dock. Parking's easy there and Frank can always leave his car if he's had a few. The rest of MIT are at The Phil but neither Frank nor Harris feels like going. She doesn't talk about the funeral.

'I think I might be.'

Harris looks at him. 'Seriously?'

Frank nods. 'Could be.'

'Wow. This could be a first.'

'I didn't say I *was* wrong,' says Frank. 'I said I could be.' He opens the door to the pub. Inside they get their drinks at the bar and find a seat. The place is busy with drinkers but most of them prefer to stand.

'Cheers,' says Harris and clinks her G & T against Frank's beer.

For a while they just sit quietly and drink. Eventually Harris asks how the funeral was and Frank tells her about Val Penaquele and the washing-up.

'You hear much from Julie lately?' says Harris. The pub as always is neutral territory. Here Keane and Harris are Frank and Emily.

'Mm,' says Frank. 'Yes. She's OK. I spoke to her yesterday.' He looks up at Harris. 'She was fine. Worried about me. And she'd been watching the news.'

'Had you told her your theories?'

'No. But she must have known something was wrong. I'd say it was intuition but you'd probably kick me.'

'Why don't we leave it as sensitivity and that way I can keep my feet on the ground? Maybe Julie just knows you well.'

Frank lets it go. A teenager comes to the table and collects some empties. The boy is around Nicky's age.

'You still think I'm wrong about Noone, don't you?' says Frank after he's gone.

Harris sucks her lower lip. 'On balance, yes. I think you got a feel about him. Maybe he's naughty on some level, I don't know. But I think you might be wrong about him being connected to the case. There's not much we can make stick, is there?'

Frank's thinking about the encounter in the toilets at Bean.

'He has been untouchable, hasn't he?'

'Because he's not guilty?'

'Well, maybe.'

Frank looks round the pub. He spots a couple of people he'd rather not see. A perennial policeman's problem. Harris is looking at him.

'You want to go?'

'Not really,' says Frank. 'We were here first.'

Harris puts a hand on his arm. That's not what she means. 'Your flat's just down the road,' she says. Frank could fall into those brown eyes if he let himself. 'You want to go there?'

Frank looks at his drink. 'But we're not drunk.'

Harris stands up. 'That's one of the reasons I'd like to go.'

It's better the second time.

Richer somehow.

They shower and get into Frank's bed.

This time there's no booze and no weed and, while Em's love-making is intense, there's no repeat of the pain and game-playing. It's different and Frank feels something give.

Afterwards they do talk, freely for once, about Julie and Linda, and about how things aren't simple. They talk about the disconnection between the person they are and the labels used to describe them. Cop. Lesbian. Married. Frank talks about the funeral. Nothing gets resolved but that feels OK too. There's something about the mood they're in, about the experiences they've gone through, that make anything feel rich in possibilities. Frank can't speak for Em but he hasn't had enough of those times in his life. The feelings that people have, and the things they say to one another at times like this, are inevitably clichés. Frank couldn't care less. I don't want this to stop, he thinks.

Fifty-Seven

From the bedroom Frank hears the vibration of his phone. One ring only – a message or an email notification. He checks his watch. It's just after two and Em's lying next to him. He doesn't need to answer the message but he wouldn't mind a cup of tea.

Careful not to disturb Em, Frank eases out of bed and pulls a pair of shorts on. He pads into the living room rubbing his face, tired but with a looseness in his shoulders that hasn't been there for a long time. This thing with Em, he doesn't know what it is or where it might go, but he likes it.

He closes the bedroom door and switches a lamp on next to the sofa. Sitting down, he picks up his phone and opens the message. It's an email notification from his public MIT account: the address he has on the card he leaves with witnesses and other officers. The address and card are new and seldom used. Until this message he hadn't even known the system pushed the notifications his way.

Frank leaves the phone on the table and puts the kettle on. As the water begins to hiss he sits down and accesses his MIT email account on his laptop.

The email is from an address with a long list of letters and numbers and has one word in the subject line: *Exeunt.*

The message is a single line: *When the players are all dead, there needs none to be blamed.*

Frank looks at it blankly. Seriously? He thought this nonsense only took place in the pages of crime fiction. He closes the laptop and leans back on the sofa, his eyes closed. It can wait until morning.

He knows it won't.

At the click of the kettle switching off, Frank gets up and makes a cup of tea. By the time he's back on the couch he's more alert.

Players.

Frank flips open the computer and looks at the email again. He opens Google and types the line into the search box.

The first answer that comes up tells him it's Shakespeare. *A Midsummer Night's Dream.*

The line's spoken by Theseus.

Frank's wide awake now.

Noone sent the email. It's as clear to Frank as if Noone were there speaking to him directly. Who else beside an actor would quote Shakespeare?

Frank looks at the email address. He'll get Rose and the computer forensics onto it in the morning, but he's willing to bet he'll draw a blank. Then he remembers that Steve Rose is pulling an all-nighter. Worth a shot.

Frank calls Stanley Road and gets put through.

'DC Rose,' says Frank, keeping his voice low.

'Boss.' Rose can't keep the surprise from his voice. 'Working late?'

'Something like that. Listen, can you see if you can trace this email address for me?'

Frank reads out the sequence of letters and numbers, Rose repeating them as he speaks.

'Give me a call when you've had a chance to take a look,' Frank says. 'I don't think there's any rush –'

He stops as Rose interrupts. 'I don't need to look it up,' he says. 'I know whose address that is. It's a Hotmail account used by Terry Peters. Seen it so often over the past week I know it off by heart.'

Frank doesn't say anything.

'Boss?'

'Yeah, OK, Steve, ta. Just something that was nagging at me. You're sure it's Peters' email?'

'Just checked, DCI Keane. It's his. That's the email most commonly used from his phone.'

'Thanks, Steve.' Frank hangs up.

Terry Peters has been dead a little more than a week.

Frank considers waking Em but thinks better of it. Instead he Googles 'Theseus'.

When the first Wikipedia page loads, Frank knows what this is about. As he reads the myth of Theseus descending into the labyrinth he knows what the email's telling him.

Nicky's in the tunnels.

Fifty-Eight

It was risky keeping hold of Terry's phone but there's no denying that it had been worth it. Just thinking about the look on Frank Keane's face as he read that bullshit message makes Noone smile.

This is the fun part. Like a movie but better because it's for real.

Noone taps some keys in New York and moves the pawns around the board in Liverpool.

He's at JFK waiting for a JetBlue connecting flight to Los Angeles and the airport's still busy with commuter traffic. Once he's sent the text to Keane, Noone carefully deletes all numbers and messages on Terry's phone and takes it into the bathroom. In a stall he places the phone under a wad of toilet paper and puts the weight of his heel on it. He wraps the pieces in the toilet paper and flushes what he can down the pan. The rest he puts into the washroom trashcan, making sure the pieces are pushed down deep.

The text should do the trick. What's the point of a performance if nobody knows it was you up there on stage? If Keane's as smart as Noone thinks he might be, then this will be enough. It doesn't occur to Noone for a second that Keane will ever be in a position to pin this thing on him.

Nothing sticks to Ben Noone. Nothing.

The whole episode on the other side of the Atlantic is already taking on the feel of a fairy tale. A spectacularly grim one, but still a fairy tale. Here, surrounded by the absolute concrete reality of America, even the idea of Liverpool seems ridiculous somehow. The messy killings belong to somebody else, a Noone trying on clothes for size. Noone's always had this capacity to separate the events in his life into neat bundles. He's pleased to see that he's not experiencing any of those post-event psychological meltdowns. If anything he's sleeping better. Fuck that *Macbeth* shit.

And he's full of ideas.

The killings have sparked off something that – now it's been dragged into the open – has been squatting at the back of his mind since his mother died. Since he found out.

It had only been the fear of taking that final step; he can see that clearly now. All the thefts, the sex games, the crap he'd been filling up the space inside with, had been swept away that night in Nicky's house.

The thing with Terry and Nicky hadn't been planned, although Noone knew the moment he bought the taser – a spontaneous decision – he was going to kill somebody. There are things he did during the killings which he was proud of in the immediate aftermath – planting the e-receipt at Burlington Road, muddying the car plates, keeping himself out of the forensics – but here in New York some of those 'clever' touches are starting to seem like the work of an amateur. The receipt, thank Christ, was charged against a PayPal account a long-departed druggie girlfriend had set up in Berlin. The girl had died – an overdose, nothing to do with Noone – and he'd used the account from time to time. This was just as well since it's obvious that with a taser being used in the killings, Frank Keane would have gone over the receipt in depth. If there'd been any link back to himself, Noone would have heard by now. But it had still been a dumb risk.

That is something that is going to change.

Noone looks at his watch. He still has more than an hour before his plane leaves. He leans back on the airport bench and goes over the killings – the first ones – in his mind.

It's Friday after the end of the third week's filming and they're all at Maxie's. They're down in the tunnels again next week and Noone's already bored out of his mind with the movie. Filming is nowhere near as much fun as he'd hoped. All that waiting around. Everyone impressed because he can act. Like it's hard.

The plain truth is that he's been acting all his life. Other than when having sex, or asleep, Noone can't recall a time when he hasn't, even for a moment, not been playing a role of one sort or another.

Child. That was one.

Isolated teen. He'd tried that for a while and then discarded emo angst for a country club tan and popularity. In his travelling twenties he'd found a skin he could live with, for a while at least, and then that too had come to a halt with the death of his mother and the secrets that had spilled out.

At the club they did some coke that Lomax had come in with. New stuff. It had been Nicky's first time and it had given the kid a serious jolt. It was fun watching him until that Aussie fuck of a barman had been giving them a hard stare and Terry got worried the guy might get an attack of conscience. Noone remembers thinking about making the barman the first one but the guy looked like he could handle himself.

Instead they leave early, in Noone's car, Lomax having already gone elsewhere. Nicky's parents are out late and he's supposed to be staying at Uncle Terry's. They'll have the place to themselves for a few hours. Terry's keen to take some photos of the fun but Noone's not going to let that happen.

He's got the taser in his pocket. Along with the receipt. A psychiatrist would say Noone knew then what was going to happen. They could go to Noone's flat but they choose to go to Southport. Did he know then? Noone's not sure. He could make the case that Nicky and Terry live in Southport so it's easier for them to go north, but when was the last time Ben Noone did someone a favour?

Nicky's talking fast in the car. Total shit coming out of his mouth. Terry's in the back leaning forward and stroking the boy's hair from time to time. Nicky doesn't mind but Noone notices he inclines his head away from Terry's palm more than once. There's an electric crackle in the atmosphere, a sense that this unfolding story is building to a climax. Noone remembers them in the car, the feeling of it all, the summer night sky still holding on to the light, the mostly empty coast road between the dunes, and his own black desires.

By the time they reach Birkdale around ten-thirty, Noone's made up his mind.

Whatever happens, he's going to kill someone tonight. He has to.

'Nice place,' says Noone as they pull up in front of Nicky's house.

He sees the dead end of the street up ahead.

Handy.

There are lights on in the house. It looks warm, inviting. A family home. Noone can feel it building in him, his blood rushing around his body. He'll kill Terry and Nicky. Later, once they've had fun. Set it up like a murder-suicide – Terry, the evil uncle, kills himself in a fit of remorse – and leave the bodies for Nicky's parents to find. If he's careful he can avoid leaving traces of himself. Once Terry's tastes come out the case would be closed.

Yes, it'll work.

Jesus, he's horny. The thought of what he's going to do afterwards gives Noone a desire beyond anything he'd experienced before. Inside, time passes, Noone's anticipation building.

More coke and they're naked in Nicky's room. Noone does some things but, to his surprise after the throbbing arousal, his heart's not in it. This isn't him. And he's conscious of where his hands have been, of leaving prints, DNA, hair.

He leaves Terry and Nicky and heads for the bathroom. Soon, soon. Maybe now.

He's in the bathroom when he senses the change in the house. There are footsteps on the stairs and voices.

'Nicky?' A woman's voice.

'Quiet, Mads. He must be asleep.' The man's voice is slurred.

The parents back home early.

Noone changes his plans.

Fifty-Nine

Frank dresses quickly and quietly in tracksuit and trainers. Even so, it's enough to wake Em, who wanders into the living room just as Frank finishes tying his shoes. She's naked, rubbing sleep from her eyes, and as Frank looks up he catches his breath. This woman is something else.

'What's going on?' Her voice is lazy, unguarded, before she's had a chance to bolt on her street armour. Frank wants to hear more of it and is stricken by the thought that this might be the last time he ever hears her – or sees her – like this. Suddenly his early morning plan feels like the most ridiculous nonsense.

Being Frank, that won't change what he's going to do. Now it's in his head it has to be checked.

He stands and holds her and kisses her softly. He thinks about telling her what he's doing but doesn't. If this is wrong he wants it to be kept quiet. His obsession with all things Noone means Frank has no choice, at least to his way of thinking.

'I can't sleep,' he says. 'I'll go for a run.'

She makes a face. 'Really?' Frank gets the feeling that if Em were more fully awake her cop senses would pick holes in his excuse in an instant. As it is, she looks confused.

'Can you be here when I get back?' says Frank. She hesitates for a split second.

'Please?' It's not a word he uses often. 'I'd like you to be.'

Em nods and wanders back into the bedroom. Frank watches her go.

With an effort he leaves.

It's cold out and he jogs across to the Albert Dock where he'd left the car last night. He turns the key in the ignition and heads up through the mostly empty city towards the Williamson tunnels. There's light just coming into the sky as Frank pulls up opposite the police station in Smithdown Road. At least the car will be safe. Probably.

Frank lifts a torch from the boot, locks the car and walks to the entrance to the Tunnels Heritage Centre. He turns into the cobbled yard and hesitates. He should be doing this properly but the idea of going back in to persuade Searle to pay for it is too much to contemplate. At least this way he can live with himself.

The door to the centre is locked. Frank lifts a small black case from his pocket and takes out a set of picks. He's very rusty so it takes almost ten minutes to slip the lock.

Frank steps through and closes the door behind him.

He's in.

Sixty

When his flight is called, Noone's thinking about the moment when he heard Nicky's parents in the house.

Until then, he realises now, despite his bravado about killing Nicky and Terry, he could still have gone either way. The moment Paul and Maddy Peters arrive home early, the course of events is set as decisively as someone pushing him off the edge of a cliff.

There is no going back.

He recalls clearly the gut-punch electric shock of hearing voices and movement outside the bathroom, and the thrilling realisation of the unalterable, immutable course of action they have set in motion. He is going to kill. It's been coming all night. It's been coming all his life.

In the tiled bathroom his own shallow breathing seems loud and he forces himself to be calm. It's a clear night outside but Noone could swear he can hear the rumble of a storm building in the distance. His nerve endings are primed and his senses wide open.

He cracks the door and sees two people paused outside Nicky's room. There's a whispered conference going on and then Nicky's parents move away towards their own bedroom.

As soon as they are out of sight, Noone darts across the landing to where his jacket is draped over the banister rail of the stairs. Neither of Nicky's parents seems to have noticed it, perhaps assuming it belongs to their son. Naked, Noone fumbles for the taser, which sticks momentarily in the pocket, caught in a fold of fabric.

Motherfucker! Come on!

There are sounds from the main bedroom. He'll be caught. There'll be a fight. *It won't be as he wants it to be!*

Then, just as panic starts to clutch him, the stubborn taser jerks free. His heart pounding, Noone slips silently into Nicky's room.

Neither the boy nor Terry has heard a thing. Both look up as Noone comes in and Terry's got that lazy post-coital grin on his face. Nicky looks fucking gone, his white face coated in a sheen of coke sweat, his carefully tended black hair wild. He's too young to be doing this. Terry's beyond hope but Noone feels a flicker of shame at his part in the teenager's dissolution. He feels unclean and Noone feels a powerful surge of anger towards Terry Peters.

Something of his thoughts must be showing on his face because Terry speaks. 'What's up?' he says. His eyes stray to the taser in Noone's hand.

And then it happens. Behind Noone the door to Nicky's room opens again and Nicky's father steps inside.

As he struggles to take in the scene in front of him, the man physically recoils.

'What?' he manages to say. He looks at Noone and then back towards Terry and Nicky, naked on the bed, his eyes wide, his face stricken. '*Terry?*'

Terry tries to say something but he looks like he's going to be sick.

Noone takes two steps forward and tasers Paul Peters in the chest.

The connection isn't perfect, but it's enough to send him jerking onto the floor, confused, disoriented. Convulsing, his eyes lock on Noone and he opens his mouth.

'Dad!' yells Nicky. Noone bends down and tasers him again, this time in the neck. Peters flings his head backwards, hitting the carpet hard. Noone thinks the man might be dead. If he isn't then he won't be waking up any time soon. The jolts he'd taken are extreme.

Now the boy stumbles up from the bed and lurches towards Noone. Although furious, he's slow and uncoordinated and much smaller than the American. Noone steps back and, stiff-armed, lets Nicky run onto the taser. Nicky twitches and gives a short yelp before folding. He drops beside his father.

'For fuck's sake, Ben!' says Terry. He's still sitting in bed, holding the duvet to his chin like a Victorian chambermaid. Noone ignores him. There's no time for him now.

From outside, there's movement. 'Get dressed,' Noone says to Terry and opens the door. To his right, three or four paces from him, is Maddy Peters, naked except for her bra, standing uncertainly in the frame of her bedroom door. She looks at Noone, fear and shock etched on her face, and makes a small sound as, naked too, he walks towards her.

His face is friendly. *Don't worry, this can all be explained.*

'It's OK, Mrs Peters,' he says. 'I'm a friend of Nicky's. I know what this must look like.'

In the bedroom she freezes as Noone comes through the door. Noone notices that she isn't covering up her nakedness. She knows this is bad, he thinks. Him seeing her like this isn't her main concern. At some level, she understands things have moved beyond that.

'Nicky,' she says, her voice quavering. 'Where's Nicky? Paul?' She looks past Noone's shoulder towards the open door. 'Paul!' she calls, her voice just hovering below a shout.

Behind Noone, Terry appears at the bedroom door. 'Terry?' says Maddy. Her voice forms the name as if it's a foreign word. She looks at him, trying to make sense of something that can't make sense. 'What's happened? What's going on?'

'Mads,' says Terry. 'I . . .'

'Nicky's fine,' says Noone, interrupting. He holds the taser behind him and sees Maddy Peters' eyes dart in that direction.

The house is detached but that doesn't mean he wants her screaming.

And then she *is* screaming, and Noone hurls himself at her. He punches her hard, catching her high on the temple. Maddy Peters groans and flops backwards onto the bed.

'No!' yelps Terry Peters. He darts forward but stops without doing anything. 'Christ Almighty, Ben!'

'Shut the fuck up!' Noone puts the taser to Maddy Peters' neck. She twitches spastically and then is still. He keeps the taser applied longer than he needs to, until he's certain that the woman is dead, or close to. Terry Peters drops into a ball and begins moaning, his hands beside his head.

Noone stands panting at the side of the bed. His heart is banging but he can't tell if it's the effort, the adrenaline or the coke. All three, most likely. After a moment he moves to the bay window and peeks through the curtains.

The street outside shows no signs of life. The houses are detached, sprawling Victorian mansions with solid walls and double-glazed windows. No one's heard a thing.

'Get up,' he tells Terry.

He considers killing the useless bastard but the thought of dealing with all of this at once is beginning to overwhelm him. He feels tired and his mind, quick and sharp in the previous few adrenaline-fuelled minutes, is slowing down. This has all got to be taken care of and, for now, he needs Terry.

Terry is still curled up on the floor. Noone pulls his head up by the hair and slaps him hard across the face.

'Get moving!' He slaps Terry again but now he stands. The two naked men face each other, breathing hard. Terry looks beaten.

Noone gets Terry's clothes from Nicky's bedroom. Nicky and Paul Peters lie on the floor. Nicky has an arm draped over his father's chest. One last embrace.

Noone returns to the main bedroom and guides Terry into his clothes. He leaves his own off. It'll be easier later, when it gets messy.

'We've got to get rid of them all,' says Noone. 'You know that, right?'

Noone doesn't believe in hell but Terry Peters' face is a snapshot of what it would be like.

'I'll take Nicky somewhere.' Peters' voice is thick. 'We can . . .'

'Go,' says Noone. 'Take him somewhere.' He wants Peters out of the house. They can deal with Nicky later. He can deal with Terry later. He has no energy spare to argue with Terry about what should happen with Nicky. A vision of what needs to be done *right now* is coming into focus. Noone feels a little dizzy and sits on the edge of the bed for a few moments, trying to think clearly. It's hard.

'Ben?' says Terry Peters. 'Not Nicky. He's just a kid, man.'

'Didn't stop you fucking him, did it, Terry?' *Jesus*. 'Bit late for a conscience now.'

Noone stands. Someone's got to get this thing done.

'This is what we do.'

241

In the hallway the keys to the family cars are sitting in a glass bowl on a side table. The two of them get the unconscious boy into the boot of the BMW in the garage. In darkness they open the garage door.

'Get rid of him,' says Noone and Terry drives away.

Once he's gone Noone finds that everything becomes simpler. Hanging on a peg on the garage wall are a pair of overalls. Noone gets an image of the dentist working on household jobs at the weekend. He slips the overalls on and opens the garage door again. After a quick glance up and down the street, Noone walks out to his car and drives it into the garage. Then, staying in the black shadow of the hedge, he goes into the garden and picks up two handfuls of damp earth. Back in the garage he places the dirt on the concrete floor and closes the door. Thanks to a thick bank of vegetation that circles the garden, Noone's confident that no one has observed anything.

In the garage Noone takes the earth from the floor and smears it across both numberplates on his own car. The numbers are just about readable but in dim light, or on CCTV, they won't be.

He feels pleased with himself for thinking this way.

Back in the house, he spends five full minutes wandering around quietly, just getting the lie of the land. It's almost half-past-twelve and the only sound he can hear is the soft ticking of a clock.

He sits down in an armchair and waits another ten minutes, thinking things through. If any of the neighbours had heard anything they'd have shrugged it off by now. He's broken into houses before and quickly discovered that panic is the most dangerous element. You can achieve a lot by simply waiting.

And there's something else. He wants to savour the moment. He was right: tonight had turned out to be the night.

Seeing the log burner he strips off the overalls and stuffs them inside. He lights a fire and watches the overalls burn. Noone turns the lever to cut the oxygen and lets the fire die down.

In the kitchen he finds some rags and cleaning products and a pair of bright yellow rubber gloves. He puts on the rubber gloves, returns to Nicky's bedroom and slowly, methodically wipes every trace of himself from the room. Noone collects and folds his clothes and places them in the bathroom. He takes the taser receipt from his pocket.

Back in Nicky's room Noone puts the receipt in a drawer under a pile of Nicky's crap. He checks Paul Peters for a pulse but can't feel anything. Hooking his hands under the man's armpits he drags him out of the bedroom. On the stairs he lets gravity slide Peters down, holding him enough to prevent too much noise.

He gets Peters into the garage and places him on the smooth cement floor.

It takes him almost ten more minutes to locate a rope. He eventually finds a length of what looks like clothes line in a room in the cellar. The rope is good quality, still inside a plastic wrapper.

Noone takes a wooden chair from the kitchen and brings it to the garage with the rope. He places it under one of the girders which form the support for the angled roof and loops a section of rope over it. It takes him several attempts to make a noose but eventually it's there. Satisfied, he drags the man to the centre of the garage underneath the noose. A ticking noise from the engine of his car is the only sound.

Noone places the noose around Paul Peters' neck and tightens it. He drags him into a sitting position on the wooden chair and hauls on the rope. The girder creaks gently as Peters is lifted by the neck upwards. When his feet are six inches above the cement floor, Noone ties the rope in position and steps back. He's sweating with the effort now but his mind feels as calm and collected as he can ever recall. It's as if the situation is evolving in front of his eyes and he is simply a part of that process.

Noone strips the hanging man and balls up his clothes. He places the chair back against the wall. It's only later he'll come to realise that's a small mistake.

Noone checks his watch and waits ten minutes in the darkened garage just to make certain the guy's dead. It's peaceful in there and Noone feels an unaccustomed sense of privilege and gratitude.

You're my first.

Noone doesn't know if he's spoken the words aloud but he thinks he may have done. He tries to gain a sense of the import of the moment but it's just time passing as always. He takes hold of the dead man's penis. He doesn't know why. This is new to him. He doesn't know how killers behave. Holding the cock in the rubber glove feels strange.

After a moment, Noone lets go and picks up the dentist's clothing before moving towards the kitchen a changed man. A virgin no longer.

In the kitchen, Noone selects a large knife from the woodblock stack on the countertop. He feels the weight of it and heads upstairs to the bedroom, the dead man's clothes under his arm.

Upstairs everything is exactly as he left it.

On the bed, to his surprise, Maddy is making small noises. He realises that while he's been busy downstairs it's possible the woman could have woken. She could have called the police if she'd been a little stronger. It's a bad mistake and Noone feels a rush of adrenaline flow through him so powerful that his hand starts to shake. He has to start being more careful. What would have happened if Paul Peters had come to?

Noone puts the taser on the bed and places the kitchen knife next to it. He finds a tie with which he gags Maddy. He uses four leather belts hanging on a rail inside the wardrobe door to strap her spread-eagled to the bed and then removes her bra.

Maddy Peters comes round as Noone's replacing her husband's clothes in the wardrobe.

She blinks, her vision unsteady, her expression confused. Her jaw looks broken. Noone expects her to struggle but she doesn't. Instead she just watches him, her eyes wide.

He walks across to the bed and looks down. He feels scared and excited at the same time and becomes aroused. He doesn't particularly want to make Maddy suffer but she probably will. Fuck, look at her, she's suffering already, looking up at him, the man who's going to kill her, the last thing she'll ever see. Noone bends in close and tries to see what she's thinking. So this is what it's like, he thinks. The power is unbelievable.

He can almost see her thinking about her child, her husband, and about her life. It makes him feel like crying, but he doesn't, because he doesn't cry. He could walk away. Disappear right now.

He could do it, too. He has the money.

But apart from the fact that she's a witness, when everything is taken into account, he really does want to kill her.

'Hello, Maddy,' he says. He keeps his voice low. 'I'm sorry about this.'

He means it. Kind of.

Sixty-One

Frank hadn't been down in the tunnels much during the search in the days following the murders. Before Dean Quinner's death there'd been little to suggest that the killings in Birkdale had anything to connect them physically to the Williamson tunnels, so the search, while thorough, had been limited.

There hadn't, Frank was certain, been anything shoddy about the search. It was just that, with finite resources, there was only so much they could do. Especially with so many other potential avenues of investigation.

And less than ten per cent of the tunnels complex is available to the public. What Frank is looking for won't be in that section, he's sure of that.

There's a map on the wall of the centre. The system extends under Edge Hill haphazardly. Frank pinpoints where he is and takes the view that if Nicky's going to be down here, he'll be as far as possible from the entrance.

Frank takes one of the printed maps from a stack on the counter and heads down a flight of bare concrete steps into the first of the caverns. He studies the map for several minutes, analysing the layout and imagining where he'd have put Nicky. There are a couple of possibilities but he has no idea if they are accessible. In all likelihood the places he's identified have already been examined.

And yet . . .

The only time he'd been in here, a quick visit at the start of the investigation, the place had been alive with activity, lights and people. Now, deserted, the bare brick dripping moisture and his torch sending shadows dancing across the blackness, it's just about the last place on earth Frank wants to be.

And if I feel like that, what must Nicky have felt like?

Say *feels*. Keep the option open at least. With food and water it's possible the boy may still be alive.

Frank follows the beam of his torch.

At the end of the first cavern he follows the path over a water-filled trough and through a twisting concrete shaft that bends to the right. Down another flight of steps and he's at a crossroads.

On the map the yellow lines indicate those tunnels that have been explored. The red lines show those that are dangerous, or filled with rubble, or otherwise unusable.

'Here goes nothing,' Frank mutters and takes the direction shown by the red line.

This shaft narrows dramatically and runs on a gentle slope for about forty metres before it opens into a cavern similar to those at the entrance. The difference here is that the space is mostly filled with builder's rubble. There has been an effort to excavate some of this but Frank sees it's got a way to go. He scrambles awkwardly up the slope until he has to crouch. Near to the top he can see that there is a narrow space. He pokes his head through. The torch beam picks up a narrow shaft, the bottom of which is covered in water.

Frank squeezes through the gap and tumbles a couple of metres into the shaft. He barks his shin against a rusted iron bar set into the wall of the shaft, and as his feet find solid ground freezing water pours over the tops of his trainers.

'Fuck!' He rubs his leg and moves slowly forward, not trusting the surface underfoot. At the end of the water-filled corridor, there is a brick arch dividing the space ahead. Below the arch, from what little Frank can see, there is another dumping ground for rubbish. Here he can go no further.

Frank looks at his map. One of his possibilities is out.

Ten minutes later he's standing at the entrance to another of his guesses. A maze of small passages seems – on the map at least – to finish in a remote dead end. Frank sees that if he is to access this he must first get through a crawl space only just large enough to fit his frame.

Frank can feel his heart rate leap at the prospect of inserting himself between the two great slabs of brick and concrete but he slides his head and shoulders in and wriggles forward. Lying there, he can almost feel the weight of the earth piled above him pressing down on the two-hundred-year-old structure. If he hears a rat he knows he's going to scream. Just the idea of being in here with a rodent is enough to jerk him into motion and he shuffles manically forward until, thankfully, he slides out into a space large enough to stand upright.

It seems to be a second dead end. Another slope of rubble with a wooden door at the top, propped against the wall. Frank scrambles up and sees that the door has been placed across a rough gap in a wall.

He gets a little lift. Someone's put this there for a reason. He pushes through the gap into a large cavern with a curved roof. There's a metal structure at one end – a box.

Big enough for someone to be inside. Frank feels his stomach lurch.

Drawing nearer, Frank can see it's some sort of industrial container. How it came to be down here he has no idea, but the tunnels are littered with the abandoned detritus of centuries of small industry. The container looks like one of the more recent additions but it's still in an advanced state of dilapidation.

Close to, the box is a solid-looking affair with a rusty locking arm placed through two steel hoops.

Frank slides the lock back and notices the metal is free of rust. It's been opened sometime recently.

It takes him an effort to free the door, and when he pries it loose, it flies back and he loses his footing. Frank's torch clatters to the floor and goes out. In the same instant, the smell hits him and he knows what's inside the container.

The next few minutes are, quite simply, the worst in Frank Keane's life.

He scrapes his hands on the rocky surface of the cavern floor, scrabbling for his torch. Once found he presses and re-presses the switch without success, each passing second alone in the dark sending him ever closer to full-blown panic.

And then he remembers his mobile. He drags it from the pocket of his zip-up and flicks it on.

In the blue-white light he sees what must be the decaying corpse of Nicky Peters lying curled in a corner of the filthy metal container, his back to the door as if, in the final hours and days, he had waited for the end without any trace of hope. He looks very small, and somehow still vulnerable.

Frank's ashamed of himself for being afraid. He's ashamed of himself for not being able to find the lost boy. Most of all, he's ashamed of himself for failing, completely, to protect the innocent.

He turns off the phone, puts his head in his hands and sits in the dark with Nicky, crying.

PART TWO

LOS ANGELES

One

About the size of a labrador, the raccoon scurries out from the trees at the foot of Fern Dell Drive and heads directly for the four lanes of traffic on Los Feliz Boulevard.

Noone, stretching before his run, watches with interest as the animal darts between the cars and trucks without breaking stride. It doesn't look right or left and none of the cars has to swerve. In less than ten seconds the raccoon has reached the safety of the other side and disappears into a thick hedge bordering a mansion on the corner of North Serrano.

A street raccoon, clearly.

Noone, wearing a long-beaked cap pulled low and a pair of dark blue Nike wraparounds, jogs along Los Feliz before turning left on the road heading up past the Greek Theatre. Just beyond there he leaves the road and takes the first of the maze of ochre-coloured hiking trails that criss-cross Griffith Park. He opens up a little on the rising ground, enjoying, as always, how the city – so close – is forgotten so quickly. There's silence up here as Noone steadily climbs through a series of winding trails. After ten minutes the white deco grandeur of the Griffith Observatory starts to appear between the trees. The building gets closer and then recedes as the tracks dance around the canyons. Finally, almost thirty minutes after leaving the city, Noone's running up a track directly below the observatory. He puts in a sprint on the last fifty yards and arrives on the lawn in front of the building breathing hard. It's a Monday morning in July and the weather is warm.

At this time of the morning there are few tourists and Noone walks through those that are here letting his muscles warm down. When his breath is back to normal he walks around to the side of the observatory facing the city. Leaning against the white wall he looks out towards the tall buildings of downtown, misty blue through the haze. To his right, lost from view, is the coast and Santa Monica. It took Noone almost forty-five minutes to drive across from there this morning but it's worth it. Up here the City of Angels is laid out below him and his mind is clear.

Pushing off from the wall of the observatory, Noone walks around to the front of the building and starts jogging down Western Canyon Road. He takes a turn back onto one of the trails and winds down in the direction of the Hollywood Reservoir. Around here the trails are less well used and Noone sees no one for almost ten minutes. With the greenery and the cypress trees and golden light, he could be in Tuscany.

He works his way up past Bugsy Siegel's old house, squatting above Mulholland Drive like a medieval castle, the Hollywood sign incongruous on the hill behind. In more recent years the place had been owned by Madonna but she is long gone too now.

Five minutes later, Noone slows his pace as he jogs past the back of a French chateau–style mansion with rolling grounds tumbling down the side of the canyon. The high, thick stone walls that surround the place have discreet, expensive-looking cameras dotted around the perimeter.

Noone can't see a way in without being seen.

He loops around the property to the front and stoops to tie a shoelace. The double-barred gate is unmarked, and from the street there's not an inch of the house that can be seen. A small sign reads simply: 'Private'. A single camera above one of the gateposts stares unblinkingly.

Noone rises and runs on.

He'll have to find another way.

One of the first things Noone had done when he got back to LA was find an agent. Even with *The Tunnels* production folding, his experience at being cast and the links with Hungry Head – and the celebrity investor – are enough to get him on the books with a solid outfit; not the best, not the biggest, but respected, and connected with some of the better productions coming out of Hollywood. Noone doesn't want any work from the agent. He wants the agent to give his appearance texture should an investigation head in his direction.

For a few weeks he settles back into the groove as smoothly as if he'd left ten weeks ago and not almost ten years.

The big difference is that now he *knows* who he is. He knows who his father is. He knows he can kill people.

Most importantly, he now knows exactly what he wants to do with his skills.

He'd got the idea quite suddenly. Going over and over the events of the last few weeks he'd been in Liverpool, it struck him how much effort he'd been putting in. And for what, exactly?

To prove he could kill?

Well, that was something. But the scale of the work needed to get away with killing someone, now that was the thing. And he'd done it just to kill some fucking suburban dentists and a fucking writer.

It was exhausting. His first thought on leaving Liverpool was to stay quiet, let time take its course and allow everyone to forget that Ben Noone was ever involved. Terry was such a wonderful outlet for blame. A child molester. A kidnapper. With nothing to connect him to the deaths, Noone is sure it will all blow over.

It was halfway over the Atlantic that the thought struck him that if it was really all over, then no one would know how well he'd done it. It was the most criminal thing about it, really. Some of the things he'd done. Jeez. For that never to be known . . .

A confession was out of the question. Confessions stunk of losers. Of failure, when what he'd done was a triumph of quick wits and planning and decisive action.

And then, thinking about the things he'd discovered when his mother died, he knew what he was going to do. It would be truly majestic. The poetry of the thing was staggering. The sweep of it, the grandeur, almost blew him away. No one would ever forget him.

So at JFK he'd made the call to that cop and started the ball rolling.

He needs a witness. Frank Keane fits the bill.

Two

While LA sweats, Monday morning in Liverpool barely staggers past ten degrees. It's raining hard with a chill wind coming in off the river. Almost four weeks since Frank found Nicky Peters' body in the Williamson tunnels and things aren't looking good for his pet theory about Ben Noone's involvement.

If Frank's honest, there's not much looking good about anything right now.

He walks to work at Canning Place from the flat at Mann Island, the much-prophesied desk move to Stanley Road no nearer to materialising. Since the relationship with Em – if that's what it was – sputtered into nothing, Frank hasn't had the heart. The time at Canning Place is time he doesn't have to deal with working alongside her. He's drifting into management by inches but Frank's finding it easier that way.

Discovering Nicky's body broke something in him that hasn't been fixed yet.

There hasn't been an hour since then that he hasn't thought about the boy.

The autopsy showed he'd been dead for less than a week. Suffocation is the cause of death. There is little additional physical evidence apart from more corroboration that places Terry Peters at the scene. There is nothing linking Ben Noone to the crime.

Frank's been through the tunnels many times since and is beginning to get a clear idea of what might have happened. Three days after Frank discovered Nicky, DC Magsi and a couple of uniforms stumble across the space where Nicky had been kept in the immediate aftermath of the Burlington Road killings. It's Frank's theory that Nicky was moved to a more secure location while Terry Peters wrestled with killing him and, perhaps, to prevent the possibility of Noone doing that. If Frank's right about Noone, there's little evidence to suggest that Terry Peters killed anyone, except perhaps Nicky. Frank's idea is that Nicky died because Terry Peters couldn't face killing his nephew directly. Instead, he left him to die of suffocation, thirty-five metres under Edge Hill.

The thing that's nagging at Frank is why Noone tipped him off that the boy was still underground. An attack of conscience? Frank doesn't believe that. The nearest he can get is that Noone wants him to stay interested.

He decides that there'll be no answer to this question while the situation remains as it is.

After getting out of the tunnels – it took almost thirty minutes – Frank had called in the SOC officers to start the investigation and had stayed on site until late in the morning. He and Em hadn't had a chance to discuss what had happened between them until the afternoon. By that time her attitude had hardened. Frank hadn't told her about the message, or about his solo trek to the tunnels. Em reads it as a slap in the face, professionally and personally, and they haven't been together outside work since. Sometimes when Frank closes his eyes he can see her walking naked towards the bedroom and wonders what might have been had he decided to stay.

Since that night Frank's been working out at the boxing club more often. It's the only thing he's enjoying right now. With Jesus gone the place is being run by Val. She's got a nephew in to help her and it's going fine.

He hasn't been to a Thursday at The Phil since finding Nicky's body. He's lost weight, the skin on his face close on the bone. He lashes out too easily, is constantly tired. Work is the raft he clings to.

At his desk, Frank does a couple of hours of emailing and paperwork before heading over to MIT at Stanley. For once his phone remains mute. The Monday briefing is at eleven.

At Stanley Road, there is a full team present for the meeting. Only DC Flanagan is absent, returned to duties at Sefton as the need for extra personnel at MIT is downgraded. Frank's managed to hang onto Saif Magsi and the young cop is showing every sign he could develop into one of the unit's best. It's good for the likes of Scott Corner and Phil Caddick to have some decent competition. Caddick especially is wary of Magsi's apparent rise and Frank has noted a few deliberate attempts by Caddick to show the new arrival in a bad light. Unless it shifts over into outright bullying, Frank won't act. If Magsi's going to do as well as Frank thinks he will, then he'll have to cope with nonsense like that. So far, Magsi seems to have Caddick's measure.

'Good morning,' says Frank. Over the past month he has become much more businesslike at the briefings, preferring Harris to lead, or Theresa Cooper if Harris isn't around. He's found that it helps him keep a distance from the team, something that he's beginning to see as essential. Footballers who make the transition from player to management often find that they can no longer be one of the boys.

He gestures for Harris to start. She nods. There's no underlying heat in their brief exchanges which may, thinks Frank, be the saddest thing of all.

As Harris outlines the various MIT cases, Frank's mulling over his meeting with Searle scheduled for this afternoon. He's going to try and make a case for going to Los Angeles to interview Noone and needs to have more than he's got right now.

There are three routes open to Frank.

The first – and the one that he knows isn't going to work with Charlie Searle, let alone the US authorities – is extradition. To make an application for extradition, Frank needs to show evidence to the court that Noone will face charges if brought back to the UK. Even in his wildest moments, Frank doesn't think he's got enough for that. There's a prickly relationship between the US and UK on extradition. In Frank's experience it's a lot easier for the Americans to extradite a Brit to the US than the other way round. He knows that there are several cases in play right now in the UK – he'd had Magsi do some background work – which have reached a seemingly interminable impasse over extradition.

Frank's second option, and the one he thinks might work, is for him to make a case to Searle that MIT makes an application to the US Justice Department under MLAT, the Mutual Legal Assistance Treaty. Under MLAT, Frank has a route by which he can go to the US and interview Noone *if* he can make a case that Noone has evidence Frank needs. MLAT is specifically designed for those investigative situations which fall short of extradition status but in which there is still evidence to be gathered. Frank's had the groundwork for this done already; DC Magsi's drawn up the paperwork and all Frank needs is Searle to OK the application. It's a workable solution but Frank would like another item or two of evidence that helps point towards Noone. So far all he has is the shaky testimony of Niall McCluskey connecting Noone to the Peters case. It might be enough, but it might not.

The last option is simply to interview Noone as a witness in the US. Frank will consider this if his MLAT application fails, but for this to work, Noone must be willing to be interviewed voluntarily. He'd also be chaperoned by the FBI. In the past this approach has worked for MIT in a few cases, the key thing being the depth of research on the witness. Frank's confident they have enough background to proceed and, weirdly, thinks that Noone would relish being interviewed. But it's not ideal.

He tunes back in to the meeting as Steve Rose is updating them on the evidence from Nicky's computer. Frank's impatient. The computer evidence has, he thought, been sifted thoroughly before now. It's been four weeks for fuck's sake. Why Rose is bringing this up when the whole of MIT (Frank excepted) is working on the assumption that Terry Peters killed his brother, sister-in-law, nephew and wife before topping himself in the fire, Frank isn't sure.

He decides to give Rose a little leeway, bites back the barb that springs to his lips and tries to concentrate on where Rose is going with it.

Although an initial forensic examination had proved fruitless, Rose has made contact with Operation Vector.

'Nicky Peters' computer was clean, as far as we could tell.' He looks at Frank, conscious perhaps that he is on old ground. Rose picks up the pace of his briefing. 'We gave it a pretty good going over. The same went for his phone. As you know, there was nothing of any significance, and Terry Peters' computers were lost in the fire.'

'Come on, Steve,' murmurs Frank. 'Cut to it.'

Rose nods. His voice becomes more urgent. 'This morning I spoke to Nia Saleed at SOCA and she passed on some information they'd got from a third party they're looking at now. The guy they have targeted has links with a North West paedophile group which they suspect Terry Peters to have been in contact with.'

'And?'

'And there's some evidence to suggest two things: one is that Nicky and Terry Peters exchanged information via an internet chat room and via Terry Peters' Hotmail account. That Hotmail account was accessed from Peters' phone after he was dead.'

'We know that,' says Frank. He leans back and puts his hands behind his head.

'But the new information is that Vector can pinpoint the call that accessed the email account and it came from outside the UK.'

Now Rose has Frank's interest. There's a ripple of noise in the room as it starts to sink in what Rose is saying.

'Go on.'

'We know you've got a thing about Noone, so I pushed them for details. The call came from New York. At the time it was made, Ben Noone was in transit at JFK.'

Steve Rose sits back, his skin flushed.

'Fuck me,' says Frank. Although filled with potential flaws, it's the first piece of concrete evidence that could positively link Ben Noone to the case. If it can be proved that he made that call on Terry Peters' phone then they have something. Maybe not a water-tight case but enough to get the fucker back here and go to work.

Frank's sure it's Noone. He flashes back to the text he got pointing him back to the tunnels. And didn't Niall McCluskey say he'd lost his phone the night he tailed Noone? Quinner's phone never showed up either. Plenty of phones have been involved in the case but very few are still around. Phones are good. Courts like phones and phone evidence. They're solid, mathematical, scientific. Frank would love to get Noone's phone or evidence relating to Noone's phone.

'Good work, Steve,' says Frank. Rose smiles and nods. He looks at Phil Caddick and surreptitiously flips him the finger. Rose's potential breakthrough pushes him to the head of the pack of DCs but Corner, Rimmer, Cooper and Magsi look as pleased as he does.

Harris pats Frank on the shoulder. 'It's enough for an MLAT application,' she says.

It is enough for Frank to accelerate the MLAT application, enough evidence that Noone could help in the enquiry. Establishing that he had been in possession of a phone linked to both Terry and Nicky Peters, used to access a paedophile chat room, would be devastating.

'They have a time at JFK?' This could be crucial. A time would allow someone to trawl the CCTV at JFK and place Noone making the call. It's a laborious and complex trail, but it is a possibility, another small but significant brick in Frank's efforts to build a case against Noone.

'Yes,' says Rose.

Harris glances at Frank and raises her eyebrows. There's really something in this. A cold Monday morning suddenly got a lot warmer.

'Let's get cracking,' says Frank.

Three

Frank, a black document case in one hand, presses the buzzer with the other.

'Keane,' he says when prompted by the disembodied voice. There's a click and he pushes open the heavy glass door. He walks through a small atrium and into a modern waiting room. It's empty. The way out of the building is through another exit. Frank's sure this is deliberate.

The receptionist behind the desk smiles briefly. Frank avoids eye contact.

'Take a seat, please, Mr Keane.'

Frank has only just sat down in the chair furthest from the reception desk when the door to one of the office suites opens and the angular frame of Angela Salt appears. She squints round the waiting room like a short-sighted heron.

'DCI Keane?'

'Call me Frank, please.'

She holds the door open for him.

Angela Salt is a forensic clinical psychologist. Frank had met her briefly in the course of an earlier MIT case and had been impressed. Now he needs a psychologist, he's called her.

They shake hands.

'Please, sit down,' says Salt. She indicates one of two comfortable-looking armchairs placed at a slight angle to each other.

'Thanks.' Frank sits in the armchair Salt indicates. He puts his case down on the floor next to the chair.

As Salt busies herself at a table laden with teapot and cups she holds up a sugar bowl. 'How do you take it?'

'Do you have coffee?'

'Of course.' She walks to the door and, opening it slightly, asks the receptionist to bring drinks. Salt moves methodically, gracefully, with the deliberation of someone who has been tall from an early age.

Angela Salt is tall, wears glasses and is dressed in a long black skirt and a charcoal sweater with buttons up the front. About sixty, she has her grey hair in a severe cut that puts Frank in mind of someone from the 1920s. Polished black boots peek out from under her skirt.

Yesterday, after Rose's good news about the phone, Frank had officially booked Salt in as an adviser to the ongoing Peters investigation using some of his precious MIT funds. With the possibility looming that he'll be heading to the US, he wants as much ammunition as possible. A report from a credible forensic psychologist like Salt will be a valuable asset.

After booking her to come in to MIT, Frank had called and changed the venue to Salt's Bebington office. He's not sure why, completely, but it probably has something to do with any searching questions Salt may ask of Frank. His prior experience of psychologists working on cases has shown him that she may well be interested in his own reactions to Noone. Given his post-tunnels reactions include insomnia, drinking and late-night crying jags, there's a distinct possibility that Salt may stray into areas that Frank does not want explored. Not in the gossip chamber of MIT at any rate. Like most coppers, Frank would rather chew his own arm off than reveal too much of his psyche.

Christ, there are things in there that even he'd rather not know about. The idea that she may get wind of his troubled relationship with a gay colleague doesn't bear contemplation.

So Bebington it is.

Salt takes her seat. She checks her watch and leans back. 'When you're ready, Frank.'

'I'm applying to go across to Los Angeles and interview a suspect I believe to be responsible, at least in part, for six deaths. The man's name is Ben Noone, an American actor. This man has returned to the US. I'm applying under MLAT – the Mutual Legal Assistance Treaty – which is an agreement between us and overseas government agencies to facilitate evidence gathering. It's basically one step down from straight-out extradition. In other words, his lawyers, and the Americans, will know that we think he's likely to be guilty but don't have enough evidence to extradite. And we don't. The US is also more protective of its citizens in the face of potential extradition by a foreign government than we are. I'm not sure if that's good or bad, but it's bad in this case, at least from our perspective.'

Angela Salt is taking notes.

'So what I'm doing is gathering anything I can to take over there. Ideally that will include some sort of psychological profile of who we're looking for.' Frank smiles. 'Which is where you can help.'

'I can try.'

Frank pauses as the receptionist comes in with a tray. She puts down the cups on the small table in between the two chairs and leaves. Frank picks up his coffee and takes a sip.

'I have to tell you that some of the people in my department, particularly my superiors, don't fully share my conviction about Noone. We already have a very credible case against another suspect, Terry Peters, who is now dead. Peters was a sexual predator and there aren't many people who are sad about his passing. Including most of MIT.'

'But you have doubts?'

'Yes, I have doubts. And some of them can't be explained away easily.'

Frank outlines his ideas about the case, placing special emphasis on the use of Terry Peters' phone after his death – from a location consistent with Noone's flight – and on the suspicions of Dean Quinner about Noone. His central idea is that Terry Peters and Ben Noone were both dangerous individuals and were involved in some way with the disappearance of Nicky Peters.

'Where I differ from some of my colleagues is in thinking that Noone was – is – the more dangerous of the two. It's feasible, to me, that Terry Peters didn't kill anyone, that it is Noone who we should be concentrating our efforts on.'

'Although from what you tell me, there is considerable evidence that Terry Peters is guilty,' Salt says.

'He was sleeping with Maddy Peters, that's true. It's also likely that he was abusing his nephew, Nicky. And I personally think he was responsible for taking Nicky underground. He was as guilty as Noone. In my view, Noone, and maybe Terry Peters, killed Paul and Maddy Peters – possibly because of what Noone and Terry had been doing with Nicky.'

'That could certainly have been a catalyst,' says Salt.

'I think that Noone killed Dean Quinner because of something he had seen. Or said. Or maybe just because Noone likes killing. And he killed Terry and Alicia to destroy any evidence that remained on Terry's computers.'

'And Nicky?'

'I'm not sure that Noone knew exactly where Nicky was. There's evidence that he was moved. I'm suggesting that Terry Peters moved his nephew without telling Noone. Nicky died of suffocation. Murder by neglect.'

'So why did Noone notify you about Nicky being in the tunnels?'

Frank shrugs. 'That's your department. I don't think Ben Noone is doing this to a plan.'

'His notifying you isn't inconsistent with a certain type of psychopathy. He could be reacting to a changing landscape more chaotically than he imagines. If he does have narcissistic personality disorder then he will oscillate between moments of imagined omnipotence and blind panic and rage at being caught. Being caught represents failure and a narcissistic personality of this type doesn't usually contemplate failure. Someone with this psychology may also need to display his cleverness and omnipotence. But we can examine that in more detail as we go on.'

Frank bends to the document case and places it on the coffee table. He unzips it and takes out a thick file which he pushes towards Salt.

'The case notes.' Frank hitches the knee of his pants and leans forward. 'Obviously this is just a summary of the main points. If you think we've missed something, just tell me. I had one of my officers boil everything down to this.'

Angela Salt flicks over the first few pages and then closes it. 'I'll go over this in detail when you're not here, Frank. I think our session time would be better spent talking and getting your input. I can do the background reading and referencing more effectively that way.'

Frank nods. 'Fine. Whatever works.'

Angela Salt leans back and crosses her legs.

'Let's go back over the reaction you had to Noone. The first time you saw him. What happened when he came in?'

'I had a feeling I'd seen him before but that might have been because he's an actor. Maybe he looks like some other actor. Nice teeth.'

'How did you feel about him?'

'As a person? I didn't dislike him. Not at first. He'd already interested me because we couldn't find much on him in the background checks we ran. It was unusual. In the interview room I felt he was performing.'

'He probably was. Everyone does, even if they don't know it.'

'He knew it,' Frank says quickly and the psychologist nods.

'A strong impression, then?'

'Yes.' Frank keeps nodding as if confirming it to himself. 'It was a performance.'

'How about your colleague? How did she react?'

'She liked him.'

'He was sexually attractive to her?'

'She's gay. Well . . .' Frank's reply fades and Salt looks up. This is why I wanted to meet here, thinks Frank.

'Well, what?'

'Nothing. My colleague's gay. But she told me that Noone was charming. She knew he was manipulating the interview and we discussed how best to prevent that.'

'Was that successful?'

'No, not really. Not in the long run.' Frank flashes back to Noone's sly smile of triumph as he and Eagles left the interview room. 'He won.'

'Let's leave that for a moment and go back to when you first formed the opinion that he was guilty. When was that, exactly?'

'In that first interview. I had been trying to ask him a question – and that's another thing he's good at, deflecting questions – and then I asked him something very direct. About him being caught with his pants down by Quinner. He got a look on his face for a second, no more, an angry and unguarded look. It was so different to the face he'd been using that it was like he was someone else. I just knew it was him.'

'You knew?'

'I knew it was him. From that moment.'

'You'd got under his skin. It's hard for someone, even an actor, to maintain control for so long. It can be done. Still, even in this case I'd suggest from what I know that Terry Peters was the more accomplished dissembler.'

'He had me fooled,' says Frank.

'But when Noone's mask slipped what you saw was his mammalian brain register your words and display his reaction unfiltered. For a second, your suspect was controlled by his limbic system. It's an incredibly telling event when it happens. We see it in here all the time. Noone was angry, embarrassed, and he let it show in a way that was so direct – to you – that there was a similar limbic reaction from you. The speed with which Noone put the mask back on and assumed his persona of control is a classic demonstration of narcissism.'

'Go on.'

'A narcissistic personality has a sense of entitlement and an ongoing need to feel in control. Letting his true self be revealed results in narcissistic rage at being challenged. The return of his control is a signifier of his narcissistic pride being restored.'

'What about his other behaviours? If what I think is true turns out to be the case?'

Angela Salt shakes her head. 'Let's keep with what we do know about Noone and see how that stacks up against the template we have for potentially damaging narcissistic behaviours. Noone's an actor, a good role for a narcissist but not in itself an indicator of personality disorder. But it does back your thesis. He's new to the job, but by all accounts, he's very good at it – good enough to have landed the role without experience. That indicates that he's coming from a place where he habitually hides his inner, true self and does it convincingly. He offers the world the version of himself that he'd most like others to see.'

Salt ticks off a finger. 'He is popular, at least from what you've mentioned regarding his circle at the nightclub that the film crew used.'

'Maxie's.'

'Yes. He seems to have had a "circle of worship" to some extent. That is another indicator of narcissism, but again, not necessarily denoting a damaging disorder. I would note, however, that all of the known material is building a reasonable platform for an identity so mired in narcissism that his capacity for empathy is diminished to dangerous levels.'

Salt breaks off. 'Apologies if some of this comes off like an official report; I'm used to talking this way.'

Frank smiles. 'Police do it all the time.'

'Another event I found interesting,' continues Salt, 'was his obtaining a high-priced lawyer from the best firm. Leaving aside the legal implications, from the thesis you've asked me to work on, that is a behaviour consistent with your idea. Getting "the best" is something he would want. And getting it quickly. When you left him in the interview room he will have had another episode of narcissistic rage. This time, once it was over, I'd suggest that he formed a strategy to demonstrate that it was he who was in control, not you. By having an expensive lawyer waiting when you got back, he could gain the upper hand. And, from what you say, that strategy worked. Does he dress well?'

'Yes, I suppose so.'

'An obvious question but it's another small pointer.' Salt checks her notes. 'On the movie set, were there any incidents prior to the killings? Thefts?'

Frank sits up. 'A wallet went missing. Belonged to a sound man.'

'Interesting.'

'Why? Did Noone do it?'

'If he's what we think he is it's credible. Narcissists have a sense of entitlement. And they enjoy risk, believing that they are ahead of the rest of us.'

'If Noone stole the wallet and Quinner saw him . . .'

'Is that a question?'

'I'm just thinking it through. We didn't check the wallet story because it was found.'

'By Noone?'

Frank shrugs. 'I'll check.'

'I'll bet you find it was,' says Salt. She looks at her watch.

'That's all I have time for, I'm afraid,' she says. 'I have an appointment in ten minutes. I'll read the file thoroughly and start putting some notes together for your submission.'

Frank gets to his feet and heads for the door.

'Not that way,' says Salt, indicating a second door on the opposite side of the room. 'This is the way out.'

Frank turns.

'He's a bad one,' he says, shaking the psychologist's hand. 'I need to get him.'

Angela Salt smiles but doesn't reply directly. Instead, still holding his hand, she says something that Frank isn't expecting.

'This must have been a traumatic experience for you, Frank. Finding the boy in the tunnels.'

Frank drops her hand as if it's hot.

'Yeah, I suppose so,' he says. 'But it's part of the job.'

'A very stressful job.'

'Perhaps.' Frank wants to leave. His shoulders turn towards the door.

'Have you ever thought about seeing someone, Frank?' says Salt. 'A therapist, I mean.'

'Me?'

Salt scribbles a name on a sheet of paper and hands it to Frank. 'You've experienced a lot of trauma recently. Even from the little you've told me, you might benefit from talking to someone. I can't do it, obviously, but I could recommend someone good.'

'If you can get your report to me as soon as possible.'

Frank, his neck flushed, opens the door, and with a brisk nod to Salt turns and walks out. As he walks away he feels embarrassed, but isn't sure if that's because the psychologist is out of line, or because he knows she's right.

He stuffs the paper with the therapist's name on it in his pocket and heads for his car.

Four

Despite himself, and despite the occasional expletive-laden rant aimed in his direction, Frank's starting to like Charlie Searle.

They'll never be drinking buddies or play a round of golf but the longer he's working under him the more Frank can see that there's a decent copper in there. Even at his relatively humble level, Frank has to deal with so much politics that it makes his head swim sometimes. What it's like for Searle is hard to imagine.

And yet, he keeps his eye on the important stuff. He might be a little too concerned with the press and a little too keen on throwing acronyms around like confetti – and Frank could definitely do without Searle palling around with Peter Moreleigh – but when he analyses the case, Searle's been with him pretty much all the way. The times he hadn't been – well, Frank might have made the same call himself had he been in Charlie Searle's seat.

'I think it's good enough, Frank.' Thursday morning and Searle's behind his desk and holding the MLAT application on Noone. 'I've had a good look at it and it falls pretty neatly into the requirements. It would help being a bit stronger in places but if we had that then maybe we'd be trying an extradition, eh?'

Frank knows the work the team's done on the MLAT application is solid. He's hoping that Searle doesn't raise any objections because he's already booked the flight for tomorrow morning.

They have anecdotal evidence now from Niall McCluskey that he was following orders from Dean Quinner when he tailed Noone – or, as Noone's lawyers would point out, someone McCluskey thought was Noone – and McCluskey's willing to testify to that. Noone leaving the country seems to have helped McCluskey's memory somewhat. That, and the fact that he had

270

been under the mistaken impression he was suspected for being involved in his cousin's death. McCluskey has also produced one Jason Reeves, aka Ghost Ninja, to back his story.

Frank also has a nice little report in from Angela Salt detailing a number of ways in which Noone fits the description of the killer. The flaw in this – which would, no doubt, be the view of Noone's lawyers – is that it rests on Noone *being* the killer. And it is only a psychologist's profile.

Lastly, and most pertinently, there is Steve Rose's work on the call to Frank's phone from Terry Peters' number. Placing the phone in New York while Noone was there is key. There can be no better reason for Frank to travel under an MLAT than needing to look at concrete CCTV evidence at JFK.

It's a neat job.

'Be careful,' says Searle, signing and handing the MLAT back to Frank. 'It's like a different country over there, Frank.' Searle shudders. 'Americans. And listen, don't let them push you around just because you're on your own.'

'Thanks, sir,' says Frank. He takes the file and gets out of the office before Searle goes any further. The last thing Frank wants Searle to know is that he already has someone on the ground in Los Angeles. On Frank's budget documentation it'll be listed as 'consultancy work' but that's bullshit.

On Monday evening, the day Rose had given him the link between Peters' phone and Ben Noone, Frank had decided that whatever happened, he'd go to Los Angeles. That evening he called Koopman and Eckhardt and persuaded them to go to the US as consultants to MIT. It's a risk: Frank's not sure it's strictly legal and he's using MIT funds for a purpose that is decidedly 'grey' but he wants help on the ground. Noone's not going to slip away because Frank hasn't tried everything.

After leaving Searle's office with the MLAT approved Frank heads back to MIT to brief the team. As time has passed, the Peters and Quinner cases have been partly submerged beneath several new murders coming into the office. Most of them are, as usual, drug-related. Which isn't to say they won't be investigated. And the investigations all take time and money. Frank often reflects on how little the public know about the role that budgets play in how well a crime is investigated. With a finite number of officers, a growing portion of Frank's job is allocation. He's done his best to move most of last year's case involving Keith Kite over to the Organised Crime Squad and they've been happy to take it on board. Normally MIT wouldn't like losing the credits on a large one like this but since one of their own officers is in it up to his neck, Charlie Searle waves it goodbye with pleasure. Most of the meeting is taken up with logistical detail and everyone's glad when it's over.

Afterwards, as they're heading back to their desks, he gets a text from Harris.

Dinner tonight at my place? 8 pm?

Frank, standing outside Em Harris's place with a bottle of wine in his hand and feeling as nervous as a teenager, presses the bell and, after a short delay, the buzzer opens the door to the block. Frank takes the stairs to Em's third-floor flat and knocks on the door.

It opens and Em's there. She looks good in tight jeans and a white shirt. Soft electro music is floating out from the living room. Frank holds up the bottle.

'Excellent,' she says, taking it from him. 'I thought you might not be drinking, when you're flying tomorrow.'

'That's why I'm drinking.'

Frank, smiling, pecks Harris on the cheek and is dismayed to sense a hesitation. Perhaps tonight isn't going to work out as he hoped it would.

Inside the living room and he sees why.

Linda's sitting on the sofa holding a glass of wine. She looks up at Frank from underneath her fringe. Her neck is flushed red.

'You're not going to throw that at me, are you?' says Frank, pointing to the wine. Linda looks past Frank to Emily.

'Play nice, Frank,' says Em. 'This isn't easy for Linda either.'

'I think you'd better get me a glass, Em.' Frank turns back to Linda. 'At least we're both armed then, eh?'

Em puts her hand on Frank's shoulder and leans in close. 'Please, Frank,' she says softly. 'For me. It's important.'

Frank holds up his hands in surrender and nods. He moves to Linda and puts out his palm. 'Frank,' he says. 'We have met, but we never got properly introduced.'

Linda's hand is small in his and soft. 'Sorry,' she says in a voice almost too quiet to hear. 'I'm Linda.'

'I know.'

Em comes across and hands Frank a large glass of red. Frank sits down next to Linda and clinks the rim of his glass with hers. She almost flinches and Frank wants to tell her it's OK. Instead he sinks back into the cushions and takes a large mouthful of the wine.

'Are we still having dinner?' he says. 'Or has that changed too?'

'We are,' says Em, 'although whether or not you're eating largely depends on your behaviour.'

'I am hungry.'

'Good.' Em sits down on an armchair at ninety degrees to Linda. 'I – we – thought this would be a good idea.'

'I didn't,' says Linda. 'It's embarrassing.'

Frank turns to her. 'I agree. What do you say we avoid talking about the subject entirely and pretend this is just a few friends having dinner? I'm all for emotional air-clearing so long as it doesn't involve me. Let's do the English thing and bury our heads in the sand.'

Em shakes her head. 'Frank –' she begins, but Linda cuts across her.

'Frank's right. Let's just have dinner.'

Em opens her mouth to speak and then closes it again. She frowns at Frank and he shrugs. 'Two against one,' he says. Linda smiles.

Over dinner they do talk. With a couple more glasses and some good food inside them talk comes easier. It helps that Frank likes Linda and she seems to be relaxing in his company. Strangely, Frank feels as if he should be the one helping her through the evening. And then he realises that this is exactly as it should be. He was the one who slept with Linda's partner. Linda's the one who's got a genuine grievance. All he got was a gobful of vinegar and a bad scare.

There were some women who wouldn't have used vinegar.

By eleven, Em and Linda are holding hands and Frank's got the picture.

They are back together. Solid. The thing with him was the result of a bad patch. For the first time since he's known Em Harris, Frank's being allowed to see the vulnerability and pressures she faces.

When Frank leaves he hugs Linda awkwardly but with warmth.

'It was nice to meet you, Frank,' she says. 'I hope we can be friends.'

At the door he hugs Em and this time there's no hesitation from her. 'Thanks, Frank.'

They disengage and Em fixes him with a stare. 'Be careful over there. If you're right about this guy, he's one of the worst. And you'll be alone.'

'I'll be fine,' says Frank. He leans back in close and cups Em's face between his hands and kisses her softly on the lips. His eyes are open and he looks right at her.

'See you in a few weeks,' he says and steps through the door. Em closes it gently behind him.

Outside, safe from view, Frank leans forward, supporting himself by placing his hands against the wall of the corridor. He lets his head hang down and he shakes it from side to side, the very essence of a broken man.

'Frank?'

Frank jerks upright and sees Em watching him from the door. She's holding his jacket.

'You forgot this.'

Frank takes it and puts it on. 'You never saw that, right?' he says.

'Saw what?' says Em and closes the door.

Five

Frank's never been a good flyer.

He's not in the category that requires sedation or hypnotherapy, but sometimes it's close.

On board he settles into his seat in economy as best he can, glad that the check-in girl noticed his flight had been paid by Merseyside Police and had given him an exit row. Airlines like policemen passengers.

The take-off is bearable as long as Frank keeps his eyes shut and doesn't move a muscle. He pretends he's asleep but only so that he can't watch the disturbing spectacle of the moors at the edge of Manchester spinning below them as the plane rises. Anyone looking at his face would assume serenity within but the grinding of his teeth gives him away.

After an eternity, the seatbelt light pings and Frank opens his eyes as the plane levels. From here it's manageable as long as they don't hit turbulence and as long as he doesn't, even for a second, think about the insanity of strapping yourself inside a cylindrical pressurised tube full of flammable material and hurtling halfway round the planet through the upper atmosphere.

Almost four hours pass without incident and then it happens.

A solid-sounding bump and the aircraft vibrates enough for the seatbelt sign to come on. Frank cinches his tight around his waist and closes his eyes.

Another bang. This time more violent and more prolonged. A couple of people squeal nervously and one or two behind Frank scream.

Frank would like to join them.

It's only forty years of conditioning as an emotionally stunted northern English male that prevents him.

The aircraft drops quickly and now some people are screaming properly. Frank feels his stomach lurch and he thinks he's going to be sick. That they're all going to die is now a given. He tries to conjure up some deep and meaningful thoughts but all he can think about are flames, and blood and smoke and tearing, screeching metal, and death.

The captain's voice comes on. 'Ladies and gentlemen, as you can see, we are experiencing some turbulence. At this point we'd advise everyone to remain seated.' His voice is calm, urbane; the voice of a privately educated Englishman. Frank is ashamed that he feels glad about that. Even in the face of death we know our place. He feels perversely proud to be from a nation in which the idea of class is so ingrained that this can be so.

There are more bumps and more bangs and the engine noise seems to alternately increase and decrease. Little by little, the passengers fall silent. Five hundred years go by.

They're going to die.

'Captain Toms again, ladies and gentlemen. Hope that that bumpy patch wasn't too troublesome. We have received advice from JFK that the weather in New York is a pleasant seventy-two degrees for our arrival. If you could just sit back and enjoy the rest of our flight we will advise on onward flight connection details. Our descent will commence very shortly.'

The lying, two-faced, upper-class *bastard*.

It's clear to anyone with a brain that they are in serious trouble.

The plane descends in near silence towards New York. Frank can't be the only one who thinks Captain Toms may have been skipping the details about three of the four engines failing, or the catastrophic icing up of some key widget, or the fucking terrorist holding a knife to his throat in the cockpit.

A small child starts crying, softly at first and then with increasing volume.

At least I don't have that worry, reflects Frank. He doesn't mind the crying. He wonders what it must be like to be worrying about not only yourself, but about another. Families are strange things when you think about it. Two strangers meeting, producing offspring and then trying to keep them from harm. Not all,

276

obviously. The cancerous Terry Peters wasn't exactly an advert for the nuclear family.

And Nicky. Poor Nicky hadn't been looked after, had he? Not that his parents had known. If Noone hadn't come along at just the wrong time, Nicky may have been 'just' damaged by Terry Peters instead of being left to die alone in the dark. Even thinking about Terry Peters makes Frank tense. He knows from the forensics that Terry met a bad end but nothing could have been appropriate punishment for that evil cunt. Frank finds he is gripping the seat so hard his fingernails are scratching the plastic veneer. And it's not because he's flying.

In the absence of Terry Peters, Frank's going to get Ben Noone.

What about Noone? What was his family background? Would there be something in Los Angeles that might help Frank understand Noone, and more importantly, stop him from killing again?

The wheels of the plane touch down and Frank's jolted back to the here and now.

Turns out the lying upper-class bastard had been telling the truth.

There's a long queue at immigration. By the time Frank's shuffled to the front he's lost the good feeling generated by the simple pleasure of having his feet on solid ground. He's got no idea what time it is in the real world but it feels like 4 am to him.

The fat uniformed woman sitting in the booth motions him forward. Frank hands his passport over and tries not to look too impatient. The immigration officer glances up at Frank without expression and places his passport face down on a scanner. She moves her head across to a computer monitor and then back to Frank.

'One moment, sir,' she says and looks across to her right to where two of her colleagues are standing. She beckons to them.

'Is there a problem?' says Frank. The woman holds up a hand, signalling him not to speak.

The other two immigration officers arrive. They look at Frank in utter distaste. One of them is Hispanic and one white. Both are enormously overweight. Both carry guns on their vast belts.

The Hispanic immigration officer takes Frank's passport and then looks at the screen and then back at Frank. He then shows the passport to the white guy and they exchange a pantomime of worried looks, all knitted brows and cold stares gleaned from TV shows.

It's almost laughable.

Frank turns briefly back in the direction of the crowded immigration hall and the smile is wiped from his face. To his right, through a thicket of passengers, he spots a face he's seen before. It's just the briefest of glimpses and then it's gone, hidden by a pillar, but it's like a slap.

'Sir. *Sir.*'

Frank turns slowly back towards the immigration officers.

'You're going to have to come with us.'

'I know I do,' says Frank. 'That's why I'm here. I'm a police officer. I'm here to see someone called Gloria Lopez. She's the FBI field agent acting as liaison. I'm sure she'll confirm my details.'

Frank flicks his gaze back to the hall trying, without success, to find the face he'd seen.

'Sir. I repeat, you will have to come with us.'

The Hispanic guy is resting his hand on the butt of his pistol.

'Seriously?' says Frank, looking down at his hand. 'This is what you're doing?'

Frank shakes his head and mutters something. The fat white officer points in the direction Frank should take. Frank starts walking and looks back but can't see anything.

Now he's wondering if he's imagined it. Why would the guy who put him on the bathroom floor in the cafe in Liverpool be in New York?

Six

Back when he'd been doing the job Frank Keane's doing now, Menno Koopman had come to Los Angeles to do a job swap in the US. He and Zoe had stayed in a chain hotel in an area of town that seemed to consist entirely of outlet stores and fast-food restaurants. It had been a depressing experience. So much so that Zoe had checked them out of the hotel and into a small rented apartment on Nichols Canyon. In the new location, the city had slowly begun to reveal its charms.

Now, sitting on the narrow balcony of the rental unit Frank had lined up for them just off San Vicente Boulevard in West Hollywood, he's having a hard time convincing the jet-lagged Warren Eckhardt about the city's good points.

'I've already been told three fucking times there's no smoking,' says Warren. 'And one of those times was on the street by a bloke wearing lime green shorty shorts and holding hands with another bloke.' He inhales deeply and blows a thick jet of smoke out into the Los Angeles night. 'I mean, it's not like my little bit of smoke is doing much to the air, is it? Fucking smog's making smokers of every bastard in the joint as far as I can see. I'm not even supposed to smoke in this fucking place and we're paying for the damn thing!'

'Merseyside Police are paying,' points out Koop, but Warren pretends not to have heard him.

Koop leans as far back from Warren's smoke as possible. Perhaps bringing Australia's most committed smoker to the least smoke-tolerant city on earth had been a mistake. For the life of him Koop couldn't see how Warren Eckhardt was going to last two days in California, let alone two weeks. And if the anti-smoking mob didn't get him, surely the Rainbow Coalition would finish the job? Right on cue, Warren starts up again.

'And did this mate of yours know he's booked us into the gayest neighbourhood outside of Darlinghurst?'

Koop shrugs.

'Did you see the little Indian guy at the desk when we checked in? Thought me and you were a pair of poofs. I could tell he wasn't happy about it.'

Koop sometimes forgot Warren was from Queensland.

He laughs.

'What's so funny?' asks Warren.

'When you filled in your address on the form you put "Queensland". That's why he was looking at you. Probably thinks it's some sort of special gay town in Australia.'

'I never thought of that.'

'You'll be safe,' says Koop. He looks at Warren's lumpy form, his fingers yellow from nicotine and eyes like two oysters past their sell-by date. 'Can't see too many of the boys making a beeline for you, mate.'

'Well, yeah.' Warren takes a couple of drags and then jabs his cigarette at Koop. 'Are you saying I'm not good enough?'

'Stop worrying.'

Warren picks up a laminated folder that lists local amenities and attractions.

'Look at this,' he says. 'Here's another thing.' He puts his cigarette in his mouth and points a thick finger the colour of earwax at a photo of a bland apartment building. 'Scene of the 1986 quadruple homicide,' he reads. 'The Packham Apartments, just fifty yards south, were the scene of 1986's most talked about killings.' He puts down the folder. 'They're fucking proud of it!'

Koop leaves Warren smoking on the balcony and goes inside to get some air. The TV's on with the sound down showing some news show. Warren's got a habit – Koop's discovered – of having the TV on at all times. Onscreen a tall man in his sixties with a grim expression is facing a barrage of microphones. Some congressional hearing. Iraq or Afghanistan. Koop recognises the guy as a politician but can't remember his name. One of the bad ones, he thinks.

On the coffee table are the fruits of their trip to the shopping mall that afternoon: three prepaid mobiles, two short-wave walkie-talkies, a camera, several cardboard files, a couple of clip-boards, two utility tool belts, two plain khaki shirts, two pairs of olive-coloured cargo pants, two green baseball caps, two pairs of workboots and the remains of a Chinese meal.

The meal was the one they'd just eaten but everything else, including the plain white panel van they'd rented, was for tomorrow. The prepaids and vehicle were Frank's suggestion but the other stuff had come from Koop. All you needed for successful stalking.

He and Warren had flown in this morning on a Qantas flight from Sydney. Frank was on his way to New York and would fly on to Los Angeles in two days' time, once he'd finished digging through the CCTV.

He wouldn't be staying with Koop and Warren. Instead Frank had booked a room at a hotel a few blocks north. Why they needed the cloak and dagger stuff, Koop didn't know. It didn't matter, really. What did matter was that tomorrow they'd take a look at the guy they'd travelled halfway round the planet to see.

For the first time in a long while, Koop is looking forward to waking up.

He takes one of the cardboard folders, sits down on the couch and reads the contents one more time.

Seven

'Gloria Lopez.' Frank's getting sick of saying the name.

He's been in the immigration interview room for an hour, sitting across the desk from the Hispanic officer. A badge on the guy's ample left tit says 'Muno-Cappiea'. Frank doesn't know if that's his name or the name of some sort of contract company.

'We haven't got anything about Agent Lopez on file,' the man says. He taps a chubby finger on the file in front of him. 'What we do have is your name on a Homeland Security watch list.'

'And I'm telling you, again, that I am a police officer with Merseyside Police in the UK and I'm here to meet with Agent Lopez. I've had an MLAT application approved by your government.' Frank looks at the badge again. 'Is that your name?'

The white officer, leaning his vast behind against a filing cabinet, taps his colleague on the shoulder and whispers something. He turns back to Frank and glares at him.

'Does that ever work?' says Frank. 'The stare? Christ.' He leans back and rubs his face. His eyes feel sandy and he's starting to feel nauseated.

'You're going to have to answer some questions.'

'Fuck off.' Frank's had it. 'Get me someone wearing a suit. Not one of you desk monkeys. Do it now before there's a diplomatic incident.' Frank leans forward and taps the file. 'What do you think is the more likely explanation? That I'm on your list and making up some bullshit story that could be disproved with a phone call, or that there's been some sort of bureaucratic mix-up? If you can't find the number for the FBI, call my office in Liverpool and they'll find it for you. Then, once they've done that, they can talk you through some more simple tasks, like tying your own

282

shoelaces, or finding your fucking face with your fucking fork. No, wait, I can see that neither of you has the slightest difficulty performing that function.'

Muno-Cappiea flushes and moves in his seat.

'Careful, big boy,' says Frank. 'You might bust an artery.'

He doesn't know what will happen next but before anyone can do anything the door to the office opens and two people enter. A man and a woman. Both are wearing business clothes and both look to be in their mid-thirties. The woman shows a badge to the immigration officers.

'FBI Agent Lopez,' she says. She turns to her partner. 'This is Agent Monroe. Apologies for this, DCI Keane. I should have been here to greet you but I got held up.'

'His name's on our list,' says the white immigration officer. 'He's ours.'

'Your list is obviously wrong,' says Lopez. 'DCI Frank Keane is here legitimately to apply for evidence from the US Justices Department under an approved MLAT. This falls under Federal jurisdiction. You two can go before I issue an obstruction of justice notice. Go on, get going.'

The immigration officers make a show of moving slowly but eventually they make the door.

'Bye,' says Frank. He makes a phone signal with one hand up to his ear. 'Let's do lunch? Call me.'

'Fuck you,' says Muno-Cappiea. He closes the door to the office with force.

'Let's get you over to your hotel,' says Lopez. 'We can go over tomorrow's details on the way.'

'No,' says Frank. 'Let's see the footage now.'

An image of the guy from Bean flashes into his head. The longer he leaves the CCTV footage, the less chance there is of getting what he needs.

'I'd rather do it straight away, Agent Lopez.'

'Whatever you want.'

MIT had emailed a list of required footage through several days ago, but no one at JFK seems to have seen it. After the clowns at immigration Frank's not surprised. He hands a new copy of the list to Lopez and they wait while Monroe tracks down the right people.

Two hours and two bad coffees later they get word that what Frank's after is in the security control room.

'This is what you asked for,' says an officer wearing a Port Authority Police uniform. He's sitting at a desk with a large computer monitor in front of him. Frank's sketchy on the details of jurisdiction but there's no disguising the cop's distaste for handing over his CCTV tapes to a couple of Feds and a foreigner.

Frank checks his notes.

'The text came through at 2.01 am UK time. We've already established that Noone was booked on the 9.30 pm flight to LA with Delta. We can assume he was at or near the gate when the call was made. He came into JFK on a Virgin Atlantic flight from Manchester, arriving at 6.27 pm.'

'There're thirty-three cameras across the terminal,' says the Port Authority cop. 'Six of them are in the area you're looking at.' He brings up six windows onscreen and clicks on one to make it bigger. 'This first one is the security gates coming through immigration. Your guy's here.'

The cop fast-forwards to a point in the digital recording. It shows the camera on the immigration desk. Ben Noone, dressed in dark clothes, looks calm and relaxed. The cop freezes the camera as Noone stares directly at the lens.

'Benjamin Noone. This is him, right?'

'That's him.'

'OK. Next time I got him is getting his bag and coming through customs.'

Another window appears and Frank watches Noone waiting for his luggage to come off a carousel. He doesn't use a phone.

'No phones permitted before clearing customs,' says the cop operating the computer. 'So he's unlikely to have used it then. Next time I can find him is just down from his onward departure gate.' An image flicks up.

Noone's sitting on a bench seat. Frank leans in close. There's something about his movements here that make Frank think this might be the likeliest place for him to have called. He watches the screen as the Port Authority cop fast-forwards through the recording. The screen jerks and suddenly there's an Asian family sitting in Noone's place.

'What happened?' Frank stands back from the screen and looks at the cop behind the keyboard. The cop rewinds and Noone reappears. He stops at the point of the jump. There's Noone and then there's a flash of white noise, electronic, and he's replaced by the family.

'Uh,' says the cop. He checks the timing and rolls back once more. He points at the timer. 'We lost some.'

Frank turns to Lopez. You seeing this? Lopez and Monroe are more alert now.

'What does that mean, "We lost some"?' Frank's trying hard to stay diplomatic but he's struggling.

'I'm just saying that's what's happened.' The cop's New York accent has hardened. 'There's been a glitch.'

'Someone's wiped a section. That's what's happened.' Frank turns to Lopez. 'What's the jurisdiction on this? Can you find out what's going on here? You're the liaison.'

Lopez sucks her lower lip. 'I'll have to check. But without a crime being committed . . .'

'Tampering with fucking evidence. That's a crime here, right?'

'If that's what's happened.' Lopez looks at the cop. 'Can you tell?'

The cop shrugs. 'I ain't an expert. You'd hafta get that kind of thing examined properly. Even then I don't know what's going to come out of it. Digital, man. Sometimes that stuff happens. A power surge, a bug, I don't know.'

'Fucking bullshit,' says Frank. He gathers his bags and turns to the door. 'I'm going to get some sleep and see if I can free up some money for a forensic examination of this.' He looks at Lopez. 'Can you at least get me a copy of what's there?'

Lopez nods. 'Leave it with me.'

'Yeah,' says Frank. He pushes through the door into the service corridor. Lopez follows him and puts an arm on his sleeve.

'Listen,' she says. 'I'll try and get something for you. Get some sleep and we'll be over in the morning.'

'You know where I'm staying?'

'We're the FBI. Yeah, we know.'

'Tell you what,' says Frank, 'give me your card and I'll call you tomorrow. How about that?'

'Whatever you like.' Lopez finds a card and hands it to Frank. 'We're on the same side.'

Frank nods and walks towards the exit to the airport terminal thinking, are we?

Eight

It's just after ten on a perfect Santa Monica morning. Noone, wearing a white shirt, black jeans and aviators, parks his jeep in a lot off Lincoln and walks around the corner to Montana, checking his reflection in the angled windows of the boutiques. He finds an outdoor table in the shade at a cafe called Grind and orders an espresso. He checks his watch, annoyed he's there before Angie and Leon. Much more stylish to be the last to arrive. He considers leaving and coming back but discards the idea in case anyone sees him doing it.

Having known Noone just over a week, Angie and Leon are now old friends in LA terms. Angie's a model on the very edge of the down slope – twenty-four – and Leon's a coming actor. He likes them both well enough and has slept with Angie – and Leon, as it happened, although that side of things didn't work out so hot. Since the thing with Terry and Nicky, Noone's gone a little cool on the bisexual thing.

Angie and Leon talk shit all the time but Noone needs company the same way he needs clothes and food and cars. The last thing he's going to be is one of those sad-assed motherfuckers sailing solo around town. The more normal Noone can appear, the easier it'll be to keep things cool until he's ready to make his play. Any investigation will not reveal a drooling loner with uncertain bathroom habits.

Besides, he needs Angie. Via his new agent Noone had gone to great lengths to engineer a meeting with her and, if he can't get what he wants through charm, is quite prepared to kill her.

As it's turning out, there should be no need for that. Angie's proving easy to manipulate.

Angie and Leon arrive just as Noone's espresso is brought out by a slim-hipped chick he hasn't seen working here before. She's cute and Noone would've liked to get her number but even Angie wouldn't stand for that so that will have to wait.

'Leon was running late,' says Angie, kissing Noone on the mouth. 'Not me.'

Angie's got her hair skinhead short and is wearing a less than opaque short dress. She's got big sunglasses pushed up on her head and some sort of retro thing going on with her shoes.

'That's OK,' says Leon, holding up his hands. 'Blame the Jew. Like always.'

'Are you Jewish?' says Noone. 'I wish you'd told me, you fucking kike.'

Leon laughs and the three of them start talking about nothing much in particular.

'They look like something off an ad,' says Menno Koopman.

He's sitting across the street at a table outside a Starbucks. He's got a laptop open in front of him and a decent view of Noone.

'Well, he is an actor,' says Eckhardt. Warren's voice sounds wheezier than ever over the tinny little speaker on the cheap phone.

'You see him too?'

'Copy. Affirmative. Subject in view,' says Warren in a terrible American accent. He lets out a wet chuckle that sounds like a reluctant throttle on a motorbike. 'Always wanted to say that. Sounds better in American, doesn't it?'

'That was American? I thought you'd had a stroke.'

Koop hangs up and looks up the street to where Eckhardt's parked the van, about eighty metres back from Grind. They've separated in case Noone continues on foot. The grid layout of Santa Monica is easy enough but until they've got their US driving heads right this is how they're playing it.

They'd picked Noone up shortly after he emerged from his house in Pacific Palisades. That had been the trickiest part: Noone's street is a winding, narrow affair with houses spaced wide apart. Not many vehicles were parked on the road and Koop and Warren felt more conspicuous than they'd like so were happy to see Noone emerge after less than an hour. It felt like a little slice of luck. Operating a two-man surveillance successfully requires as much luck as you can get. It's an inexact science, especially when conducted in a foreign country with no backup and jet lag.

From Starbucks Koop studies Noone properly for the first time.

Since Frank's phone call, he's been wondering about the man who'd got under Frank's skin enough to bring Koop and Warren from Australia as backup. Koop gives weight to Frank's policing instincts but he also knows that instinct alone can be fatal to a good copper. Koop's been guilty of coming up short a couple of times himself when he 'knew'.

That said, there's still the time line evidence and the phone, which all fits. Frank had emailed a detailed case file compiled by DC Magsi to Koop.

The killings of Terry and Alicia Peters don't feel like a murder-suicide to Koop. And if someone killed Terry then maybe Frank is on to something with Noone. The phone call from JFK is the most damning piece of evidence but it's not much without corroboration. In the absence of any forensics, or conclusive witnesses, or CCTV, there's not a lot a prosecutor could do except drop the case. With Noone being affluent – and Koop's just beginning to see how affluent – then good lawyers will shred the case as it stands. Koop doesn't attach much importance to the report from the psychologist. It's probably accurate and it might help them predict a few things, but it will only come into its own if and when Noone is caught.

From what Koop's seen of the man so far he doesn't look like someone who's particularly worried about anything. Which is why Koop is leaning towards Frank's view. Noone's behaviour this morning is a display of nonchalance. If, Koop reasons, it had been himself under suspicion of multiple murder – even a multiple murder he'd left behind in Liverpool – he's sure he'd have been more nervous than Noone appears to be.

Ten minutes pass. The area of the cafe that Koop's sitting in is set back, giving him a view through the windows of part of the cross-street. There's a dark blue Toyota half-hidden behind a shop sidewalk display board, a man in the driver's seat, his head a silhouette. Although it's the first time he's noticed him – consciously at least – Koop gets the feeling he might have been there a while. It's probably nothing.

Twenty minutes later Noone's little party is dispersing. Koop watches Noone head towards Lincoln and the other two down Montana in the direction from which they'd arrived.

'You think he's going for his car?' asks Warren over the phone.

'Looks that way.'

Koop's just about to move when he notices the blue Toyota pull out. It swings a U and heads in the direction taken by Noone.

'Wait,' says Koop into the phone. He watches the Toyota turn into Lincoln.

Once the car is out of sight Koop hurries towards their van. He slides into the passenger seat.

'There's someone else following our boy,' says Koop. As Eckhardt moves the van towards the intersection Koop points the vehicle out. 'There.'

He doesn't have to tell Eckhardt what to do. Warren waits and then makes a left onto Lincoln as the Toyota tails Noone's silver jeep. Koop and Eckhardt hang back.

'Who do you think it is?' says Eckhardt. 'FBI?'

'Could be. Frank's had the MLAT application in for a few weeks. Maybe they think Noone's worth some examination.' Koop points to the right. 'He's turning.'

Noone pulls the jeep left and the Toyota follows. It's tricky, keeping them both in view, so Eckhardt just stays with the Toyota.

Koop's looking at the sat nav.

'I think he's headed home. The Pacific Coast Highway's this way.'

'Maybe we should drop back more? Play it safe.'

'No, stick with them.'

Koop's glad they do. A minute later and Noone's on the Santa Monica Freeway heading east. The traffic's heavy but that helps Eckhardt. He keeps the van tucked out of sight using a truck about a hundred metres behind the blue Toyota as a shield. In the traffic, everything's moving the same pace.

'Just make sure we don't follow the wrong Toyota,' says Eckhardt. 'There's a fucking lot of the bastards.'

Eckhardt's right, Los Angeles seems to be full of blue Toyotas, but Koop keeps it in sight. The only worry is not doing something dumb that draws attention to the white van. Koop's pretty sure whoever's tailing Noone is an expert. Anything untoward in the rear-view will be noticeable.

'You done much driving on this side of the road?' Koop asks.

Eckhardt shrugs. 'I have now.' He fumbles for a cigarette.

'Wait,' says Koop. 'I'll do it.' Koop hates smoke but denying Eckhardt would be like depriving a diver of oxygen. And it'll help Eckhardt concentrate.

Koop lights up and coughs. He hands the cigarette to Eckhardt, who looks at the filter dubiously. 'Bit wet, isn't it?' Then he shrugs again and sticks it hungrily in his mouth.

It takes thirty-five minutes of stop-start driving before Noone gets off the freeway.

'Careful,' says Koop but there's no need; Eckhardt's smooth. He swings onto the down ramp and pulls in right behind the Toyota at the stoplight on the looped exit.

'What the fuck are you doing?' says Koop.

'Easy, chief.' Eckhardt blows a plume of smoke out of the window. 'If he's wondering about us this'll stop him. When did you ever see a tail pull up close like this? Besides, if I hadn't it would have looked weird. In this traffic you take your slot when it comes.'

Eckhardt's got a point. Avoiding the Toyota would have been strange.

Waiting for the lights they take the time to study the man following Noone. He's white, short-haired and with wide shoulders. His clothing is dark. There's nothing personal on show in the car and nothing on the outside that indicates where the vehicle's from, other than a generic California plate. No bumper stickers, no insignia. Koop writes down the tag.

'He's some sort of law,' says Eckhardt. 'Far as I can tell.'

'Maybe. Military?'

'Why the fuck would some military bloke be following our bloke?'

The lights change and the Toyota moves lanes to get a little nearer to Noone's jeep. The caterpillar of cars bends through the intersection and up onto La Cienega.

'How do you pronounce that?' says Eckhardt, glancing up at the green street sign. 'Hard "c"? Or "ch"?'

'Search me. Do you always discuss pronunciation during a tail?'

'What else are you going to do?' says Warren. 'It's a pretty long tail and you have to pass the time somehow. I haven't got a never-ending supply of snappy dialogue like you. Besides, I really want to know. *Chee-enn-ah-gah*. I reckon that's it.'

'Fuck off. Concentrate on the road.' Koop checks his watch. Almost twelve-thirty.

Noone drives north and after a couple of turns pulls into a quiet residential street off Sunset Boulevard. The place looks like it belongs somewhere else out in the Midwest. There are white picket fences and fresh-painted porches with double-seat swings on them. Koop remembers his surprise at the contrast between the main arteries and the side roads in LA from his first trip. For Eckhardt it's all new.

He rolls the van past the end of the street and stops out of sight of the side road on Sunset.

'We can't stop down there,' he says. 'Might as well be driving an ice-cream truck.'

'Wait here,' says Koop. He puts on a khaki cap and grabs a clip-board and tool belt. 'I'll call and let you know what's happening. For all we know he's taking a short cut.'

The tree-lined street, despite connecting Hollywood and Sunset, is almost eerily quiet. Koop, in his make-do uniform, feels exposed, fake. Looking north he can see the blue Toyota stationary on the right-hand side of the road. Noone's jeep is parked about eighty metres further on. Maybe two minutes have passed since Eckhardt stopped the van.

A nearby house has a Halloween pumpkin on the porch. There's something familiar about the place but Koop can't work out what and has no idea why there'd be a pumpkin there in July. It adds to his sense of unease as he tries to look convincing in his role as some kind of tradesman.

He's getting closer to the Toyota. He can see clearly the silhou-ette of the man in the front seat and Koop has no choice but to walk past. His phone vibrates in his pocket but he lets it go. He can't talk to Eckhardt now – he's three paces from the car and the driver's window is down.

Shit.

Drawing level, Koop tries to appear engrossed in something on his clipboard. Out of the corner of his eye he glimpses the driver's face.

He gives Koop a level glance and then turns back to the view through the windscreen. Up ahead, a white open-topped minibus with 'Starline' written on the side in red turns into the street. Packed with tourists holding cameras it passes Noone's jeep and drives slowly down the street. As it approaches the house that the blue Toyota is parked outside, the bus slows to a halt and Koop can hear the tour guide's excited commentary. The house is the one used in the horror movie *Halloween*.

The bus is temporarily blocking the road.

Noone's jeep pulls out and turns into Selma Avenue. As he does, the blue Toyota, frustrated by the bus, blares his horn. The bus driver holds up an apologetic palm, puts the bus into gear and moves forward. By the time a gap has opened up, Noone and the jeep are gone.

Smooth, thinks Koop, as the blue Toyota accelerates towards the intersection.

Koop walks away from the tour bus, takes his phone out of his pocket and calls Warren. There's no answer.

Koop walks around the block and comes out onto Sunset. After the shade of the side streets the sun is blinding. There's no sign of Warren.

'Shit,' mutters Koop.

Nine

At the cafe Noone finally gets what he wanted from Angie.

The guest list for the Fundraiser.

The Fundraiser. Always with a capital 'F'. Angie is sleeping with one of the lawyers on the fundraising committee. It's all she's been talking about for days.

Noone's given Angie a good Hollywood reason for the guest list: he wants to network. A lot of names at the party. His status as a new arrival, and his story to Angie about the unlucky end to his big break on *The Tunnels*, rings true. Noone doesn't have to lay anything on too thick; Angie believes him. And, since he's exactly the sort of moneyed contributor the party machine is interested in, she hands the guest list over without a murmur. Ben had explained his need for the list to her; there's no way he's going to stump up a wad for the ticket – thirty grand – without knowing who he's rubbing shoulders with. He tells her it's just between the two of them. He doesn't want every fundraising body in town chasing him. When Leon goes to the bathroom, Angie slips Noone the list.

As they're leaving Grind, Noone makes the guy following him. He glances across towards Starbucks in the reflection in a dry-cleaning store and sees the blue Toyota move off.

So fucking obvious.

A black curtain descends. Noone's had enough of this shit. If someone's going to follow him at least make a show of being professional. Who sits in a car outside a coffee shop for that length of time? Go inside and order coffee. Make it look respectable. He'd clocked the car earlier as well as the tall guy with the laptop. Since laptop boy didn't make a move Noone figures he got that one wrong.

Noone fingers the short-bladed knife he carries inside his jacket. He's got plans today that don't involve being tailed.

By the time he's in West Hollywood the Toyota's still there. Noone gets to North Orange Grove Avenue, turns in and accelerates hard for the intersection with Selma. He'd had a thing with a girl here when he was twenty and knows the area well. He parks close to the corner with Selma, leaving the jeep in full view. As expected the Toyota pulls into North Orange Grove behind him and parks at the lower end of the street when he sees Noone's jeep at the kerb up ahead. The driver's hoping that Noone hasn't seen him. He pulls in on the left-hand side so as to remain half-hidden by the two vehicles between his car and Noone's jeep.

Noone's prepared to wait twenty minutes but he's in luck. To his right, one of the tourist buses that plague the area dawdles slowly down Selma Avenue and turns into North Orange Grove. Noone turns away from the camera-happy tourists as the bus passes. In the rear-view he watches it reach the *Halloween* house, blocking the Toyota, and pulls out quickly into Selma. He makes a right and then another and pops back out onto Sunset heading west towards I-10 and Palm Springs, confident he's not being watched.

Ten

'Fucking piece of shit!'

Warren throws the prepaid mobile onto the passenger seat in disgust. Noone's jeep is back on Sunset. It just popped out right in front of him and accelerated west. The sudden appearance of the car causes Warren to drop the lit stub of his cigarette onto his lap. By the time he's found the thing and burnt his fingers, Noone's almost out of sight.

'Shit.'

Warren looks around but there's no sign of Koop or the blue Toyota. From the speed Noone's going, Warren's guessing that he's slipped the tail.

There's nothing for it. Warren pulls out and follows. Conscious of driving in foreign traffic, he tries to call Koop again but there's nothing. He can't work out if it's the signal, the battery, or some other thing. One-handed there's not much he can do except stay with Noone. Koop will just have to work it out for himself.

Now Noone's really moving through the traffic and Warren has trouble keeping pace. There's a dizzying rush of freeway entrances and exits and then they're on I-10 burning through what looks like the outer suburbs. Pomona, Ontario, Colton. The names blow past like leaves in the wind.

About an hour in and the smog lifts like a theatre curtain rising. There's a clarity and sparkle to the air here that makes Warren feel he's just cleaned his sunglasses. To either side of the road scrubby desert starts to dominate between the industrial units.

Warren checks his fuel. Half-full. On the GPS he presses through the menu to give him a high view of the map. The only place he can see up ahead is a place called Palm Springs. Today's not working out exactly as expected.

On the side of the road giant white wind turbines sprout like alien wildflowers; thousands of them. To Warren's right, a mountain range with snow clinging to the clefts at the ridge. The temperature gauge has been climbing for thirty minutes: 69 in LA, it's 112 now. Warren takes a minute to work it out and then turns the aircon higher. Whatever it is, it's fucking hot out there. The Sonny Bono Memorial Freeway. Jesus. Warren only knows the name because of that one song: 'I Got You Babe'. Is that all it takes to get a freeway named after you?

Warren squints into the distance. It's hard keeping track of Noone but he's pretty sure he's still got him in sight. There's an exit coming up and Noone takes it. Warren eases back and waits until he sees Noone loop around and back over the freeway, heading north on something called Twentynine Palms Highway. After a few minutes the road starts to climb, and in the more powerful vehicle, Noone pulls ahead. By the time Warren gets to somewhere called Morongo, Noone's gone.

Warren tries Koop again on the phone but this time it's definitely a signal problem. He pushes on another five minutes but it's useless. Warren pulls into a gas station outside Twentynine Palms – which turns out to be a town – and refuels. He buys a pack of cigarettes and uses the payphone inside to call Koop and leave a message.

'I lost him,' says Warren. 'I'm at somewhere called Twentynine Palms, wherever that is. No idea if he's gone further or turned off so I'm heading back. I'll see you at the apartment. Call me if you get this message before then.'

Warren hangs up and stretches. Outside, the air is dry and hot, but pleasant in a way. Better than the humidity back home, anyway. Warren walks off the station forecourt and onto a patch of scrub. He takes a cigarette from the fresh pack and lights up. Warren stands looking at the distant mountain range while he smokes. When he's finished he grinds the butt underfoot, taking care that it's dead. This country looks like it could burn easy.

He sees a sign for the bathroom and follows the building to a back lot that faces a section of rising scrub. Drain the snake before the slog back.

He's at the urinal when the door opens behind him.

Warren glances over his shoulder.

It's Noone.

The man looks at Warren, a neutral expression on his face.

Warren nods affably and turns his back.

In a long career, not without incident, it's one of the hardest things he's ever done. It's like turning his back on a Bengal tiger. For a second or two Warren looks at the white tile of the restroom wall and wonders if it will be the last thing he sees. Wouldn't be a great way to bow out.

And then Noone takes his place at a stall two down. Neither man speaks.

Warren finishes, forces himself to move slowly, and washes his hands. His back itches in anticipation of the knife but it doesn't come. He dries his hands under the blower, the noise from the motor filling the restroom. As Noone moves to the washbasins, Warren leaves and walks out into the heat. Everything looks better than when he went inside. He can almost hear the angels singing.

Hall-e-fucking-lujah!

Warren walks to the van and climbs inside. As he starts the engine, he looks in the wing mirror and sees Noone leaving the restroom. Warren pulls out and joins the traffic on the highway. He points the van back towards Los Angeles, fumbling a cigarette from his pack, and lights up, his fingers trembling. Drawing the smoke down deep, he feels his overworked heart thumping in his chest.

A few minutes later, Warren sees Noone's jeep blow past as the road winds down the mountain pass towards the desert plain and the freeway beyond. He doesn't give chase. If Noone sees the white van tailing him his cover is gone. Now that Noone's seen it, they'll have to change the vehicle for something else.

Besides, Warren thinks he might be about to have a heart attack.

Eleven

Frank wakes from a dreamless sleep at 4 am with a jolt of fear. He has a feeling he shouted something in the moment before waking but what it is he can't remember.

It takes him a few minutes to focus on where he is before he gets out of the hotel bed. The view through the window looks like something from a 'Batman' movie. Gotham's dark but there's activity everywhere.

So it's true. This city doesn't sleep.

Frank takes a long shower and gets dressed and spends a couple of hours going over the case notes. It's not until he turns on his laptop that he finds the email from Koop.

'Problems,' it says, cryptically. 'Call me when you get this. Whatever the time is. Your phone's not working. Urgent.' The email has the numbers for Koop and Eckhardt's new prepaids.

Frank picks up his mobile and checks it. It seems like it's fine but when he tries to dial Koop there's nothing there. Frank picks up the receiver by his bed and presses for an outside line. He starts to dial before hesitating and replaces the receiver.

There are things happening that are worrying him. Dark shapes drift beneath the waiting surfer. Maybe using the hotel phone isn't such a good idea.

Frank emails Koop to say he'll be travelling to LA later once he's heard from Lopez.

At seven, Lopez calls and asks him to meet downstairs in the hotel bar.

'I thought I was going to call you?' says Frank.

'Does it matter?'

She's drinking coffee when Frank gets there. There's no sign of Monroe and Lopez doesn't offer an explanation.

Frank orders coffee and sits down.

'Did you find anything?' he says. He already knows the answer by looking at Lopez.

The agent hands Frank a padded envelope. Inside is a DVD.

'The footage from JFK,' says Lopez.

'The same as yesterday?' says Frank. 'Or is this the full director's cut?'

Lopez shakes her head. 'There's nothing more on there than you've already seen.'

'This is crap,' says Frank. He moves to stand but Lopez puts a hand on his wrist. Frank sits back in the chair.

'There's no more footage,' says Lopez. 'Believe me, I looked.'

'But someone wiped it?'

'That's not what I'm saying. I have no evidence of that.'

Frank waves the padded envelope. 'There's this.'

'It's not good, I'll give you that.'

'So what am I still sitting down for?'

Lopez looks around the room. There are about ten other tables occupied from maybe fifty. 'I'm here alone.'

Frank doesn't say anything.

'Monroe wouldn't come,' says Lopez in a low voice. 'Do you know what I'm saying?'

Frank raises an eyebrow. 'No,' he says. 'I don't.'

'He's ambitious,' continues Lopez. 'Being seen with you isn't good.'

'I'm not sure . . .'

'You should be careful, DCI Keane.'

'Is that a threat?'

Lopez digs a nail into Frank's hand and he flinches. 'I'm taking a risk coming today, asshole. Our advice was to leave you alone. Not do anything, just leave you alone. The agent who told me to do that is my boss. He looked scared and he's not a guy who I've ever seen look like that before.' Lopez moves her hand away and then gets to her feet. 'But just letting you ride doesn't feel right to me, so I thought I could come along and at least make you aware of the field you're playing on. Someone big enough to scare my boss is a truly frightening concept.

'Be careful,' she says and leaves Frank sitting at the table alone.

Twelve

Koop crosses Sunset and walks towards a main intersection. At a cafe he sits at the counter, orders orange juice – he's caffeined to the gills after the stint at Starbucks this morning – and gets the number of a cab company from the waitress. As he waits for the cab he calls Eckhardt but the phone rings out.

Back at the apartment Koop calls Frank. It's just after two in Los Angeles, three hours behind New York.

'Koop,' says Frank. He's at the departure gates waiting for the flight to LA. 'I called earlier but there was no reply.'

'Yes, we're having some trouble with these prepaids. Listen, can you talk? I mean, are you alone?'

'Yes. I'm on my way to Los Angeles.'

'CCTV no good?'

'It's been erased. Lopez – she's the FBI field agent here – says it's "unfortunate". Says she's sure it's coincidental. She said it in a voice that might have been sarcastic.'

'Uh-huh.'

'Well, right, exactly. We have him on tape but not calling. It's not a massive thing; his lawyer would still say that doesn't prove he was using Peters' phone but it means we can't triangulate the times. Anyway, what's your news?'

'I think you might be right about Noone.'

'What?'

Koop fills Frank in on the details of Noone giving the blue Toyota the slip.

'Warren's still on him, I think. I can't get through. But that's what I'd have done.'

'Does he know he had two tails?'

'No,' says Koop. 'I'm pretty sure. But there's something going on here, Frank. I mean more than our boy being a fucking nut. The guy in the Toyota tailing Noone was a pro. Do you think LAPD or the FBI are doing something?'

'Possibly. But I think it's unlikely.' Frank's thinking of budgets and bureaucracy. Not to mention Lopez's warning. Assigning a tail on Noone because some Brit wants to talk to him is not going to happen. Too expensive and too time-consuming. It doesn't feel right.

Frank thinks about what would happen if the information was coming the other way, if the Americans were interested in someone in Liverpool. Would he authorise surveillance? Probably not.

'Let me try a few things,' says Koop. 'I'm at the apartment. I'll wait here to hear from Warren and I'll make some calls. Don't worry, I'll be discreet.'

'OK, I'll be there tonight. I'll come to the apartment from the airport. Around eleven your time if there are no delays. Lopez is handing me on to the LA field agent but I'm not seeing them until tomorrow, Sunday. We need to get our heads together. I thought we'd have a bit more time than this.'

'Maybe our boy is hurrying things along? Could be he's on a schedule.'

'What makes you think that?'

'The drive out to Palm Springs? I don't know. Do people drive there and turn round like that? It felt to me like he was going there for a reason.'

'Could be. Look, I'll talk later. The flight's being called.'

After Frank's call Koop rings Warren again but there's no answer. Koop puts down the phone and yawns. He feels like he could sleep for a week. Jet lag. If he's meeting Frank tonight he'll have to get some sleep. But not yet; there are things to do. Koop takes a shower to wake himself up and is stepping out when the phone rings. It's Warren. Koop presses redial and this time he connects.

'We need a new car,' says Warren. 'And I need a new ticker.'

Thirteen

Since Warren's going to exchange the rental for something else it'll take him three hours or more to get back to the apartment, so Koop spends the time doing some digging.

The first thing he does is call Sam Dooley.

In 2001 Koop had spent six months on an all-expenses-paid holiday to Los Angeles. At least that was the way his MIT colleagues had seen it at the time. Merseyside Police and the LAPD, as part of some now forgotten political initiative, had joined an information and skills program, the IPPP. The acronym stood for the International Police Pooling Program. Koop had applied during a time when he was beginning to think about retirement. Six months in California sounded fantastic and it was. Dooley had been Koop's liaison at the LAPD. Now he's a senior detective on the Gang Detail working out of the City of Burbank Police Department.

Koop calls him, and after some bullshit about being in LA on holiday and agreeing to meet for drinks, he asks Dooley to check the plate number on the blue Toyota.

'Now?' Dooley's tone, warm until this point, drops a couple of degrees. 'Why? You're on vacation, Koop.'

'Can you find that information, Sam?' Koop feels bad asking, but it can't be helped.

'Yeah, I guess. But I don't like it, Koop.'

Koop doesn't say anything. Dooley doesn't have to like it, just so long as he does what Koop asks. There's a pause.

'It's registered to a company. Daedalus.' Dooley spells out the word letter by letter and gives Koop the address.

'OK. Thanks.'

'That's it? No details on why?'

'It was nothing, Sam. You know what cops are like. I thought I saw something funny today but a woman told me it was for reality TV. I wanted to check.'

'Right.' Dooley is outright frosty now. Koop finishes the call awkwardly and, alone in the apartment, shakes his head. Another tiny little relationship dies in the name of information. It's happened too many times down the years. Good coppers are always losing friendships.

Koop sits with the phone for a minute and then calls Sam Dooley again.

'Sam,' says Koop, when Dooley picks up, 'I feel bad about doing that.'

'Yeah, well, maybe you should. What is it now? You want something else? Tickets to Disney?'

'Don't be bitter. I said I was sorry; I'm not going to send you flowers. Listen, I want to talk to you about something you might be interested in. An exchange of information.' Koop does feel bad about using Dooley but knows that to get traction on this thing over here they're going to have to have some allies. Frank always was a lone gun type but it's not going to work in Los Angeles. Dooley's a friendly face and, besides being the right thing to do, eating a little humble pie might help the cause.

'I'm listening,' says Dooley.

'Not now,' says Koop. 'It's too complicated. Can you meet for coffee or lunch tomorrow?'

Dooley's got a court appearance at eleven so he arranges to meet Koop at one at a coffee shop down the street from the Burbank Courthouse. By the time he rings off Koop's recovered some of the ground he'd lost from the first call.

After the call, Koop gets online and tries for information on Daedalus. It doesn't take long.

Daedalus is the name of a large private security and intelligence gathering service with links to the US Department of Corrections and a number of high-profile blue-chip companies. From what Koop can see, Daedalus do everything the modern CEO might want in the way of security, from supplying shopping mall guards to preventing insurgents blowing up your oil pipeline. Daedalus is owned by an even larger parent company called Loder Industries. Loder has interests in a wide swathe of industries, chief among them engineering and supply logistics. To Koop it sounds about as interesting as accountancy but the numbers are huge. Current valuation of Loder stands at over $120 billion. Loder's biggest customer is the US government.

Koop puts the information on Loder to one side and concentrates again on Daedalus.

There are a number of news items but he has no luck finding anything that mentions Noone, even tangentially.

Koop gets a Coke from the fridge and drains it in an attempt to stay awake longer.

He switches his attention back to Noone. After Frank had contacted him about coming to LA, Koop had done as much background as he could on Ben Noone. Koop pulls up some of that information onscreen again now and reads over it once more. Like DC Magsi, Koop had found information on Noone difficult to come by.

The bare facts are that he was born in LA in 1983. Noone's father, Larry Grant, an LA native, had died before Noone was born, leaving him to be brought up by his mother, Deborah Sterling, originally from Connecticut. Deborah had died two years ago leaving Noone, her only child, to inherit.

Koop stares for several minutes at the screen, the cursor blinking at the end of the word 'inherit'.

He leans back and folds his hands behind his head. An old phrase came to him, so overused that it had become a mantra. In all the fire and blood and sex of the crimes committed in Liverpool, Koop thinks there's perhaps one thing they hadn't truly examined in enough detail. So intensely personal, so mired in gore and perversion are the crimes, that Frank may have forgotten the mantra of all investigations, the words that should be tattooed on the hand of every cop on the planet.

Follow the money.

Fourteen

A beer never tasted so good.

Frank clinks the neck of his bottle against Koop's and then leans across the balcony table to do the same with Warren.

The three men drink and Frank rubs his neck. He landed an hour and a half ago and took a taxi to the apartment. His brief, unsuccessful stop in New York, followed by another long flight, has done nothing to improve his outlook, but the beer's helping.

And being with friends is good. Warren he only met ten minutes ago but if Koop's happy with him then that's good enough for Frank. Hearing Koop's Liverpool accent – even one softened at the edges by three years in Australia – also helps.

Five floors below the sounds of a different city drift up to the apartment and, despite it all, Frank gets a tang of that holiday feeling. It always surprises him when he travels that places don't look like they're supposed to, as if somehow there's a conspiracy to hide the real version of a place from everyone. But LA is exactly like LA should be. There are palm trees and smog and cars and neon and all the thousands of tiny visual details Frank, like everyone else in the western world, has been absorbing frame by frame their entire lives. As with New York, everything looks like a film set and, consequently, nothing appears real. Taxidrivers, waitresses, cops – everyone seems to be playing a role in some vast production.

It's dangerous thinking, Frank knows that. But for now, sitting back with a cold beer as the clock ticks towards midnight, it's OK to let his mind drift along those paths.

'Frank.' Koop's voice jerks his eyes open.

'You need some sleep.'

Frank nods. He sits up and rolls the kinks out of his neck. He glances back into the apartment where the TV's showing football. Not proper football: the American kind.

'I got into this a bit when I was over here,' says Koop, following Frank's eye. 'Started watching it.'

'It's like rugby,' says Warren. 'For poofs.'

Frank can't work out if Warren's kidding. From the little he's seen it's hard to tell with the Australian.

'How so?' says Frank.

'He's from Queensland,' says Koop, by way of explanation.

Warren ignores Koop. 'All that padding, helmets and the like. Seems a bit . . . girly.'

Frank looks at Koop, who shakes his head.

'Queensland.'

Warren winks at Frank. 'He's easy to stir up.'

They go over what they have and decide what to do in the morning. Frank's got to meet his liaison at LAPD headquarters so it's down to Koop or Warren to tail Noone.

'Do you think it was coincidence, him being in the toilet at the petrol station?' asks Frank.

Warren takes a pull on his beer. 'I was thinking about that on the way back here.' He drags on his cigarette and speaks through a cloud of smoke. 'And the conclusion I reached was no. I mean, what are the odds?'

'So what was it?' asks Koop.

'I think he wanted a close look at me. See if I was a cop.'

Warren looks down at himself. He's out of shape, dressed in the shirt and khakis Koop had bought as cover. 'I think he was reassured. I didn't say anything in case the accent spooked him.' Warren doesn't tell them how scared he'd been.

'You think he's definitely our bloke?' he says. 'He didn't look like a loony.'

'He's the one,' says Frank. 'Not sure that loonies generally look like loonies.'

'Did you hear that story about the Queen visiting Ashworth?' Koop looks at Frank.

Frank shrugs.

Koop turns to Warren. 'Ashworth's a high-security mental hospital in Frank's patch.' He turns back to Frank. 'Anyway, the Queen visits and the head guy introduces her to this bloke, John. John's a trustee, says the head guy; very well behaved. He's going to show you round today, Your Majesty. So John shows the Queen around and is very well spoken and all in all seems to be a pretty nice feller. If you don't mind me asking, John, says the Queen, what did you do to get locked away inside here?'

'Is this going to be a long one?' says Warren, getting to his feet. 'Because I could do with another beer.' He pushes inside and takes a fresh one from the fridge.

'So John says to the Queen: funny you should say that, Your Majesty, but there's been a terrible mistake. I didn't commit the crime they say I did but no one will believe me. All I need is for someone to check a few facts and I would be a free man. The Queen nods and says she'll do whatever she can tomorrow. Thanks, says John, and the tour continues. An hour later, the tour over, the Queen's heading for the Bentley when a brick hits her on the back of the head. She turns round to see John waving at her. "You won't forget now, will you?" he yells.'

Warren laughs. Frank smiles. He's heard it before.

'OK, fair enough,' says Warren.

'If Frank says Noone's the guy, then Noone's the guy,' says Koop.

Frank moves to the couch and stares blankly at the TV. His eyes are heavy, and although he can hear Koop and Warren talking, he can't make out what they're saying. The last thing he sees as he drifts into unconsciousness is a graphic onscreen with the words 'pass interference'.

Fifteen

Money makes the world go round.

There's money somewhere in the picture, Koop's sure of that. For Frank, who'd been on the ground back in Liverpool, the money doesn't seem important. Nicky Peters dying like that. Sexual abuse. The abattoir scene. McCluskey's finger. All of this means that Frank has this case wired as a hot one. Hot in the sense of being about blood and violence and instability. Money, at best, is a means for Ben Noone to evade capture by hiring expensive lawyers.

Menno Koopman's not so sure.

In the morning, early, Warren heads to Santa Monica in the new rental to keep an eye on Noone as best he can. Frank never made his hotel and slept on the couch. Koop shakes him awake and pushes him towards the shower. By seven-thirty he's in a taxi heading to his hotel before meeting the liaison officer at nine. Frank's due at LAPD headquarters on West 1st Street to start selling his contact on elevating the MLAT to an extradition order at some point. What he's hoping is to find a sympathetic ear for his theories, someone willing to consider the circumstantial evidence. The fact that the liaison is willing to meet on a Sunday is promising.

Alone in the apartment, Koop's first act is to book a second car rental with a hire company who'll deliver the vehicle at nine. He gives himself an hour to get across to Burbank to meet Dooley at eleven.

Koop pours a cup of coffee and settles in front of the computer to do some online background chasing of his own before the meeting. Noone's Los Angeles address had been part of the package of information that Frank's already received. While the lack of an attempt to conceal the address might not mean much, it's an indicator to Frank that Noone's confident about any investigation.

Koop starts with Noone's house in Santa Monica. He doesn't have Frank's faith that Noone's lack of concern means that it's a dry well. In Koop's experience, if there's property, there's a paper trail. Or digital.

On the LA County Assessor's website he finds the steps to follow after someone has died and left property. It takes time but he digs up the Change of Ownership Statement filed when Deborah Sterling died. It's all on public record once he knows where to look. Benjamin Noone's listed as the new owner. The property was assessed at a value of just under four million at time of transfer. There's nothing Koop can see that raises any flags and he's sure that this is all material accessed by Frank's team in Liverpool.

He finds a news item about Sterling's death. Noone's mother died of colorectal cancer and spent the last four months of her life at the Palisades Palliative Care facility not far from her home. While Noone is hardly shaping up as a model child, he's out of the picture as far as killing his mother is concerned.

Koop's starting to build up some material. He's tech-savvy but likes a paper copy. He searches online and finds an electronics store two blocks away. Thirty minutes later he's back in the apartment with a sixty-dollar printer hooked up to the laptop.

Koop switches his attention to the name.

Sterling.

It's been bugging him that Noone has a different name to that of his father and mother. On a hunch that the death of his mother prompted the name change, Koop limits his investigation to the time period immediately after Deborah Sterling's death. He's wrong. An hour later he discovers that Ben Sterling changed his name shortly after his mother died, after lodging a court petition with the LA Superior Court. It's a standard procedure with no barriers except if there's evidence that the name change will be used to commit fraud. The website offers an example: sex offenders are one category barred from changing their names. Presumably Ben Sterling came up clean, because one week after completing the paperwork, he became Ben Noone.

Koop, with DC Magsi's original report in front of him, smiles. No wonder Frank went apeshit at Magsi. To be fair, Koop isn't working with an additional caseload and there's some information he has access to now that Magsi didn't then. Still.

The Sterlings sound to Koop like they'd inherited money but he can't locate anything to support that. There's something of a gap in the material on Larry Grant. All Koop can get is that he was in the military, an enlisted man who died in an on-base auto accident at Fort Bragg. No money there.

Deborah Sterling must have had the cash – but when Koop tries to find it, he comes up blank. All he discovers is a 2011 blog post from a Deborah Sterling referring to a movie she'd seen about domestic servants in pre-civil rights Mississippi. Sterling refers to her own experiences as a nanny. If this is Noone's mother posting, then there's no money in her family either.

It's only when Koop reads through the whole post that he sees it buried right near the end. A throwaway reference to Sterling's old employer being in trouble tickles Koop's memory. She uses a particular word to describe him.

Minotaur.

Sixteen

Frank's meeting at LAPD headquarters with the liaison agent in attendance is even less productive than the Sunday timing had threatened. After the warning from Lopez in New York, he had expected some element of turf protection to be in evidence, but what he isn't prepared for is the open hostility. Lopez's west coast counterpart, Federal Agent Ross Hagenbaum, is clear from the outset about his lack of sympathy with Frank's ideas. As far as Hagenbaum and Lieutenant Mills, the wiry veteran whose office the meeting takes place in, are concerned, Frank's MLAT application is at best a fishing trip and at worst completely baseless. Frank doesn't think either man has been warned to go hard on him; that's something that comes naturally to both.

To compound matters, neither Hagenbaum nor Mills are fools, or anything close to being fools. They are both well informed about the data and both have a firm understanding of the weaknesses in Frank's case against Noone.

'That's why I'm here,' he says. 'To gather some harder evidence. I'm looking for your help.'

'We don't see what we can do.' Hagenbaum looks at his watch. 'Noone has committed no crime. You have nothing.' Hagenbaum is younger than Frank, around thirty. He's smart and knows it. Frank wants to smash his perfect white teeth in.

Instead he counts to ten. 'We have Noone involved in a case with six dead. We have a witness who was assaulted by Noone. We have a psychologist's report which matches Noone's profile. And we have him at JFK at a time when Terry Peters' phone was used to make a call. It's more than nothing.'

'I'll give you the phone,' says Mills. 'And what you say about the CCTV at the airport is a concern.' He looks at Hagenbaum. 'You think?'

'It's not good.' Hagenbaum pauses. 'But it's not enough to push me to your view, Frank.'

Frank doesn't remember telling Hagenbaum he could call him by his first name but he lets it pass. It's an old trick that Frank uses himself to subtly remind subordinates of their unthreatening status. Searle employs it all the time. Except that Searle is Frank's boss and Hagenbaum isn't.

'So what can you give me?' Frank checks his watch now. If this is going to be a complete pile of shit he might as well get moving.

'We will of course extend all hospitality,' says Mills.

'What does that mean, exactly?'

'You can use Lieutenant Mills' interview rooms. We can facilitate any meetings with Benjamin Noone or his representatives.'

'And we can help you with any secretarial and logistical requirements.' Mills says this as if he's offering Frank a gift of emeralds.

'Secretarial?' It's hard to keep the scorn from his voice. He shakes his head and then looks at the two men in the room in turn.

'You're both officers of the law, right? You both want the same things as me, at least on paper. I'm telling you straight that Ben Noone is a killer. Now, what do I have to do to get you on our team?'

Hagenbaum stands and adjusts the sleeve of his black jacket.

'Bring us something,' he says. 'Something we can use.' He extends his hand and shakes Frank's. 'Frank,' he says, then nods towards the lieutenant. 'Lieutenant Mills.'

As the door closes behind him, Frank turns to Mills.

'Fucking Feds,' says Mills and shrugs. 'What can you do?'

'I want to talk to Noone,' says Frank. 'Will you be able to help me with that?'

Mills nods. 'We can call him,' he says.

Frank stands and shakes Mills' hand.

'If it's not too much trouble,' he says.

Seventeen

'You heard how Warren's doing?'

Frank steps into the car and Koop pulls out of the parking lot into the LA traffic as if he's done it all his life. After his meeting with Hagenbaum and Mills, Frank had called Koop and is coming with him to meet Dooley.

'Noone's still at home as far as Warren can tell.'

Frank raises his eyebrows.

'I think Warren's a bit spooked from yesterday,' Koop offers by way of explanation. 'Must have been a big moment Noone walking in on him like that.'

'Very big.'

The two of them are quiet for a moment as Koop negotiates a busy intersection.

'So not too productive?' asks Koop.

'Terrible,' agrees Frank. 'But at least we know where we are. And they've agreed to "facilitate" a meeting with Noone. Once we have something more.'

Koop smiles like he's trying not to. He's got something, thinks Frank. He was always like this when he'd made progress; a child at Christmas. Frank feels his pulse tick up a notch.

'What?' says Frank. 'Spit it out.'

'I think we might have an opening.' He fills Koop in on what he's found out about Noone's tail and his theory about the money being a key. It's good, but not good enough to have Koop grinning like a demented chimp.

'Daedalus,' says Frank. 'Why is that ringing a bell?'

Koop jerks a thumb towards the back seat. 'The file's in my bag,' he says.

Frank sees the sheaf of freshly printed material. 'Been shopping?'

He flicks through the printouts. Koop's got information on Daedalus, on Noone's name change, on the Santa Monica property and a secondary sheaf of paper on some congressional hearings in progress in Washington.

Frank holds these up with a questioning expression.

'Just read it,' says Koop. 'See if you see it the same way I do.'

Eighteen

It's just after five-thirty on the morning of 20 March 2003, and Baghdad begins to explode. The first air strikes are called in by commandos from the CIA Special Activities Division, who had been on the ground for weeks, possibly months. The preparations by this unit, and others like it, have been plotted by the Northern Iraq Liaison Element and are crucial to the campaign. By 12 April Iraq has fallen and Saddam's statue is being toppled in Firdos Square.

The invasion is not the end, but the beginning of a decade of bloodshed and horror affecting millions.

Frank looks up from the file.

'Iraq?'

'Keep reading,' says Koop.

The unit that had called in the first strikes was composed of veterans in the field. One of those vets retires from active service three months after the invasion. Returning to the US he starts a private company specialising in the protection of private contractors flown in to begin the gigantic infrastructure rebuild across Iraq. It's a boom time, at least for those involved in this kind of business. The company recruits more retired veterans as well as specialists from other western countries.

'Does this make sense somewhere?' asks Frank.

'It gets better.' Koop follows the GPS prompts and turns a corner.

Daedalus, although later to the game than some of the companies formed after the Afghanistan invasion two years previously, is doing more things right. In the toxic atmosphere of the war it blossoms, a multi-layered, complex cactus. Inside five years it is the dominant player in the US industrial overseas security sector. In 2009 it's gobbled up by Loder Industries and becomes a multi-billion-dollar outfit in its own right.

At the end of 2010 there are questions raised about defence contract procedures by one of Loder's competitors when Daedalus is awarded sole rights to the Iraqi and Afghanistan private security requirements. The man at the centre of the controversy is Dennis Sheehan, one-time US Secretary of State. Sheehan, the majority shareholder of Loder Industries, is a broad-shouldered, silver-haired man in his seventies, with the build of an athlete run to fat. He had the reputation of a bruising, unforgiving politician and that's carried over into his private business, which he runs with ruthless efficiency.

'Interesting,' says Frank. 'But I don't see what use it is to us.'

'Look at the last sheet.'

Frank flips over the page.

It's a photo of Sheehan taken – judging from the clothes – sometime around 1970. Sheehan's in a business suit and smiling as he stands behind Richard Nixon. He's much thinner, there are no glasses, and his hair is black. In the photo he looks around thirty years old.

'Sweet Mary, Mother of God,' whispers Frank.

Nineteen

Just as Frank and Koop arrive at the cafe to meet Dooley, Warren calls to let them know Noone's on the move.

'Just track him,' says Frank. Koop's got Warren on speaker.

'I hope he's not going to the fucking desert again,' says Warren. 'I don't want to do that drive twice in two days.'

'We found something' says Frank. What he's just seen on Koop's printouts has shaken him and he wants Warren to be aware of what they are dealing with. He tells Warren about the Daedalus connection.

'Be careful,' says Frank.

'You think?' says Warren and signs off.

Poms. Jesus.

Noone's heading back into the city but this time he leaves the freeway and sticks to Santa Monica Boulevard.

Warren checks the GPS and thumps the dashboard in frustration. The fucker *could* be going to Palm Springs again.

Instead, when Noone reaches Beverly Boulevard, he exits and parks at a place called the Farmers Market. Warren watches him leave the jeep in a paying lot and walk towards a shopping centre.

As quickly as he can, Warren pulls into the lot and parks. He walks over to the jeep and sees that Noone has bought a two-hour ticket.

Warren walks in the direction taken by Noone, conscious that, out of the car, he's all too visible. About fifty metres away he glimpses Noone's head disappearing through a walkway leading into an old-fashioned market. Warren follows, breathless in his effort to keep up, and finds himself in the middle of a bewildering wooden maze of cafes and shops and delicatessens. He's stand-ing next to a Korean barbecue stand. Warren didn't even know there was such a thing as Korean barbecue. It smells wonderful.

To his left is a row of shops. The low-ceilinged space is busy with what looks like a predominantly local crowd. On the GPS Warren had noticed that the place was smack up against the TV giant CBS. Several of the passers-by wear T-shirts with the names of TV shows written on them.

He can't see Noone anywhere.

'Fuck.' Warren thinks about calling Koop again and dismisses the thought. He's been a cop for too long to keep running to someone else every time there's a problem.

From what he can see the place is set out on a square grid. At either end there are areas full of tables with umbrellas. Warren takes the chance that Noone is meeting someone here and is at one of the tables.

He buys a baseball cap from a souvenir stand and jams it on his head. It's not much but it's something. Warren approaches the cafe area slowly, keeping himself hidden behind the brightly lit shelves of a bakery.

He's just about to move on when he spots Noone looking directly at him.

Warren curses under his breath and, doing his best to look unconcerned, lets his eyes skate across Noone's. Warren turns to the bakery shelves and in the reflection from a chrome edging sees Noone walking in his direction.

Warren slips down the side of the bakery and turns left, moving as quickly as he can through a narrow passageway. At the end he finds himself outside an old-style ice-cream shop called Bennetts. A glance over his shoulder tells him that Noone's still coming his way. Warren darts down the side of Bennetts and heads right down a passageway with a sloping roof. His breath is coming hard now. At the end of the passageway he turns and doubles back on himself. If Noone's following then Warren's banking on him not expecting this.

To his relief, when Warren emerges into the Farmers Market there's no sign of Noone.

Warren zigzags back towards the Korean barbecue joint. He pauses at the end of a service alley and leans against a wall to get his breath back.

A hand clamps itself over his mouth and another grips his nose hard and Warren is dragged back through a doorway. Inside it's freezing cold and Warren realises that he's in a cold storage area servicing the market. Noone has Warren's head clamped between wiry, muscled arms and the Australian can't get free. He reaches up, frantically clawing at his attacker, but it's no good. Warren's badly out of shape and Noone isn't.

A few frantic, panicky seconds tick by. Noone is breathing hard close to Warren's ear. He smells of expensive cologne. Warren can hear his own blood pumping madly through his lousy veins and then a black tunnel starts to form at the edges of his vision and the sound of his blood is drowned by a distant humming and all he can think is how stupid it is that after all the anti-smoking warnings, he's going to die, like this, with his feet in the air in the cold storage area behind a Korean barbecue. Warren's phone starts to ring, muffled inside his pocket, but it's too late, much too late.

Twenty

Sam Dooley's already at a booth when they arrive at the coffee shop.

He's an imposing black guy about Frank's age with a belly and a taste for smart clothes. Next to him Frank feels scruffy. He's not what he imagined from Koop's description of his role.

After the introductions are made and coffee ordered for Frank and Koop, Dooley fills Koop in on some of his history. The Gang Detail had been formed in the wake of the Rampart Division corruption scandal of the late nineties in which a large number of officers were implicated in gang crime. Dooley's one of the results of the overhaul. Recruitment standards were raised and pride restored. It's clear to Frank that Dooley's proud of his contribution.

He listens politely but Frank's mind keeps flashing on to the old photo of Dennis Sheehan and the implications for his case. It's a fucking time bomb and Frank feels out of his depth. This – if what they think is true turns out to be so – is way beyond his pay grade.

'Keane,' says Dooley. 'Am I boring you?'

'Sorry,' says Frank. 'Jet lag.'

'Yeah.' Dooley purses his lips. He turns to Koop. 'I guess I might have been talking too much.' He juts his chin at Koop's file. 'What you got?'

Before they'd arrived at the coffee shop Frank and Koop had agreed to keep the Sheehan photo under wraps until a point in the meeting with Dooley when it feels right. With Frank's stock apparently so low with the US authorities, he needs time before making any wild assertions about the Noone case to a sceptical local.

'We need a friend,' says Koop. 'You're it.'

Frank outlines the case he's chasing and fills Dooley in on bringing Koop and Warren in as consultants. As Frank's talking he can feel Dooley closing off. Dooley sits back in the booth, his body language indicating growing discomfort.

Frank can't blame him; if a US cop had shown up on Merseyside with two freelancers in tow and a hinky story like this, Frank would have been less than happy. But he perseveres.

'I know it's not something that you'd like,' he says, 'but I'm beginning to think that Noone's planning to kill again.'

'If he's your guy.'

'He's our guy, believe me.' Frank tells Dooley about Noone's trip to Palm Springs and about the way he shook off the blue Toyota. 'There's something he didn't want anyone to see.'

'Probably a boyfriend,' says Dooley. 'Palm Springs is a big gay town.'

'Maybe. It wouldn't be something that would surprise me. But I don't think it is. Noone's being followed by people from Daedalus. They're a –'

'I know who they are,' interrupts Dooley. 'We deal with them all the time through the D of C. Rent-a-cops, mostly.'

'Maybe here,' says Koop. 'But the Daedalus core business is several rungs higher than that. Ex-Special Forces, CIA, hardcore military intelligence people. They're running big operations in Afghanistan and Iraq. All of it legal as far as we know, and the people are top quality. It would be a mistake to see them as amateurs.'

Dooley's expression hasn't changed but Frank can sense they've got him at least paying attention.

'OK, then I guess the question is,' says Dooley, 'why are Daedalus following Noone?'

Koop looks at Frank and raises his eyebrows.

'Show him,' says Frank.

'Daedalus is owned by Loder Industries,' says Koop. 'Loder Industries' majority shareholder is Dennis Sheehan.'

Dooley's fully with the program now. He's leaning forward, eager. 'Ex-Secretary of State?'

'The same.' Koop takes out a photo showing Sheehan giving evidence to the congressional hearings. He places it on the table and rotates it so that Dooley can see.

'OK,' says Dooley. 'But I'm still not getting the connection.'

Koop takes out another sheet. This time it's a photo of Noone taken from the Hungry Head pre-production publicity website for *The Tunnels*. Noone's smiling, looking right at the camera. Koop puts it next to the shot of Sheehan.

Dooley shrugs.

Koop places the photo of Dennis Sheehan with Richard Nixon and puts it next to the one of Noone. Dooley bends closer, his eyes widening. He takes the photo of Noone and slides it across to take out Nixon.

'You see it, right?' Frank leans forward and taps a finger on the image of the young Sheehan. 'We think Dennis Sheehan is Ben Noone's father.'

Twenty-One

Noone, breathing hard, lets go of the dead guy and lowers him to the floor of the cold storage room. Conscious that someone could walk right in at any time, he bends and takes out the man's wallet, holding it by the edges. He lets it flip open and sees the guy's driver's licence. It's not a California issue.

Warren Eckhardt.

Australia?

What the fuck is an Australian doing snooping around Los Angeles?

For the first time in a while Noone wonders if he's done the right thing. Maybe this guy is a tourist after all. Then he flashes on the restroom in Morongo and knows that Eckhardt's no tourist.

A further inspection of the wallet reveals Eckhardt's ID card, still showing him as a Queensland police officer. What the fuck?

Noone places the wallet on the floor and finds a cheap prepaid phone in the dead man's jacket pocket. He slips the phone into his own pocket. Then he replaces the wallet in Eckhardt's jacket after wiping the corners to remove any trace of his own prints.

Standing, he checks that the alley is empty before wiping the handle of the storage room door and slipping out. Noone's last act is to push the door shut behind him with the toe of his boot before walking calmly away.

Noone takes the long route around and back to a cafe in the centre of the market. He sits at the counter and orders a coffee from the Latino server. A few minutes later and there's a tap on his shoulder.

'Ben.'

Noone turns and sees his agent, Fiona Berens. She's a small, dark-haired woman in her thirties, dressed in grey. Like almost everyone working in the LA media she has the body of a gym rat. She pushes her sunglasses up on her head and kisses Noone's cheek.

'You're cold,' she says.

Noone shrugs.

'Been here long?' says Berens.

'I just arrived,' says Noone. 'Good meeting?'

Berens is the one who'd suggested coffee here after her meeting at CBS.

She smiles brightly and cocks her head on one side. 'It was a meeting. They're all good, aren't they?'

Both of them laugh. Berens orders an espresso and places her phone flat on the counter so she can see any messages as they arrive. Hollywood etiquette: phone on silent, but messages can be glanced at.

'And now you got another one.' Noone makes an apologetic face.

'Oh, meetings with you aren't meetings, silly. They're fun.'

Berens isn't kidding. She does enjoy Noone's company. He is fun. If she wasn't happily married she might even have slept with him.

He looks sceptical.

'You're not pushy,' says Berens. 'Most of my clients . . .' She lets the sentence drift. It's true. Ben Noone doesn't have the desperation most of the actors on her books have. She imagines it's the family money that gives him that confidence but there's something else there that Berens can see. A deeper sense that Noone knows exactly who he is and what he wants. She'd seen it before in other actors who made the grade. They just know.

The possibilities for her new client excite her.

As the espresso arrives there is a commotion over towards a Korean place. Berens and Noone glance across to where a small crowd has gathered.

'Always something in LA,' says Noone.

Berens nods. She takes a sip of coffee and starts talking business.

Noone barely listens – he has almost zero interest in obtaining roles now that he is playing the biggest role of his life – but he lets her chirp on about developing projects and meetings with casting directors. From time to time he interjects with some sort of encouraging word while, over Berens' shoulder, he watches an ambulance arrive and take away the man he's just killed.

Noone hopes the Australian cop won't be a problem.

There's less than a week before the big one.

Twenty-Two

Frank's not the only one worried about the scale of the thing they appear to have stumbled into. Dooley's veneer of cool has evaporated like spit on a desert road. It's like Koop's put down a grenade on the table.

'Uh-huh, no, no fucking way.' He pushes the photos back across the table as if needing to put a physical distance between himself and the knowledge of the connection between Sheehan and Noone.

He leans back, shaking his head. 'Have you any idea of the amount of shit something like that could bring down? You guys are fucking deluded if you think I'm gonna go near that mess. I'm not happy you even told me.' He looks around as if expecting a SWAT team at any moment. 'I mean what the fuck, man? Sheehan?' His voice is low, urgent. 'Are you fucking kidding me?'

Koop holds up his hands. 'Listen, Sam, there's no reason to go off. We're just trying to make sense of this. We have zero proof that Sheehan is Noone's father. And even if we did, it doesn't add anything to the case against Noone. Sheehan might be covering up that he'd fathered a child. At the time of Noone's birth Sheehan was married. He's a conservative and he stood on a platform of family values. There's every reason for him to cover it up but so far we can't see any crime he's committed.'

'If we're right,' says Frank, 'it explains a lot about the case. If Daedalus were tailing Noone they might have seen things relating to the deaths that I'm investigating. They were doing something similar in Liverpool, I'm pretty sure.' Frank flashes on the American putting him on the bathroom floor in Bean. 'At the very least it would be good to talk to them.'

'You need to take this to the Feds,' says Dooley. 'I can't do anything. Even if I wanted to. Which I definitely don't.'

'Noted,' says Frank. 'But we still want you to remember that we showed you this. In case it does get really nasty. In case something happens.'

Dooley rolls his eyes.

'Oh, you don't think it could?' says Koop. 'Some of these guys were underground in Baghdad for months. Do you think they'll worry about knocking off a few nosy Brits and Aussies?'

'We're going to take it to the FBI,' says Frank. 'But I suspect that they'll just take it away from us and do nothing. Now that might be OK if Noone isn't planning to carry on killing. It might also be OK if he hadn't killed six people in Liverpool including a sixteen-year-old boy. And if the Feds don't want to do anything about Noone, I do. I want that fucker – I mean, I *really* want him – and you can help us without doing very much. You don't have to do anything except track the records on Deborah Sterling. It'll take us forever. I'm going to ask my official connections here to do the same but I have a suspicion that the evidence might go the same way that the CCTV footage did at JFK.'

Frank looks at Dooley. 'Get us a connection between Sterling and Sheehan before someone sees to it that there is no connection. That's it.'

Dooley slides out of the booth and gets to his feet.

'I'll think about it,' he says, and leaves.

Twenty-Three

From the coffee shop in Burbank, Frank and Koop head back to see Mills at West Street.

'I have to give them this,' says Frank.

Koop agrees. Information as explosive as this might prove to be needs to be passed along. Still, Koop's conscious that it's speculative. Without further evidence of the connection between Sheehan and Noone's mother, it's all conjecture. Coming hard on the heels of Hagenbaum's words about bringing something solid back to the table, both Frank and Koop aren't sure how this will play.

Mills, to his credit, sees Frank immediately, while Koop waits with the car. Frank's not ready to reveal openly he has help on the ground just yet. For all he knows, the Feds are fully aware of Koop and Warren but there's no need to make it easy for them.

The landscape of the investigation is shifting underneath his feet. Frank can feel it. Information is becoming currency and it doesn't come in any larger denominations than Dennis Sheehan. As the tectonic plates shift, Frank needs to retain some sort of edge, even if it's only to make him feel better.

Everything's a long way from the murders in Burlington Road. It's not a good feeling.

'Quick work,' says Mills when Frank hands over the file of print-outs. 'You had this before our meeting earlier?'

Frank shakes his head. 'I'll need copies of those,' he says.

Mills puts the papers down on his desk and rubs his face. His reaction isn't so different from Dooley's.

There's a silence in the office. Frank can see the business of the department going on through the glass windows of Mills' office and he gets a sudden yearning to be tucked up nice and safe at Stanley Road.

'What do you want me to do with this?' says Mills.

Frank repeats what he asked Dooley. 'If I can establish the connection between Sheehan and Noone it'll help me obtain – or try to obtain – information from any Daedalus employees who might have been following Noone in Liverpool.'

'It's thin,' says Mills. 'I mean from the point of view of your case. As information . . .' Mills mimes an explosion with his hands. 'We'll have reporters crawling through the fucking air vents to get their hands on this.' He seems to be talking to himself so Frank says nothing.

Mills looks at him. 'Who else knows?'

'Just me,' says Frank. Mills looks unconvinced. 'Really? Because I'd have told someone if I was sitting on this.'

Is Mills making a threat? Frank decides not. And he has a point. Maybe it's a warning.

'I may have emailed my team,' says Frank. 'As a matter of protocol.'

'Protocol, hey?'

Mills pushes the material back across the desk. 'You keep this,' he says. 'If I need copies I can look up what you looked up.' He folds his hands across his stomach. 'The fewer people who know about this the better. It's political with a capital Fuck Me. Making a fishing trip to find witnesses – which I'm not saying is wrong – is one thing. Coming up with assertions like this Sheehan connection? That's trouble, right there. For you, for me, for Sheehan, for your department.'

'My department?'

'If this goes public watch how soon your actions get looked at. You Brits have a nosy press, right?'

Frank thinks of McSkimming sniffing at his heels when Nicky Peters was missing.

'But you'll pass this along to Hagenbaum?'

'Yes,' says Mills. 'As quickly as possible. I don't want any part of this if I can help it.'

'And the meeting with Noone?'

'We'll fix it.'

As Frank stands Mills speaks. 'I'm curious,' he says. 'What do you think Noone's gonna do? Assuming you're right about him?'

'Kill his father,' says Frank quickly, surprising himself. Until Mills had asked, Frank hadn't known that was what he thought.

'Why?'

Frank shrugs. 'I don't know.' He pushes open Mills' door and walks out, thinking: I need to speak to Salt.

Twenty-Four

'Look at this,' says Koop, pointing to the laptop.

They've been back at the apartment for an hour. It's almost five. Koop's been working the internet while Frank makes calls. There's been nothing from Warren and Frank needs to wait a little longer until he can call MIT. He wants Harris to do some more digging and he wants to register their progress with the case files. He's already spoken to DC Rose, who's once again pulling a late one in Liverpool, but this is something Frank wants to go through with Harris. She'll be in around seven in the morning, 11 pm in LA.

'What is it?' says Frank.

'I was digging around into Sheehan and saw this.'

Frank follows Koop's finger. It's a news item about a presidential fundraiser dinner to be held in Los Angeles at the weekend, in four days' time. LA is a Democrat stronghold and the president will be in attendance at a dinner hosted by a movie star. Tickets for the best tables are being snapped up at $30,000 a pop. Despite his involvement as a witness in the congressional hearings, Dennis Sheehan will be attending.

'I thought he was a Republican?'

'Was,' says Koop. 'He retired from politics. Maybe now that he's just a humble businessman he likes to keep on the right side of whoever's winning.'

Frank reads out loud. 'Following an afternoon charity garden party hosted by the First Lady and her daughters in support of US veterans, the president will attend an evening dinner for the Hollywood community, whose contributions will make this the most expensive dinner in political history.'

'Daddy's coming to town,' says Koop. 'Might be worth talking to him.'

'Hmm.'

Frank sinks back onto the couch and pinches the bridge of his nose tightly. He's drowning here. All the work he's put in and all the effort involved in getting Koop and Warren out from Australia seems to have been swallowed up by the magnitude of Noone's connection to Sheehan. Frank tries to pinpoint what it is he's feeling and the answer is that he feels exactly as he did blundering through the darkened tunnels under Edge Hill. There's the same sense of being underneath a great weight. There are forces moving around him that he is barely aware of.

There's something else too that's been nagging him.

Why did Noone send the Theseus email? What's in it for him?

Before Frank can chase those thoughts down their particular rabbit holes, the phone rings.

It's Dooley.

'Deborah Sterling was employed as a nanny for Dennis and Mary Sheehan's youngest child, Cody,' says Dooley. 'Between June of 1982 and January of 1983.'

'Noone was born in July '83,' says Frank. 'Good.' It's not conclusive but it's a link, probably not enough to lever open the Daedalus machinery but a start.

'There's more,' says Dooley. He sounds reluctant, but Frank can also hear the note of triumph at a job well done.

'More?'

'I fished around into the listed father.'

'Larry?'

'Uh-huh, yeah. I can't find anything that shows that Deborah and Larry even met. Which don't mean they didn't hook up and make a baby one night without telling anyone, right?'

'True.'

'And then Larry conveniently died before Noone was born.'

'We know that.'

'But what you don't know,' says Dooley, 'and what maybe they didn't know either is that Larry had surgery in 1981 at Cedars-Sinai. Double inguinal orchiectomy. Larry had no nuts when he was supposed to be fathering your guy.'

'That would be . . . tricky,' says Frank.

'Fuck, yeah,' says Dooley.

'Would they have picked him, knowing he couldn't have kids?'

'Not if they knew, no. But you know what it's like with this kind of information. If the medical history didn't show it – and this was before computers, y'know? – then maybe they wouldn't know at the time. I got it from an updated records system. They may know now but it's so long ago they might figure it doesn't matter any more.'

'Makes sense. Thanks, Sam. Listen, I handed the information I gave you to my contact at West Street LAPD, Lieutenant Mills. I'm not going to mention you unless you want me to?'

'No, no mentions. You can get this stuff yourselves if you push Mills. Claim you thought it up yourselves, whatever the fuck you want. Leave me out. Peace.'

'Peace,' mutters Frank self-consciously as Dooley rings off. Koop smiles.

'You hear all that?' says Frank. 'Larry Grant couldn't have fathered Noone.'

'Dooley's a good feller,' says Koop.

Frank's phone rings again. It's Dooley.

'Sam,' says Frank. 'We were just . . .'

'Stop,' says Dooley. There's something different in his voice. 'Something else just came into the office. We get updates on all deaths in the divisions around Burbank. One of them caught my eye. They found a dead guy in a cold store at the Farmers Market this morning. Heart attack. Reason I noticed it is that the dude was an Australian.'

Frank feels sick.

'He was a cop,' says Dooley. 'Warren Eckhardt.'

Twenty-Five

Warren looks healthier dead than he had done alive.

Koop supposes there must have been a young Warren Eckhardt once, a Warren without the layering of lard and the shattered lungs and underpowered ticker, but he finds it hard to imagine. Warren, to Koop, will permanently be the wheezing wreck slumped in the armchair of the house in Nashua, cradling a beer in his nicotine-stained fingers.

Lying flat on the slab under the green sheet his skin looks smoother, his wrinkles less pronounced. His expression is mildly sardonic, as if dying is a sly joke and he'd just been told the punchline.

Koop nods at the doctor holding the sheet clear of Warren's face. 'It's him.'

They're at Cedars-Sinai Medical Center on Beverly Boulevard, the same place Larry Grant had been operated on in the eighties.

Frank and Koop walk slowly through the double doors of the mortuary display room and back into the warmer environment of the main hospital building. Frank's already argued with the medical staff about Warren being moved from the storage room. His insistence that Warren's death is a murder is getting little sympathy.

'Heart failure, Mr Keane,' says the doctor. 'It's simple. Your friend had a massive cardiac infarction.'

'Behind a Korean barbecue?'

The doctor holds his hands up in supplication. 'Not my area of expertise. All I can tell you is that there is overwhelming evidence that Mr Eckhardt died from natural causes. If you can say that about someone who smoked as he did. If you feel differently, please speak to the police.'

'Leave it, Frank,' says Koop. 'It's not this man's fault.' Koop turns to the doctor and shakes his hand. 'Thank you.'

Fifty minutes later Frank and Koop emerge from the hospital and stand in the concrete canyon outside the emergency room. It's almost midnight.

'What now?' says Frank. 'I should call Mills and Hagenbaum. See if they can place Noone at the Market . . .'

Koop puts a hand on Frank's arm. 'You think that's going to happen? They call the hospital and the doctor tells them what he just told us. Look at what Warren was like. Maybe Noone was involved. Maybe Warren mistook the storage room for the toilets and had a heart attack. Either way, he's dead and we have nothing to give to the Americans that would help even if they were inclined to investigate. We can't get them to help much with the six dead in Liverpool and we know they were murdered. We're a long way from home.'

'So we do nothing?'

'Not now,' says Koop. 'Not until tomorrow, Frank. I'm going to find a bar and drink something. You coming?'

They leave the car in the hospital lot and walk without purpose until they find somewhere off the main drag. The doorman gives them the once-over but waves them inside without a problem. Inside the bar is half-full. Mostly men, with a scattering of women.

'You know this is a gay bar, Koop?' says Frank.

Koop's already ordering at the bar. 'Who gives a shit?' He's been in plenty of gay bars with Zoe.

Drink follows drink and bar follows bar in an endless spiral of oblivion. Koop tells stories Warren told him. There is some singing and an argument with a barman who won't serve them. Frank's sick outside the last place and they make it to the apartment around four.

Koop is unconscious within seconds of lying down but Frank is still restless. He drinks a large glass of water and sits heavily on the couch, the lights off, and stares stupidly at a spot on the wall opposite. His phone is wedged uncomfortably in his pocket and he fishes it out.

For a few seconds he sits with it held loosely in his hand. Then, concentrating hard to find the number, he calls Warren's phone and puts it to his ear. It rings and Frank can picture Warren's phone sitting in a plastic bag of his belongings on a shelf in an office at Cedars.

Just as Frank's about to hang up someone answers. In his drunken state Frank says, 'Warren?'

Whoever has answered says nothing. Frank sobers up fast. He sits up, listening intently to the silence on the other end of the call.

'Noone,' says Frank. 'I know that's you. We're coming, fucker. You hear that? We're coming.'

There is silence and then the call is ended. Frank looks at the phone for a long time.

Tomorrow things are going to change.

Twenty-Six

Noone presses 'end' on the cheap prepaid he took from the Australian and puts it back in his jacket pocket.

It had been worth taking if only to discover that Keane's out there.

DCI Frank Keane. Noone's not sure of the connection between Keane and Eckhardt but he now knows that there is one. It's useful. As is the knowledge that Keane's followed him over here. Not to mention that the dumb fuck is drunk and mouthy. Brits and booze. Jesus.

'Who was that?' Angie's voice is sleep-heavy.

'No one.' Naked, Noone pads across the room, gets back into the bed and puts one hand behind his head. The other he drapes over the curve of Angie's hip, his fingers brushing the soft skin of her thigh.

'Someone was speaking,' murmurs Angie.

'No one important. Shh.'

They're at Angie's place, ten or more blocks back from the pricey Venice properties. Noone prefers coming here to taking Angie home. He doesn't really like anyone coming into his own house. Not that there's anything much to hide. Noone has none of those handy Hollywood serial killer rooms at his place, no walls full of photos, no blueprints in the cabinet, no smoking gun.

That's not who he is.

In the dark he doesn't feel powerful, doesn't feel 'evil', whatever the fuck that might be. He just feels like he's in the right place at the right time.

Angie reaches down and takes hold of his cock.

'I thought you were asleep?' Noone says.

'Your phone woke me up, remember?'

'Go back to sleep.'

Angie slides down the bed under the covers. She runs her tongue along Noone's lower stomach. Despite himself he can feel the blood flowing. His cock grows and Angie flicks her tongue at the tip.

'Still want me to go back to sleep?' Her voice is muffled.

Noone doesn't reply. Instead he pushes his hips so that Angie takes him in her mouth.

'What?' says Angie.

'Nothing.' Noone hadn't realised he'd made a sound. He reaches down and turns Angie so that his head is between her legs and licks her pussy gently, two of the beautiful people passing time. As with everything he does, pretty much anyway, not all of Ben Noone is present. He can see himself in bed with Angie, can see what they look like, can analyse what they're doing, as if checking his performance while it's happening.

'Ben,' says Angie. 'Come back.'

Noone squirms out from underneath her, leaving her on all fours. He positions himself behind her and Angie guides him inside. While they fuck he's wondering if she knows him too well.

He hopes not.

Twenty-Seven

Frank can feel the rocks pressing down, can feel the back of his knuckle scrape along the sweating sandstone walls of the narrow shaft. For some reason he can't quite grasp, he finds himself past the point of no return; the angle and shape of the tunnel conspiring to force him forward. Gravity, muscle, weight, all push him in one direction. There is no going back.

Ahead of him, if he cranes his neck and strains his eyes, is a wider cavern, and in it, their skin green-white and corpse-clammy, are the murder victims from Birkdale and Garston and Los Angeles. Nicky Peters is talking softly to Warren Eckhardt while smoke from Eckhardt's cigarette coils around his head and shoulders. Terry Peters is slumped, his head down, at a distance from the others. The rest of the Peters family, and Dean Quinner, stand uncertainly to one side.

As Frank shuffles towards the cavern he feels something sliding along his skin.

It's a thread being pulled away from him, back the way he came, and Frank knows that if the end of it slips from his grasp he's finished. His fingers scrabble frustratingly on the stone and then, just as the thread is in his grasp, he sees the Minotaur come into the chamber.

It's monstrous. A beast. Frank can see every quivering hair on its flaring nostrils, hear the air within the creature's lungs. He wants to cry, to call out, to warn Nicky and Warren, but the words won't come. He can help, but only if he lets go of the thread.

He jerks awake, a noise on his lips.

Outside he can hear the Los Angeles traffic. He sinks back into the pillow feeling about as rough as he's felt in a long time.

Which is exactly how he wants it. He deserves to feel bad after dragging Warren into this. He's going to tell Koop to go home today. There are things he's thinking of doing that could end very badly and he doesn't want anyone else's blood on his hands.

Frank showers and stands under the jets for five minutes. He shaves and dresses in jeans and a T-shirt. Today there're going to be no meetings if he can help it, no being patronised by the likes of Hagenbaum.

Frank's plan lasts as long as the time it takes for him to walk from the bedroom to the kitchen.

Koop's already up and looking like he spent the previous night tucked up with a cup of nothing more toxic than tea. He's sitting at the kitchen table with two men in suits.

Neither of them says anything as Frank walks in.

'Did I miss something and you got lucky last night?' says Frank, looking at Koop. 'No wonder you wanted us to go to that bar.'

'Frank, this is Mr Ashland and Mr Baines. They're from – well, I'm not sure exactly – where are you from again?'

'We didn't say,' says the older of the two. 'I'm Ashland.' He points at the other guy. 'He's Baines.'

Ashland looks about fifty, Baines a few years younger. Both carry themselves like ex-military.

'They were in the room when I woke up,' says Koop.

'We understand that you're here on an MLAT with the intention of gathering evidence against Benjamin Noone,' says Ashland.

'Is that a question?' says Frank. He starts making coffee. If he doesn't get some caffeine soon he's going to faint. That wouldn't look good for his tough guy stance.

'No,' says Ashland. 'It's not.'

'We're acting under the umbrella of Homeland Security, DCI Keane,' says Baines. 'Agent Hagenbaum of the FBI has passed along the concerns you have about Benjamin Noone to us.'

'You know that Noone killed one of my consultants yesterday?'

'We know that a man died, yes. Heart attack. And we're concerned that you have consultants working with you. We think that's contrary to the application you made.'

'How did you get in here?' says Frank. He pours a cup of coffee and sits at the table. 'Are you with Daedalus? Do you work for Sheehan?'

Ashland folds his arms on the table. 'DCI Keane, you have strayed into some very deep waters indeed over here. There are things in that water that you have little or no understanding of. It's dangerous for you to be swimming. And besides, what you are doing is, we believe, borderline illegal. Mr Koopman and the deceased Mr Eckhardt have no permission to investigate anything on American soil. Your permission is only to investigate through the US authorities, not to go freelancing the fuck out of everything.'

'And if Noone's planning something else?'

'That's in our hands now, DCI Keane. We're aware of the link between Benjamin Noone and Dennis Sheehan. It's immaterial.'

'Immaterial?' says Frank. 'You know that Sheehan's at the fundraising dinner this weekend? What if Noone is planning an appearance?'

'He is,' says Baines. 'Ben Noone has made no secret of the fact that he's attending. He contributes heavily to the party. He's going for the simple reason that he bought a ticket.'

'And you think that's OK? Noone, who I suspect has killed seven people, will be at a party attended by the president and his estranged father?'

'Of course not,' says Ashland. 'Which is why we spoke to Mr Noone less than an hour ago, along with his attorney. Mr Noone will hand his ticket back to the committee and has made it clear that, in the light of your concerns and baseless accusations, he will not be attending the function. His attorney did speak about a possible lawsuit against you and your force. I think he might have a case.'

Frank can't think of anything to say.

Ashland leans back.

'That's not going to go down well back in jolly old Blighty, is it, DCI Keane? The press might like to hear about your little trip.'

'Do you two have any ID?' says Frank.

'No,' says Ashland, getting to his feet. 'We don't.' He and Baines take a few steps towards the door. 'You know in the movies when you see the spooky guys behind the scenes? The ones pulling all the strings? The ones with enormous amounts of power? The ones who can put people on planes equipped with complicated and painful apparatus and then have those people just . . . disappear? That's us. But feel free to call Agent Hagenbaum and Lieutenant Mills. I'm sure they'll put your mind at ease. In the meantime, the MLAT has been revoked and we strongly suggest that you and Mr Koopman return home at your earliest opportunity.'

'Always a pleasure,' says Koop as Ashland and Baines walk to the door of the apartment. 'Drop by any time.'

Ashland points a finger at Koop and winks. 'That'd be some of that famous British humour, right? Or do I mean Australian?' He's not smiling. 'Get the fuck out of Dodge. Understand?'

Twenty-Eight

When Koop closes the door behind Ashland and Baines, Frank starts to speak but stops as he sees Koop put a finger to his lips.

'Let's get breakfast,' says Koop.

In the car both remain silent as they drive haphazardly round the maze of residential streets. It's peculiar weather, foggy, more like November in England than August in Los Angeles, and the palm trees are ghosts in the grey-white mist. Without the regular washed-out blue of the sky and the hard angles of shadows on the stucco, LA softens into an urbanised Japanese watercolour, the brake lights of the traffic bleeding through the gloom as Koop and Frank make an effort to shake off the tail they know must be there.

After ten minutes zigzagging through the streets, Frank pulls the rental into a cafe off Santa Monica Boulevard and they walk through the busy dining room towards an empty-looking rear courtyard space.

'There's no smoking out there,' says the waitress as they pass the counter, mistaking their intentions. The words make them both think of Warren.

'That's OK,' says Frank. They order coffee – double shot for Frank – and find a corner table. In the relative cool they are the only outside customers.

'Fog in LA,' says Frank. 'No one mentioned that in the brochure.'

'It happens sometimes. Or so they told me when I was here. Never saw it until now.'

The waitress brings their drinks and they fall silent while she puts down the cups.

'Anything else I can get you?' she says.

They shake their heads and she returns to the main building.

'You think they bugged the apartment?' says Frank once she's out of earshot.

'I don't know,' says Koop. 'But given the type of people we think they are, would it surprise you?'

'No, probably not.'

'I think we should work as if everything we say from now on is being listened to.'

'From now on? That sounds like we're staying.' Frank puts a spoon of sugar in his coffee and stirs. Christ, his head hurts.

'Aren't we?' says Koop. 'It's just getting interesting.'

'I was planning to send you home,' says Frank, massaging the sides of his head. 'I don't want anything else to happen. Besides, someone has to take Warren back.'

'There's no one there for him.' Koop winces as he sips the coffee. He wishes he could have a cup of his own North Coast brew right now, but from here Australia seems as preposterous a place to believe in as Narnia. Zoe, too, to a degree. 'There's a sister he doesn't talk to. Somewhere out west.' Koop looks up at Frank. 'And there's not much back there for me either.'

'You and Zoe'll patch things up.'

Frank's uncomfortable on this territory.

Back in Liverpool he and Koop would never have talked like this. As the investigating officer, Frank had heard things during the Stevie White case about Koop's private life that he would rather not have done.

Private was better.

His line of thought makes him think about Angela Salt and the suggestion she'd made at their last meeting. His wallet's resting on the table and Frank can see the white edge of the scrap of paper Salt had given to him. He wonders if he'll ever use it and why he hasn't thrown it away.

'I know that's what you're supposed to say,' says Koop. 'But I don't think it's true, Frank. Not this time. You must have seen it happen to people who've been through what Zoe went through?'

Frank nods and then grimaces. Judging by the jolt of pain that shoots down the side of his head, Frank still has some way to go to recover from last night's excesses.

'Still hurting?' says Koop.

'Yes,' says Frank. 'A lot.' He folds his arms. 'Are we still talking about my head?'

Koop shrugs. The two men are quiet for a time.

'This fucking stinks,' says Frank.

'I've tasted worse,' says Koop, putting his cup down.

'You know what I mean.'

'What do you make of all this?' Koop says. 'All the run-around, I mean. Not Warren's death. I mean the visit from the two spooks, the cooperation you're getting – or not getting – from Mills and Hagenbaum, everything.'

'It's bullshit.'

'Of course it's bullshit. What I mean is, why is it happening?' Koop's talking in the same way he used to in the MIT operations room. Think. It's an invitation for Frank to heighten his observational senses.

Frank leans back and looks up at a tropical plant of some sort rising from a massive pot, as if he's hoping to read a message of inspiration on the underside of its leaves. Thinking clearly is not something that's coming easy right now.

'You remember the case against Don Hilton?' Koop's talking about a murder in Liverpool linked to large-scale fraud in the council planning department.

'Yes, why?'

'You remember we had three fires at the homes of MIT officers and that it turned out to be Hilton who set those fires?'

'Of course, yeah. He was doing it to get our attention focused somewhere else. Stupid, but that's the reason.'

Koop says nothing and waits for Frank.

'Pass interference,' says Frank. He's remembering the TV graphic from a few days ago.

'OK,' says Koop. 'It's not what I was thinking but you're right. All of this stuff is just . . .'

'Slowing us down.'

A couple who look like students come into the courtyard but sit too far from Frank and Koop to make them wary.

'You're going to check their story with Mills and Hagenbaum?' asks Koop.

Frank nods. 'But not right away. If we assume that those two jokers were telling the truth – that they do have the authority – then we can assume that Hagenbaum will be in touch to back their story up.'

'OK.'

'I think we have a day, maybe two, before they reel us in and force us out.'

'Or put us into that torture plane.'

'Yeah, or that.' Frank taps a finger on the table. 'I wasn't kidding about you not having to do this, Koop. You can go, today, if we can fix the flight.'

'I wasn't thinking about going, Frank.' Koop smiles but there's no humour in it. 'I was thinking of taking the offensive. Put the fuckers on the back foot.'

'What's the plan?'

Koop drains his cup. 'That depends on how far you're prepared to go.'

Outside the cafe, with the passing traffic making talking difficult, Koop calls the funeral directors whose number the morgue had given him and makes the arrangements for Warren's body to be flown back to Australia. Warren's only relative, an estranged sister, proves too difficult to locate in the circumstances, and Koop calls Zoe to ask her to arrange for Warren's body to be picked up by a funeral home. It's the first time Koop's spoken to his wife in weeks and the call isn't smooth. Koop can't believe the distance, both geographical and emotional, there is between them. Zoe sounds like a stranger and, although she agrees to help with the arrangements, she leaves Koop in no doubt that in her current state of mind there's little left between them. All those years.

After the calls Frank books the two of them onto flights on Sunday neither of them has any intention of taking. Everything is done to convey the impression to Ashland and Baines that they are heeding Ashland's warning. Assuming that they're looking.

'What now?' It's Koop talking, Frank driving. They've decided to treat the car as 'safe'. With just two of them on the ground and two days before they get booted out, they have to cut some corners. If the car's bugged then it's bugged.

'I don't know,' says Frank. This is the side of investigations that never gets reported: the drifting into stasis. Back home Frank could get busy on gathering data and making sure the MIT team were crunching the statements and following lines of enquiry. Here, alone, the lines of enquiry are limited. As things stand, Koop and Frank have little. As experienced investigators they know that the choice they make now about what approach to go with will, in all likelihood, mean the difference between success and failure. Do they concentrate efforts on working on Lieutenant Mills, hoping to turn him round to Frank's point of view? Or do they work on the Sheehan angle?

Frank decides that the only way is to go with Noone. Frank's been on him for over a month and is still convinced that Noone's got something bad brewing.

'I think we keep digging,' says Frank. 'I want to speak to Angela Salt again. She doesn't know anything about the Sheehan connection and it's possible she'll have something to say.'

'That'll work.' Koop checks his watch. It's almost 11 am, seven pm in Liverpool. 'Let's swap,' he says. 'I'll drive. You call her now before it gets too late.'

They pull up, and Koop steps out of the car. Frank shuffles across to the passenger side. 'Where are we going now?' says Frank as Koop slides into the driver's seat.

'The library,' says Koop. 'Do it the old way. And who knows what tracking they've got on our computers at the apartment?'

While Koop looks up the GPS route to the LA city library, Frank calls Salt's office. As expected she's finished for the day, so he calls MIT in the UK and gets Rose to find the psychologist's home number. Rose tries to chat but Frank closes him down.

By the time Rose calls back they're at the library on San Vicente Boulevard next to the blue glass block of the Design Center. Frank takes Rose's call while Koop heads inside. Frank finds a shady spot and sits on a low concrete wall.

'Frank.' Salt's voice is as clear as if she's sitting next to him.

'Thanks for agreeing to talk,' says Frank. 'I know it's out of office hours but it's something of an emergency.'

'I rarely get emergency calls,' says Salt. 'It's fine. Besides, I'll be

348

billing your department. Now, since this is an emergency, what is it all about? I'm assuming it's concerning Ben Noone?'

'We have some new information. And I believe Noone has killed again.' Frank fills Salt in on the details of Warren Eckhardt's involvement and his death.

'It's being ruled a heart attack,' says Frank. 'And they're probably right. But with him following Noone I don't believe that his death was accidental.'

'And there's other new information?'

Frank looks around him to check there's no one eavesdropping. 'We think that Ben Noone is the illegitimate son of Dennis Sheehan, the former US Secretary of State.'

There's a silence on the end of the line. 'Dr Salt?' says Frank.

'How sure are you? That's quite an assumption.'

'We're sure.' Frank tells Salt about the Nixon photograph. 'If it was just a physical resemblance – even a striking one – then we'd have nothing. But we did more digging on Noone's mother. She was employed as a nanny for Dennis and Mary Sheehan's youngest child, Cody, in '82, '83. The timing's right for the pregnancy. Sterling had no money. We suspect the man listed as her husband is a cover. We can't find any evidence the two even met. And yet, once the child is born, Deborah Sterling is loaded. She'd been bought to silence her. There's nothing illegal about any of that, but it's pertinent to my investigation.'

'And Noone lives a life of wealth, privilege and protection. Without a father.'

'Correct.'

'And what about the name? If his mother's name is Sterling, where does Noone come from?'

'Noone changed his name shortly after his mother's death. Nothing illegal about it.'

'But suggestive on several counts,' says Salt. 'Not least of which the choice of name.'

'What do you mean?'

'Noone,' says Salt. '*No one.* You probably already thought of that?'

'No,' says Frank, feeling stupid. It was so fucking obvious now Salt had pointed it out. 'I didn't see it.'

'Well anyway, it's a significant – if adolescent – event. Coming hard on the death of his mother. That could have been the rationale.' Salt isn't talking to Frank now, she's musing to herself, so Frank just listens. 'But if Noone is a narcissistic psychopath, as we suspect, then I wonder if he discovered the truth about his father on the death of his mother. That would explain the acceleration from bad behaviour – relatively minor criminality and destructive patterns – into full-blown violence and murder.'

'His father's been protecting him,' says Frank. 'At least that's what we think. Again, we have nothing concrete.'

'And the Americans? What was their response?'

'They've closed ranks. Those who believe us about the connection to Sheehan are shying away. He's too powerful, even out of office. Our contacts here – the official and unofficial ones – have pulled their skirts up and run. We're the untouchables. And we had a visit from a couple of people who scared us. And we don't scare easily.' Frank tells Salt about the visit from Ashland and Baines.

'Sheehan's due to visit the city tomorrow. A presidential fundraiser no less.' Frank lowers his voice. 'I think Noone's going to do something. And that's the emergency, Dr Salt. I need to know what he's likely to do.'

'It doesn't work like that, Frank. You must know that.'

'Yes, I do. But we need to do something. And I'm not ready to let Noone get away with the killings in Liverpool.'

'OK, I can't say I like it, but here goes. For what it's worth, I don't think his father will be the target. Noone's narcissistic personality disorders are, essentially, a scream for attention. Having an absent father – no matter how indulgent – will anger Noone. His acts of rebellion in an accelerating series of criminal actions show that although he thinks he can get away with anything, he has an underlying desire to be caught. That sounds trite, but Noone wants attention from the one person who has denied him that attention – his father. He is choosing – Noone, I mean – to get that attention through classic adolescent behaviours. In many ways narcissists remain stuck in adolescent patterns. What's dangerous here, if we're right about Noone, is that those adolescent behaviours are being acted out in killing. The best way Noone can get attention is by pointing out the way he has been "badly treated", in his eyes. He may try to shine a harsh light on his own abandonment by Sheehan by doing something extreme. Killing his father wouldn't do that. It's not grandiose enough. He'll want something big, something that will demonstrate to everyone how special he is, how unique. The best way to do that – assuming he's performing the way you describe – is to have his day in court. Noone's not going to be someone happy to arm himself and die in a hail of bullets. He wants everyone to see not only how poorly he's been treated – and don't forget Noone will see every financial and physical benefit he has been given as something he is "entitled" to – but how clever he's been, how ingenious. He'll want to survive.'

'Survive what?'

'From what you tell me, Noone wants to survive when he kills the president.'

Twenty-Nine

Three days to go.

Noone's lawyer, an aggressive, supremely confident man called Max Perot, arrives at Noone's house at nine with two people from the committee who make the trip to Santa Monica to apologise. The thirty thousand Noone had splashed on the fundraising ticket had been worth every cent. He makes the most of handing it back, playing the aggrieved but magnanimous donor to perfection. He can afford to: he doesn't need the ticket. Never has.

'I expect a good seat next time,' Noone jokes, seeing them to the door. 'One with a good line of sight and an easy exit route.'

They laugh and shake hands.

When they've gone, Noone drives into the city, making sure he slips any of the Daedalus tails that still remain. He's not even sure they're there but he does it anyway.

In a theatrical outfitters on Sunset he buys several items he needs for Thursday.

Back home Noone puts his purchases down on the metal-topped kitchen counter and gets a low-cal soda from the Sub-Zero and watches the waves rolling in on Santa Monica Beach down below as he drinks. Further away, a jetliner, its fuselage gleaming in the afternoon sun, slides out of the hazy clouds at the edge of the Pacific and drifts down towards LAX. The traffic's light on the distant highways, no sound reaching up to this rarefied stratosphere.

It's perfect, a snapshot of the American Dream, California style.

Noone's neighbours are global names. Movie stars. Politicians. Even a stray rapper, the Palisades' nod to inclusion. Tom Hanks at the PTA, Schwarzenegger coaching soccer, Christian Bale buying bagels at Vons. Noone'll miss it, he will, all the clothes and money and shiny, shiny *stuff*, but it's bullshit compared to immortality.

The TV is on and is tuned to a news channel. Noone turns and watches a report from outside the house the president will be staying at prior to the fundraiser. It's a fucking zoo: camera crews, reporters, photographers, gawkers, cops, agents. The place is sewn up tighter than a Beverly Hills facelift.

Noone's glad his plan makes all that go away.

Lateral thinking.

The deaths in Liverpool, his first baby steps, now seem pathetically amateur.

Killing fucking dentists. Jesus.

What was going to happen if he got caught for those childish stunts? It wouldn't even make a dent in Sheehan's Kevlar-coated reputation.

With the deep pockets of Loder Industries, his father might even emerge stronger from any court case in Liverpool. A deranged son. A tragedy. Sheehan could be forgiven, pitied even, for his bad fortune. A couple of appearances on a TV couch and some repentant noises in the press, the right marketing advice, and Ben Noone's name would be gone on the wind.

It's not enough. Someone like him needs a bigger stage. A crime that will echo across the globe and down the decades. A crime so terrible that even Dennis Sheehan will be taken down. A JFK, a 9/11, a Utøya Island.

He opens the bag from the theatrical shop and lays out his purchases. Seeing them there on the counter makes it all seem very real. Noone smiles.

This fucker's going to work.

Thirty

Koop's in front of a public access computer at a desk in the LA Central Library. As Frank approaches, Koop glances up and then turns back to the screen. Frank pulls up a chair and leans forward.

The room is busy but Frank can't detect anyone there who shouldn't be. After the conversation with Angela Salt his paranoia levels are rising to a point that Frank thinks might be unsustainable. He feels ill.

'Look at this,' says Koop, gesturing at the screen. There's a photograph of a Greek vase. Wrapped around the curving black surface, two orange-tinted figures – one human, one a hybrid creature, half-man, half-bull – are fighting.

'Theseus and the Minotaur,' says Koop. Both he and Frank are talking in whispers.

'Theseus is sent by the King of Athens to slay the Cretan Minotaur. He's half-bull, half-man and every seventh year devours seven of Athens' youth. The Minotaur lives in an underground labyrinth created by Daedalus.'

Frank leans closer. 'As in Sheehan's company.'

'And Sheehan's nickname – the one Deborah Sterling called him – is Minotaur.'

Franks reads the text that runs underneath the image.

Theseus, unarmed, takes the place of one of the youths offered to the monster. On arrival in Crete, Ariadne, the daughter of King Minos, falls in love with Theseus. Daedalus, the creator of the labyrinth, tells Ariadne to hand Theseus a ball of twine in order for him to find his way out of the labyrinth if he manages to slay the Minotaur. Theseus follows her instructions and finds the Minotaur.

Producing a hidden sword he fights the beast, slays it and returns to the surface using the string.

'Noone's email was a quote from Theseus,' says Koop. 'I thought it might be interesting to see what the background was. We thought it was just a reference to the kid in the tunnels but it looks like there's a bit more to it than that.'

'You can say that again.' Frank's head is reeling with possibilities. An unarmed warrior slaying a monster in the heart of his protective maze.

Frank tells Koop Salt's conclusions.

'We can't go to them with this,' says Koop. 'It's interesting stuff if you think the way we do but you can imagine the reaction.'

'I still think we have to tell them,' says Frank. 'In fact we're going to tell them.'

Koop leans back and folds his arms across his chest.

'You're right,' he says. 'But there's one thing I think we should do before we call Hagenbaum.'

'And that is . . .?'

'Break into Noone's house.'

Thirty-One

Noone parks the jeep – its plates muddied just like he'd done back in Birkdale after killing the Peters couple – and walks a block to a blue and green bungalow on one of the neat suburban roads way the fuck out in Corona. He'd been put onto this dealer by an obliging Samoan biker he'd met in Manhattan Beach. After getting the guy laid and handing him enough coke to choke a Russian supermodel, Noone had fed him some bullshit about an independent movie he was making that needed a gun. Did the Samoan know anywhere he could get his hands on a particular weapon?

The Samoan didn't give a supersonic shit why Noone needed the weapon so long as the money was good and Noone kept up the supply of top-grade pussy and blow. The only downside with the Samoan's contact is him living out in the boonies.

The bungalow has a Ford mini-van parked outside and looks well cared for. The garden is trimmed, and there's shade from a couple of orange trees. 'Just go in and knock,' the Samoan had said. 'It'll be cool. Money's always cool, bro. But be polite, y'hear? There's kids around.'

Noone plans to be polite. He's not so green that he's about to piss off an arms supplier with biker links.

The place doesn't look like somewhere you'd get high-grade assault weapons. There's a rainbow sticker on the window and Noone can see brightly coloured plastic children's toys inside. There's music playing, something familiar he can't quite identify, a nursery rhyme.

Noone knocks at the door. After a few seconds it's opened by a small white woman in her early sixties with a wide rear end. She's wearing glasses and carrying an Hispanic child about two years old.

'Elliot?' she says. Her voice has a muted southern twang.

Noone nods.

'Come on in. I'm Gena. Traffic heavy?'

'Some,' says Noone.

'Wait till Thursday when that big ol' presidential dinner starts. You don't want to be moving anywhere *then*.'

'I was expecting someone else,' says Noone. He's not keen on talking about the president. 'Gene.'

'A guy, right?'

Noone nods. 'I suppose.'

'Well, you'll have to settle for me, young man. Happened before. Gene. Gena. Mickey doesn't always speak real clear. Come through.'

Gena pushes through a door into a living room. There are two children about three years old sitting in front of a large TV showing cartoons. It's an old show: *ThunderCats*. The theme tune is what Noone had heard through the door. He remembers watching it first time round.

The kids turn their moon faces towards him when he comes into the room and look at him, their expressions blank. One of them turns back to the screen after a couple of seconds.

'Take a seat,' says Gena. 'Don't mind the kids. I run a kind of amateur kindergarten. Lot of working moms in the neighbourhood.'

Noone sits down on a fat sofa. The floor is strewn with toys and he moves a couple out from under his feet. Gena puts the kid she's carrying down on the floor next to the other two.

'Play nice, Hector,' she says. 'Watch the show.'

She waddles out of the room. The kid who's been staring at him continues to watch Noone. Hector looks like he might have a few issues. He picks his nose and watches Noone too. The TV is loud but not unpleasant.

'*ThunderCats*,' says Hector and points at the screen.

Noone nods. 'Yeah.'

Hector seems happy with the response and resumes the examination of his nose.

The house is clean and comfortable. Noone had been half-expecting a slum.

Gena comes back in carrying a solid-looking wooden box. She puts it down on the coffee table and clears a couple of cartons of juice out of the way. The effort of this task makes Gena breathe hard and she rises after placing the box, looking like she might pass out.

'You OK?' says Noone. Not that he gives a shit about the old woman but he doesn't want to have to deal with whoever's behind Gena if she dies right here. And there will be someone behind Gena. It's a tactic – so Mickey the Samoan told Noone – for suppliers of illegal weaponry to run them through a front. The front will get a hike in his – or her – pension and is completely expendable in the event of a crisis. 'Plus they have more balls than some young guys,' Mickey said. 'Dependable.'

'I'm fine,' says Gena. She puts her hands on her hips and sucks in some oxygen. 'Cancer,' she says in the voice other people might say 'flu'. She waves her hand to dismiss the subject and then leaves the room again.

Hector pulls himself up using the edge of the coffee table and puts his chubby hands on the box.

'Don't, kid,' says Noone. Hector ignores him so Noone growls in a low, urgent way and Hector sits back down.

Gena returns with two more boxes, one wooden, one waxed card. She places these down next to the larger box and, with difficulty, manoeuvres her behind into a leather armchair.

'Watch TV, Hector,' she says, flapping her hand at the tube. 'Be good, chico.'

She passes Hector a carton of juice with a straw in the top and he takes it, although he doesn't turn away from the box or sit down. Gena shrugs and flicks the clasp on the lid.

Inside, lying on a bed of shaped foam, is the most simultaneously beautiful and ugliest object Noone has ever seen. Hector leans forward, interested, the juice carton clamped to his mouth.

'Micro Tavor X95S,' says Gena. 'Just like you ordered.' In the presence of the Micro Tavor, her voice takes on a reverential tone and she transfers some of that to Noone.

He's paid upwards of twenty-five grand for this weapon alone when he could have had a fully automatic Uzi for a tenth of that.

The money doesn't matter; he'd have paid double once he'd seen the gun online. It is utterly, completely, one hundred per cent, the most badass gun a person could own.

'Israeli made. Ten point eight inch barrel, nine millimetre, integrated silencer, twelve hundred rounds a minute. Maximum range around four hundred metres. This one came from Operation Defensive Shield. Hector, don't touch; you got sticky fingers, chico.'

Gena pushes Hector's hands out of the way, lifts the gun out and passes it to Noone.

'Mine,' says Hector.

'Not now, honey,' says Gena in a soothing tone. 'Fucking sweet, hey?' she says, turning to Noone. She's not talking about Hector.

The weapon is a short-barrelled, snub-nosed, squat lump of absolute evil energy. The power of it fills the room like smoke and Noone feels his heart beat faster, the cold black muzzle of the gun seeming to draw energy inwards. No one – Hector and his compadres excepted – would ever be within fifty yards of this thing and not know exactly where it was pointed.

The weapon's made of dark grey composite material and is surprisingly light in Noone's hands. Back in Liverpool, when he'd handled the taser for the first time, he had felt the thrill then of having violent power at his fingertips, but the Micro Tavor is a beast of another species. When Noone had been researching assault weapons, the Micro Tavor had screamed out to him. Here, in Gena's living room, having one actually in his hands almost makes him cry.

He cradles it lovingly, a mother and her new born, and the ergonomically crafted weapon sits in his grasp as snugly as if it was always supposed to have been there. Noone can't believe he'd never thought of getting hold of guns before. Put together with his capacity for killing, the Micro Tavor pushes him towards godhood.

Gena taps a finger on the gun's stock. 'You ever fired anything like this before, son?'

He shakes his head.

'Uh huh, nothing like this.' He doesn't let Gena know he's never so much as handled a gun before. Gena takes the weapon from Noone and he has to suppress a momentary desire to grab it back.

Gena explains the technicalities of the gun for twenty minutes, breaking off now and again to change the TV channel or take one of the kids to the bathroom. By the end of it Noone feels comfortable. He wants to load the Mic now and feel the juddering roar as it spits.

He wants to shoot Gena and the brats just to feel what it's like.

He won't, for so many reasons, but the temptation to load and fire is there. Noone doesn't think he can wait until Saturday.

Gena puts the gun back in its box and taps a finger on a second box.

'There are three clips in here, darlin'. More than enough to get the job done.' Gena flicks a glance at Noone. They're straying into territory that neither of them wants to occupy, the reason Noone wants the gun. Gena hurries towards the third box. He lifts the lid.

'Glock 22 RTF2. Also nine millimetre. This one's fully legal.'

Noone picks up the Glock.

It's beautiful too but can't be compared to the Mic. Gena runs through the basics with Noone and their business is complete. No money changes hands; Mickey's taken care of all that beforehand. Cash money only makes everything dirtier.

'Let me go get my vehicle,' says Noone. 'I parked it round the corner until . . . well, until I was sure of how this'd work out.'

Gena nods. 'Sure. Don't blame you, hun.' Hector's pulling at her hip and Gena rubs his head fondly. 'Good kid,' she says to Noone but he just smiles and heads out.

He gets the jeep and backs it onto Gena's short drive, the trunk almost at the mouth of the carport shade. He opens the Jeep back gate and puts the boxes inside in a steel lock-up box. He doesn't shake hands or say anything else to Gena before he leaves and she looks comfortable with that. Hector's face is impassive.

Noone pulls off, leaving Gena and the kid watching him drive away through the rainbow sticker on the window.

Thirty-Two

'I'm in the wrong business.'

It's the first time Frank's seen Ben Noone's house at Pacific Palisades. Warren and Koop had been handling that side of things.

It's late afternoon. The two of them are parked in a car lot on the beachside of the Pacific Highway. Instead of peering at the ocean Frank's got the binoculars up to his eyes and is looking at a glass and steel house high on the hillside a little north of Santa Monica. The morning fog is long gone and the temperature has been climbing steadily.

'Not bad.'

Frank puts the binoculars down.

Both men look up at the house. Two large glass boxes set at a ninety degree angle to each other with an infinity pool between them. There's a cantilevered steel bridge connecting the two parts of the building, one part of which juts out into space. In front, the grounds drop down the steep slope of the canyon. Lush landscaping hugs a curving driveway that opens out into an expanse of concrete on which stands a car Frank can't identify but imagines would cost more than his house. Next to it – so says Koop who has seen the place from close up – is the space where Noone's jeep usually sits and next to that an older vehicle that looks too basic to be at the property.

A Santa Monica police cruiser rolls into the lot and drives past Frank and Koop's car. Frank resists the instinct to nod at the patrolman.

Koop unfolds a shiny tourist map and makes a show of looking at it.

The cruiser comes back after doing a circuit of the lot and, with a last glance in their direction, drifts back onto the highway and south towards Venice.

They step out and lean against the guard rail in front of a bike track which runs along the ocean front between the highway and the water.

'You still OK with this?' Frank asks Koop.

'No,' says Koop. 'But I'm still going to do it.'

Frank's about to say something else when there's movement. Frank lifts the binoculars.

'Someone's moving.'

A Hispanic woman walks out of Noone's house and to the back of the white car. She loads a box of what might be cleaning products into the trunk, gets in and reverses out of the driveway.

Frank and Koop get back into the rental and wait. A minute later, the cleaner's white car passes them in the rear-view mirror.

'Now or never,' says Frank. He pulls the car out into traffic and swings across the intersection before taking the turn into the street behind Noone's place. Koop's already done a recce. Noone's property backs onto a couple of undeveloped lots and a sliver of the Topanga State Park reaching down towards the coast like a green finger. They park in a quiet corner of a cul-de-sac and move into the trees.

Three minutes later they're at the edge of Noone's property.

Frank hands Koop one of the ski masks they'd bought at an outlet mall on the way over.

'I feel stupid,' says Koop, but he rolls it down over his face. Noone may have security cameras. Frank has a small bag of tools they got at Home Depot. It's not perfect but they'll work. Frank doesn't want to think about what might happen if Noone comes back home but the way things are going they don't have much choice.

They hop over the small wire fence and jog down the embankment to the house. There's a hot tub set on an escarpment overlooking the Pacific. Behind it is a small door that looks like a good entry point. Frank takes out a short-handled sledge hammer.

'Ready?' he asks.

Koop gives the thumbs up and Frank splinters the lock. They

both tense, waiting for an alarm that doesn't come. When there's nothing, neither man relaxes. Most alarms in a place like this would be silent, linked to a central operations room.

Frank's banking on Noone not having this arrangement. It's risky, but after Warren's death they're both in the mood. Besides, if Noone does have the place linked to security, there's nothing he or Koop can do about it.

Inside they find themselves in a short corridor of polished concrete. A translucent glass door at the end opens into the main body of the house. It's an open plan, industrial-scale building with almost 360 degrees of glass.

'Not the best place to stay hidden,' says Koop.

'The cocky fucker probably doesn't think he needs to,' replies Frank. He thinks of what Salt told him; this man does not believe you can beat him. He's had everything he's wanted all his life – except, perhaps, his father's attention. There's no reason he wouldn't have a glass house; from his perspective, he's normal.

Frank takes the upper level, Koop down.

Upstairs the rooms are divided more privately but it's still a very open arrangement. In the main bedroom Frank opens the walk-in wardrobe. It's like a department store both in the amount of clothes and in the precise arrangement. Everything looks brand-new. Expensive. But there's nothing of interest.

He moves to the bedside cabinet and finds a similar story. Neat, nothing overly personal. In the bathroom there are cupboards stocked with enough toiletries to open a drugstore. Even the toothbrush looks box fresh. Frank spends another ten minutes searching without finding anything. His stomach is knotted with tension.

Downstairs Koop has a similar story. Fridge well-stocked. Everything stored exactly where it is supposed to be. The only sign of any personality is a small pinboard in the kitchen. On it are the usual banal detritus of a householder. Two power bills. A delivery order menu from an upmarket deli. Five or six business cards, most of them for tradesmen: electrician, plumber, pool. One has a black and white photo of a young woman. Frank lifts it from the pin holding it and flips it over. Angie Santamaria. Angie lists herself as a model/actor.

'That's who we saw him with a few days ago,' says Koop. 'At the cafe.'

Frank writes down Angie's number and replaces it on the pinboard. It's a pathetic haul from the daring raid. After the build-up, both of them feel slightly foolish.

'There's nothing,' Frank says. 'Unless you have any bright ideas?'

'No,' says Koop. 'Let's go. I don't know about you,' he says, pointing to the ski mask, 'but I feel a complete tit in this thing.'

They reach the car unobserved, removing their ski masks under cover of the trees.

'What now, boss?' says Koop. He's driving.

Frank leans an arm on the sill of the passenger window and watches the Pacific Ocean slide past. The landscape, used in so many TV shows and movies, is curiously familiar. It's an odd feeling.

He shakes his head. 'No idea.' He turns his gaze back to the road.

Their whole investigation feels dead. Frank's just about had it. He turns the radio on. The DJ's in the middle of talking about the guest list for tomorrow's presidential fundraiser. *Air Force One* arrives at LAX inside the hour and the traffic is expected to be horrible. Frank switches it off and they sit in silence for a while.

'What about the girl on the card?' says Koop. 'We should talk to her.'

Frank shrugs. 'Why not?'

It's not like they've got anything else to do.

Thirty-Three

After getting the guns from the old woman in Corona, Noone heads up the Riverside Freeway until he intersects with the connecting roads onto I-10 going east.

The traffic's heavy here but moving steady enough. Noone passes the turn for Twentynine Palms and curves south until he enters Joshua Tree National Park around eleven. The green National Parks sign, like many in the area, is studded with a matrix of rusty bullet holes and dents. Guns and high spirits. Noone had heard ads for survivalist outfitters on the drive over – *Off the Grid, for all your survival needs!* – and seen posters for candidates running for election on anti–gun control tickets.

'Fucking right,' Noone had smiled, the guns snug in the lockbox of the Jeep. In this landscape it's practically compulsory to be packing. He'd always sneered at rednecks but now, a gun-owner himself, he feels he may have misjudged.

He drives for ten minutes into the park and stops at the station to buy a Parks pass from the ranger station. The pass will enable him to continue across to Twentynine Palms almost an hour north. About halfway through, just past somewhere called Fried Liver Wash, Noone swings the Jeep east and bumps along a sand road to a dead end far from the main route. He parks and steps out of the car.

Foggy in LA when he left, the summer heat out here is unreal.

There is a complete absence of sound. No wind today, and too far from anything to hear or, more importantly, be heard. After taking the assault weapon from the lockbox, Noone stands for a moment contemplating the panorama. The landscape in the high desert is composed of vicious spinifex, twisted, tormented Joshua trees and Flintstone-like rock formations looking like they've been drawn in place.

The big sky and wide open space make him feel small. An uncomfortable experience but a familiar one. I could stop all this right here, he thinks. Pack up and work it out some other way, a voice whispers. Forget all this killing and complexity and rage. You can't unkill those already dead, and you can't become someone you're not, but you're not a monster, Ben, are you? Not like Terry.

If he hadn't been holding the new gun he might have got right back in the car and gone back to LA.

But the gun is there.

Its solid black presence, its fat weight in his hands, is so real, so viscerally satisfying, that it's enough to see him through the moments of doubt.

He remembers seeing a movie about Mark Chapman, the dumb fat fuckwit who killed Lennon. Chapman had doubts too; set out a couple of times to do the deed and even decided that he wasn't going to pull the trigger. Got John to sign and walked away, happy to be the spectator not the performer.

Then he just did it. Told the cops later that he just decided he really did want to know where the ducks went in winter and the time was *now*; global fame in the couple of seconds it took to unload the .38. Five shots and he's better known than Salinger. On equal billing with Lennon, for a time.

In Norway, Anders Breivik had moments of doubt.

Just like Noone, Breivik hadn't thought of himself as a monster. He had a mission which transcended his own humanity and overcame his revulsion at the way that task had to be achieved.

And like Breivik, Noone's not ready to die. Not before he's explained everything; delivered the monologue, played Hamlet.

The quiet of the landscape, the geological weight, gives Noone confidence. He doesn't *want* to do what he's planning to do. It's something he must do.

It's inevitable.

He puts the assault weapon in his backpack and sets off on foot. After ten minutes he arrives at a fold in the landscape. This will do.

366

Energised, Noone takes out the gun and slides the clip in as Gena had told him. He makes sure the suppressor is snug, thumbs the automatic switch and takes aim at a dry log resting on a sandbank.

Mother*fucker!*

The Micro Tavor comes alive, there's no other way to describe it. It just *erupts*. Heavy bullets pour out like liquid and the sand in front of Noone explodes. He can feel the impact through the soles of his boots.

Noone takes his finger off the trigger, frightened and exhilarated at the same time. He resets himself, this time taking more care, and rips the log in half with a short burst.

It's better than sex.

He spends five more minutes handling the weapon before reluctantly heading back to the Jeep. Although confident he's not being observed out here, you never know. He doesn't want to risk a stray hiker making a report about some nut with an assault weapon.

Having fired the Micro Tavor for the first time, Noone now wants to put his plan into action more than he's ever wanted to do anything in his life. He can almost hear the soundtrack playing behind him. The doubts of twenty minutes ago seem as substantial as this morning's fog. Thursday can't come soon enough.

But before then there's business to take care of in Twentynine Palms.

Thirty-Four

The town, straggling along the highway, sits between the edge of Joshua Tree National Park on one side and the massive, largely unseen, Marine Corps Air Ground Combat Center on the other.

It's high desert country here. If you climb the ridges of the rolling scrub to the south and look across the Yucca and Morongo valleys you can see Palm Springs and the snow-capped ridge line of Mount San Jacinto, and, on a clear day, the Salton Sea and the Colorado Desert beyond.

Noone gets there from Joshua Tree around one.

He gets a drive-through McDonald's and pulls the Jeep up on a dusty lot across the way to eat alongside a detailed mural depicting the fall of Baghdad painted on the back wall of a Japanese massage joint. The mural's done in the style more often seen in Soviet propaganda except now these soldiers are Marines and wear the stars and stripes. The spindly palms that rise above the stucco facade and the dusty desert hills lend the painting a disorienting geographical shift. Only the fast-food joints across the intersection spoil the illusion. Twentynine Palms is a Marine town.

Noone eats a burger and drains a jumbo Diet Coke. He balls the wrappers and throws them in the back before checking the GPS and heading north up the Adobe Road. He follows the directions until he gets to the Bagdad Highway.

'Spelt the goddam American way too,' murmurs Noone as he passes the sign. 'Fucken A.'

He'll have to be careful out here; the road runs close to the base and intruders aren't welcome. Especially intruders with assault weapons stowed in the trunk.

Five minutes down the highway he turns off down a scrub road so sand-strewn that it is difficult to differentiate between asphalt and desert. There are few buildings out here and those that are are scattered far and wide. Some trailers, a few low-roofed adobe shacks. The base itself, from what Noone can gather, is a shadowy presence, its exact location sketchy on Google Maps and the GPS. There are frequent live-fire operations and training in the hills and scrub around the Marine Combat Center.

But it's not the base that Noone's looking for.

Approximately eight miles along the highway, Noone drives past a small white house sprouting a giant satellite dish on the roof. The dish is so big Noone is sure it must be supported by some sort of bracing underneath to prevent it plunging through the roof. Noone parks the Jeep at the side of the road about half a mile away. It's a risk leaving the vehicle here so close to the base, especially with the guns, but he hopes what he needs to do won't take long. He props the hood open to make it look like a breakdown.

Noone puts on a baseball cap and starts walking in a wide arc around to the rear of the white house. By the time he gets close he's sweating heavily. He's taken the long way round, trying to keep out of sight as much as possible. Although the landscape is mostly flat, there are undulations in the terrain that enable him to get within thirty yards relatively confident that no one has observed him.

This will be the tricky bit.

Noone kneels in the sand and watches the house but, after five hot minutes, has seen no movement. It's the second time he's been along this road in recent weeks and neither time has he seen anyone on the Bagdad Highway. A helicopter clockworks its way towards the Combat Center to Noone's left, too far away to worry about.

Close up against the house, tucked into the shade of a corrugated lean-to, is a dark blue mini-van. Noone stays kneeling for another minute until he feels he's going to boil away like spit on a rock. It's almost one-thirty in the afternoon now and this isn't an environment you want to be hanging around in.

Noone stands and starts walking purposefully towards the building. He moves slowly; if he's challenged he's going to say his car broke down. Sprinting would be hard to explain and Noone has no doubt whoever is inside the house is armed. Guns are mandatory in this part of the world.

Noone himself has nothing except a fat short-bladed knife with a rubberised grip in a looped sheath on his belt. There's no point bringing any of his new guns. The last thing he wants is any noise, and the Micro with the suppressor fitted is too visible.

At a distance of some ten yards from the back of the property a straggling line of rocks marks out some sort of nominal garden. There is nothing growing inside the designated area and nothing to separate it from the ground beyond, yet it's clear that the rocks now tell anyone that they are inside a private zone.

Noone steps across the rocks and as soon as he does a shape rolls out from the dense black shadow of the lean-to and onto a section of concrete in the sun. A slim, heavily bearded man of approximately thirty years of age wearing army surplus pants, a check shirt and reflective sunglasses glides a few yards towards Noone on a bulky motorised wheelchair. He has a red bandanna wrapped around his head and holds a shotgun comfortably across his knees. Although it's not pointing directly at Noone the man in the wheelchair has his trigger finger resting inside the guard.

The guy's name is Kenny Hoy.

Kenny's the reason Noone's in Twentynine Palms. Even with the beard he looks much younger and fitter than Noone had envisaged. Noone wonders how long Kenny Hoy's been watching him.

'Stop,' says Hoy. His voice is neutral but precise. The voice of someone who knows what they're doing. In the glare of the sun every detail seems hyper-real.

Noone stops and holds up both his hands in a placatory gesture. 'Hey, man,' he says. 'I'm stopped.'

'You can step back a couple,' says Hoy. 'That way you won't be on my property and I'll feel a little better.'

Noone moves back over the rocks.

'What the fuck you doing arriving over my back fence like that?' Again, despite the words, Hoy's voice is controlled.

'I broke down,' says Noone, jerking a thumb in the direction of the highway. 'I'm looking for a buddy of mine lives out on Monte Vista.' Noone plucks the name of a road he's seen on the GPS.

370

'I know some folks over there. What's his name?'

'Sheehan,' says Noone without hesitation. 'Dennis Sheehan.'

'Like the politician.'

'Yeah, except this guy's about forty. Most people call him Shorty on account of being tall.'

'Don't know him,' says Hoy. Noone notices that he no longer has his finger in the trigger guard.

'He's ex-corps,' says Noone. He knows Hoy's military past. 'You?'

'What division?'

Noone shrugs. 'I don't know, man. I never served. I do what I can for Shorty when I can and he moved over here a few weeks ago. He's got some . . . well, he's got some problems since getting home from Kandahar. You know.'

Hoy nods. He does know. But he's not about to put the shotgun down anytime soon.

'So what you doing at my place? Breakin' down don't mean you have to sneak round back.'

'Like I said, I broke down. This looked the quickest way here. And my phone's got no reception.'

'That can happen, I guess,' says Hoy. He looks over in the direction of the Marine Base. 'On account of all the electronics they got. Star Wars shit and all manner of doo-dahs in there. Fuck up the radio waves something bad. You need a booster like I got on the roof.'

'Listen, man,' says Noone, 'I know it's a lot to ask but could you call a tow truck for me from Twentynine Palms?'

'OK,' says Hoy. Instead of moving, Hoy slides a hand inside the top pocket of his shirt and pulls out a smartphone. 'I know a guy who'll get it done. What's your name? You got any ID?'

Noone takes out his wallet, steps a little closer to Hoy and flips it open to his driver's licence.

'Ben Noone,' he says. Hoy asking for ID is clever. Noone once again makes a note not to underestimate him.

Hoy takes a good look at the licence.

'Santa Monica? Fancy.' Hoy's smiling but he looks like he thinks the ID is for real. Noone is who he says he is.

Noone can almost see Hoy relax.

He knows that he's going to have to do it now before the call's connected and his name's out there. Noone plants his hands on his hips and, covered by the angle of his right palm, thumbs open the flap on the knife sheath.

Hoy tries to dial one-handed but it's tricky with the sun gleaming on the glass front of the phone. He angles his head down to look more closely.

Noone takes the opportunity to take out his knife and put it behind his back. He stands like his hands are clasped together. Behind his back, Noone's left hand lightly grasps his right wrist. With his right he takes a firm grip on the rubberised handle of the knife.

Hoy looks up. 'What was the name again?' He's relaxing a little. 'Noone. Ben Noone.'

As Hoy glances back down at the phone, Noone sprints the four paces towards the wheelchair. It's quiet out here and the sound of Noone's boots on the grit is loud.

Hoy looks up and sees Noone almost upon him. He drops the phone and swings the shotgun up but Noone's already right there and he blocks the barrel of Hoy's gun with his left forearm.

'Motherfucker!' screams Hoy. He punches Noone in the kidneys with a hard left that has real power. Hoy picked up his disability on his second tour of duty in Kandahar. The metal frag had nicked his spinal column and left him paralysed from the waist down. Hoy hasn't let the injury stop him; he plays basketball and does everything himself. His upper body is hard and his reactions are fast. He might be in a chair but he's still a Marine.

Noone gasps and almost drops right then. Instead, he pushes down on the barrel of the shotgun with his left and swings the knife blindly back-handed at Hoy with his right.

It's a wild, panicky shot because Noone knows now that taking on the Marine is a serious mistake. He should have brought the gun, got up close and disarmed the man before trying a stunt like this.

To Noone's astonishment and relief, he gets lucky: the blade plunges directly into Hoy's left eye. The man jerks spasmodically and makes a low guttural animal noise. Noone can feel Hoy's hot

blood running down his wrist. With his left hand, his own movements clumsy and awkward, Noone takes the shotgun by the barrel
and directs it towards the ground while Kenny Hoy twitches underneath him. He doesn't want Hoy to pull the trigger in a reflex spasm.

Noone keeps the knife in Hoy's eye socket until there's no
movement and then, satisfied the man is dead, pulls it out.

Noone bends double and tries to control his breathing.

The place on his side where Hoy had caught him hurts like a
bastard but he's glad; it'll help him to focus more when the next
time comes. After a minute or two his breathing becomes regular.
His own phone rings and Noone jumps. He takes the cell out and
doesn't recognise the number onscreen. He lets it ring out. There's
no one he wants to talk to at the moment.

He stands in the absolute silence of the desert and looks at the
dead man in the wheelchair. He still marvels at it; alive a minute or
two ago and dead now.

There.

Not there.

It's a magic trick and he's the conjuror.

He is trembling with adrenaline. This is the first kill where he
hasn't used the taser and he feels flush, proud that he has brought
it off and had the control to finish the job. A fucking *Marine*, dude.

The only blood Noone has on him is on his right hand and wrist.
He pockets Hoy's phone, places his shotgun on the floor and hauls
Noone off the wheelchair and lets him fall onto the sand. Noone
angles his head to let the eye wound bleed out.

Leaving the dead man, Noone finds a rag hanging in the carport
next to a broom and uses it to clean up as best he can. With his
hands relatively dry he kneels to wipe the blood off the knife in the
sand. He stands and replaces it in the sheath.

Noone double-checks the call to the tow truck guy hadn't been
made. The screen is blank. Noone switches the phone off and slips
it back into his own pocket.

He drags Hoy's chair into the space between the mini-van and
the shack. It's a lot cooler here and Noone's conscious of how over-
heated he's become. He opens the door into the house and finds the
fridge. He takes out a can of soda and drains it.

The house is small but as neat as a barrack room on inspection day. The floor is polished concrete and the fixtures designed for a man in a wheelchair. There are no dirty dishes, no piled laundry, nothing out of place. Hoy's Marine background shows through everywhere. An organised man.

Noone walks back to his jeep and brings it onto Hoy's property. He parks it behind the mini-van and out of sight of the sand-covered highway.

He wraps Hoy's head in a beach towel to minimise the mess from the blood and lifts him back onto the wheelchair. Noone takes Hoy to a battered metal shed twenty yards behind the house. The shed is larger than the house. The door is padlocked so Noone goes back into the house and finds the keys hung neatly on a hook at waist height near the rear door.

Inside the shed is a professional-looking set of gym equipment: mostly weights and some specialised stuff that Noone guesses Hoy must have had made for him. Although it's broiling inside there is a huge aircon unit set into one of the walls. Standing against the opposing wall is a jumbo freezer cabinet. Noone had been planning to simply leave Hoy in the shed but the freezer will be perfect.

Noone moves items around inside the freezer to make space and then hauls Hoy's body from the chair and places it inside the cabinet under a layer of frozen meat. He closes the lid. The body won't be missed by anyone who's looking carefully but Noone's not overly concerned. If everything goes to plan he'll only need Hoy's place for less than forty-eight hours.

Noone pushes the wheelchair outside, locks the door of the shed and heads into the house. As he's doing so his phone rings again and this time it's his lawyer, Perot. Noone lets it ring out and then listens to the message. Call me.

Putting the phone back in his pocket he places the wheelchair in the centre of the air-conditioned kitchen and wipes it down with another towel. Apart from a puddle of blood on one edge of the seat it's relatively clean. Noone bundles the bloody towel into the trash.

The wheelchair is a robust-looking machine, with rugged tyres, the seat very similar in appearance to a regular car seat. Underneath is a boxed area that houses the motor and the electronics. There is also a space for storing items but Noone isn't interested in that. He finds a box cutter in Hoy's pristine garage cum workshop and uses it to carefully slice open the back edge of the seat along the seam. He makes a cut of about eight inches in length. This done, Noone drops to his knees and prises open the leather. Inside the seat is a foam pad. Noone manoeuvres this out through the gap he's opened up and places it on the kitchen floor.

He retrieves the Micro Tavor from the Jeep and places it on top of the pad. If he breaks it down into the two component parts as Gena had demonstrated and lays it diagonally across the foam, it just fits. Using the box cutter, Noone hollows out a space in the yellow foam and places the gun inside. After a few adjustments he gets it to sit in naturally. He replaces the foam padding and gun inside the seat of the wheelchair and stands back to see how it looks.

From the front and sides there's nothing to see. At the back, only the gap where he'd made the cut gives anything away. It takes another ten minutes but Noone finds a sewing kit in one of the kitchen cupboards. Taking his time he carefully sews the gap closed, keeping the thread as close to the raised seam as possible. By the time he's finished it's almost impossible to detect there has been any tampering with the chair.

Noone sits on the wheelchair and switches it on. He can feel the gun beneath his buttocks. He spends twenty minutes driving the chair around Hoy's house. Satisfied that he has control of the chair he parks it in an angle of the hallway, out of view of any of the windows. In Hoy's bedroom there's a battery charger for the chair. Noone brings it into the hallway and hooks it up to the wheelchair.

He's going to have to leave the Micro here overnight but that can't be helped. In any case it keeps it out of trouble.

There's something else he needs from Hoy: the invitation.

Noone had been hoping it'd be propped up on the kitchen counter or some such dopey shit, but it's not there. It takes him five minutes but he eventually finds it in a side drawer of the cabinet next to Hoy's bed. A crisp white envelope and a sheet of card inside. Noone checks the details and replaces it in the drawer. He'll pick it up on Thursday. No sense in keeping any of Hoy's stuff in Santa Monica.

His last task is to move Hoy's mini-van inside the garage. He's hoping that if anyone does call by they'll assume Hoy is out. It's a risk, but it can't be helped.

Noone tidies up any sign he's been inside the house and, satisfied there's nothing that would be discovered by a casual inspection, finds the bathroom. In the bathroom he cleans himself up properly. He takes off his clothes and inspects them carefully, looking for blood or anything suspicious. There's a smear on the side of his shirt so he balls it up and finds a replacement in Hoy's bedroom. He puts his own shirt in the laundry basket. He steps into the shower and washes himself. He dries himself and dresses in his own clothes and Hoy's shirt.

Leaving the bathroom as tidy as he found it, Noone leaves the house, locking the door behind him. He puts Hoy's keys in his pocket. On his way out he throws sand over the bloodstains in the yard.

In the Jeep he's thirty minutes west of Palm Springs when his phone rings once more and this time Noone answers.

It's his lawyer, Perot.

The cops are at his place.

Thirty-Five

Noone, tired and edgy, gets back around seven.

He pulls into the drive and parks on the concrete pan next to a Santa Monica PD cruiser.

'Ben,' says Perot, shaking his hand. Noone reciprocates. Perot glances at his dusty jeans and boots. 'Been hiking?'

'Something like that.' He turns his head in the direction of the police car. 'What's this all about?'

'Cops got a call from one of your neighbours,' says Perot. 'They saw someone acting suspicious, heading up over the back through the park. She thought they were coming from your property so she told the cops to come here. They did and found signs of a forced entry. Nothing taken from what they can see.'

'Why are you here?'

'The Santa Monica PD called you but got no answer. They had my name on file as your lawyer and that was the only contact number they had for you. I called you and thought you might need some support.' Perot smiles. 'All part of the service.'

Noone doesn't reply. He's still feeling wary this close to D-day. 'You been inside?'

Perot, following behind, shakes his head. 'Uh-huh, no.'

At the junction with the steel walkway, Noone heads left and down a set of stairs to where a cop is looking closely at the broken lock.

'Mr Noone?' says the cop. Noone nods.

'I'm Patrolman O'Brien. My colleague, Patrolman Vento, is inside. Looks OK but we'd like you to check around and see if anything's gone.'

Noone goes in. The place looks exactly as he'd left it. There's nothing incriminating on the property of any kind other than

377

a small stash of recreational dope. He walks through each of the rooms and emerges back into the downstairs kitchen area shaking his head.

'Can't see anything missing.'

O'Brien points up at one of the security cameras. 'How about checking your camera feed?'

Noone shakes his head. 'It's not hooked up,' he says. 'Dumb, huh?'

'It happens a lot,' says Vento. 'I suggest you get that fixed as soon as possible, Mr Noone.'

Ten minutes later, after filling out a short incident report form, the cops leave, followed by Perot.

Noone heads straight for his office. He opens his computer and establishes a link with the security camera feed, which is working perfectly. He resets the digital counter to when he left this morning and fast forwards until he finds an image of two men at the door. He watches them smash the lock and then follows their progress around the house. It's clear they've found nothing.

Noone doesn't think it's anyone from Daedalus. It's too clumsy for them. But there's something familiar about one of the burglars and Noone thinks he knows who it is.

Keane.

Right on cue.

Noone smiles and checks his watch. The president will be touching down around now. Noone knows every step of the itinerary. After landing, the president will be taken to a private home in Century City. The place has been loaned by one of the city's biggest agents. It's not the venue for tomorrow night's party, which will be in the Hollywood Hills.

There's one final touch that Noone wants to make to ensure he gets a clear run at the target. When he'd thought of it he could have hugged himself, so perfect was it in its simplicity.

He picks up the phone and dials the number he never thought he'd need to call.

Thirty-Six

Angie's not picking up.

Frank tries all the way back into West Hollywood but gets nowhere.

He leaves a message for her to call. He tells her he's a friend of Ben's from Liverpool.

At the apartment he and Koop don't say much. The cloud of failure is hovering. Koop turns the TV on and switches it to CNN on mute.

'I'm going to get cleaned up,' he says. He flicks a thumb at the TV. 'See if anything happens ahead of schedule.'

While Koop's in the shower, Frank makes another call. On the TV a straw-haired reporter is standing outside a police cordon at LAX. He looks excited.

'Em,' Frank says when Harris picks up. He keeps his voice down but he doesn't really know why.

Em Harris's voice is sleep-clogged. 'Frank,' she says and then pauses. 'Do you know what time it is?'

'Sorry.'

Frank hears a few muffled words. Em has her hand over the phone and is speaking to someone.

'Em?'

'I'm here,' she says after a moment. 'I'm in the living room. You woke us up.'

'How is Linda?'

'She's fine. Look, Frank, you haven't phoned for a chat, have you? I only got to sleep a couple of hours ago. If you imagine you're getting a warm welcome at three in the fucking morning you've got another think coming.'

'I need you to listen to a story,' says Frank. 'It might take a while. But it's business, Em, so pay attention.'

'OK, fire away.'

Frank outlines the events leading up to this moment in time. He leaves out the break-in at Noone's. If the apartment is being bugged it's the only thing he doesn't want them to hear. Pretty much everything else they already know and he wants them to know he's passing it on to Harris, to someone.

When he's finished Em lets out a long low breath. Frank can hear it across the miles, can see the air leaving her lips. On the screen a procession of limousines and police motorcycles sweeps past the cameras in a blaze of red and blue flashing lights. Despite the way the case has gone Frank feels a ludicrous elation at being so close to the centre of power. Is this what it feels like to be American? Is that why they are as they are? The Romans must have felt like this, and the English a hundred years ago.

'You have to take it to Homeland Security, the FBI, someone, Frank. You have no choice. If something happens and you don't make every effort to warn them there'll be . . . well, there'll be trouble.'

'I know,' says Frank. 'The next call I make is to Hagenbaum. But I suspect that what will happen is that I'll be warned off again, this time more seriously. There may even be violence. Daedalus seem to be somewhat maverick when it comes to due process. I need you to know what I think and to have it down tomorrow morning in an MIT report. And if this place is bugged then that saves me the trouble of going through the whole stupid dance again.'

'I'll get it on the system now,' says Harris. 'I'm awake anyway.'

Maybe something of Frank's desperation is coming through in his voice because Harris's has softened when she speaks next.

'Superintendent Searle has been asking for an update. One involving a possible assassination attempt on the US president might make him sit up and take notice.'

Koop comes back into the room wearing jeans and no shirt. He stands rubbing the back of his head with a towel and watches the presidential motorcade as CNN follows its progress through south LA.

'Yeah, well,' says Frank, 'let's hope they're right and I'm dead wrong about this.'

'Take care, Frank.'

'Will do,' he says and hangs up before he starts blubbing.

'Big party,' says Koop without taking his eyes off the TV. He turns to Frank.

'You'll have to call them.'

'Put a shirt on, for fuck's sake, Koop. I can see you've got a tan. No need to rub it in.' Frank waves the phone. 'And I'm calling them now, OK?'

Koop makes a gesture of supplication and heads back to his room.

After a couple of dead ends, Frank gets Agent Hagenbaum on the line.

'I was just about to call you,' says Hagenbaum before Frank can get a word out.

'Good,' says Frank. He waits.

'Are you there?' says Hagenbaum, an irritated edge in his voice.

'I was waiting for you, Hagenbaum. I thought you said you were about to call me.'

'You need to come in. You and the consultant. We're not far from you. At the Beverly Hilton on Wilshire.'

'FBI must be paying well. And what's it about?'

'Just get here right away, Keane. Like, now. Ask for me at the desk. They'll point you in the right direction.'

After Hagenbaum hangs up, Frank turns back to the TV but he's not listening.

What now?

Thirty-Seven

A river of cars backs up on the freeway. Outriders flashing blue and red block each exit and entrance as the motorcade sweeps through the paused city from the south. Overpasses are sealed. Two Navy helicopters monitor from above. It is the embodiment of power, and the Angelenos are only too pleased to be observers along the route. Even those held up in the grotesque traffic snarls feel privileged somehow.

The 405 to Santa Monica Boulevard. North Beverly to Coldwater Canyon, the caravan slowing as it winds up the hills in late-afternoon sun, the morning fog a distant memory.

At a property big enough to be invisible from the road, the gates are open and the motorcade swings in without stopping, its comet tail of media sputtering to a halt and then directed to the allotted parking by stern-faced cops in sunglasses. The gates close and the media swarm from the vehicles to join those already in place.

The president is in Los Angeles.

Thirty-Eight

It takes them almost an hour to get to the Beverly Hilton thanks to the presidential traffic extending back onto Wilshire Boulevard. They let the car be valet parked because there's no other way to do it.

Despite both Frank and Koop possessing the Liverpool sense that nowhere is too good for them, the Beverly Hilton does its best to dispossess them of their customary lack of nerves. It's not so much that it is particularly imposing, or that it is overly luxurious, it is more the sense that everyone – *everyone* – in there is connected, important, beautiful or loaded.

'Fuck me,' Koop whispers as they cross the lobby and a slimline supermodel type drifts past them in a cloud of perfume and attitude.

'Try and keep it together, you peasant,' mutters Frank. 'We are flying the flag, remember.'

At the desk Frank asks for Hagenbaum.

'Room 322. They're expecting us.'

'One moment, sir,' murmurs the desk clerk and picks up a phone. He speaks into it and then replaces the receiver. 'Suite 322 is on the third floor, sir. The elevators are to your left.'

'Suite,' says Frank, sotto voce, as they stand waiting. '*Suite* 322, sir.'

At the third floor they exit the lift and follow the signs for 322. The corridor is lit with soft lamps and the carpet underfoot is thick. Frank feels a little knot of tension in his gut.

'You don't think this is where we get the waterboard treatment, do you, Koop?' he murmurs.

'What's all this "we" stuff, you English prick?' Koop winks. 'If it goes belly up, remember I'm an Aussie now, mate. It might confuse them long enough for me to slide out.'

At 322 Frank takes a breath and raps a knuckle on the door. When it opens Hagenbaum is there.

'DCI Keane,' he says and looks pointedly at Koop. 'Mr Koopman.'

Frank doesn't remember ever mentioning Koop's name to Hagenbaum but says nothing.

'This is all a bit James Bond, isn't it, Hagenbaum?' says Frank as they walk into the suite. Hagenbaum doesn't reply.

Frank turns the corner and sees a large room with two couches facing each other over a coffee table. Leaning against the wall opposite the floor-to-ceiling window is Ashland. Baines, his arms folded, is standing next to the window. Frank turns and stops dead.

On one of the couches is Ben Noone, dressed in black and grey. He's leaning back and holding a beer bottle, looking comfortable. Catching sight of Frank he waves a lazy hand. Frank doesn't respond. Instead he looks at the man on the seat facing Noone.

He's an older man who Frank recognises from the TV. He stands as Frank and Koop approach. He's tall and dressed in what looks like a very expensive suit. Everything about him exudes power and privilege.

'DCI Keane,' says the man in the expensive suit as he extends a hand. 'Dennis Sheehan.'

Thirty-Nine

The police have established an exclusion zone around the side road leading up to the house where the president is staying the night. A long line of TV trucks and cars straggle down the road on either side of the intersection. The vehicles bristle with satellite dishes, radio antenna and electronics. Around each vehicle reporters and crew turn lights on and off as they do their piece to camera. Further down the street there are barriers keeping the curious from moving any nearer. Locals must pass through a temporary checkpoint to access their property but there aren't many who do; this area belongs to the very rich and most people in the surrounding couple of streets have wisely left overnight to avoid the zoo.

Four perimeters have been established by the presidential protection team radiating out from the man himself. The key perimeter is the one closest to the president, composed of the Secret Service agents who accompany him everywhere. The house and gardens, of course, have been swept and sniffed and examined many weeks previously. The house in which the president will host the fundraiser tomorrow evening has had the same treatment.

The second security perimeter is an obvious one, composed of highly visible police units, Federal agents and more Secret Service agents. This team patrols the borders of the property and has established checkpoints at all entrances. Police dogs patrol the gardens. There are SWAT snipers on the roof and concealed in strategic points. In areas where there is deemed to be a weakness, motion sensors and infra-red cameras are installed.

The third layer of security is less visible. Federal agents patrol a wider perimeter behind and within the publicly accessible areas. Their brief is to look for red flag signifiers, suspicious activity, or even faces on their watch list. Operatives from Homeland Security working out of two large mobile bases monitor electronic transmissions in the area. Mobile phones are difficult to use close to the president. Internet connection is often suspended.

Finally there are the helicopters and aircraft maintaining an exclusion zone in the airspace around the house. The normally busy skies above this part of Los Angeles are temporarily quiet. Flights are diverted around the exclusion zone and air traffic for hundreds of miles in any direction is patrolled by fighter jets from Edwards Air Force Base.

The scale of operation required to protect the leader of the free world is breathtaking.

The possibility of anyone penetrating that ring of steel is almost zero.

Almost.

Forty

'You look like you need a drink,' says Sheehan to Frank. His voice is deep and rich and authoritative. 'Can we get you something?'

'I'll take a scotch,' says Koop. 'I don't know about Frank, but I could certainly use something.'

'Mr Ashland,' says Sheehan. 'If you would.'

Ashland nods and walks towards what appears to be a fully stocked bar. He makes no sign of being disappointed to be performing barman duties.

'Same for me,' says Frank.

'I'll take one too,' says Noone. He holds his bottle up and waggles it back and forth.

Sheehan shakes hands with Koop.

'Please,' he says, indicating the couch. 'Sit down.'

Frank and Koop sit on the couch facing Noone.

'No lawyer?' says Frank to Noone.

Noone shrugs as Dennis Sheehan takes an armchair at ninety degrees to his son. 'The fewer people who know about this meeting, the better. And that includes lawyers. We're kind of in new territory here.'

Frank studies Noone. It's been so long since he's seen his prey in the flesh that he has forgotten how visceral his response was to him back in the interview room at Stanley Road. He's almost glad to get the same feeling now. It's reassuring.

Ashland comes over and hands drinks to Frank and Koop. There's no trace of animosity on his face and no reference to their conversation earlier in the day.

'Things have changed since Mr Ashland and Mr Baines visited you,' says Sheehan as if he had read Frank's thoughts. Sheehan looks at Noone. 'And what's changed is that Ben called me.'

Noone's face is blank. 'I thought it might be a way out of all this . . . mess,' he says.

'I understand that you feel my son is connected in some way with killings in the UK,' says Sheehan. 'And that now you think he has some plan to harm me.' Sheehan leans back and extends his arms. 'Does it look like he's harming me?'

Sheehan's not expecting a reply, which is just as well because Frank's not sure he's got one. 'There are some things you should know, DCI Keane. One is that I have been taking care of my son ever since he was born. Due to my public duties I could not reveal what had happened. Even now it would be a problem for me; not a disastrous one, but a problem. So this meeting is to reassure you that you are simply barking up the wrong tree. Ben did not kill anyone. I will allow that he has, in the past, been somewhat wild and I have done my best to keep those excesses within reason. If he got caught up in a local matter in England that is unfortunate but it's not his fault.'

'He did it,' says Frank.

The words come out faster than he wants them to. He breathes deeply and gets himself under control. 'He killed the Peters family. He killed Dean Quinner. And he killed Warren Eckhardt a few days ago at the Farmers Market, right here in Los Angeles.'

Sheehan looks at Noone, who shrugs. You see what I'm dealing with?

It's Ashland who speaks next. 'Let me reiterate what I told you this morning. You have nothing on Mr Noone. Nothing. It's all conjecture and hearsay and coincidence. There are no forensics. There are no motives that you can come up with. And I think your friend agrees with me, don't you, Mr Koopman?'

Koop pulls a face. 'It's not looking very strong right now, I agree. Although I'm with Frank when it comes to thinking he did it.'

'And here's the other thing,' says Sheehan.

He rotates an iPad lying on the coffee table and the video of the break-in at Noone's house comes onscreen. Sheehan taps the screen. 'You committed a felony, DCI Keane. You too, Koopman. We could dig around and get some positive forensics from your visit; my organisation has very deep pockets and we'd find hair samples, fibres, something that puts you inside my son's house. If we didn't, we'd plant it. We're not subtle.'

Sheehan leans forward and smiles a shark smile and for the first time Frank considers the notion that Sheehan knows all about his son's past . . . and doesn't care. 'Or I could get Mr Ashland here to put you on a round-the-world trip to pain, DCI Keane.' Sheehan clicks his fingers. 'Just like that. Who do you think you're dealing with here?' Sheehan's eyes are cold and Frank can feel the dark power of the man. 'I controlled armies, DCI Keane. Armies. I have my own army now. If I chose to I could drop you and Mr Koopman naked at the Afghan border with the Stars and Stripes tattooed on your foreheads. You'd be there by tomorrow morning.' Sheehan snaps his fingers again.

There's a short silence.

'I can't speak for Frank,' says Koop. 'But I'd prefer it if you didn't.'

'This official FBI policy, Hagenbaum?' says Frank.

'Listen to Mr Sheehan, Keane,' Hagenbaum says. 'Really. You need to. You're out of your depth. We all are.'

Sheehan smiles again, a warmer one this time, and shifts back in his seat. 'I'm sure there'll be no need for anything so crude, DCI Keane. But I did want to make you aware that this investigation, from your point of view, has run its course. There will be no further investigation. There will be no pursuing of your little MLAT application. You got it wrong. You will go home. You will not come back. There is, literally, nothing you can do to attach blame to Ben for your local troubles. I hope you get the guy who did it, I really do. But it wasn't Ben. My son does not represent a threat to either me or the president. We have spoken with the White House security people and Ben has passed on attending the fundraiser. They see that as being a very generous gesture on his part after paying thirty thousand dollars for it. They have no concerns about him as the only worries have been raised by you without producing one credible piece of evidence. And you're a burglar. In fact, they expressed the idea that it is you who may represent a more credible threat. The word obsession was used.'

Frank drains his glass and gets to his feet. 'I hope you're right, Mr Sheehan. Because I think your son is a fucking psychopath.'

'We going?' says Koop, looking at Frank. 'I was beginning to enjoy myself.'

Dennis Sheehan stands and extends his hand to both men. 'Please don't misunderstand me, gentlemen. Coming down hard on decent law enforcement officers is not something that gives me pleasure. But try and consider that, in this case, we are right and you are wrong. And, if you find you can't do that, then you'll have to be content with the idea that you can't do a fucking thing about it.'

Noone stands and offers his hand to Frank. 'No hard feelings, sport?'

Frank glances at Noone's hand. There's a small, fresh-looking scratch on the back of his knuckle. Frank turns towards the door. He doesn't have any smart comeback. He just feels ill.

Forty-One

Back at the apartment around nine, Frank feels as tired as he's ever felt. Worse, he feels beaten. He'd rather have had a physical encounter than the comprehensive humiliation he's just been put through.

Koop doesn't feel good either but as the lead investigator it's Frank who's shouldering the greater burden. Koop leaves him watching coverage of the presidential visit, which seems to consist of overexcited reports from outside the agent's home and cutaways to the agenda for the rest of the week.

Koop heads into his room and calls Zoe. She's not exactly turning handsprings to hear him but at least she's talking. It'll do for now.

Afterwards, in front of the TV, Koop's about to suggest a beer somewhere when Frank gets a call.

It's Angie.

Angie's clearly a night owl. It's past ten when she calls, replying to the message left on her phone. Frank lies about being a friend of Ben's from his travelling days in Liverpool and persuades her to meet him at a coffee shop just around the corner from her apartment. Angie won't make the trip into the city from her place in Santa Monica at this time – not simply for safety reasons but because it'll take her too long and she's not *that* interested in catching up with one of Ben's buddies. Frank guesses she has an hour to fill. Or maybe there's some relationship thing with Noone that Angie's not happy about. Frank knows that women will do a lot to get information about someone they care about. If Noone's Santa Monica property is anything to go by, maybe Angie has her sights on becoming more than a girlfriend. Whatever the reason, she says she'll meet.

'What do you reckon?' says Frank. 'Worth a shot?'

'No idea,' says Koop. 'But what else are we going to do? Pack?'

They take a circuitous route, conscious that since the meeting with Sheehan the stakes have been raised considerably. Only when they are sure they have shaken any tail do they drive to Santa Monica; and even then Frank makes them park four blocks away.

Neither of them is anxious to take that day trip to Kandahar.

Now Frank and Koop are sitting at stools in a late-night diner. Koop's got his laptop open and they both have coffee on the go.

Just after eleven Angie walks in and they recognise her from the photo on Noone's wall. He waves and she nods.

'Angie? Frank.'

She sits down. A punked-up waitress arrives at the table and pulls out a pad. Angie orders tea, Frank and Koop get more coffee.

'I like your accent,' Angie says to Frank. 'Cute.'

'What about mine?' says Koop. Angie gives Koop a glance and smiles pityingly.

He's been weighed, measured, and found wanting, all inside the three seconds it's taken to say the sentence. Koop sits back and lets Frank take the lead. It's been a long day.

'I have a confession,' Frank starts. He lowers his voice and beckons Angie closer. He takes out his wallet and shows her his Merseyside police ID. 'I'm not a friend of Ben's, Angie. Far from it.'

Angie inspects Frank's badge and pulls back, wary.

'You're in a great deal of danger, Angie,' says Frank. 'Ben Noone has killed six people in England, and myself and my colleague are here to investigate further. I strongly suspect that he's killed one of my investigators already.'

'No,' says Angie. 'Ben wouldn't do that.'

'Yes. He would.' Frank takes out the case file and lays some images of Nicky Peters' body taken in the metal box inside the Williamson tunnels. 'He and an accomplice imprisoned this boy underground and let him die. After they'd fucked him and filled him full of coke.'

Angie looks like she's going to be sick. Tears are in her eyes. It's an old trick but Frank's got no time to come up with anything clever. His main aim is to shock Angie into giving up what she knows – if she knows anything – and do it as quickly as possible.

'He killed the boy's parents,' says Frank, and shows her a photo from the blood-soaked bedroom in Birkdale. Angie puts her hand to her mouth. Frank pushes on. He places a photo of Dean Quinner on the mud at Garston and another of the charred corpses of Terry and Alicia Peters. He explains in a low, urgent voice what he believes Noone to have done. By the end of it, Angie is silently weeping. The waitress looks over, attitude on her face, but Frank's dark-eyed glare is so intense that she retreats behind the relative safety of the counter.

'Angie,' says Frank. 'I need to know anything that might help me. And I think that if you're being honest with yourself, there's part of you that knows that what I'm saying about Ben could be true. In fact I'm willing to bet that's the case. If you think there's absolutely no chance that Ben Noone could kill anyone then just walk away now. I won't stop you and I won't bother you again. But before you do, ask yourself this: did Ben Noone request anything from you related to the presidential fundraiser?'

Angie's head jerks upright. 'What?'

'The fundraiser. Did he want anything from you? Do you have anything to do with the fundraiser?'

'Yes,' says Angie. 'Well, sorta. I know one of the guys who is organising something.'

A case that Frank and Koop felt had gone forever is suddenly back on track.

'What do you mean?' says Frank.

'Ben was very interested that I knew this lawyer on the organising committee. Said he was going to go to the fundraiser too. Showed me the ticket and everything so I thought it was all right.' She looks at the two men. 'I haven't done anything wrong, have I?'

Frank pats Angie's arm. 'No, Angie. You're doing fine. Tell us what Ben wanted off you.'

'Well that's what's so weird about all this,' says Angie. 'He wanted to see the guest list.'

'And you had that list?' Frank's surprised. A list like that would surely be more closely guarded.

'Well, there was no real secret about it,' says Angie. 'I mean it's supposed to be kept confidential but there's no way you can do that.

Not with an event that big. And it's not like it was the list for the party that the president is going to or anything.'

'What's the list for?' says Koop.

'The fundraiser, of course.' Angie looks at them both as if they're crazy.

'Wait,' says Koop, holding up a hand. 'I'm confused. Ben Noone wanted to see this guest list, right? Ben Noone bought a ticket for the event. The president's going to be there.'

Angie shakes her head. 'Uh, no. He's not. This friend of mine who works for the fundraising committee? He's not doing the presidential event in Hollywood. He's doing the other one.'

'The other one?'

'There're about four fundraising events this week. All sorta linked to the big one but the one that my friend is helping organise is out of town. This one's for the CCC. The Children's Climate Community – they're a charity?' Angie says this as though it's a question. 'It's a picnic. Like, a big one?'

'Where is it, Angie?'

'Mount San Jacinto,' says Angie. Frank and Koop look at her blankly.

'Palm Springs,' says Angie. 'That's the one Ben was asking about.'

Forty-Two

'A dummy,' says Frank. 'The devious fucker.'

'What?'

Frank looks at Koop. 'Noone buying the ticket. He sold us a dummy. Thirty grand gets him a clear run. He never intended that his ticket would be used. Whatever he's got going on is going to happen out at . . .' Frank looks at Angie. 'What's the name of that mountain again?'

'Mount San Jacinto. Nice place. Got a cute cable car running up the side of it.'

'I thought it was desert out there?'

'They have hills too,' says Angie. 'Do you think we should call someone? The cops. I mean, like, our cops?'

'We will,' says Frank. 'We just want to check the details first.' He doesn't tell Angie that Dennis Sheehan has already ensured that all official routes are effectively blocked. The lines are blurred between the public and private here in a way that is not reassuring for an outsider like Frank. Ashland and Baines, for example. Frank wouldn't like to guess where their desks are. And, what's more, he'll probably never know.

The list Angie's got, the one Noone asked for, was in an email, which is why she still has a copy.

'Will I get in trouble?' she says. 'Showing Ben the list, I mean. Part of my friend's job was to forward this on to the media. Ben could've got it somewhere else.'

'That's OK, Angie,' says Frank. 'You're fine.'

Koop thinks of something. 'It's mid-summer. Won't it be too hot for a picnic? Out in the desert?'

Angie frowns. 'No. The picnic's up at the top of the mountain. It's like, cooler up there? I mean, way cooler. They get snow sometimes all year.'

Koop opens the park details up on the laptop. 'It's more than eight thousand feet,' he says. Photos show an almost Alpine wilderness in stark contrast to the desert below. There are streams and pine trees and squirrels. The park is reached by a cable car rising up from just above Palm Springs to the ranger station at the top. From there, hiking trails fan out into the park itself.

'I don't get it,' says Frank. 'Why would Noone be interested in a picnic at the top of a mountain?'

Angie shakes her head in disbelief. 'The First Family, of course,' she says, looking at Frank and Koop as if they are mentally impaired. 'It's being hosted by the president's wife.'

Angie downloads the guest list from her email account using Koop's laptop.

'There,' she says, and rotates it towards Frank. Despite her initial disbelief about Noone, Angie seems to now regard herself as one of the team. Frank wonders if she thinks this is an episode of *CSI*. In LA it can be hard for some people to know the difference between reality and TV.

Frank runs his eye down the long list looking for something to jump out. There are approximately four hundred names on the list. Most of them, judging by the school name following their own, are children from the Palm Springs area. Frank disregards those. On a first pass through the rest there's nothing he can see. Representatives of fundraising committees, local dignitaries, veterans associations. Then a number of addresses strike a memory.

Twentynine Palms.

Warren had lost Noone on the highway before Twentynine Palms. Frank's assumption for the last half-hour since he'd found out about the San Jacinto fundraiser had been that any trip Noone was making out there was to look at the mountain.

'Get Twentynine Palms up there,' he says to Koop.

Koop gets the map onscreen and Frank looks at the distance between San Jacinto and Twentynine Palms. The two places are more than eighty kilometres apart.

Noone must have had a good reason to go there. From what Warren had said it wasn't a tourist spot – other than a jump-off point for Joshua Tree National Park – and Frank has a hard time seeing Noone as a hiker.

There are twelve names on the list of people who live at Twenty-nine Palms. Four are women and six of the others, Frank guesses, might be military veterans. The six names are followed by a rank.

'Let's see what we can get on these guys,' says Frank.

'Can I go?' says Angie. 'You guys look like you're gonna be here all night.'

'Thanks, Angie,' says Frank and watches her leave. So does most of the restaurant.

Forty-Three

'We shouldn't be involved in something like this,' says Frank after Angie's gone. It's past midnight and the diner's almost empty. 'I'm from Bootle, Koop. People from Bootle don't end up doing this sort of stuff.'

'Where do people who do this sort of stuff come from?'

'No idea. But it isn't fucking Bootle.'

'I'm still not sure what it is exactly that we are doing,' says Koop. 'To be honest.'

'Me neither. I just think we're going to.' Frank toys with the ketchup bottle on the counter. 'How about the names from Twenty-nine Palms? Did you get anything there?'

'I don't know,' says Koop. He flicks open some of the information he's got but it's all over the place. Personal blogs, the odd news report, people with the same names, all the internet can spew out. Without access to official databases the six names don't mean much. 'What are we looking for? You think one of those names might be working with Noone?'

Frank shrugs. 'Maybe. Or a target.'

Koop doesn't respond. It doesn't sound convincing. They're fishing without bait. Or hooks.

'We have a day before the picnic,' says Koop. 'I could try Dooley again, see if he can help.'

'If we try Dooley I think Sheehan will find out.'

'We could do nothing. Go home.' Koop doesn't expand on where this would be for him. The Northern Rivers don't feel like home now so much.

'We could do that.' Frank's nodding. He's serious. They could do nothing.

They *should* do nothing.

'In the movies they'd just ride out and fix it. A showdown. High Noon.'

'How?'

'No idea. But that's what happens in the movies. Bruce Willis gets on a spaceship armed with a nuke. They act.'

'I could call MIT,' says Frank. 'See what they say.' He taps a finger on his phone, which is lying on the plastic surface of the table.

'No Bruce Willis ending?'

Frank checks his watch and picks up his phone. Past midnight here, morning in Liverpool.

'Not very Hollywood,' says Frank. 'I'll take this outside.' He leaves and Koop orders a beer.

Pacing in front of the diner Frank gets through to Charlie Searle. He's in a meeting but Frank insists that it's urgent.

'Frank,' says Searle. His voice is brisk but not yet hostile. He's going to give Frank some room to explain why he needed to be dragged out of a meeting but Frank can tell there won't be much leeway. 'News?'

'Something like that, sir.' Frank moves to a quieter area of the street and explains the information from Angie and his feeling that Noone is planning an attack on the fundraiser picnic.

'That's it?' says Searle when Frank stops talking. 'That's all you have? A list of invites to a picnic? It's not exactly a smoking gun, is it, Frank? Jesus.'

'I think he's –'

'Stop. Just stop, Frank.' Charlie Searle sounds tired. 'I don't want to hear anything else. Here's what's going to happen. I'll call the Americans and forward your concerns – no, wait, don't interrupt – and they can take whatever steps they deem appropriate. Is that clear? Good. You will return home immediately as planned. You will send Koopman back to the colonies. You will not take any action on this, not even calling your liaison. I don't want to turn on the news and see one of my officers being marched into court wearing orange pyjamas.'

Searle hangs up. He hadn't sworn once. Frank thinks this may be the most disturbing part of the whole conversation. He pockets the phone and goes back inside.

Koop looks up as Frank sits. There's a beer in front of Frank.

'Thanks,' he says and takes a pull.

'So?'

Frank shrugs. 'He said we should do exactly what I thought the situation required.'

'And that is?'

'Do you have any mountain climbing experience?'

'You have to be kidding.'

Frank shakes his head and Koop raises his beer. 'Yippee ki-ay, motherfucker.'

The two of them sit in silence.

'We're going to need vests,' says Koop.

Forty-Four

Ben Noone spends Wednesday doing the things he should be doing. He goes to the gym at Pacific Palisades and talks to people. He acts normal. Afterwards he has lunch in Santa Monica and calls in at his bank. He buys some clothes and gets the shop assistant's phone number. He takes the shop assistant out for an early dinner and cocktails and they spend the night at the Hotel Shangri-La on Ocean Avenue.

Noone doesn't sleep well but it's more excitement than nerves. He imagines that all truly great performers feel this way the morning of a career-defining show. You'd have to be a monster not to.

Leaving the girl asleep Noone leaves the Shangri-La at five and drives the short distance home. By six he's in the Jeep with a backpack containing what he needs in the footwell of the passenger seat and is driving east. Once again he takes care not to attract any unwarranted attention and makes certain he isn't followed. In Culver City he parks the Jeep in a multi-level car park and picks up the white Ford saloon he bought for cash the previous week from a used car lot in the Valley. In recent days his paranoia has increased to the point where he feels precautions like this are required. Daedalus are more than capable of installing tracking devices. If they have they will already know he's been out to Twentynine Palms. In itself, that shouldn't be too much of a problem but Noone doesn't want to take any more chances like that. The Jeep in Culver City will keep them focused there for a while and by then it will be too late.

The morning traffic builds as Noone crosses the city but he misses the main rush and gets to Kenny Hoy's place around nine.

He parks the Ford at the back of the mini-van and takes his backpack into the house. He puts the bag down on the kitchen table and heads out to the shed. Hoy's body is still there in the freezer, his features coated with a thin ream of ice, the blood around his eye glittering black. Noone closes the lid, locks the shed and goes back into the house.

In Hoy's bedroom he selects clothes from the dead man's wardrobe. He and Hoy are close in build and Noone picks out a pair of khakis, immaculately laundered, and an olive-coloured long-sleeve shirt with a vaguely military feel. Hoy only has one tie, a black one, so this is the one that Noone uses. He takes the pants, shirt, tie and a leather flying jacket and lays out the clothes neatly on the bed.

Hoy's boots are several sizes too small so Noone wears his own. He takes these off and puts them with Hoy's clothes. He takes off the rest of his own clothes and puts them to one side.

Above the TV set in the living room Hoy has a number of framed photographs. Several show him in uniform, some in formal dress and others taken overseas. In these images Hoy is dressed in the bulky battle-dress of the Marines. There is only one image that shows Hoy in a wheelchair and it's him receiving some sort of award. Noone lifts this photo off the wall and takes it into the bathroom along with his backpack.

He places the photo of Hoy on the bathroom cabinet above the mirror and takes out a number of items from a theatrical make-up supplier from the backpack. Hoy's face isn't much like Noone's but he has a beard and long hair. With sunglasses and a cap it'll be difficult for anyone who doesn't know Hoy to tell it's not him. Noone finds a Marine Corps cap on a shelf in Hoy's room.

Noone looks in the mirror and sees Kenny Hoy staring back at him.

'Hey,' says Noone, trying to get Hoy's laconic tone. He tries it a slightly different way. 'Hey.' Better. 'Hey, bro. Semper Fi.'

He dresses carefully in Hoy's clothes and once more inspects himself. For some reason he's not as happy with this but he thinks he knows why. He retrieves the wheelchair from the hallway and sits in it again. This time in the lowset mirror in the living room, Noone sees Kenny Hoy once more. He drives the wheelchair around the house and out a few times using the ramps, getting to know the feel of the machine. He spends a long time working out how the chair gets in and out of the mini-van and how Hoy gets himself in and out. If anyone observes him he wants to make it look at least partway convincing.

Hoy's phone vibrates and Noone checks the ID. It's a text message from someone called Mike. Nothing important. Since pocketing Hoy's phone yesterday it's only the third call he's received and one of those was a promotional thing from the phone company. Hoy was clearly not someone with a busy social calendar.

Noone checks his watch. Ten after twelve.

Time to go.

Forty-Five

With over fifteen hundred expected at the Mount San Jacinto picnic, the cable car to the plateau at two thousand metres has been shuttling groups up since seven-thirty. With the First Family in attendance, security is tight at the base station. The event is invitation only.

The access from the Palm Springs side via the Aerial Tramway can be easily policed. There are no roads past the base station and all access to the peak from the east is by cable car. The existing electronic ticket system in place already does most of the security work: without a ticket, you can't get on the cable car.

Additional cops are on hand but they are mainly there to facilitate the movement of people. Local Lions Clubs and Veterans Associations have set up tents at the base serving hot dogs, coffee and soda. Almost half the guests are children from the surrounding areas belonging to church groups, schools and environmental groups with junior memberships. The rest are local dignitaries, representatives of climate groups, veterans, academics and press. Although the main gig is going on in Los Angeles later that day there are a lot of TV stations covering the picnic.

Noone's pleased to see that there is some national TV there in addition to the locals. Driving Hoy's mini-van with a prominent disabled sticker on the windshield, he's directed to one of the designated parking spots close to the tramway station.

As he pulls into the slot, a cop approaches. 'You need a hand with anything, buddy?'

'Thanks, man,' says Noone, 'but I like to do things myself.'

'I hear you,' says the cop. He holds up a hand and disappears.

It takes Noone a few minutes to get settled in the chair. He opens the rear gate on the van and a ramp descends to the floor. Noone rolls the chair out into the sun. It's cooler here than in the valley but still warm; on the road up from Palm Springs the signs advise drivers to switch off their aircon as they climb the two thousand feet to the base station.

Noone's sweating in the leather flying jacket so he takes it off and places it across his knees. He'll need it when he gets to the summit. Up there it's forty degrees cooler.

The crowds part as he moves the chair towards the disabled ramp. It's like being Moses. Noone almost thinks it could be worth being disabled if this is how it works. The veterans badge on his cap adds to his aura, more than one patriot slapping his shoulder as he passes. At his age there's only one conflict where he could have picked up his injuries and, this close to the Marine Combat Center, there are friendly faces everywhere. Noone tries to keep his head down. He doesn't want to meet anyone who knows Kenny Hoy. This is the biggest risk in the whole scheme but it can't be helped.

Inside the ticket office to the cable car Noone shows his invitation at the first checkpoint. A Parks Service agent, a stocky woman in her forties, smiles broadly and waves him through. In the chair he's fast-tracked to the front of the queue. At the final check before the cable car there are two policemen scrutinising invitations against ID. Noone fishes out Hoy's wallet and shows the cop. He takes off the cap and sunglasses without being asked.

'You're good, Mr Hoy,' the cop says. 'You enjoy yourself, up there, y'hear?'

Noone nods and replaces the cap. 'I aim to,' he says. He slips the sunglasses back into place and moves into the holding room for the next car. When it arrives he is allowed on first and directed to a spot at the back of the car.

'Don't matter where you are,' says the operative. 'The cable car rotates 360 degrees every few minutes. You'll get a good view. Just make sure your wheels aren't crossing the gap.'

Noone sketches a salute and locks the wheelchair in place. He tries to shift his weight in the chair without appearing to use his legs. The gun under the seat is uncomfortable and Noone's back is already strained with the effort of keeping his legs motionless. Behind him the car fills up with the remaining passengers. Noone's pleased to note there are no other disabled travellers. For some irrational reason he fears they would know he was faking. Exactly why this would be, Noone's unsure, but the feeling's there.

The cable car closes its doors and moves upwards. There is a cheer from a group travelling together and a few squeals from a bunch of schoolkids. Noone sits quietly and watches the desert move away from him. Palm Springs stretches across the valley floor, shimmery in the August heat. The car bumps over the first stanchion and there are more squeals. Noone's point of view swings round to face Mount San Jacinto. The terrain below is steep and unforgiving.

They're nearly there.

Forty-Six

They decide it's too risky to call on Dooley which means they're on their own and that leaves both Frank and Koop feeling vulnerable. It's one thing to give the appearance of not caring about the consequences. It's a completely different thing actually doing it.

After the call with Searle, Frank knows that the only option he has is to do as his superior officer ordered. On the basis of the evidence Searle's right.

Except he's not.

All coppers live their lives making compromises and seeing the guilty walk free. Frank's no exception. He's not some newborn mewling infant who expects everything to work out exactly as he wants.

But this one is different and Frank knows that he is incapable of doing nothing about Noone, even if that's just heading out to Mount San Jacinto to see if they can spot anything. Nicky Peters and his parents won't let him. Dean Quinner won't let him. Warren Eckhardt won't let him.

'Searle doesn't need to know,' says Frank. 'If I'm wrong about Noone then we get on the flights tomorrow and no one is any the wiser.'

'And if we're right about Noone?' says Koop. 'Won't it take some explaining how you happened to be on the spot? Or how about if we're wrong and we get mistaken for terrorists?'

'I thought you were all Bruce Willis about this?'

They're driving back to the apartment through the relatively traffic-free streets.

'I think we should go,' says Koop. 'But all that action hero stuff is just talk. I think the best we can hope to do is spot Noone. If he's there we'll know something's up.'

'And what then?'

'Fucked if I know,' says Koop.

On Wednesday they go to the library to dig a little deeper into the six names from Twentynine Palms. They don't get far. Even discovering the addresses is problematic. After almost two hours they have two addresses and they decide to switch tactics and concentrate on the location.

'We come at it from the south,' says Koop. He points at the screen. 'This road takes us within eight kilometres of the top cable car station. It's tricky terrain but it's got trails that can be followed, even by us. Given the size of the area there is no way for the security forces to be able to seal off access on the wider perimeter.'

As with most potential security threat assessments, the biggest factor stopping a determined intruder is pure luck. Which doesn't mean it will be easy.

'We just walk in?' says Frank. 'That doesn't sound right.'

'I don't have a better idea.' Koop turns back to the layout of the park. 'And unless they've got most of the Army patrolling the mountain there has to be a way in.'

He hesitates. Frank's not going to like the next bit.

'There is something else,' says Koop. 'I think if we can get past the first level of security there's a way round to the plateau they won't be watching.'

'Why?' Frank's been around Koop long enough to know when he's hiding something. 'What's the problem?'

Koop zooms in on a section of the mountain. It's hard to tell from the satellite images but it's clear that this is the edge of a steep drop-off.

'Just here,' says Koop. 'There's a gap. Quite a well-known one. There are photos.' He clicks a side panel and an image appears.

'Fuck me,' says Frank. He looks pale.

'It's not that bad. We can jump that easy.'

'Are you fucking mental? It's impossible.'

'We'll talk about it tomorrow,' says Koop. 'But it's what we should do.'

408

'What's this place called?'

'Er . . .'

'What's it called, Koop?'

'Gallows Drop.'

Frank feels sick.

He's got a thing about heights.

'No way.'

'We'll talk about it,' says Koop.

In the afternoon, back in the apartment, the discussion about Gallows Drop suspended, Frank books flights for himself and Koop to England and Australia. They keep the talk to discussions of return plans. Frank emails MIT to update them on his return. It'll be enough – he hopes – to keep both Charlie Searle and Sheehan's goons off their backs. On Wednesday evening they pack before going to eat at a grill around the corner. In hushed tones they go over the details of tomorrow's plan.

Leaving around six on Thursday, Frank and Koop head towards the airport before losing any tail they may have. Once sure they're unobserved they head east and get to the turnoff at Banning by eight-fifty. They stop at an outlet mall en route and buy hiking gear at a sports and camping store. Koop picks up a compass and a detailed map of the San Jacinto trails.

They take the car as far as it will go and park it just off a trail road leading up from Idyllwild. They change into their new gear and start the climb towards the peak. Hot as it was at the mall it's almost cold this high up the mountain.

'Jesus,' says Frank. 'I didn't think it'd be as cool as this.' He's glad of the fleece jacket that seemed such a ridiculous purchase at the mall.

'We're climbing to almost ten thousand feet,' says Koop. He checks the map almost constantly, glad he bought the most detailed he could find. It would be easy to get lost up here.

As they climb Frank feels his lungs struggling to extract enough oxygen from the thin air. It's not unpleasant but already everything is taking just that little bit of extra effort. After an hour hiking he feels like a smoker. Poor old Warren, God rest his cig-gobbling soul, would have needed oxygen just waiting in the car. The air is crisp and the thickly forested mountain seems a world away from Los Angeles. If they weren't tracking a dangerous killer, Frank would have enjoyed it.

By eleven they're within a mile of the plateau. Ten minutes after that they're stopped by a parks ranger standing next to a 'trail closed' sign.

'Sorry, folks,' she says. 'No access to the cable car today. Invitation only.'

'That's OK,' says Frank. 'We're just hiking.'

'Where's that accent from?' says the ranger.

'England.' Putting on another accent is beyond Frank. It's easier just to tell the truth.

'You sound like the Beatles.'

Frank smiles but doesn't reply.

'What's the best way back down to Idyllwild from here?' says Koop. He unfolds his map and pretends interest while the ranger points out some good lookouts on the way down.

They retreat a few hundred yards down the way they came until they are out of sight of her.

'Why isn't there more security?' says Frank. He gestures at the two of them. 'Why didn't Noone come in this way?'

'Maybe he didn't come at all.' Koop takes a long look around. He points up the mountain. 'I think the main security will be focused on being close to the president's family. You know what it's like.'

Frank does know. Protection – complete protection – of anyone is an illusion. For the president, cocooned inside the house in Los Angeles and transported inside a rolling convoy every time he moves, there is a level of security that would stop most attacks. But when the president presses the flesh, or attends a rally, the risk appreciates steeply and anyone who has ever been involved in any sort of protection plan is aware that that's all it is: a plan. Frank's been involved in security preparations in Liverpool at various times and knows that much of it is conveying the idea that to attempt an attack is too risky. That's why the visual is so important. Armed officers, black uniforms, dogs, high visibility.

In the case of the First Family, at an event such as the Mount San Jacinto picnic, full protection is simply not an option.

410

With an unfenced outside location there are too many entry points, too many variables, for even the heavily resourced White House to plug with the help of local agencies.

Locating the event on the plateau helps. Access via the cable car from the Palm Springs side means that they can at least control the majority of the visitors. Anyone coming in uninvited from the west will be turned away.

If Frank had been in control of security he would identify the easiest trails first and close them off, just as had happened a few minutes ago. That would be the first level; park rangers, local patrol officers, perhaps even volunteers from local organisations to pad out the manpower. At the next level there would be agents stationed at possible entry points. You may not be able to cover them all but you could have a presence. Anyone found at these entry points would be treated as hostile. The third ring would be on the plateau itself, where the concentration would be on establishing a perimeter around the central point. The final level of security would be the immediate vicinity of the First Family.

It wouldn't be easy. If Frank's right about Noone, he had come to the same conclusion. He must have found a way in but exactly what that is, Frank doesn't know. Unlike them, he's been planning this for some time.

They'll just have to walk in.

On the map Koop points out the trails that wind towards the plateau. 'They'll have people here and here and here,' he says. 'And then I'm guessing that there'll be agents in the forest but there's too much ground for them to protect it all. It'll be bad luck if we run into anyone.' Koop's finger traces an off-trail route. 'This is our route.'

'The fucking Gallows Drop one? No fucking way. We'll have to find another one.'

'TINA,' says Koop, setting off along the trail.

'What?'

'There Is No Alternative. Get moving. It'll be a doddle.'

Forty-Seven

Coming off the cable car, the whole damn thing almost falls apart when Noone's wheelchair grinds to a halt on the motherfucking exit ramp. The car attendant and a couple of cops push Noone and the heavy chair to one side as the rest of the passengers stream past. The attendant pats him on the shoulder and returns to the cable car leaving Noone with the cops.

'It done this before?' asks one of the cops. He's a big guy, fat around the middle but with experience in his eyes. He bends low and speaks in a precise way. Noone's only been in the wheelchair for an hour and he's already noticing how patronising almost everyone is. He has a moment's empathy with Kenny Hoy before remembering that he'd stabbed him in the eye and stuffed his corpse in the freezer.

'Sometimes,' says Noone. He lends a slackness to the tone, reinforcing the mistaken assumption that he is mentally impaired. It might be useful right now.

'Let me see,' says the second cop, a younger Hispanic guy. 'I'm pretty good at electronics.' He smiles paternally at Noone and bends to the area below the seat which houses the workings of the chair. Noone wonders what will happen if they start poking around there. What if there's some fucking cable or something running into the cushion? He fights the urge to run and forces an idiot grin onto his face.

'Hey,' says the younger cop from behind the chair. Noone can't see either of them. 'What do you think?'

'Try it.'

Noone feels something being pushed on the back of the chair and the machine gives a satisfying hum. He presses the control lever and it shifts forward.

'Yeah!' says the Hispanic cop. He leans over Noone and gives him a cartoon thumbs up. 'Looks like you're all set, buddy. Just had a loose wire back there.'

'Thanks,' says Noone. He shakes hands with both cops and pushes the control lever forward. To one side, next to the gift shop, is a lift which Noone takes down one level. From there he moves along a hallway to a set of double doors. An old woman holds them open as he approaches and Noone finds himself outside on a platform overlooking the plateau. The platform is thick with excited visitors, mostly children. Music is coming from somewhere below. A large green banner reading *Welcome CCC Picnicers!* flutters in the slight breeze.

'You know which way to go, honey?' says the old woman. She points to a wide concrete path that zigzags down the side of the slope. 'Down that way. You can't miss it. If you like I can get someone to help you?'

'That won't be necessary, ma'am,' says Noone. He salutes the old woman and turns down the path.

At the end of the concrete Noone arrives at a wide expanse of rolling grassland dotted with pine trees and granite boulders. Three white marquees without walls have been erected close to the path and a temporary disabled access platform has been installed to continue the path into the tents. There are people everywhere and, on a low stage in front of the tents, a jazz band is playing. Noone turns away from a TV camera which swivels his way but the cameraman is only working out some sort of shot. Here and there reporters are interviewing people. Noone feels there is an air of Christmas Eve about the place although that may simply be the crisp air and Alpine setting.

A group of children wearing some sort of semi-military uniform rush past in a blur of screams and excitement. A man with a bullhorn is calling out instructions to a group of organisers dressed in khaki.

'You OK, son?' A large man in his late sixties with a red face and a silver moustache is right up in Noone's face.

'Yeah, I'm good, thanks.'

'Because I can get someone to help you, if you'd like. Always happy to help a military man. You get the, uh, injury, in Iran?'

'You mean Iraq.'

413

'Yeah, Iraq, right.'

'No,' says Noone. 'Afghanistan.'

'You're a patriot, soldier,' says the old coot.

Noone can hardly wait to start shooting.

Forty-Eight

Gallows Drop must be close to a thousand feet straight down.

Frank wants to be sick.

They're so close to the picnic they can hear the music drifting in and out on the breeze. They have seen a couple of agents on patrol but by simply standing still and waiting until they passed by they are able to continue.

'Come on,' says Koop. 'Just forget about the drop. Concentrate on the distance.'

'That's what I'm fucking looking at, you fucking maniac!' Frank rubs a hand across his mouth and breathes heavily through his nose. 'Just look at the fucking thing! It's fucking massive! You'd have to be fucking . . . fucking . . . FUCK! Who the fuck is the fucking long jump champion?'

'You'll be fine.'

To be honest, now they're here, Koop's not sure they can get across. The gap is more like a chasm, a split between a monstrous cliff that effectively marks the end of this trail. From one side to the other Koop estimates the distance to be around two metres. Only an idiot would try to jump this.

'You jumped longer than that at school,' says Koop.

'Aye, into a fucking sandpit, dickhead!'

Frank approaches the edge, his legs weak, and looks down into the void. 'Sweet Jesus!' he hisses. 'There's no fucking way.'

Koop sprints past Frank and leaps across, his feet landing squarely on the other side.

'See?' he says. 'Easy.' He tries not to let Frank see his trembling hands. That had been fucking scary. 'Just don't think about it.'

Frank is shaking his head from side to side. 'Uh-nuh, no, no. Can't do it. No, no, no.'

Then, as Koop is considering jumping back across Gallows Drop, Frank strides purposefully away in the direction they've come from.

'Frank!' Koop hisses.

When he's twenty paces from the gap, Frank turns and sprints.

He can sense the loose gravel under his shoes giving way, can almost see the ledge he's on beginning to crumble and then the fatal stumble as his fingers try and fail to hold on to something solid. He imagines the fall as he spins down onto the rocks below. And then he sees Nicky, dead in the tunnels and then he's airborne. There is a flash of green glimpsed below and then he's there on the other side being grabbed by Koop.

'Fuck!' says Koop. 'I never thought you'd make it! That's a fucking *massive* gap! Massive!'

Frank half-runs, half-skips away towards the safety of a tree and vomits.

'That's the way,' says Koop. 'Get it all out.'

Frank flips Koop the finger and tries to control his breathing.

Koop looks at the map.

'I think we're inside the perimeter.'

Koop takes off his backpack and shoves it into a gap between two rocks. Frank, breathing a little easier now, stands upright and follows suit. Both of them take off their fleece jackets and stow them with the backpacks. In the khaki workpants and shirts they bought at the sports outlet they look like maintenance workers. Koop wishes he'd remembered a clipboard. It's an old truism that you can go a long way armed with a clipboard.

'Now we just walk like we belong here,' says Koop. He can see groups of children playing tag in a clump of trees about eighty yards away.

They walk down the slope and find themselves looking at the three white tents. There's a large crowd, maybe twelve hundred people, and even from a distance Frank can sense the anticipation.

They walk across the clearing and are soon enveloped in the crowd. A cop glances at them but it's nothing more than that. Frank finds a woman handing out green CCC caps and he takes two. With them in place he and Koop are even less noticeable.

'What are we looking for?' says Koop.

'A tall psychopath with a gun. Should be easy to spot, I reckon.'

Inside each tent are several large tables stacked with food. Helpers are busy behind each table. There are a number of people in wheelchairs and one or two severely disabled people with their carers.

'Can't see any,' says Koop. He's about to say something else when a man using a bullhorn starts trying to assemble the crowd in the tents. High above the plateau at the cable car station there is movement, a buzz, people moving.

The First Family has arrived.

Forty-Nine

Noone, antenna twitching, adrenaline spiking, spots Keane and another guy he doesn't recognise almost as soon as they arrive in the clearing. It's pure chance seeing them. Noone can't work out if it's a good or bad thing.

He watches them pick up the baseball caps. Noone tries to keep as many people as possible between himself and Keane. How the fuck the guy has figured it out he doesn't know, but the fact is he's here. The text from JFK doesn't seem such a good idea now. Noone had never intended Frank Keane to be able to maintain his crusade for this length of time, only for him to put in an appearance in court, to testify to Noone's cleverness.

On the plus side, Noone's willing to bet Keane isn't armed. As long as he doesn't ID Noone – and given the cap, beard, hair and glasses, not to mention the fact that he's in a wheelchair – everything will be fine. Noone slides himself inside one of the tents and tries to put people between himself and Frank Keane.

'Your hair looks funny.'

Noone refocuses.

The voice is coming from a child standing at his elbow. She's black, chubby, maybe ten years old, Noone can't really tell. He doesn't know any children. How she arrived there unseen he has no idea.

'What?'

'Your hair looks fake,' repeats the girl. 'Like a doll. Is it real? Did you have chemo? My cousin's hair fell out when he had chemo. He died.' Her voice seems, to Noone, to be younger than her looks suggest. Maybe she's a fucking retard?

'It's real. There's no chemo.'

'OK.' The girl shakes her head from side to side. 'But it still looks kinda fake. What happened to your legs?'

'They broke. Is your mom around? Why don't you go find your mom?'

'Were you in the Corps? My daddy was in the Corps. My daddy let me fire his gun sometime. Out in the desert. We used to shoot at rocks.'

'Yeah, I was in the Corps. You got someone you should be with?'

The kid leans her arm on the back of Noone's chair. He has to twist round to see her.

'What division was you in? My daddy's was the 11th when we was up at Las Pulgas.'

Noone doesn't reply but the kid's lost interest in his Marine division.

The girl bends down behind Noone's chair. 'Did you know your chair's all busted?' The girl is looking at the stitching along the seam where Noone has picked some of it loose. She pokes an exploratory finger inside the seam.

'Stop that, you little cunt!' hisses Noone. This shit has gone on long enough.

The savagery makes the child jerk upright and stare at him. There is fear and moisture in her eyes. And anger too.

'That's not a nice word. I heard it before. Derrek called me that one time on the bus and Momma hit him real good when I tole her.'

Noone glances round. There are one or two people looking in their direction. Although he's certain no one overheard what he said, an elderly woman looks at him funny, as if he's molested the brat.

'Look, kid, I'm sorry,' says Noone. He taps his legs. 'I get bad-tempered sometimes. On account of what happened.'

'In Iraq? Daddy was in Iraq.'

'Yeah, yeah, Iraq. Like daddy.' Noone smiles. 'So are we good?' The child nods. 'I guess.'

'OK. You have fun now.'

Noone turns as he hears a crackle of excitement and chatter. The president's family has arrived at the cable car station.

It's time.

419

The tent begins to empty. Noone needs to get to the restrooms. The disabled stall will give him the privacy he needs to assemble the gun.

Frank Keane and the other guy are in the way.

Fuck it.

They're not looking for anyone in a wheelchair. As he passes they move out of the way, barely glancing at him, their attention focused on the arrival of the First Family. Noone keeps his head down and is swallowed up in the crowd.

He runs through the sequence once more.

After he assembles the gun in the restroom his first action will be to take the wheelchair to the middle of the central tent. With everyone focused on the stage Noone will conceal the weapon under his flying jacket until he's in position. Once in position in the opening of the tent he will stand and shoot the First Family and then the police and agents in the immediate area. They are mostly lined up in front of the stage so it will be easy. Then he will kill as many of the crowd as possible. In the tightly packed tent the deaths will run into the hundreds from that first attack. He has noted the positions of the TV cameras and will make sure no bullets are aimed in their direction.

He has given himself just one minute to shoot. After that, he is sure, he will be targeted by the police and agents approaching the carnage from the perimeter. He may be killed before the minute is over but he thinks that the lack of noise from the weapon and the panic of the mob will help. His position inside the shaded tent will also hamper any heroes outside. The crowds inside will prevent the cops firing into the tent until they are sure they have a good shot. By the time that happens it will be over. He will drop his weapon and hold his hands above his head.

Noone wants to survive, to have the cameras on him, to have his days, weeks and months in court, to have his father's name linked forever with a killer, a monster.

Fifty

'See anything?' says Koop.

Frank peers through the crowd.

'This is impossible. He could be anywhere.'

From somewhere near the cable car station there's a ripple of applause. People around the clearing start to move towards the path coming down from the cable car.

'They've arrived,' says Koop.

'Shit.'

A guy in a wheelchair comes past and Frank moves to one side.

'Sorry,' says Frank but the vet doesn't respond and rolls through the crowd in the direction of a temporary restroom block.

'Do we go and see what's happening?'

'I don't know,' says Frank. He's still looking at the wheelchair but without knowing why. Jumping at ghosts, he thinks, and turns back to Koop.

From the cable car station a phalanx of people is moving down the path. A dark swathe of Secret Service agents is at the front looking exactly, Frank notes, as they do in the movies. Sunglasses, suits and earpieces. Behind them are a woman and two children: the First Lady and her two pre-teens. Even from this distance they look relaxed and happy to be up in this cool air paradise.

As they arrive at the level of the clearing the crowd starts being herded gently into the tents and encouraged to face the stage.

The band is playing upbeat music that Frank doesn't recognise. There is cheering and every second person has an iPhone held aloft.

Frank's finding it hard to concentrate. There's something in his head that won't come out. Something important. Something about shoes.

The First Family entourage arrive onstage and wave to the crowd. For many at the back it is their first clear look at them and there is a roar of applause. They look, to Frank, like a pleasant family. The two children are tentative in their acknowledgement of the crowd but it's clear they have been in public on many occasions. A man in a suit and shiny cowboy boots steps to the microphone and makes an announcement.

'Ladies and gentlemen, boys and girls. Please stand for the national anthem.'

As the band strikes up the first familiar chord, Frank remembers what is bothering him about the guy in the wheelchair. Not shoes.

Boots.

Dust-covered boots worn by a man who can't walk.

'The guy in the wheelchair,' he says, grabbing Koop by the arm and moving through the singing crowd. 'It's him.'

Fifty-One

The toilet block, a temporary structure about ten metres long, moves slightly on its base as Noone rolls the wheelchair up the access ramp and inside. The place is empty; a stroke of luck. Noone wasn't sure what he'd have done if the disabled stall was occupied. A row of metal basins is against one wall and stalls along the other.

Noone goes into the disabled toilet at the end and bolts the door behind him. Now the time is here, he feels euphoric.

This is going to happen.

There's a gap above and below the door but it can't be helped. Noone stands and rubs some feeling back into his legs before squatting behind the wheelchair and ripping out the stitching from the seat cushion.

He pulls out the Micro Tavor and tries to remember how to put the two pieces together. After a couple of false starts – *relax* – he's relieved to hear the casing click into place with a solid-sounding *snik*. He takes out one of the clips and snaps that into position. He puts the spare clips inside the pockets of the flying jacket. He won't get time to use more than three.

With everything in place Noone tries to get himself prepared. Despite everything going to plan he feels nauseated. There are so many ways this could still go wrong.

There's a sound from outside the door. A furtive sound, the creak of someone trying to conceal a footstep. Noone freezes, his senses fully open.

Another creak.

Noone moves quickly and opens the toilet door a crack.

There, in the centre of the restroom, her eyes wide, is the girl.

'Your legs,' she says. Her voice is tiny. Whatever her learning problems she knows she made a bad mistake coming in here and it's too late to fix it now.

Noone swings the gun towards her.

Outside, louder than Noone expected, the band begins the familiar opening to *The Star-Spangled Banner*. Noone's finger rests on the trigger, the automatic weapon centred on the girl's round face.

Do it.

Do it now.

'Fuck!' Noone drops the barrel of the gun so it's pointed at the floor and reaches out to grab the brat. She scrabbles backwards, frantic.

'Mommy!' she yells, heading for the door, her voice loud in the bathroom. Although it's covered by the music from outside, there's still a chance someone might hear. Noone feels his scheme beginning to unravel.

Noone darts forward, grabs hold of the girl by the hair and hauls her backwards. She's screaming like a siren now and Noone backhands her savagely across the room, cutting the noise off almost as soon as it starts. The girl hits the wall and crumples to the ground. She may be dead, Noone doesn't know. He fucking hopes she is, the fucking interfering bitch.

Shit. Shit. Shit.

Noone paces the restroom.

Relax. It's OK. A bump in the road. Put the kid in the stall and carry on. No problem.

Then things start happening quickly.

The kid isn't dead. That's one thing. She's on her feet and screaming like a bastard again, just as a heavyset woman wearing a volunteer uniform comes in.

'*Mommy!*'

The woman looks at Noone, her face distorted in horror. 'What the hell?'

Noone shoots her. Two ripples of bullets cut across her midsection and the kid screams as her mother crumples.

Noone is turning the gun towards the kid when Koop runs in. Instinctively, Koop knocks the child sideways, away from the gun.

Her head clangs against a handbasin and the child drops like a stone beside her dead mother as Koop puts himself between her and Noone.

Noone presses the trigger.

Frank, coming in a beat behind, sees a soft blap of bullets rip through Koop's left arm. Blood and bone spatter across the plasterboard walls of the restroom and onto Frank.

Koop makes a deep, guttural sound and his left hand falls free from his wrist, ripped clear by the spray of bullets. Four or five holes appear in the wall and a cloud of plasterboard particles billows across the restroom. Koop falls heavily on top of the girl.

Frank skids on the rubberised floor.

Time solidifies.

Then Noone, jerking free of the momentary paralysis, opens up with the Micro Tavor. In the confines of the restroom, his movement is baulked by the door of one of the stalls and his bullets splinter a metal handbasin next to Frank. Water begins spraying across the floor from a cracked pipe.

Frank feels a hot liquid sensation in his face. Half-falling, half-jumping, he throws himself to one side, hitting the door of one of the stalls hard. It opens inwards and Frank falls awkwardly against the pan. Behind him, the toilet door slams shut.

It happens so fast that no one, not Frank, not Koop, not Noone, has time to analyse what to do. There is just pain and panic and disbelief and raw gut instinct. Blood and water pools across the floor of the restroom.

Frank can feel blood in his mouth. Prone on the toilet floor, he glances at the girl, whose head is bleeding freely, and at Koop, his eyes opening and closing while blood pumps out of his mangled arm onto the unconscious child. All he can see of the mother is the sole of her shoes. They are dusty. Like Noone's boots.

Frank sees all this: the dead, the dying, the injured, and the pointless hyper-sharp details, all in a micro-second, his senses open to maximum capacity.

The thread guiding Frank back out of the tunnel is sliding from his grasp; he can feel it, slick and wet and treacherous, spooling from between his scrabbling fingers, moment by tortuous moment.

Where the fuck are the police?

Then Frank realises that the whole stop-go carnage has taken place in near silence. The sound of the gun is masked by the squat suppressor, the girl's screams and the noises of the ricochets and movements, covered by the music from outside. It occurs to Frank that it is very likely he won't live to hear the end of the anthem.

Frank can hear Noone coming towards him now to finish him off.

He pushes himself upright and slams the toilet door back on its hinges. He's in luck. The edge of the door catches the American, smashing him backwards into a metal handbasin. The gun is jolted from Noone's fingers and lands heavily on the floor.

Frank doesn't hesitate. He takes a step forward and cracks his elbow into Noone's skull and the man buckles, moaning. Frank opens his mouth to shout for help but only hears himself gurgle. He's lost more blood than he thought. His head swims.

Noone punches Frank in the face. He's twisted away so the blow isn't powerful but it lands where the sink fragments have hit Frank's face and Frank feels a hot pulse of almost unbearable pain rip through his body. He reaches his arm around Noone's throat and fastens onto his own wrist to create a chokehold.

It stops Noone moving but the American has just enough of his chin down to make the choke only partly effective.

'Please,' Noone croaks but Frank's not sure Noone knows he's said anything. In any case he can't reply even if he wants to.

The floor of the restroom is slick with blood and water.

Frank can't tell if Koop and the girl are dead or alive. Everything's happening in a series of flash frames.

His face is tight against Noone's, so close he can hear the American's breath rasping through his throat, feel the synthetic hair of Noone's wig in his nostrils, and smell his odour of sweat and blood and cologne. Frank recalls sparring with Chrissy Cahill back in Liverpool. In the clinches you hear your opponent's heartbeat, sense the heat of his breath and . . .

Concentrate.

Fuck everything else. None of it matters. Frank can hear Jesus's voice in his head. *Just the here and now, Frankie lad, that's all there is.*

426

Just the here and now.

Frank forces himself to shut out everything except the fight. For twenty seconds the only sound inside the restroom is the panicked breathing from both men, the rustle of clothing and the squeak from boots skidding on wet rubber.

Frank's losing strength.

Sensing a weakness, Noone redoubles his efforts. He pushes against the handbasins and uses his body weight to drive Frank back into the disabled stall, part of which buckles as they hit. They land awkwardly on Hoy's wheelchair and Frank feels something sharp gouge into his side and something bad happens to his elbow. He makes an agonised grunt and clings on but there's no doubt that Noone is gaining the upper hand.

Heaving with the effort, Noone gradually works his head out from Frank's loosening grasp and elbows him square in the face as he does. Frank falls back and smacks his head against the toilet. Noone reaches down and punches him. Frank feels his nose break.

Frank grabs hold of Noone's shirt, pulls him close and crunches the thick bone of his forehead into the American's nose. There's a satisfying sound but the effort makes Frank's head swim.

'Motherfucker!' Noone hisses, reeling backwards. *Muddafudder.*

He clamps a hand over his busted nose, blood spurting from between his fingers. Frank gets to his knees and aims two quick punches to Noone's ribs. They land but there's no solid connection; there's nothing left in the tank.

Blood is pouring from the wounds on his scalp and it washes down over his eyes. He can feel the life-force pumping out of him. Fuck, this is too hard. He needs rest.

Frank leans back against the wall and then slides down. He tries to shout but all that comes out is a wet croak. Noone staggers upright and kicks Frank square in the ribs. Frank can hear the bone break and rolls up into a ball. All he can do now is hang on. He squints through a curtain of blood at Noone. He's done. He's gone, his vision blurred, his breathing shallow.

All Noone has to do is get the gun and finish Frank.

Behind Noone a figure comes into focus.

It's the girl.

She's a nightmare. The walking dead, her head and shoulders coated in blood, her face a red mask, teeth bared in a rictus snarl of agony and grief and retribution. Fat drops of blood slap the floor.

Frank looks at her and can't see a child. The bloodied wreck in front of him holds the Micro Tavor in her hands, the black muzzle aimed squarely at Noone.

Outside the anthem draws to a close. There is cheering and Noone turns to see what Frank is looking at.

When he sees the girl he laughs. 'You got to be fucking kidding.' He steps forward.

'Put the gun down,' barks Noone. 'This isn't a fucking rap video, you little bitch. You're not going to shoot anyone.' The girl takes a pace forward, lifts the gun and bullets disintegrate a door next to Noone. The gun shakes in her grip but she holds onto the Micro. *My daddy let me fire his gun sometime.*

'Jesus!'

Noone scrambles away, slipping on the wet floor. Backed up against the wall he holds his hands up in a gesture of surrender.

The girl points the gun at Noone.

'You shot my mom,' says the girl.

'No, I didn't,' says Noone, as if by simply saying the words they will be so. He smiles winningly. 'Come on, kid.'

'Wait,' says Frank, but the word is slippery in his mouth and he's not sure anyway what it is he wants to convey. A warning? A plea? With the anthem over there will be someone coming to the restroom soon. They could call for help. Get this dealt with.

'You can't do this,' says Frank. 'He's not worth it.'

The girl looks at Frank, turns back to Noone and shoots him in the chest. Noone is flung backwards against the wall. He looks disbelievingly at the hole in his chest and then back at the girl.

She leans against the wall facing Noone and slowly slides down into a sitting position. On the plasterboard an abstract expressionist brushstroke of red follows her downward path. She sits, catatonic, the Micro Tavor held neatly across her lap.

The only sound in the room comes from the burst pipe and from the wet sucking noises from Noone's open chest.

Noone tries to say something but Frank can't hear him. The girl keeps her big eyes on Noone until he dies. Not long after, the door to the restroom opens and someone wearing a uniform comes in.

It's over.

Fifty-Two

A metal fragment from the handbasin had ripped through Frank's cheek and taken off the top part of his right ear. Another gouged a shallow trench in the thick part of his skull and more splinters from the restroom slaughterhouse are lodged in the fleshy part of his shoulder. His nose is broken and he has dislocated his elbow, ripping the tendons in the fight with Noone. It takes six separate operations over a two-month period to repair the damage.

The room he's in looks like a high-end private hospital room, but there are touches that tell Frank he's not in a civilian medical centre. The TV does not have outside reception. The only channels are movie channels. No news. There's no phone. The call to Searle takes place on a handset brought in for him by an orderly and then removed. The solid metal door to the room is always locked.

The doctors, nurses and orderlies don't answer his questions.

They're not hostile, just evasive. Sometimes they'll just point blank tell Frank that they don't have the authorisation to give him the information he's asking for. From their careful demeanour he guesses that he is being observed via CCTV.

As he starts to become more mobile he is given access to a second room containing another, larger TV, a shelf of books, an exercise bicycle and, thrillingly, a sealed window. From here Frank can see mountains in the distance, some fences and the occasional military vehicle. Planes can be seen coming and going but it's not an airport. Frank's guessing he's on some kind of US airbase.

In the time between operations he is visited on several occasions by Ashland and Baines, who pick over the details of his investigation into Noone. One day they turn up with what looks like a genuine MIT file on the murders in Liverpool. When Frank asks them about it they don't answer. As he gets stronger the visits from the pair decrease.

At no time does Frank see anyone from the police or federal authorities. One day, about a month in, and to Frank's great surprise, Ashland brings a phone and allows him to speak to Charlie Searle. Searle tells Frank in no uncertain terms to keep quiet, take the treatment and return home when they let him. If they let him.

'This is not a fucking game, Frank,' says Searle. 'I had a call from the PM. He said he hopes you get well soon and don't suffer any – and I quote – "adverse reactions" to your wounds. Adverse reactions. Are you understanding what I'm saying here, Frank?'

Frank can hear the tension in Charlie Searle's voice all the way across the Atlantic. He had thought that being mixed up in all of this was beyond his own pay grade. What he's discovering is that it's beyond Searle's too.

'Where am I? They won't tell me.'

'I don't know,' says Searle. 'A military hospital, they said. You'll be released when you're fit enough to travel. Officially, you're nowhere. You're off the grid.'

'Jesus.' Searle doesn't know where Frank is?

'And what about Koopman? The girl and her mother?'

'We don't know about Koopman. The Australians are dealing with his affairs. There's some doubt about the jurisdiction as Koopman had a citizenship application approved but not finalised. The others I don't know about. I have no details.'

Searle signs off and that's all Frank gets. He pushes for more information but they ignore him. After the warnings from Charlie Searle, Frank doesn't push hard. The thread guiding him back out of this labyrinth is stretched so fine that Frank's not sure it exists at all any more. Off the grid. Terra Incognita.

Here be monsters.

A week after the last operation on his shoulder Frank is watching TV. He's dressed in trackpants and sweatshirt and is feeling as good as he's felt during his hospitalisation. Or imprisonment.

The door opens and Dennis Sheehan walks in.

He looks a little older than Frank remembers but there's no disputing who is the alpha male in the room.

Sheehan holds out a hand. 'Don't worry,' he says. 'I'm not contagious.'

Frank shakes the man's hand.

'You're looking better,' says Sheehan. He sits on an armchair and Frank takes a seat on the couch.

'Compared to what?'

'Compared to when you were brought in. I saw you being prepped for theatre the first night. You'd lost some blood.'

'Your son shot holes in me,' says Frank. 'Blood leaks out when that happens.'

Sheehan nods. A fleeting look of pain passes over his face before the mask is replaced.

'He didn't shoot you,' says Sheehan. 'At least that's not the story that anyone will ever hear.'

'Unless I tell them.'

Sheehan shrugs. 'You can try,' he says. 'You might even succeed in convincing somebody. There are people out there who believe we're ruled by a race of alien lizards. I have dozens of websites dedicated to proving how evil I am. You could throw your hand in with those nuts, see how it goes.'

Sheehan adjusts his jacket. 'You must have wondered why you were brought here,' he says. He waves a hand around the room. 'Do you remember me talking to you in Los Angeles? I mentioned that you were swimming in very deep waters.'

Frank nods. 'I was right about your son. He wanted to hurt you. We just didn't know that he wanted to do that by killing others and shining a light onto you.'

'That's true. You were right about Ben. And you're a tenacious bastard, I'll say that for you. But only you and Koopman and a couple of other people will ever know what happened. The events at Mount San Jacinto didn't take place. There are no witnesses. The girl? Too young to be reliable. The mother who walked in the restroom? Disappeared. Presumed to have fallen from one of the lookouts. A tragedy. Happens all the time. Mr Ashland and Mr Baines fixed it all because that's what they do. We'll look after the girl; she'll never be the same but we'll see she gets the best. The guy who discovered the scene and the cop who arrived and the emergency team who got you out are covered under the magic word of Homeland Security. No one questions anything. You saw something? Homeland Security requires you unsee it. You think you know something? Homeland Security requires you don't.'

'Why don't I just disappear?' says Frank. 'There was some talk of a plane ride to Afghanistan.'

Sheehan purses his lip. 'I thought about it. It could still happen too if you're dumb enough to take me on. But in the end I opted not to. You saved me. I'm not a monster, Frank, despite what you might think. I'm a patriot. No, really, I am. You hear that phrase about "the greater good" all the time but it's just a glib expression for most people. You're looking at the greater good made concrete. People like me keep the wheels turning. We make the decisions that others cannot or will not make no matter how painful they might be. My people do things . . . well they do things you don't want to think about. Believe it or not, and as painful as it is for me to admit it, this stuff with Ben is just local stuff, unimportant. If he'd killed the First Family that would have been a different story and we'd have had to cope with that. But every day I, and people like me, make decisions that cost or save thousands, sometimes millions of lives.'

'You should get a medal, Sheehan.'

Sheehan smiles. 'I have plenty of those. I got some of them for making the difficult decisions.'

'Like abandoning your son.'

'Exactly. Ben had everything but wanted something I couldn't give him.'

'Attention.'

'I watched over him as best I could – money, schools, health – but it wasn't good enough. I thought about stopping him; put plans in place to do just that, but even I . . . well, even I found that a step too far. Killing your only son. Too far.'

Frank closes his eyes and sees Nicky Peters.

'Did you know? About the killings in Liverpool, I mean?'

'We knew he was going off reservation. Since his mother died and he found out about our connection . . . he hadn't been dealing with it well. I did what I could.'

'Did you know?'

Sheehan nods. 'I could tell you I didn't; that we were unsure of his involvement, that although we had him under observation we never saw him killing, but I'd be lying to myself. I knew it was him, deep down.'

'And when I showed up here?'

'We thought we could control it. We never thought he had such . . . grandiose ambitions. We were wrong. I was wrong.' Sheehan pauses. 'We're very grateful for what you and your team did, Frank. Very grateful. But there's a wider picture which you can't see, and believe me, I sometimes wish I didn't see it either.'

Sheehan gets to his feet.

'How long will I stay here?' says Frank.

'You're leaving,' says Sheehan. 'Today.'

'Do you mean I'm leaving as in getting on a plane and flying home? Or is that some sort of complicated way of saying you're going to have me fall off a cliff?'

'I'm not playing games with you, Frank. I'm a human being. This isn't fucking James Bond. My son died trying to kill the president's family and I'd rather not have the fallout from that. It's not a selfish decision; if I go because of this then things will happen that end up with larger casualties.'

'According to you.'

'Yes, that's right. According to me. If not me, then who? Look, I'm past caring about games. You'll be flown back to the UK today on a regular commercial flight. When you get back there'll be no questions from your superiors, although you'll probably get visited by one of your more shadowy agencies. They'll want to know details and I suggest you tell them everything. Some of it they'll know anyway and the rest, well I can live with them knowing. There's no evil empire plan. If I wanted you gone you'd already be dead. Besides, you have qualities we admire, Frank. We're always interested in expanding our operational capacity.'

'This is a fucking job offer? Wouldn't it have been easier to put an ad up?'

Sheehan smiles bleakly. 'Possibly. I'll bear that in mind next time. I don't normally get involved at this level, you understand.'

'And Menno Koopman? Where's he? What's happened to him?'

'He's alive,' says Sheehan. 'He's lost an arm. His recovery will take longer than yours. When he's fit enough we'll assess his attitude and deal with it accordingly. Hopefully he will see things our way.'

'And if he doesn't?'

At the door Sheehan pauses.

'Everyone does. In the end.'

Fifty-Three

He never finds out the name of the base where he'd been kept.

From the medical unit he is taken in a windowless helicopter and flown to Atlanta's Hartsfield Jackson Airport. Ashland goes with him. After Sheehan leaves, Frank's given new clothes: Nikes, jeans, a blue cotton shirt and a windcheater; the choice of a conservative. They were waiting for him in the room when Sheehan had gone, along with his passport and wallet and some basic toiletries in a green washbag.

At Atlanta the helicopter lands in a corner of the airfield. An airport authority bus takes Frank and Ashland to a Delta 777 waiting at the terminal. Ashland leads Frank through a door and up to the plane. He hands a document to a member of the cabin crew who looks at Frank as if he may explode. Frank wonders if Ashland will say anything but he doesn't. Leaving Frank standing in the doorway of the 777, Ashland turns and walks back down the connecting air bridge.

'This way, sir,' says the flight attendant. She turns left and heads to the nose of the aircraft and directs Frank to the front seat. At least Sheehan isn't cheap, reflects Frank. It's his first time at the pointy end.

He notices the flight attendant glancing at the bruising on his face. In the mirror back at the military base it hadn't seemed so bad but out in the real world he guessed it was different, especially on board a plane. He traces the line of the scar across the right side of his scalp. His hair had been shaved to treat the wound and, although it is starting to grow back, it's still short enough for the ridge to show. Frank's nose is crooked and there's more bruising around his eyes. He's bone tired but doesn't want to sleep. He's afraid the line of dead will return. They've been coming into his dreams with increasing frequency: Paul, Maddy, Nicky, Alicia, Dean, Warren, even Terry.

In his seat, Frank is only dimly aware of take-off, his old fear of flying gone forever. There are more things to be afraid of out there. He watches Atlanta drift past underneath the aircraft and then it's gone. He doesn't feel like he's going home. He feels like he's being exiled. Maybe it's the medication.

An hour and a half into the flight another attendant approaches with a glass of water on a tray.

'I'm OK,' says Frank but the man ignores him and places the tray on the table.

Next to the glass is a white A4 envelope. The steward nods politely and moves back down the plane towards the galley. Frank twists in his seat and watches the man return to his duties.

Frank looks at the envelope for a few minutes before touching it. Eventually he picks it up and slides his thumb under the sealed flap.

Inside is a single sheet of paper.

In the centre of the sheet there are a few lines of black type.

CCBDB Central Credit Banque de Belgique
www.creditbanquedebelgique.com
Account number: 434-99843-221-000
Access code: gREEk24
PO Box 2334, Liverpool City Post Office
Pick up the phone.

Frank looks at the media console to his right. Above the TV screen is a phone recessed into a plastic casing. He looks around the cabin but nobody seems remotely interested in him.

After a few seconds Frank reaches forward and unclips the handset from its housing. He lifts it to his ear. There's an electronic hiss and then a voice starts to talk. The voice is digital.

Frank. The sheet of paper has details of a bank account. This is in your name. You can access it online via the website. It is linked to a separate and completely legitimate UK account in the name of a security consulting company called Northern Security.

This company is owned by you and is also completely legitimate. In the post office box in Liverpool there is paperwork detailing a highly successful two years you traded in stocks to explain the funds in the accounts. If you do not access the account nothing will happen. If you do access it, the contents are yours to do with as you wish. If you report the account to your superiors nothing will happen: the account is absolutely legal. You have, according to the UK tax records, reported the earnings and paid the correct tax. The account contains twenty-five million US dollars. There are no strings.

The voice stops. Frank waits but there's nothing else. Unsure of what to do he replaces the handset before picking it up again and listening. There's nothing. Frank taps the mechanism. Nothing. He replaces the handset.

With the sheet of paper in his hand, his face illuminated by the soft glow of the overhead reading light, Frank looks out of the window at the darkening sky. The 777 is heading east into the night. Frank switches off the light and watches the plane get swallowed by a towering stack of black cloud.

Acknowledgements

As with the first book in this series, there are a number of people who have, again, been instrumental in getting me to this point.

I'm grateful to clinical psychologist and one-time Maghull High stud poker champion, Dr Andrew Peden for the psychological detail and suggestions, as well as for some pithy early readings of the text. For valuable detail on Merseyside Police procedures, and for guiding me through the workings of the Mutual Legal Assistance Treaty, I have Stewart Newton Parkinson to thank. Graham Herring also provided some worthwhile police information that prevented me looking more foolish than normal.

In Los Angeles, I have Mark Cigolle and Kim Coleman to thank for their local knowledge, gracious hospitality and extremely good margaritas.

There are also people who didn't object to being murdered (Jonny and Catherine Lea who, although not named, were the inspiration for the unfortunate dentists), and a host of people who loaned me their names (Peter Moreleigh, Sebastian Ross-Hagenbaum and Angela Salt among them). Needless to say, none of them are remotely like their characters in this book.

Other people who deserve thanks are Tara Wynne, my agent at Curtis Brown; Bev Cousins and Georgina Hawtrey-Woore, my publishers at Random House (Australia and UK respectively); Margrete Lamond for early readings and encouragement; my editors, Elena Gomez and Elizabeth Cowell; my son, Danny, for keeping me focused with some of my wilder ideas; my daughter, Sophie, for ensuring the medical side of things was kept within believable limits and, most deservingly, my wife Annie, for everything.

ALSO AVAILABLE IN ARROW

A Dark Place to Die

Ed Chatterton

No escape. No rescue. No mercy.

On a cold winter morning, Detective Inspector Frank Keane is called to Liverpool's shoreline where a body, brutally tortured and burned, has been found. Keane and his team are soon on the hunt for a sadistic killer, but this is just the beginning of a vicious cycle of violence.

When the corpse turns out to be the son of Frank's former boss, the case becomes more complicated as the lines between justice and revenge start to blur.

Frank's former boss has not been forgotten in his old hunting ground – not by his colleagues or by his enemies. And, as the body count rises, Keane is caught up in a web of deceit as his search for the killer becomes a fight for survival.

arrow books